Barrington
Vol. 1

by

Charles James Lever

Barrington
Vol. 1
by Charles James Lever

Copyright © 2023

All Rights reserved.

ISBN: 978-93-60465-57-5

Published by

DOUBLE 9 BOOKS

2/13-B, Ansari Road
Daryaganj, New Delhi – 110002
info@double9books.com
www.double9books.com
Tel. 011-40042856

ABOUT THE AUTHOR

Charles James Lever was an Irish author and storyteller who lived from August 31, 1806 to June 1, 1872. Anthony Trollope said that Lever's books were like his conversations. Lever was born on Amiens Street in Dublin. He was the second son of architect and builder James Lever and went to special schools. He had many adventures at Trinity College, Dublin, from 1823 to 1828. It was there that he got his medical degree in 1831. Some of the stories of his books are based on these experiences. The character of Frank Webber in the book Charles O'Malley was based on Robert Boyle, a friend from college who later became a priest. Lever and Boyle made extra money by singing original songs in the streets of Dublin. They also pulled off a lot of other jokes, which Lever wrote about in more detail in his books O'Malley, Con Cregan, and Lord Kilgobbin. Before he really started studying medicine, Lever went to Canada on an emigrant ship as an untrained surgeon. He has used some of what he learned in Con Cregan, Arthur O'Leary, and Roland Cashel. When he got to Canada, he went into the woods and joined a Native American group. But he had to leave because his life was in danger, just like his character Bagenal Daly did in his book The Knight of Gwynne.

CONTENTS

CHAPTER I
THE FISHERMAN'S HOME

If there should be, at this day we live in, any one bold enough to confess that he fished the river Nore, in Ireland, some forty years ago, he might assist me by calling to mind a small inn, about two miles from the confluence of that river with the Barrow, a spot in great favor with those who followed the "gentle craft."

It was a very unpretending hostel, something wherein cottage and farmhouse were blended, and only recognizable as a place of entertainment by a tin trout suspended over the doorway, with the modest inscription underneath, — "Fisherman's Home." Very seldom is it, indeed, that hotel pledges are as honestly fulfilled as they were in this simple announcement. The house was, in all that quiet comfort and unostentatious excellence can make, a veritable Home! Standing in a fine old orchard of pear and damson trees, it was only approachable by a path which led from the highroad, about two miles off, or by the river, which wound round the little grassy promontory beneath the cottage. On the opposite side of the stream arose cliffs of considerable height, their terraced sides covered with larch and ash, around whose stems the holly, the laurel, and arbutus grew in a wild and rich profusion. A high mountain, rugged with rock and precipice, shut in the picture, and gave to the river all the semblance of a narrow lake.

The Home, as may be imagined, was only resorted to by fishermen, and of these not many; for the chosen few who knew the spot, with the churlishness of true anglers, were strenuously careful to keep the secret to themselves. But another and stronger cause contributed to this seclusion. The landlord was a reduced gentleman, who, only anxious to add a little to his narrow fortune, would not have accepted a greater prosperity at the cost of more publicity, and who probably only consented to his occupation on finding how scrupulously his guests respected his position.

Indeed, it was only on leave-taking, and then far from painfully, you were reminded of being in an inn. There was no noise, no bustle; books, magazines, flowers, lay about; cupboards lay open, with all their cordials free to take. You might dine under the spreading sycamore beside the well, and have your dessert for the plucking. No obsequious waiter shook his napkin as you passed, no ringleted barmaid crossed your musing steps, no jingling of bells, or discordant cries, or high-voiced remonstrances disturbed you. The hum of the summer bee, or the flapping plash of a trout, were about the only sounds in the stillness, and all was as peaceful and as calm and as dreamy as the most world-weary could have wished it.

Of those who frequented the spot, some merely knew that the host had seen better days. Others, however, were aware that Peter Barrington had once been a man of large fortune, and represented his county in the Irish Parliament. Though not eminent as a politician, he was one of the great convivial celebrities of a time that boasted of Curran, and Avanmore, and Parsons, and a score of others, any one of whom, in our day, would have made a society famous. Barrington, too, was the almoner of the monks of the screw, and "Peter's pence" was immortalized in a song by Ned Lysaght, of which I once possessed, but have lost a copy.

One might imagine there could be no difficulty in showing how in that wild period of riotous living and costly rivalry an Irish gentleman ran through all his property and left himself penniless. It was, indeed, a time of utter recklessness, many seeming possessed of that devil-may-care spirit that drives a drowning crew to break open the spirit-room and go down in an orgie. But Barrington's fortune was so large, and his successes on the turf so considerable, that it appeared incredible, when his estates came to the hammer, and all his personal property was sold off; so complete his ruin, that, as he said himself, the "only shelter he had was an umbrella, and even that he borrowed from Dan Driscoll, the sheriff's officer."

Of course there were theories in plenty to account for the disaster, and, as usual, so many knew, many a long day ago, how hard pressed he had been for money, and what ruinous interest he was obliged to pay, till at last rumors filtered all down to one channel, and the world agreed that it was all his son's doing, and that the scamp George had ruined his father. This son, his only child, had gone out to India in a cavalry regiment, and was celebrated all over the East for a costly splendor that rivalled the great Government officials. From every retired or invalided officer who came back from Bengal were heard stories of mad Barring-ton's extravagance: his palace on the Hooghly, his racing stud, his elephants, his army of retainers, — all narratives which, no matter in what spirit retailed, seemed to delight old Peter, who, at every fresh story of his son's spendthrift magnificence, would be sure to toast his health with a racy enthusiasm whose sincerity was not to be doubted.

Little wonder need there be if in feeding such extravagance a vast estate melted away, and acre followed acre, till all that remained of a property that ranked next to the Ormonds' was the little cottage over whose door the tin-trout dangled, and the few roods of land around it: sorry remnant of a princely fortune!

But Barrington himself had a passion, which, inordinately indulged, has brought many to their ruin. He was intensely fond of law. It was to him all that gambling is to other men. All that gamesters feel of hope and fear, all the intense excitement they derive from the vacillating fortunes of play, Barrington enjoyed in a lawsuit. Every step of the proceeding had for him an intense interest. The driest legal documents, musty declarations, demurrers, pleadings, replies, affidavits, and counter-affidavits were his choicest reading; and never did a young lady hurry to her room with the last new novel with a stronger anticipation of delight than did Barrington when carrying away to his little snuggery a roll of parchments or rough drafts, whose very iterations and jargon would have driven most men half crazy. This same snuggery of his was a curiosity, too, the walls being all decorated with portraits of legal celebrities, not selected with reference to their merit or distinction, but solely from their connection with some suit in which he had been engaged; and thus under the likeness of Chief Baron O'Grady might be read, "Barring-ton versus Brazier, 1802; a juror withdrawn:" Justice Moore's portrait was inscribed, "Argument in Chambers, 1808," and so on; even to the portraits of leading counsel, all were marked and dated only as they figured in the great campaign,—the more than thirty years' war he carried on against Fortune.

Let not my reader suppose for one moment that this litigious taste grew out of a spirit of jarring discontent or distrust. Nothing of the kind. Barrington was merely a gambler; and with whatever dissatisfaction the declaration may be met, I am prepared to show that gambling, however faulty in itself, is not the vice of cold, selfish, and sordid men, but of warm, rash, sometimes over-generous temperaments. Be it well remembered that the professional play-man is, of all others, the one who has least of a gamester in his heart; his superiority lying in the simple fact that his passions are never engaged, his interest never stirred. Oh! beware of yourself in company with the polished antagonist, who only smiles when he loses, whom nothing adverse ever disturbs, but is calmly serene under the most pitiless pelting of luck. To come back: Barrington's passion for law was an intense thirst for a certain species of excitement; a verdict was to him the odd trick. Let him, however, but win the game, there never was a man so indifferent about the stakes.

For many a year back he had ceased to follow the great events of the world. For the stupendous changes in Europe he cared next to nothing. He scarcely knew who reigned over this empire or that kingdom. Indifferent to art, science, letters, and even society, his interest was intense about all that went on in the law courts, and it was an interest so catholic that it took in everything and everybody, from the great judge upon the bench to the small taxing-officer who nibbled at the bill of costs.

Fortunately for him, his sister, a maiden lady of some eighteen or twenty years his junior, had imbibed nothing of this passion, and, by her prudent opposition to it, stemmed at least the force of that current which was bearing him to ruin. Miss Dinah Barrington had been the great belle of the Irish court,—I am ashamed to say how long ago,—and though at the period my tale opens there was not much to revive the impression, her high nose, and full blue eyes, and a mass of wonderfully unchanged brown hair, proclaimed her to be—what she was very proud to call herself—a thorough Barrington, a strong type of a frank nature, with a bold, resolute will, and a very womanly heart beneath it.

When their reverses of fortune first befell them, Miss Barrington wished to emigrate. She thought that in Canada, or some other far-away land, their altered condition might be borne less painfully, and that they could more easily bend themselves to humble offices where none but strangers were to look on them; but Barrington clung to his country with the tenacity of an old captain to a wreck. He declared he could not bring himself to the thought of leaving his bones in a strange land, but he never confessed what he felt to be the strongest tie of all, two unfinished lawsuits, the old record of Barrington v. Brazier, and a Privy Council case of Barrington and Lot Rammadahn Mohr against the India Company. To have left his country with these still undecided seemed to him—like the act of a commander taking flight on the morning of a general action—an amount of cowardice he could not contemplate. Not that he confided this opinion to his sister, though he did so in the very fullest manner to his old follower and servant, Darby Cassan. Darby was the last remnant of a once princely retinue, and in his master's choice of him to accompany his fallen fortunes, there was something strangely indicative of the man. Had Darby been an old butler or a body-servant, had he been a favorite groom, or, in some other capacity, one whose daily duties had made his a familiar face, and whose functions could still be available in an humble state, there would have seemed good reason for the selection; but Darby was none of these: he had never served in hall or pantry; he had never brushed the cobweb from a bottle, or led a nag to the door. Of all human professions his were about the last that could address themselves to the cares of a little household; for Darby was reared, bred, and passed fifty-odd years of his life as an earth-stopper!

A very ingenious German writer has attempted to show that the sympathies of the humble classes with pursuits far above their own has always its origin in something of their daily life and habits, just as the sacristan of a cathedral comes to be occasionally a tolerable art critic from his continual reference to Rubens and Vandyck. It is possible that Darby may have illustrated the theory, and that his avocations as earth-stopper may have suggested what he assuredly possessed, a perfect passion for law. If a suit was a great game to Barrington, to Darby it was a hunt! and though his personal experiences never soared beyond Quarter Sessions, he gloried in all he saw there of violence and altercation, of vituperative language and impassioned abuse. Had he been a rich man, free to enjoy his leisure, he would have passed all his days listening to these hot discussions. They were to him a sort of intellectual bull-fight, which never could be too bloody or too cruel. Have I said enough, therefore, to show the secret link which bound the master to the man? I hope so; and that my reader is proud of a confidence with which Miss Barrington herself was never intrusted. She believed that Darby had been taken into favor from some marvellous ability he was supposed to possess, applicable to their new venture as innkeepers. Phrenology would perhaps have pronounced Darby a heaven-born host, for his organ of acquisitiveness was grandly developed. Amidst that great household, where the thriftless habits of the master had descended to the servants, and rendered all reckless and wasteful alike, Darby had thriven and grown almost rich. Was it that the Irish climate used its influence over him; for in his practice to "put by something for a rainy day," his savings had many promptings? As the reputation of having money soon attached to him, he was often applied to in the hunting-field, or at the kennel, for small loans, by the young bloods who frequented the Hall, and, being always repaid three or four fold, he grew to have a very high conception of what banking must be when done on a large scale. Besides all this, he quickly learned that no character attracts more sympathy, especially amongst the class of young squires and sporting-men, than a certain quaint simplicity, so flattering in its contrast to their own consummate acuteness. Now, he was simple to their hearts' content. He usually spoke of himself as "Poor Darby, God help him!" and, in casting up those wonderful accounts, which he kept by notches on a tally-stick, nothing was more amusing than to witness his bewilderment and confusion, the inconceivable blunders he would make, even to his own disadvantage, all sure to end at last in the heart-spoken confession that it was "clean beyand him," and "he 'd leave it all to your honor; pay just what ye plaze, and long life to ye!"

Is it that women have some shrewd perception of character denied to men? Certainly Darby never imposed on Miss Barrington. She read him like a book, and he felt it. The consequence was a very cordial dislike, which strengthened with every year of their acquaintance.

Though Miss Barrington ever believed that the notion of keeping an inn originated with her brother, it was Darby first conceived the project, and, indeed, by his own skill and crafty intelligence was it carried on; and while the words "Peter Barrington" figured in very small letters, it is true, over the door to comply with a legal necessity, to most of the visitors he was a mere myth. Now, if Peter Barrington was very happy to be represented by deputy,—or, better still, not represented at all,—Miss Dinah regarded the matter in a very different light. Her theory was that, in accepting the humble station to which reverse of fortune brought them, the world ought to see all the heroism and courage of the sacrifice. She insisted on being a foreground figure, just to show them, as she said, "that I take nothing upon me. I am the hostess of a little wayside inn,—no more!" How little did she know of her own heart, and how far was she from even suspecting that it was the *ci-devant* belle making one last throw for the admiration and homage which once were offered her freely.

Such were the three chief personages who dwelt under that secluded roof, half overgrown with honeysuckle and dog-roses,—specimens of that wider world without, where jealousies, and distrusts, and petty rivalries are warring: for as in one tiny globule of water are represented the elements which make oceans and seas, so is it in the moral world; and "the family" is only humanity, as the artists say, "reduced."

For years back Miss Barrington had been plotting to depose Darby. With an ingenuity quite feminine, she managed to connect him with every chagrin that crossed and every annoyance that befell them. If the pig ploughed up the new peas in the garden, it was Darby had left the gate open; it was *his* hand overwound the clock; and a very significant hint showed that when the thunder soured the beer, Mr. Darby knew more of the matter than he was likely to tell. Against such charges as these, iterated and reiterated to satiety, Barrington would reply by a smile, or a good-natured excuse, or a mere gesture to suggest patience, till his sister, fairly worn out, resolved on another line of action. "As she could not banish the rats," to use her own words, "she would scuttle the ship."

To explain her project, I must go back in my story, and state that her nephew, George Barrington, had sent over to England, some fifteen years before, a little girl, whom he called his daughter. She was consigned to the care of his banker in London, with directions that he should communicate with Mr. Peter Barrington, announce the child's safe arrival, and consult with him as to her future destination. Now, when the event took place,

Barrington was in the very crisis of his disasters. Overwhelmed with debts, pursued by creditors, regularly hunted down, he was driven day by day to sign away most valuable securities for mere passing considerations, and obliged to accept any conditions for daily support He answered the banker's letter, briefly stating his great embarrassment, and begging him to give the child his protection for a few weeks or so, till some arrangement of his affairs might enable him to offer her a home.

This time, however, glided over, and the hoped-for amendment never came,—far from it. Writs were out against him, and he was driven to seek a refuge in the Isle of Man, at that time the special sanctuary of insolvent sinners. Mr. Leonard Gower wrote again, and proposed that, if no objection would be made to the plan, the child should be sent to a certain convent near Namur, in the Netherlands, where his own daughter was then placed for her education. Aunt Dinah would have rejected,—ay, or would have resented such a proposal as an insult, had the world but gone on better with them. That her grand-niece should be brought up a Catholic was an outrage on the whole Barring-ton blood. But calamity had brought her low,—very low, indeed. The child, too, was a heathen,—a Hindoo or a Buddhist, perhaps,—for the mother was a native woman, reputed, indeed, to be a princess. But who could know this? Who could vouch that George was ever married at all, or if such a ceremony were possible? All these were "attenuating circumstances," and as such she accepted them; and the measure of her submission was filled up when she received a portrait of the little girl, painted by a native artist. It represented a dark-skinned, heavy-browed child, with wide, full eyes, thick lips, and an expression at once florid and sullen,—not any of the traits one likes to associate with infancy,—and it was with a half shudder Aunt Dinah closed the miniature, and declared that "the sight of the little savage actually frightened her."

Not so poor Barrington. He professed to see a great resemblance to his son. It was George all over. To be sure, his eyes were deep blue, and his hair a rich brown; but there was something in the nose, or perhaps it was in the mouth,—no, it was the chin,—ay, it was the chin was George's. It was the Barrington chin, and no mistake about it.

At all events, no opposition was made to the banker's project, and the little girl was sent off to the convent of the Holy Cross, on the banks of the Meuse. She was inscribed on the roll as the Princess Doondiah, and bore the name till her father's death, when Mr. Gower suggested that she should be called by her family name. The letter with the proposal, by some accident, was not acknowledged, and the writer, taking silence to mean consent, desired the superior to address her, henceforth, as Miss Barrington; the first startling intimation of the change being a strangely, quaintly written note, addressed to her grand-aunt, and signed "Josephine Barrington." It was a cold, formal letter,—so very formal, indeed, as to read like the copy of a document,—asking for leave to enter upon a novitiate of two years' duration, at the expiration of which she would be nineteen years of age, and in a position to decide upon taking the veil for life. The permission, very urgently pressed for by Mr. Gower in another letter, was accorded, and now we have arrived at that period in which but three months only remained of the two years whose closure was to decide her fate forever.

Barrington had long yearned to see her. It was with deep and bitter self-reproach he thought over the cold neglect they had shown her. She was all that remained of poor George, his boy,—for so he called him, and so he thought of him,—long after the bronzed cheek and the prematurely whitened hair had tempered his manhood. To be sure, all the world said, and he knew himself, how it was chiefly through the "boy's" extravagance he came to ruin. But it was over now. The event that sobers down reproach to sorrow had come. He was dead! All that arose to memory of him were the traits that suggested hopes of his childhood, or gave triumph in his riper years; and oh, is it not better thus? for what hearts would be left us if we were to carry in them the petty rancors and jealousies which once filled them, but which, one day, we buried in the cold clay of the churchyard.

Aunt Dinah, moved by reasons long canvassed over in her own mind, at last began to think of recalling her grand-niece. It was so very bold a project that, at first, she could scarcely entertain it. The Popery was very dreadful! Her imagination conjured up the cottage converted into a little Baal, with false gods and graven images, and holy-water fonts at every turn; but the doubtful legitimacy was worse again. She had a theory that it was by lapses of this kind the "blue blood" of old families grew deteriorated, and that the downfall of many an ancient house was traceable to these corruptions. Far better, she deemed it, that the Barringtons should die out forever than their line be continued by this base and ignoble grafting.

There is a *contre* for every *pour* in this world. It may be a weak and an insufficient one, it is true; but it is a certainty that all our projects must come to a debtor or creditor reckoning, and the very best we can do is to strike an honest balance!

How Miss Dinah essayed to do this we shall learn in the next chapter and what follows it.

CHAPTER II
A WET MORNING AT HOME

If there was anything that possessed more than common terror for Barrington, it was a wet day at the cottage! It was on these dreary visitations that his sister took the opportunity of going into "committee of supply," — an occasion not merely for the discussion of fiscal matters, but for asking the most vexatious questions and demanding the most unpleasant explanations.

We can all, more or less, appreciate the happiness of that right honorable gentleman on the Treasury bench who has to reply to the crude and unmeaning inquiries of some aspiring Oppositionist, and who wishes to know if her Majesty's Government have demanded an indemnity from the King of Dahomey for the consul's family eaten by him at the last court ceremonial? What compensation is to be given to Captain Balrothery for his week's imprisonment at Leghorn, in consequence of his having thrown the customs officer and a landing waiter into the sea? Or what mark of her Majesty's favor will the noble lord recommend should be conferred upon Ensign Digges for the admirable imitation he gave of the dancing dervishes at Benares, and the just ridicule he thus threw upon these degrading and heathenish rites?

It was to a torture of this order, far more reasonable and pertinent, however, that Barrington usually saw himself reduced whenever the weather was so decidedly unfavorable that egress was impossible. Poor fellow, what shallow pretexts would he stammer out for absenting himself from home, what despicable subterfuges to put off an audience! He had forgotten to put down the frame on that melon-bed.

There was that awning over the boat not taken in. He 'd step out to the stable and give Billy, the pony, a touch of the white oils on that swelled hock. He 'd see if they had got the young lambs under cover. In fact, from his perturbed and agitated manner, you would have imagined that rain was one of the rarest incidents of an Irish climate, and only the very promptest measures could mitigate the calamity.

"May I ask where you are off to in such haste, Peter?" asked Miss Dinah one morning, just as Barrington had completed all his arrangements for a retreat; far readier to brave the elements than the more pitiless pelting that awaited him within doors.

"I just remembered," said he, mildly, "that I had left two night-lines out at the point, and with this fresh in the river it would be as well if I 'd step down and see—"

"And see if the river was where it was yesterday," broke she in, sneeringly.

"No, Dinah. But you see that there 's this to be remarked about night-lines—"

"That they never catch any fish!" said she, sternly. "It's no weather for you to go tramping about in the wet grass. You made fuss enough about your lumbago last week, and I suppose you don't want it back again. Besides,"—and here her tongue grew authoritative,—"I have got up the books." And with these words she threw on the table a number of little greasy-looking volumes, over which poor Barrington's sad glances wandered, pretty much as might a victim's over the thumb-screws and the flesh-nippers of the Holy Inquisition.

"I've a slight touch of a headache this morning, Dinah."

"It won't be cured by going out in the rain. Sit down there," said she, peremptorily, "and see with your own eyes how much longer your means will enable you to continue these habits of waste and extravagance."

"These what?" said he, perfectly astounded.

"These habits of waste and extravagance, Peter Barring-ton. I repeat my words."

Had a venerable divine, being asked on the conclusion of an edifying discourse, for how much longer it might be his intention to persist in such ribaldries, his astonishment could scarce have been greater than Barrington's.

"Why, sister Dinah, are we not keeping an inn? Is not this the 'Fisherman's Home'?"

"I should think it is, Peter," said she, with scorn. "I suspect he finds it so. A very excellent name for it it is!"

"Must I own that I don't understand you, Dinah?"

"Of course you don't. You never did all your life. You never knew you were wet till you were half drowned, and that's what the world calls having such an amiable disposition! Ain't your friends nice friends? They are always telling you how generous you are,—how free-handed,—how benevolent. What a heart he has! Ay, but thank Providence there's very little of that charming docility about *me*, is there?"

"None, Dinah,—none," said he, not in the least suspecting to what he was bearing testimony.

She became crimson in a minute, and in a tone of some emotion said, "And if there had been, where should you and where should I be to-day? On the parish, Peter Barrington,—on the parish; for it 's neither *your* head nor *your* hands would have saved us from it."

"You're right, Dinah; you're right there. You never spoke a truer word." And his voice trembled as he said it.

"I did n't mean *that*, Peter," said she, eagerly; "but you are too confiding, too trustful. Perhaps it takes a woman to detect all the little wiles and snares that entangle us in our daily life?"

"Perhaps it does," said he, with a deep sigh.

"At all events, you needn't sigh over it, Peter Barring-ton. It's not one of those blemishes in human nature that have to be deplored so feelingly. I hope women are as good as men."

"Fifty thousand times better, in every quality of kindliness and generosity."

"Humph!" said she, tossing her head impatiently. "We 're not here for a question in ethics; it is to the very lowly task of examining the house accounts I would invite your attention. Matters cannot go on as they do now, if we mean to keep a roof over us."

"But I have always supposed we were doing pretty well, Dinah. You know we never promised ourselves to gain a fortune by this venture; the very utmost we ever hoped for was to help us along,—to aid us to make both ends meet at the end of the year And as Darby tells me—"

"Oh, Darby tells you! What a reliable authority to quote from! Oh, don't groan so heavily! I forgot myself. I would n't for the world impeach such fidelity or honesty as his."

"Be reasonable, sister Dinah,—do be reasonable; and if there is anything to lay to his charge—"

"You 'll hear the case, I suppose," cried she, in a voice high-pitched in passion. "You 'll sit up there, like one of your favorite judges, and call on Dinah Barrington against Cassan; and perhaps when the cause is concluded we shall reverse our places, and *I* become the defendant! But if this is your intention, brother Barrington, give me a little time. I beg I may have a little time."

Now, this was a very favorite request of Miss Barring-ton's, and she usually made it in the tone of a martyr; but truth obliges us to own that never was a demand less justifiable. Not a three-decker of the Channel fleet was readier for a broadside than herself. She was always at quarters and with a port-fire burning.

Barrington did not answer this appeal; he never moved,—he scarcely appeared to breathe, so guarded was he lest his most unintentional gesture should be the subject of comment.

"When you have recovered from your stupefaction," said she, calmly, "will you look over that line of figures, and then give a glance at this total? After that I will ask you what fortune could stand it."

"This looks formidable, indeed," said he, poring over the page through his spectacles.

"It is worse, Peter. It *is* formidable."

"After all, Dinah, this is expenditure. Now for the incomings!"

"I suspect you 'll have to ask your prime minister for *them*. Perhaps he may vouchsafe to tell you how many twenty-pound notes have gone to America, who it was that consigned a cargo of new potatoes to Liverpool, and what amount he invested in yarn at the last fair of Graigue? and when you have learned these facts, you will know all you are ever likely to know of your *profits!*" I have no means of conveying the intense scorn with which she uttered the last word of this speech.

"And he told me—not a week back—that we were going on famously!"

"Why wouldn't he? I 'd like to hear what else he could say. Famously, indeed, for *him* with a strong balance in the savings-bank, and a gold watch—yes, Peter, a gold watch—in his pocket. This is no delusion, nor illusion, or whatever you call it, of mine, but a fact,—a downright fact."

"He has been toiling hard many a year for it, Dinah, don't forget that."

"I believe you want to drive me mad, Peter. You know these are things that I can't bear, and that's the reason you say them. Toil, indeed! *I* never saw him do anything except sit on a gate at the Lock Meadows, with a pipe in his mouth; and if you asked him what he was there for, it was a 'track' he was watching, a 'dog-fox that went by every afternoon to the turnip field.' Very great toil that was!"

"There was n't an earth-stopper like him in the three next counties; and if I was to have a pack of foxhounds tomorrow—"

"You 'd just be as great a foot as ever you were, and the more sorry I am to hear it; but you 're not going to be tempted, Peter Barrington. It's not foxes we have to think of, but where we 're to find shelter for ourselves."

"Do you know of anything we could turn to, more profitable, Dinah?" asked he, mildly.

"There 's nothing could be much less so, I know *that!* You are not very observant, Peter, but even to you it must have become apparent that great changes have come over the world in a few years. The persons who formerly indulged their leisure were all men of rank and fortune. Who are the people who come over here now to amuse themselves? Staleybridge and Manchester creatures, with factory morals and bagman manners; treating our house like a commercial inn, and actually disputing the bill and asking for items. Yes, Peter, I overheard a fellow telling Darby last week that the ''ouse was dearer than the Halbion!'"

"Travellers will do these things, Dinah."

"And if they do, they shall be shown the door for it, as sure as my name is Dinah Barrington."

"Let us give up the inn altogether, then," said he, with a sudden impatience.

"The very thing I was going to propose, Peter," said she, solemnly.

"What!—how?" cried he, for the acceptance of what only escaped him in a moment of anger overwhelmed and stunned him. "How are we to live, Dinah?"

"Better without than with it,—there's my answer to that. Let us look the matter fairly in the face, Peter," said she, with a calm and measured utterance. "This dealing with the world 'on honor' must ever be a losing game. To screen ourselves from the vulgar necessities of our condition, we must submit to any terms. So long as our intercourse with life gave us none but gentlemen to deal with, we escaped well and safely. That race would seem to have thinned off of late, however; or, what comes to the same, there is such a deluge of spurious coin one never knows what is real gold."

"You may be right, Dinah; you may be right."

"I know I am right; the experience has been the growth of years too. All our efforts to escape the odious contact of these people have multiplied our expenses. Where one man used to suffice, we keep three. You yourself, who felt it no indignity to go out a-fishing formerly with a chance traveller, have to own with what reserve and caution you would accept such companionship now."

"Nay, nay, Dinah, not exactly so far as that—"

"And why not? Was it not less than a fortnight ago three Birmingham men crossed the threshold, calling out for old Peter,—was old Peter to the good yet?"

"They were a little elevated with wine, sister, remember that; and, besides, they never knew, never had heard of me in my once condition."

"And are we so changed that they cannot recognize the class we pertain to?"

"Not *you*, Dinah, certainly not you; but I frankly own I can put up with rudeness and incivility better than a certain showy courtesy some vulgar people practise towards me. In the one case I feel I am not known, and my secret is safe. In the other, I have to stand out as the ruined gentleman, and I am not always sure that I play the part as gracefully as I ought."

"Let us leave emotions, Peter, and descend to the lowland of arithmetic, by giving up two boatmen, John and Terry—"

"Poor Terry!" sighed he, with a faint, low accent

"Oh! if it be 'poor Terry!' I 've done," said she, closing the book, and throwing it down with a slap that made him start.

"Nay, dear Dinah; but if we could manage to let him have something,— say five shillings a week,—he 'd not need it long; and the port wine that was doing his rheumatism such good is nearly finished; he'll miss it sorely."

"Were you giving him Henderson's wine,—the '11 vintage?" cried she, pale with indignation.

"Just a bottle or two, Dinah; only as medicine."

"As a fiddlestick, sir! I declare I have no patience with you; there 's no excuse for such folly, not to say the ignorance of giving these creatures what they never were used to. Did not Dr. Dill tell you that tonics, to be effective, must always have some relation to the daily habits of the patient?"

"Very true, Dinah; but the discourse was pronounced when I saw him putting a bottle of old Madeira in his gig that I had left for Anne M'Cafferty, adding, he 'd send her something far more strengthening."

"Right or wrong, I don't care; but this I know, Terry Dogherty is n't going to finish off Henderson's port. It is rather too much to stand, that we are to be treating beggars to luxuries, when we can't say to-morrow where we shall find salt for our potatoes." This was a somewhat favorite illustration of Miss Barrington,—either implying that the commodity was an essential to human life, or the use of it an emblem of extreme destitution.

"I conclude we may dispense with Tom Divett's services," resumed she. "We can assuredly get on without a professional rat-catcher."

"If we should, Dinah, we'll feel the loss; the rats make sad havoc of the spawn, and destroy quantities of the young fish, besides."

"His two ugly terriers eat just as many chickens, and never leave us an egg in the place. And now for Mr. Darby—"

"You surely don't think of parting with Darby, sister Dinah?"

"He shall lead the way," replied she, in a firm and peremptory voice; "the very first of the batch! And it will, doubtless, be a great comfort to you to know that you need not distress yourself about any provision for his declining years. It is a care that he has attended to on his own part. He 'll go back to a very well-feathered nest, I promise you."

Barrington sighed heavily, for he had a secret sorrow on that score. He knew, though his sister did not, that he had from year to year been borrowing every pound of Darby's savings to pay the cost of law charges, always hoping and looking for the time when a verdict in his favor would enable him to restore the money twice told. With a very dreary sigh, then, did he here allude "to the well-feathered nest" of one he had left bare and destitute. He cleared his throat, and made an effort to avow the whole matter; but his courage failed him, and he sat mournfully shaking his head, partly in sorrow, partly in shame. His sister noticed none of these signs; she was rapidly enumerating all the reductions that could be made,—all the dependencies cut off; there were the boats, which constantly required repairs; the nets, eternally being renewed,—all to be discarded; the island, a very pretty little object in the middle of the river, need no longer be rented. "Indeed," said she, "I don't know why we took it, except it was to give those memorable picnics you used to have there."

"How pleasant they were, Dinah; how delightful!" said he, totally overlooking the spirit of her remark.

"Oh! they were charming, and your own popularity was boundless; but I 'd have you to bear in mind, brother Peter, that popularity is no more a poor man's luxury than champagne. It is a very costly indulgence, and can rarely be had on 'credit.'"

Miss Barrington had pared down retrenchment to the very quick. She had shown that they could live not only without boatmen, rat-catchers, gardener, and manservant, but that, as they were to give up their daily newspaper, they could dispense with a full ration of candle-light; and yet, with all these reductions, she declared that there was still another encumbrance to be pruned away, and she proudly asked her brother if he could guess what it was?

Now Barrington felt that he could not live without a certain allowance of food, nor would it be convenient, or even decent, to dispense with raiment; so he began, as a last resource, to conjecture that his sister was darkly hinting at something which might be a substitute for a home, and save house-rent; and he half testily exclaimed, "I suppose we 're to have a roof over us, Dinah!"

"Yes," said she, dryly, "I never proposed we should go and live in the woods. What I meant had a reference, to Josephine—"

Barrington's cheek flushed deeply in an instant, and, with a voice trembling with emotion, he said,—

"If you mean, Dinah, that I'm to cut off that miserable pittance—that forty pounds a year—I give to poor George's girl—" He stopped, for he saw that in his sister's face which might have appalled a bolder heart than his own; for while her eyes flashed fire, her thin lips trembled with passion; and so, in a very faltering humility, he added: "But you never meant *that* sister Dinah. You would be the very last in the world to do it."

"Then why impute it to me; answer me that?" said she, crossing her hands behind her back, and staring haughtily at him.

"Just because I 'm clean at my wits' end,—just because I neither understand one word I hear, or what I say in reply. If you 'll just tell me what it is you propose, I 'll do my best, with God's blessing, to follow you; but don't ask me for advice, Dinah, and don't fly out because I 'm not as quick-witted and as clever as yourself."

There was something almost so abject in his misery that she seemed touched by it, and, in a voice of a very calm and kindly meaning, she said,—

"I have been thinking a good deal over that letter of Josephine's; she says she wants our consent to take the veil as a nun; that, by the rules of the order, when her novitiate is concluded, she must go into the world for at least some months,—a time meant to test her faithfulness to her vows, and the tranquillity with which she can renounce forever all the joys and attractions of life. We, it is true, have no means of surrounding her with such temptations; but we might try and supply their place by some less brilliant but not less attractive ones. We might offer her, what we ought to have offered her years ago,—a home! What do you say to this, Peter?"

"That I love you for it, sister Dinah, with all my heart," said he, kissing her on each cheek; "that it makes me happier than I knew I ever was to be again."

"Of course, to bring Josephine here, this must not be an inn, Peter."

"Certainly not, Dinah,—certainly not. But I can think of nothing but the joy of seeing her,—poor George's child I How I have yearned to know if she was like him,—if she had any of his ways, any traits of that quaint, dry humor he had, and, above all, of that disposition that made him so loved by every one."

"And cheated by every one too, brother Peter; don't forget that!"

"Who wants to think of it now?" said he, sorrowfully.

"I never reject a thought because it has unpleasant associations. It would be but a sorry asylum which only admitted the well-to-do and the happy."

"How are we to get the dear child here, Dinah? Let us consider the matter. It is a long journey off."

"I have thought of that too," said she, sententiously, "but not made up my mind."

"Let us ask M'Cormick about it, Dinah; he's coming up this evening to play his Saturday night's rubber with Dill. He knows the Continent well."

"There will be another saving that I did n't remember, Peter. The weekly bottle of whiskey, and the candles, not to speak of the four or five shillings your pleasant companions invariably carry away with them,—all may be very advantageously dispensed with."

"When Josephine 's here, I 'll not miss it," said he, good-humoredly. Then suddenly remembering that his sister might not deem the speech a gracious one to herself, he was about to add something; but she was gone.

CHAPTER III
OUR NEXT NEIGHBORS

Should there be amongst my readers any one whose fortune it has been in life only to associate with the amiable, the interesting, and the agreeable, all whose experiences of mankind are rose-tinted, to him I would say, Skip over two people I am now about to introduce, and take up my story at some later stage, for I desire to be truthful, and, as is the misfortune of people in my situation, I may be very disagreeable.

After all, I may have made more excuses than were needful. The persons I would present are in that large category, the commonplace, and only as uninviting and as tiresome as we may any day meet in a second-class on the railroad. Flourish, therefore, penny trumpets, and announce Major M'Cormick. The Major, so confidently referred to by Barrington in our last chapter as a high authority on matters continental, was a very shattered remnant of the unhappy Walcheren expedition. He was a small, mean-looking, narrow-faced man, with a thin, bald head, and red whiskers. He walked very lame from an injury to his hip; "his wound," he called it, though his candor did not explain that it was incurred by being thrown down a hatchway by a brother officer in a drunken brawl. In character he was a saving, penurious creature, without one single sympathy outside his own immediate interests. When some sixteen or eighteen years before the Barringtons had settled in the neighborhood, the Major began to entertain thoughts of matrimony. Old soldiers are rather given to consider marriage as an institution especially intended to solace age and console rheumatism, and so M'Cormick debated with himself whether he had not arrived at the suitable time for this indulgence, and also whether Miss Dinah Barrington was not the individual destined to share his lot and season his gruel.

But a few years back and his ambition would as soon have aspired to an archduchess as to the sister of Barrington, of Barrington Hall, whose realms of social distinction separated them; but now, fallen from their high estate, forgotten by the world, and poor, they had come down—at least, he thought so—to a level in which there would be no presumption in his pretensions. Indeed, I half suspect that he thought there was something very high-minded and generous in his intentions with regard to them. At all events, there was a struggle of some sort in his mind which went on from year to year undecided. Now, there are men—for the most part old bachelors—to whom an unfinished project is a positive luxury, who like to add, day by day, a few threads to the web of fate, but no more. To the Major it was quite enough that "some fine day or other"—so he phrased it—he 'd make his offer, just as he thought how, in the same propitious weather, he 'd put a new roof on his cottage, and fill up that quarry-hole near his gate, into which he had narrowly escaped tumbling some half-dozen times. But thanks to his caution and procrastination, the roof, and the project, and the quarry-hole were exactly, or very nearly, in the same state they had been eighteen years before.

Rumor said—as rumor will always say whatever has a tinge of ill-nature in it—that Miss Barrington would have accepted him; vulgar report declared that she would "jump at the offer." Whether this be, or not, the appropriate way of receiving a matrimonial proposal, the lady was not called upon to display her activity. He never told his love.

It is very hard to forgive that secretary, home or foreign, who in the day of his power and patronage could, but did not, make us easy for life with this mission or that com-missionership. It is not easy to believe that our uncle the bishop could not, without any undue strain upon his conscience, have made us something, albeit a clerical error, in his diocese, but infinitely more difficult is it to pardon him who, having suggested dreams of wedded happiness, still stands hesitating, doubting, and canvassing,—a timid bather, who shivers on the beach, and then puts on his clothes again.

It took a long time—it always does in such cases—ere Miss Barrington came to read this man aright. Indeed, the light of her own hopes had dazzled her, and she never saw him clearly till they were extinguished; but when the knowledge did come, it came trebled with compound interest, and she saw him in all that displayed his miserable selfishness; and although her brother, who found it hard to believe any one bad who had not been tried for a capital felony, would explain away many a meanness by saying, "It is just his way,—a way, and no more!" she spoke out fearlessly, if not very discreetly, and declared she detested him. Of course she averred it was his manners, his want of breeding, and his familiarity that displeased her. He might be an excellent creature,—perhaps he was; *that* was nothing to her. All his moral qualities might have an interest for his friends; she was a mere acquaintance, and was only concerned for what related to his bearing in society. Then Walcheren was positively odious to her. Some little solace she felt at the thought that the expedition was a failure and inglorious; but when she listened to the fiftieth time-told tale of fever and ague, she would sigh, not for those who suffered, but over the one that escaped. It is a great blessing to men of uneventful lives and scant imagination when there is any one incident to which memory can refer unceasingly. Like some bold headland last seen at sea, it lives in the mind throughout the voyage. Such was this ill-starred expedition to the Major. It dignified his existence to himself, though his memory never soared above the most ordinary details and vulgar incidents. Thus he would maunder on for hours, telling how the ships sailed and parted company, and joined again; how the old "Brennus" mistook a signal and put back to Hull, and how the "Sarah Reeves," his own transport, was sent after her. Then he grew picturesque about Flushing, as first seen through the dull fogs of the Scheldt, with village spires peeping through the heavy vapor, and the strange Dutch language, with its queer names for the vegetables and fruit brought by the boats alongside.

"You won't believe me, Miss Dinah, but, as I sit here, the peaches was like little melons, and the cherries as big as walnuts."

"They made cherry-bounce out of them, I hope, sir," said she, with a scornful smile.

"No, indeed, ma'am," replied he, dull to the sarcasm; "they ate them in a kind of sauce with roast-pig, and mighty good too!"

But enough of the Major; and now a word, and only a word, for his companion, already alluded to by Barrington.

Dr. Dill had been a poor "Dispensary Doctor" for some thirty years, with a small practice, and two or three grand patrons at some miles off, who employed him for the servants, or for the children in "mild cases," and who even extended to him a sort of contemptuous courtesy that serves to make a proud man a bear, and an humble man a sycophant.

Dill was the reverse of proud, and took to the other line with much kindliness. To have watched him in his daily round you would have said that he liked being trampled on, and actually enjoyed being crushed. He smiled so blandly, and looked so sweetly under it all, as though it was a kind of moral shampooing, from which he would come out all the fresher and more vigorous.

The world is certainly generous in its dealings with these temperaments; it indulges them to the top of their hearts, and gives them humiliations to their heart's content. Rumor—the same wicked goddess who libelled Miss Barrington—hinted that the doctor was not, within his own walls and under his own roof, the suffering angel the world saw him, and that he occasionally did a little trampling there on his own account. However, Mrs. Dill never complained; and though the children wore a tremulous terror and submissiveness in their looks, they were only suitable family traits, which all redounded to their credit, and made them "so like the doctor."

Such were the two worthies who slowly floated along on the current of the river of a calm summer's evening, to visit the Barringtons. As usual, the talk was of their host. They discussed his character and his habits and his debts, and the difficulty he had in raising that little loan; and in close juxtaposition with this fact, as though pinned on the back of it, his sister's overweening pride and pretension. It had been the Major's threat for years that he 'd "take her down a peg one of these days." But either he was mercifully unwilling to perform the act, or that the suitable hour for it had not come; but there she remained, and there he left her, not taken down one inch, but loftier and haughtier than ever. As the boat rounded the point from which the cottage was visible through the trees and some of the outhouses could be descried, they reverted to the ruinous state everything was falling into. "Straw is cheap enough, anyhow," said the Major. "He might put a new thatch on that cow-house, and I 'm sure a brush of paint would n't ruin any one." Oh, my dear reader! have you not often heard—I know that I have—such comments as these, such reflections on the indolence or indifference which only needed so very little to reform, done, too, without trouble or difficulty, habits that could be corrected, evil ways reformed, and ruinous tendencies arrested, all as it were by a "rush of paint," or something just as uncostly?

"There does n't seem to be much doing here, Dill," said M'Cormick, as they landed. "All the boats are drawn up ashore. And faith! I don't wonder, that old woman is enough to frighten the fish out of the river."

"Strangers do not always like that sort of thing," modestly remarked the doctor,—the "always" being peculiarly marked for emphasis. "Some will say, an inn should be an inn."

"That's my view of it. What I say is this: I want my bit of fish, and my beefsteak, and my pint of wine, and I don't want to know that the landlord's grandfather entertained the king, or that his aunt was a lady-in-waiting. 'Be' as high as you like,' says I, 'but don't make the bill so,'—eh, Dill?" And he cackled the harsh ungenial laugh which seems the birthright of all sorry jesters; and the doctor gave a little laugh too, more from habit, however, than enjoyment.

"Do you know, Dill," said the Major, disengaging himself from the arm which his lameness compelled him to lean on, and standing still in the pathway,—"do you know that I never reach thus far without having a sort of struggle with myself whether I won't turn back and go home again. Can you explain that, now?"

"It is the wound, perhaps, pains you, coming up the hill."

"It is not the wound. It's that woman!"

"Miss Barrington?"

"Just so. I have her before me now, sitting up behind the urn there, and saying, 'Have you had tea, Major M'Cormick?' when she knows well she did n't give it to me. Don't you feel that going up to the table for your cup is for all the world like doing homage?"

"Her manners are cold,—certainly cold."

"I wish they were. It's the fire that's in her I 'm afraid of! She has as wicked an eye in her head as ever I saw."

"She was greatly admired once, I 'm told; and she has many remains of beauty."

"Oh! for the matter of looks, there's worse. It's her nature, her temper,— herself, in fact, I can't endure."

"What is it you can't endure, M'Cormick?" cried Barrington, emerging from a side walk where he had just caught the last words. "If it be anything in this poor place of mine, let me hear, that I may have it amended."

"How are ye,—how are ye?" said the Major, with a very confused manner. "I was talking politics with Dill. I was telling him how I hated *them* Tories."

"I believe they are all pretty much alike," said Barring-ton; "at least, I knew they were in my day. And though we used to abuse him, and drink all kind of misfortunes to him every day of our lives, there was n't a truer gentleman nor a finer fellow in Ireland than Lord Castlereagh."

"I'm sure of it. I've often heard the same remark," chimed in Dill.

"It's a pity you didn't think so at the time of the Union," said M'Cormick, with a sneer.

"Many of us did; but it would not make us sell our country. But what need is there of going back to those times, and things that can't be helped now? Come in and have a cup of tea. I see my sister is waiting for us."

Why was it that Miss Barrington, on that evening, was grander and statelier than ever? Was it some anticipation of the meditated change in their station had impressed her manner with more of pride? I know not; but true it is she received her visitors with a reserve that was actually chilling. To no end did Barrington exert himself to conceal or counteract this frigidity. In all our moral chemistry we have never yet hit upon an antidote to a chilling reception.

The doctor was used to this freezing process, and did not suffer like his companion. To him, life was a huge ice-pail; but he defied frost-bite, and bore it. The Major, however chafed and fidgeted under the treatment, and muttered to himself very vengeful sentiments about that peg he had determined to take her down from.

"I was hoping to be able to offer you a nosegay, dear lady," said Dill,— this was his customary mode of address to her, an ingenious blending of affection with deference, but in which the stronger accent on the last word showed the deference to predominate,—"but the rain has come so late, there's not a stock in the garden fit to present to you."

"It is just as well, sir. I detest gillyflowers."

The Major's eyes sparkled with a spiteful delight, for he was sorely jealous of the doctor's ease under difficulties.

"We have, indeed, a few moss-roses."

"None to be compared to our own, sir. Do not think of it."

The Major felt that his was not a giving disposition, and consequently it exempted him from rubs and rebuffs of this sort. Meanwhile, unabashed by failure, the doctor essayed once more: "Mrs. Dill is only waiting to have the car mended, to come over and pay her dutiful respects to you, Miss Dinah."

"Pray tell her not to mind it, Dr. Dill," replied she, sharply, "or to wait till the fourth of next month, which will make it exactly a year since her last visit; and her call can be then an annual one, like the tax-gatherer's."

"Bother them for taxes altogether," chimed in Barrington, whose ear only caught the last word. "You haven't done with the county cess when there's a fellow at you for tithes; and they're talking of a poor-rate."

"You may perceive, Dr. Dill, that your medicines have not achieved a great success against my brother's deafness."

"We were all so at Walcheren," broke in M'Cormick; "when we 'd come out of the trenches, we could n't hear for hours."

"My voice may be a shrill one, Major M'Cormick, but I'll have you to believe that it has not destroyed my brother's tympanum."

"It's not the tympanum is engaged, dear lady; it's the Eustachian tube is the cause here. There's a passage leads down from the internal ear—"

"I declare, sir, I have just as little taste for anatomy as for fortification; and though I sincerely wish you could cure my brother, as I also wish these gentlemen could have taken Walcheren, I have not the slightest desire to know how."

"I 'll beg a little more tea in this, ma'am," said the Major, holding out his cup.

"Do you mean water, sir? Did you say it was too strong?"

"With your leave, I 'll take it a trifle stronger," said he, with a malicious twinkle in his eye, for he knew all the offence his speech implied.

"I'm glad to hear you say so, Major M'Cormick. I'm happy to know that your nerves are stronger than at the time of that expedition you quote with such pleasure. Is yours to your liking, sir?"

"I 'll ask for some water, dear lady," broke in Dill, who began to think that the fire was hotter than usual. "As I said to Mrs. Dill, 'Molly,' says I, 'how is it that I never drink such tea anywhere as at the—'" He stopped, for he was going to say, the Harringtons', and he trembled at the liberty; and he dared not say the Fisherman's Home, lest it should be thought he was recalling their occupation; and so, after a pause and a cough, he stammered out—"'at the sweet cottage.'" Nor was his confusion the less at perceiving how she had appreciated his difficulty, and was smiling at it.

"Very few strangers in these parts lately, I believe," said M'Cormick, who knew that his remark was a dangerous one.

"I fancy none, sir," said she, calmly. "We, at least, have no customers, if that be the name for them."

"It's natural, indeed, dear lady, you shouldn't know how they are called," began the doctor, in a fawning tone, "reared and brought up as you were."

The cold, steady stare of Miss Barrington arrested his speech; and though he made immense efforts to recover himself, there was that in her look which totally overcame him. "Sit down to your rubber, sir," said she, in a whisper that seemed to thrill through his veins. "You will find yourself far more at home at the odd trick there, than attempting to console me about my lost honors." And with this fierce admonition, she gave a little nod, half in adieu, half in admonition, and swept haughtily out of the room.

M'Cormick heaved a sigh as the door closed after her, which very plainly bespoke how much he felt the relief.

"My poor sister is a bit out of spirits this evening," said Barrington, who merely saw a certain show of constraint over his company, and never guessed the cause. "We've had some unpleasant letters, and one thing or another to annoy us, and if she does n't join us at supper, you 'll excuse her, I know, M'Cormick."

"That we will, with—" He was going to add, "with a heart and a half," for he felt, what to him was a rare sentiment, "gratitude;" but Dill chimed in,—

"Of course, we couldn't expect she'd appear. I remarked she was nervous when we came in. I saw an expression in her eye—"

"So did I, faith," muttered M'Cormick, "and I'm not a doctor."

"And here's our whist-table," said Barrington, bustling about; "and there 's a bit of supper ready there for us in that room, and we 'll help ourselves, for I 've sent Darby to bed. And now give me a hand with these cards, for they 've all got mixed together."

Barrington's task was the very wearisome one of trying to sort out an available pack from some half-dozen of various sizes and colors.

"Is n't this for all the world like raising a regiment out of twenty volunteer corps?" said M'Cormick.

"Dill would call it an hospital of incurables," said Barrington. "Have you got a knave of spades and a seven? Oh dear, dear! the knave, with the head off him! I begin to suspect we must look up a new pack." There was a tone of misgiving in the way he said this; for it implied a reference to his sister, and all its consequences. Affecting to search for new cards in his own room, therefore, he arose and went out.

"I wouldn't live in a slavery like that," muttered the Major, "to be King of France."

"Something has occurred here. There is some latent source of irritation," said Dill, cautiously. "Barrington's own manner is fidgety and uneasy. I have my suspicion matters are going on but poorly with them."

While this sage diagnosis was being uttered, M'Cormick had taken a short excursion into the adjoining room, from which he returned, eating a pickled onion. "It's the old story; the cold roast loin and the dish of salad. Listen! Did you hear that shout?"

"I thought I heard one awhile back; but I fancied afterwards it was only the noise of the river over the stones."

"It is some fellows drawing the river; they poach under his very windows, and he never sees them."

"I 'm afraid we 're not to have our rubber this evening," said Dill, mournfully.

"There's a thing, now, I don't understand!" said M'Cormick, in a low but bitter voice. "No man is obliged to see company, but when he does do it, he oughtn't to be running about for a tumbler here and a mustard-pot there. There's the noise again; it's fellows robbing the salmon-weir!"

"No rubber to-night, I perceive that," reiterated the doctor, still intent upon the one theme.

"A thousand pardons I ask from each of you," cried Barrington, coming hurriedly in, with a somewhat flushed face; "but I 've had such a hunt for these cards. When I put a thing away nowadays, it's as good as gone to me, for I remember nothing. But here we are, now, all right."

The party, like men eager to retrieve lost time, were soon deep in their game, very little being uttered, save such remarks as the contest called for. The Major was of that order of players who firmly believe fortune will desert them if they don't whine and complain of their luck, and so everything from him was a lamentation. The doctor, who regarded whist pathologically, no more gave up a game than he would a patient. He had witnessed marvellous recoveries in the most hopeless cases, and he had been rescued by a "revoke" in the last hour. Unlike each, Barrington was one who liked to chat over his game, as he would over his wine. Not that he took little interest in it, but it had no power to absorb and engross him. If a man derive very great pleasure from a pastime in which, after years and years of practice, he can attain no eminence nor any mastery, you may be almost certain he is one of an amiable temperament Nothing short of real goodness of nature could go on deriving enjoyment from a pursuit associated with continual defeats. Such a one must be hopeful, he must be submissive, he must have no touch of ungenerous jealousy in his nature, and, withal, a zealous wish to do better. Now he who can be all these, in anything, is no bad fellow.

If Barrington, therefore, was beaten, he bore it well. Cards were often enough against him, his play was always so; and though the doctor had words of bland consolation for disaster, such as the habits of his craft taught him, the Major was a pitiless adversary, who never omitted the opportunity of disinterring all his opponents' blunders, and singing a song of triumph over them. But so it is,—*tot genera hominum,*—so many kinds of whist-players are there!

Hour after hour went over, and it was late in the night. None felt disposed to sup; at least, none proposed it. The stakes were small, it is true, but small things are great to little men, and Barrington's guests were always the winners.

"I believe if I was to be a good player,—which I know in my heart I never shall," said Barrington,—"that my luck would swamp me, after all. Look at that hand now, and say is there a trick in it?" As he said this, he spread out the cards of his "dummy" on the table, with the dis-consolation of one thoroughly beaten.

"Well, it might be worse," said Dill, consolingly. "There's a queen of diamonds; and I would n't say, if you could get an opportunity to trump the club—"

"Let him try it," broke in the merciless Major; "let him just try it! My name isn't Dan M'Cormick if he'll win one card in that hand. There, now, I lead the ace of clubs. Play!"

"Patience, Major, patience; let me look over my hand. I 'm bad enough at the best, but I 'll be worse if you hurry me. Is that a king or a knave I see there?"

"It's neither; it 's the queen!" barked out the Major.

"Doctor, you 'll have to look after my eyes as well as my ears. Indeed, I scarcely know which is the worst. Was not that a voice outside?"

"I should think it was; there have been fellows shouting there the whole evening. I suspect they don't leave you many fish in this part of the river."

"I beg your pardon," interposed Dill, blandly, "but you 've taken up my card by mistake."

While Barrington was excusing himself, and trying to recover his lost clew to the game, there came a violent knocking at the door, and a loud voice called out, "Holloa! Will some of ye open the door, or must I put my foot through it?"

"There is somebody there," said Barrington, quietly, for he had now caught the words correctly; and taking a candle, he hastened out.

"At last," cried a stranger, as the door opened,—"at last! Do you know that we've been full twenty minutes here, listening to your animated discussion over the odd trick?—I fainting with hunger, and my friend with pain." And so saying, he assisted another to limp forward, who leaned on his arm and moved with the greatest difficulty.

The mere sight of one in suffering repressed any notion of a rejoinder to his somewhat rude speech, and Barrington led the way into the room.

"Have you met with an accident?" asked he, as he placed the sufferer on a sofa.

"Yes," interposed the first speaker; "he slipped down one of those rocks into the river, and has sprained, if he has not broken, something."

"It is our good fortune to have advice here; this gentleman is a doctor."

"Of the Royal College, and an M.D. of Aberdeen, besides," said Dill, with a professional smile, while, turning back his cuffs, he proceeded to remove the shoe and stocking of his patient.

"Don't be afraid of hurting, but just tell me at once what's the matter," said the young fellow, down whose cheeks great drops were rolling in his agony.

"There is no pronouncing at once; there is great tumefaction here. It may be a mere sprain, or it may be a fracture of the fibula simple, or a fracture with luxation."

"Well, if you can't tell the injury, tell us what's to be done for it. Get him to bed, I suppose, first?" said the friend.

"By all means, to bed, and cold applications on the affected part."

"Here's a room all ready, and at hand," said Barrington, opening the door into a little chamber replete with comfort and propriety.

"Come," said the first speaker, "Fred, all this is very snug; one might have fallen upon worse quarters." And so saying, he assisted his friend forward, and deposited him upon the bed.

While the doctor busied himself with the medical cares for his patient, and arranged with due skill the appliances to relieve his present suffering, the other stranger related how they had lost their way, having first of all taken the wrong bank of the river, and been obliged to retrace their steps upwards of three miles to retrieve their mistake.

"Where were you going to?" asked Barringtou.

"We were in search of a little inn they had told us of, called the 'Fisherman's Home.' I conclude we have reached it at last, and you are the host, I take it?"

Barrington bowed assent.

"And these gentlemen are visitors here?" But without waiting for any reply,—difficult at all times, for he spoke with great rapidity and continual change of topic,—he now stooped down to whisper something to the sick man. "My friend thinks he'll do capitally now, and, if we leave him, that he'll soon drop asleep; so I vote we give him the chance." Thus saying, he made a gesture for the others to leave, following them up as they went, almost like one enforcing an order.

"If I am correct in my reading, you are a soldier, sir," said Barrington, when they reached the outer room, "and this gentleman here is a brother officer,—Major M'Cor-mick."

"Full pay, eh?"

"No, I am an old Walcheren man."

"Walcheren—Walcheren—why, that sounds like Malplaquet or Blenheim! Where the deuce was Walcheren? Did n't believe that there was an old tumbril of that affair to the fore still. You were all licked there, or you died of the ague, or jaundice? Oh, dummy whist, as I live! Who's the unlucky dog has got the dummy?—bad as Walcheren, by Jove! Is n't that a supper I see laid out there? Don't I smell Stilton from that room?"

"If you 'll do us the honor to join us—"

"That I will, and astonish you with an appetite too! We breakfasted at a beastly hole called Graigue, and tasted nothing since, except a few peaches I stole out of an old fellow's garden on the riverside,—'Old Dan the miser,' a country fellow called him."

"I have the honor to have afforded you the entertainment you speak of," said M'Cormick, smarting with anger.

"All right! The peaches were excellent,—would have been better if riper. I 'm afraid I smashed a window of yours; it was a stone I shied at a confounded dog,—a sort of terrier. Pickled onions and walnuts, by all that 's civilized! And so this is the 'Fisherman's Home,' and you the fisherman, eh? Well, why not show a light or a lantern over the door? Who the deuce is to know that this is a place of entertainment? We only guessed it at last."

"May I help you to some mutton?" said Barrington, more amused than put out by his guest's discursiveness.

"By all means. But don't carve it that way; cut it lengthwise, as if it were the saddle, which it ought to have been. You must tell me where you got this sherry. I have tasted nothing like it for many a day,—real brown sherry. I suppose you know how they brown it? It's not done by sugar,—that's a vulgar error. It's done by boiling; they boil down so many butts and reduce them to about a fourth or a fifth. You haven't got any currant-jelly, have you? it is just as good with cold mutton as hot. And then it is the wine thus reduced they use for coloring matter. I got up all my sherry experiences on the spot."

"The wine you approve of has been in my cellar about five-and-forty years."

"It would not if I 'd have been your neighbor, rely upon that. I'd have secured every bottle of it for our mess; and mind, whatever remains of it is mine."

"Might I make bold to remark," said Dill, interposing, "that we are the guests of my friend here on this occasion?"

"Eh, what,—guests?"

"I am proud enough to believe that you will not refuse me the honor of your company; for though an innkeeper, I write myself gentleman," said Barrington, blandly, though not without emotion.

"I should think you might," broke in the stranger, heartily; "and I'd say the man who had a doubt about your claims had very little of his own. And now a word of apology for the mode of our entrance here, and to introduce myself. I am Colonel Hunter, of the 21st Hussars; my friend is a young subaltern of the regiment."

A moment before, and all the awkwardness of his position was painful to Barrington. He felt that the traveller was there by a right, free to order, condemn, and criticise as he pleased. The few words of explanation, given in all the frankness of a soldier, and with the tact of a gentleman, relieved this embarrassment, and he was himself again. As for M'Cormick and Dill, the mere announcement of the regiment he commanded seemed to move and impress them. It was one of those corps especially known in the service for the rank and fortune of its officers. The Prince himself was their colonel, and they had acquired a wide notoriety for exclusiveness and pride, which, when treated by unfriendly critics, assumed a shape less favorable still.

Colonel Hunter, if he were to be taken as a type of his regiment, might have rebutted a good deal of this floating criticism; he had a fine honest countenance, a rich mellow voice, and a sort of easy jollity in manner, that spoke well both for his spirits and his temper. He did, it is true, occasionally chafe against some susceptible spot or other of those around him, but there was no malice prepense in it, any more than there is intentional offence in the passage of a strong man through a crowd; so he elbowed his way, and pushed on in conversation, never so much as suspecting that he jostled any one in his path.

Both Barrington and Hunter were inveterate sportsmen, and they ranged over hunting-fields and grouse mountains and partridge stubble and trout streams with all the zest of men who feel a sort of mesmeric brotherhood in the interchange of their experiences. Long after the Major and the doctor had taken their leave, they sat there recounting stories of their several adventures, and recalling incidents of flood and field.

In return for a cordial invitation to Hunter to stay and fish the river for some days, Barrington pledged himself to visit the Colonel the first time he should go up to Kilkenny.

"And I'll mount you. You shall have a horse I never lent in my life. I'll put you on Trumpeter,—sire Sir Hercules,—no mistake there; would carry sixteen stone with the fastest hounds in England."

Barrington shook his head, and smiled, as he said, "It's two-and-twenty years since I sat a fence. I'm afraid I'll not revive the fame of my horsemanship by appearing again in the saddle."

"Why, what age do you call yourself?"

"Eighty-three, if I live to August next."

"I'd not have guessed you within ten years of it. I've just passed fifty, and already I begin to look for a horse with more bone beneath the knee, and more substance across the loins."

"These are only premonitory symptoms, after all," said Barrington, laughing. "You've many a day before you come to a fourteen-hand cob and a kitchen chair to mount him."

Hunter laughed at the picture, and dashed away, in his own half-reckless way, to other topics. He talked of his regiment proudly, and told Barrington what a splendid set of young fellows were his officers. "I'll show you such a mess," said he, "as no corps in the service can match." While he talked of their high-hearted and generous natures, and with enthusiasm of the life of a soldier, Barrington could scarcely refrain from speaking of his own "boy," the son from whom he had hoped so much, and whose loss had been the death-blow to all his ambitions. There were, however, circumstances in that story which sealed his lips; and though the father never believed one syllable of the allegations against his son, though he had paid the penalty of a King's Bench mandamus and imprisonment for horsewhipping the editor who had aspersed his "boy," the world and the world's verdict were against him, and he did not dare to revive the memory of a name against which all the severities of the press had been directed, and public opinion had condemned with all its weight and power.

"I see that I am wearying you," said Hunter, as he remarked the grave and saddened expression that now stole over Barrington's face. "I ought to have remembered what an hour it was,—more than half-past two." And without waiting to hear a reply, he shook his host's hand cordially and hurried off to his room.

While Barrington busied himself in locking up the wine, and putting away half-finished decanters,—cares that his sister's watchfulness very imperatively exacted,—he heard, or fancied he heard, a voice from the room where the sick man lay. He opened the door very gently and looked in.

"All right," said the youth. "I 'm not asleep, nor did I want to sleep, for I have been listening to you and the Colonel these two hours, and with rare pleasure, I can tell you. The Colonel would have gone a hundred miles to meet a man like yourself, so fond of the field and such a thorough sportsman."

"Yes, I was so once," sighed Barrington, for already had come a sort of reaction to the late excitement.

"Isn't the Colonel a fine fellow?" said the young man, as eager to relieve the awkwardness of a sad theme as to praise one he loved. "Don't you like him?"

"That I do!" said Barrington, heartily. "His fine genial spirit has put me in better temper with myself than I fancied was in my nature to be. We are to have some trout-fishing together, and I promise you it sha'n't be my fault if *he* doesn't like *me*."

"And may I be of the party?—may I go with you?"

"Only get well of your accident, and you shall do whatever you like. By the way, did not Colonel Hunter serve in India?"

"For fifteen years. He has only left Bengal within a few months."

"Then he can probably help me to some information. He may be able to tell me—Good-night, good-night," said he, hurriedly; "to-morrow will be time enough to think of this."

CHAPTER IV
FRED CONYERS

Very soon after daybreak the Colonel was up and at the bedside of his young friend.

"Sorry to wake you, Fred," said he, gently; "but I have just got an urgent despatch, requiring me to set out at once for Dublin, and I did n't like to go without asking how you get on."

"Oh, much better, sir. I can move the foot a little, and I feel assured it 's only a severe sprain."

"That's all right. Take your own time, and don't attempt to move about too early. You are in capital quarters here, and will be well looked after. There is only one difficulty, and I don't exactly see how to deal with it. Our host is a reduced gentleman, brought down to keep an inn for support, but what benefit he can derive from it is not so very clear; for when I asked the man who fetched me hot water this morning for my bill, he replied that his master told him I was to be his guest here for a week, and not on any account to accept money from me. Ireland is a very strange place, and we are learning something new in it every day; but this is the strangest thing I have met yet."

"In *my* case this would be impossible. I must of necessity give a deal of trouble,—not to say that it would add unspeakably to my annoyance to feel that I could not ask freely for what I wanted."

"I have no reason to suppose, mind you, that you are to be dealt with as I have been, but it would be well to bear in mind who and what these people are."

"And get away from them as soon as possible," added the young fellow, half peevishly.

"Nay, nay, Fred; don't be impatient. You'll be delighted with the old fellow, who is a heart-and-soul sportsman. What station he once occupied I can't guess; but in the remarks he makes about horses and hounds, all his knowing hints on stable management and the treatment of young cattle, one would say that he must have had a large fortune and kept a large establishment."

In the half self-sufficient toss of the head which received this speech, it was plain that the young man thought his Colonel was easily imposed on, and that such pretensions as these would have very little success with *him*.

"I have no doubt some of your brother officers will take a run down to see how you get on, and, if so, I'll send over a hamper of wine, or something of the kind, that you can manage to make him accept."

"It will not be very difficult, I opine," said the young man, laughingly.

"No, no," rejoined the other, misconstruing the drift of his words. "You have plenty of tact, Fred. You'll do the thing with all due delicacy. And now, good-bye. Let me hear how you fare here." And with a hearty farewell they parted.

There was none astir in the cottage but Darby as the Colonel set out to gain the high-road, where the post-horses awaited him. From Darby, however, as he went along, he gathered much of his host's former history. It was with astonishment he learned that the splendid house of Barrington Hall, where he had been dining with an earl a few days ago, was the old family seat of that poor innkeeper; that the noble deer-park had once acknowledged him for master. "And will again, plase God!" burst in Darby, who thirsted for an opportunity to launch out into law, and all its bright hopes and prospects.

"We have a record on trial in Trinity Term, and an argument before the twelve Judges, and the case is as plain as the nose on your honor's face; for it was ruled by Chief Baron Medge, in the great cause of 'Peter against Todd, a widow,' that a settlement couldn't be broke by an estreat."

"You are quite a lawyer, I see," said the Colonel.

"I wish I was. I'd rather be a judge on the bench than a king on his throne."

"And yet I am beginning to suspect law may have cost your master dearly."

"It is not ten, or twenty—no, nor thirty—thousand pounds would see him through it!" said Darby, with a triumph in his tone that seemed to proclaim a very proud declaration. "There's families would be comfortable for life with just what we spent upon special juries."

"Well, as you tell me he has no family, the injury has been all his own."

"That's true. We're the last of the ould stock," said he, sorrowfully; and little more passed between them, till the Colonel, on parting, put a couple of guineas in his hand, and enjoined him to look after the young friend he had left behind him.

It is now my task to introduce this young gentleman to my readers. Frederick Conyers, a cornet in his Majesty's Hussars, was the only son of a very distinguished officer, Lieutenant-General Conyers, a man who had not alone served with great reputation in the field, but held offices of high political trust in India, the country where all his life had been passed. Holding a high station as a political resident at a native court, wielding great power, and surrounded by an undeviating homage, General Conyers saw his son growing up to manhood with everything that could foster pride and minister to self-exaltation around him. It was not alone the languor and indolence of an Eastern life that he had to dread for him, but the haughty temper and overbearing spirit so sure to come out of habits of domination in very early life.

Though he had done all that he could to educate his son, by masters brought at immense cost from Europe, the really important element of education, — the self-control and respect for other's rights, — only to be acquired by daily life and intercourse with equals, this he could not supply; and he saw, at last, that the project he had so long indulged, of keeping his son with him, must be abandoned. Perhaps the rough speech of an old comrade helped to dispel the illusion, as he asked, "Are you bringing up that boy to be a Rajah?" His first thought was to send him to one of the Universities, his great desire being that the young man should feel some ambition for public life and its distinctions. He bethought him, however, that while the youth of Oxford and Cambridge enter upon a college career, trained by all the discipline of our public schools, Fred would approach the ordeal without any such preparation whatever. Without one to exert authority over him, little accustomed to the exercise of self-restraint, the experiment was too perilous.

To place him, therefore, where, from the very nature of his position, some guidance and control would be exercised, and where by the working of that model democracy — a mess — he would be taught to repress self-sufficiency and presumption, he determined on the army, and obtained a cornetcy in a regiment commanded by one who had long served on his own staff. To most young fellows such an opening in life would have seemed all that was delightful and enjoyable. To be just twenty, gazetted to a splendid cavalry corps, with a father rich enough and generous enough to say, "Live like the men about you, and don't be afraid that your checks will come back to you," these are great aids to a very pleasant existence. Whether the enervation of that life of Oriental indulgence had now become a nature to him, or whether he had no liking for the service itself, or whether the change from a condition of almost princely state to a position of mere equality with others, chafed and irritated him, but so is it, he did not "take to" the regiment, nor the regiment to him.

Now it is a fact, and not a very agreeable fact either, that a man with a mass of noble qualities may fail to attract the kindliness and good feeling towards him which a far less worthy individual, merely by certain traits, or by the semblance of them, of a yielding, passive nature is almost sure to acquire.

Conyers was generous, courageous, and loyal, in the most chivalrous sense of that word, to every obligation of friendship. He was eminently truthful and honorable; but he had two qualities whose baneful influence would disparage the very best of gifts. He was "imperious," and, in the phrase of his brother officers, "he never gave in." Some absurd impression had been made on him, as a child, that obstinacy and persistency were the noblest of attributes, and that, having said a thing, no event or circumstance could ever occur to induce a change of opinion.

Such a quality is singularly unfitted to youth, and marvellously out of place in a regiment; hence was it that the "Rajah," as he was generally called by his comrades, had few intimates, and not one friend amongst them.

If I have dwelt somewhat lengthily on these traits, it is because their possessor is one destined to be much before us in this history. I will but chronicle one other feature. I am sorry it should be a disqualifying one. Owing in great measure, perhaps altogether, to his having been brought up in the East, where Hindoo craft and subtlety were familiarized to his mind from infancy, he was given to suspect that few things were ever done from the motives ascribed to them, and that under the open game of life was another concealed game, which was the real one. As yet, this dark and pernicious distrust had only gone the length of impressing him with a sense of his own consummate acuteness, an amount of self-satisfaction, which my reader may have seen tingeing the few words he exchanged with his Colonel before separating.

Let us see him now as he sits in a great easy-chair, his sprained ankle resting on another, in a little honeysuckle-covered arbor of the garden, a table covered with books and fresh flowers beside him, while Darby stands ready to serve him from the breakfast-table, where a very tempting meal is already spread out.

"So, then, I can't see your master, it seems," said Con-yers, half peevishly.

"Faix you can't; he's ten miles off by this. He got a letter by the post, and set out half an hour after for Kilkenny. He went to your honor's door, but seeing you was asleep he would n't wake you; 'but, Darby,' says he, 'take care of that young gentleman, and mind,' says he, 'that he wants for nothing.'"

"Very thoughtful of *him*, —very considerate indeed," said the youth; but in what precise spirit it is not easy to say.

"Who lives about here? What gentlemen's places are there, I mean?"

"There's Lord Carrackmore, and Sir Arthur Godfrey, and Moore of Ballyduff, and Mrs. Powerscroft of the Grove—"

"Do any of these great folks come down here?"

Darby would like to have given a ready assent,—he would have been charmed to say that they came daily, that they made the place a continual rendezvous; but as he saw no prospect of being able to give his fiction even twenty-four hours' currency, he merely changed from one leg to the other, and, in a tone of apology, said, "Betimes they does, when the sayson is fine."

"Who are the persons who are most frequently here?"

"Those two that you saw last night,—the Major and Dr. Dill. They 're up here every second day, fishing, and eating their dinner with the master."

"Is the fishing good?"

"The best in Ireland."

"And what shooting is there, —any partridges?"

"Partridges, be gorra! You could n't see the turnips for them."

"And woodcocks?"

"Is it woodcocks! The sky is black with the sight of them."

"Any lions?"

"Well, maybe an odd one now and then," said Darby, half apologizing for the scarcity.

There was an ineffable expression of self-satisfaction in Conyers's face at the subtlety with which he had drawn Darby into this admission; and the delight in his own acuteness led him to offer the poor fellow a cigar, which he took with very grateful thanks.

"From what you tell me, then, I shall find this place stupid enough till I am able to be up and about, eh? Is there any one who can play chess hereabout?"

"Sure there's Miss Dinah; she's a great hand at it, they tell me."

"And who is Miss Dinah? Is she young,—is she pretty?"

Darby gave a very cautious look all around him, and then closing one eye, so as to give his face a look of intense cunning, he nodded very significantly twice.

"What do you mean by that?"

"I mane that she'll never see sixty; and for the matter of beauty—"

"Oh, you have said quite enough; I 'm not curious about her looks. Now for another point. If I should want to get away from this, what other inn or hotel is there in the neighborhood?"

"There's Joe M'Cabe's, at Inistioge; but you are better where you are. Where will you see fresh butter like that? and look at the cream, the spoon will stand in it. Far and near it's given up to her that nobody can make coffee like Miss Dinah; and when you taste them trout, you 'll tell me if they are not fit for the king."

"Everything is excellent,—could not be better; but there's a difficulty. There's a matter which to me at least makes a stay here most unpleasant. My friend tells me that he could not get his bill,—that he was accepted as a guest. Now I can't permit this—"

"There it is, now," said Darby, approaching the table, and dropping his voice to a confidential whisper. "That's the master's way. If he gets a stranger to sit down with him to dinner or supper, he may eat and drink as long as he plases, and sorra sixpence he'll pay; and it's that same ruins us, nothing else, for it's then he 'll call for the best sherry, and that ould Maderia that's worth a guinea a bottle. What's the use, after all, of me inflaming the bill of the next traveller, and putting down everything maybe double? And worse than all," continued he, in a tone of horror, "let him only hear any one complain about his bill or saying, 'What's this?' or 'I didn't get that,' out he'll come, as mighty and as grand as the Lord-Liftinint, and say, 'I 'm sorry, sir, that we failed to make this place agreeable to you. Will you do me the favor not to mind the bill at all?' and with that he'd tear it up in little bits and walk away."

"To me that would only be additional offence. I 'd not endure it."

"What could you do? You'd maybe slip a five-pound note into my hand, and say, 'Darby my man, settle this little matter for me; you know the ways of the place.'"

"I 'll not risk such an annoyance, at all events; that I 'm determined on."

Darby began now to perceive that he had misconceived his brief, and must alter his pleadings as quickly as possible; in fact, he saw he was "stopping an earth" he had meant merely to mask. "Just leave it all to me, your honor,—leave it all to me, and I 'll have your bill for you every morning on the breakfast-table. And why would n't you? Why would a gentleman like your honor be behouldin' to any one for his meat and drink?" burst he in, with an eager rapidity. "Why would n't you say, 'Darby, bring me this, get me that, fetch me the other; expinse is no object in life tome'?"

There was a faint twinkle of humor in the eye of Conyers, and Darby stopped short, and with that half-lisping simplicity which a few Irishmen understand to perfection, and can exercise whenever the occasion requires, he said: "But sure is n't your honor laughing at me, is n't it just making fun of me you are? All because I'm a poor ignorant crayture that knows no better!"

"Nothing of that kind," said Conyers, frankly. "I was only smiling at thoughts that went through my head at the moment."

"Well, faix! there's one coming up the path now won't make you laugh," said Darby, as he whispered, "It's Dr. Dill."

The doctor was early with his patient; if the case was not one of urgency, the sufferer was in a more elevated rank than usually fell to the chances of Dispensary practice. Then, it promised to be one of the nice chronic cases, in which tact and personal agreeability—the two great strongholds of Dr. Dill in his own estimation—were of far more importance than the materia medica. Now, if Dill's world was not a very big one, he knew it thoroughly. He was a chronicle of all the family incidents of the county, and could recount every disaster of every house for thirty miles round.

When the sprain had, therefore, been duly examined, and all the pangs of the patient sufficiently condoled with to establish the physician as a man of feeling, Dill proceeded to his task as a man of the world. Conyers, however, abruptly stopped him, by saying, "Tell me how I'm to get out of this place; some other inn, I mean."

"You are not comfortable here, then?" asked Dill.

"In one sense, perfectly so. I like the quietness, the delightful tranquillity, the scenery,—everything, in short, but one circumstance. I'm afraid these worthy people—whoever they are—want to regard me as a guest. Now I don't know them,—never saw them,—don't care to see them. My Colonel has a liking for all this sort of thing. It has to his mind a character of adventure that amuses him. It would n't in the least amuse me, and so I want to get away."

"Yes," repeated Dill, blandly, after him, "wants to get away; desires to change the air."

"Not at all," broke in Conyers, peevishly; "no question of air whatever. I don't want to be on a visit. I want an inn. What is this place they tell me of up the river,—Inis—something?"

"Inistioge. M'Cabe's house; the 'Spotted Duck;' very small, very poor, far from clean, besides."

"Is there nothing else? Can't you think of some other place? For I can't have my servant here, circumstanced as I am now."

The doctor paused to reply. The medical mind is eminently ready-witted, and Dill at a glance took in all the dangers of removing his patient. Should he transfer him to his own village, the visit which now had to be requited as a journey of three miles and upwards, would then be an affair of next door. Should he send him to Thomastown, it would be worse again, for then he would be within the precincts of a greater than Dill himself,—a practitioner who had a one-horse phaeton, and whose name was written on brass. "Would you dislike a comfortable lodging in a private family,—one of the first respectability, I may make bold to call it?"

"Abhor it!—couldn't endure it! I'm not essentially troublesome or exacting, but I like to be able to be either, whenever the humor takes me."

"I was thinking of a house where you might freely take these liberties—"

"Liberties! I call them rights, doctor, not liberties! Can't you imagine a man, not very wilful, not very capricious, but who, if the whim took him, would n't stand being thwarted by any habits of a so-called respectable family? There, don't throw up your eyes, and misunderstand me. All I mean is, that my hours of eating and sleeping have no rule. I smoke everywhere; I make as much noise as I please; and I never brook any impertinent curiosity about what I do, or what I leave undone."

"Under all the circumstances, you had, perhaps, better remain where you are," said Dill, thoughtfully.

"Of course, if these people will permit me to pay for my board and lodging. If they 'll condescend to let me be a stranger, I ask for nothing better than this place."

"Might I offer myself as a negotiator?" said Dill, insinuatingly; "for I opine that the case is not of the difficulty you suppose. Will you confide it to my hands?"

"With all my heart. I don't exactly see why there should be a negotiation at all; but if there must, pray be the special envoy."

When Dill arose and set out on his mission, the young fellow looked after him with an expression that seemed to say, "How you all imagine you are humbugging me, while I read every one of you like a book!"

Let us follow the doctor, and see how he acquitted himself in his diplomacy.

CHAPTER V
DILL AS A DIPLOMATIST

Dr. Dill had knocked twice at the door of Miss Barrington's little sitting-room, and no answer was returned to his summons.

"Is the dear lady at home?" asked he, blandly. But, though he waited for some seconds, no reply came.

"Might Dr. Dill be permitted to make his compliments?"

"Yes, come in," said a sharp voice, very much with the expression of one wearied out by importunity. Miss Barrington gave a brief nod in return for the profound obeisance of her visitor, and then turned again to a large map which covered the table before her.

"I took the opportunity of my professional call here this morning—"

"How is that young man,—is anything broken?"

"I incline to say there is no fracture. The flexors, and perhaps, indeed, the annular ligament, are the seat of all the mischief."

"A common sprain, in fact; a thing to rest for one day, and hold under the pump the day after."

"The dear lady is always prompt, always energetic; but these sort of cases are often complicated, and require nice management."

"And frequent visits," said she, with a dry gravity.

"All the world must live, dear lady,—all the world must live."

"Your profession does not always sustain your theory, sir; at least, popular scandal says you kill as many as you cure." "I know the dear lady has little faith in physic."

"Say none, sir, and you will be nearer the mark; but, remember, I seek no converts; I ask nobody to deny himself the luxuries of senna and gamboge because I prefer beef and mutton. You wanted to see my brother, I presume," added she, sharply, "but he started early this morning for Kilkenny. The Solicitor-General wanted to say a few words to him on his way down to Cork."

"That weary law! that weary law!" ejaculated Dill, fervently; for he well knew with what little favor Miss Barrington regarded litigation.

"And why so, sir?" retorted she, sharply. "What greater absurdity is there in being hypochondriac about your property than your person? My brother's taste inclines to depletion by law; others prefer the lancet."

"Always witty, always smart, the dear lady," said Dill, with a sad attempt at a smile. The flattery passed without acknowledgment of any kind, and he resumed: "I dropped in this morning to you, dear lady, on a matter which, perhaps, might not be altogether pleasing to you."

"Then don't do it, sir."

"If the dear lady would let me finish—"

"I was warning you, sir, not even to begin."

"Yes, madam," said he, stung into something like resistance; "but I would have added, had I been permitted, without any due reason for displeasure on your part."

"And are *you* the fitting judge of that, sir? If you know, as you say you know, that you are about to give me pain, by what presumption do you assert that it must be for my benefit? What's it all about?"

"I come on the part of this young gentleman, dear lady, who, having learned—I cannot say where or how—that he is not to consider himself here at an inn, but, as a guest, feels, with all the gratitude that the occasion warrants, that he has no claim to the attention, and that it is one which would render his position here too painful to persist in."

"How did he come by this impression, sir? Be frank and tell me."

"I am really unable to say, Miss Dinah."

"Come, sir, be honest, and own that the delusion arose from yourself,— yes, from yourself. It was in perceiving the courteous delicacy with which you declined a fee that he conceived this flattering notion of us; but go back to him, doctor, and say it is a pure mistake; that his breakfast will cost him one shilling, and his dinner two; the price of a boat to fetch him up to Thomastown is half a crown, and that the earlier he orders one the better. Listen to me, sir," said she, and her lips trembled with passion,— "listen to me, while I speak of this for the first and last time. Whenever my brother, recurring to what he once was, has been emboldened to treat a passing stranger as his guest, the choice has been so judiciously exercised as to fall upon one who could respect the motive and not resent the liberty; but never till this moment has it befallen us to be told that the possibility—the bare possibility—of such a presumption should be met by a declaration of refusal. Go back, then, to your patient, sir; assure him that he is at an inn, and that he has the right to be all that his purse and his want of manners can insure him."

"Dear lady, I'm, maybe, a bad negotiator."

"I trust sincerely, sir, you are a better doctor."

"Nothing on earth was further from my mind than offence—"

"Very possibly, sir; but, as you are aware, blisters will occasionally act with all the violence of caustics, so an irritating theme may be pressed at a very inauspicious moment. My cares as a hostess are not in very good favor with me just now. Counsel your young charge to a change of air, and I 'll think no more of the matter."

Had it been a queen who had spoken, the doctor could not more palpably have felt that his audience had terminated, and his only duty was to withdraw.

And so he did retire, with much bowing and graciously smiling, and indicating, by all imaginable contortions, gratitude for the past and humility forever.

I rejoice that I am not obliged to record as history the low but fervent mutterings that fell from his lips as he closed the door after him, and by a gesture of menace showed his feelings towards her he had just quitted. "Insolent old woman!" he burst out as he went along, "how can she presume to forget a station that every incident of her daily life recalls? In the rank she once held, and can never return to, such manners would be an outrage; but I 'll not endure it again. It is your last triumph, Miss Dinah; make much of it." Thus sustained by a very Dutch courage,—for this national gift can come of passion as well as drink,—he made his way to his patient's presence, smoothing his brow, as he went, and recalling the medico-chimrgical serenity of his features.

"I have not done much, but I have accomplished something," said he, blandly. "I am at a loss to understand what they mean by introducing all these caprices into their means of life; but, assuredly, it will not attract strangers to the house."

"What are the caprices you allude to?"

"Well, it is not very easy to say; perhaps I have not expressed my meaning quite correctly; but one thing is clear, a stranger likes to feel that his only obligation in an inn is to discharge the bill."

"I say, doctor," broke in Conyers, "I have been thinking the matter over. Why should I not go back to my quarters? There might surely be some means contrived to convey me to the high-road; after that, there will be no difficulty whatever."

The doctor actually shuddered at the thought. The sportsman who sees the bird he has just winged flutter away to his neighbor's preserve may understand something, at least, of Dr. Dill's discomfiture as he saw his wealthy patient threatening a departure. He quickly, therefore, summoned to his aid all those terrors which had so often done good service on like occasions. He gave a little graphic sketch of every evil consequence that might come of an imprudent journey. The catalogue was a bulky one; it ranged over tetanus, mortification, and disease of the bones. It included every sort and description of pain as classified by science, into "dull, weary, and incessant," or "sharp lancinating agony." Now Conyers was as brave as a lion, but had, withal, one of those temperaments which are miserably sensitive under suffering, and to which the mere description of pain is itself an acute pang. When, therefore, the doctor drew the picture of a case very like the present one, where amputation came too late, Conyers burst in with, "For mercy's sake, will you stop! I can't sit here to be cut up piece-meal; there's not a nerve in my body you haven't set ajar." The doctor blandly took out his massive watch, and laid his fingers on the young man's pulse. "Ninety-eight, and slightly intermittent," said he, as though to himself.

"What does that mean?" asked Conyers, eagerly.

"The irregular action of the heart implies abnormal condition of the nervous system, and indicates, imperatively, rest, repose, and tranquillity."

"If lethargy itself be required, this is a capital place for it," sighed Conyers, drearily.

"You have n't turned your thoughts to what I said awhile ago, being domesticated, as one might call it, in a nice quiet family, with all the tender attentions of a home, and a little music in the evening."

Simple as these words were, Dill gave to each of them an almost honeyed utterance.

"No; it would bore me excessively. I detest to be looked after; I abhor what are called attentions."

"Unobtrusively offered, — tendered with a due delicacy and reserve?"

"Which means a sort of simpering civility that one has to smirk for in return. No, no; I was bred up in quite a different school, where we clapped our hands twice when we wanted a servant, and the fellow's head paid for it if he was slow in coming. Don't tell me any more about your pleasant family, for they 'd neither endure me, nor I them. Get me well as fast as you can, and out of this confounded place, and I 'll give you leave to make a vascular preparation of me if you catch me here again!"

The doctor smiled, as doctors know how to smile when patients think they have said a smartness, and now each was somewhat on better terms with the other.

"By the way, doctor," said Conyers, suddenly, "you have n't told me what the old woman said. What arrangement did you come to?"

"Your breakfast will cost one shilling, your dinner two. She made no mention of your rooms, but only hinted that, whenever you took your departure, the charge for the boat was half a crown."

"Come, all this is very business-like, and to the purpose; but where, in Heaven's name, did any man live in this fashion for so little? We have a breakfast-mess, but it's not to be compared with this,—such a variety of bread, such grilled trout, such a profusion of fruit. After all, doctor, it is very like being a guest, the nominal charge being to escape the sense of a favor. But perhaps one can do here as at one of those 'hospices' in the Alps, and make a present at parting to requite the hospitality."

"It is a graceful way to record gratitude," said the doctor, who liked to think that the practice could be extended to other reminiscences.

"I must have my servant and my books, my pipes and my Spitz terrier. I 'll get a target up, besides, on that cherry-tree, and practise pistol-shooting as I sit here. Could you find out some idle fellow who would play chess or écarté with me,—a curate or a priest,—I 'm not particular; and when my man Holt comes, I 'll make him string my grass-mat hammock between those two elms, so that I can fish without the bore of standing up for it. Holt is a rare clever fellow, and you 'll see how he'll get things in order here before he's a day in the place."

The doctor smiled again, for he saw that his patient desired to be deemed a marvel of resources and a mine of original thought. The doctor's smile was apportioned to his conversation, just as he added syrups in his prescriptions. It was, as he himself called it, the "vehicle," without special efficacy in itself, but it aided to get down the "active principle." But he did more than smile. He promised all possible assistance to carry out his patient's plans. He was almost certain that a friend of his, an old soldier, too,—a Major M'Cormick,—could play écarté, though, perhaps, it might be cribbage; and then Father Cody, he could answer for it, was wonderful at skittles, though, for the present, that game might not be practicable; and as for books, the library at Woodstay was full of them, if the key could only be come at, for the family was abroad; and, in fact, he displayed a most generous willingness to oblige, although, when brought to the rude test of reality, his pictures were only dissolving views of pleasures to come.

When he took his leave at last, he left Conyers in far better spirits than he found him. The young fellow had begun to castle-build about how he should pass his time, and in such architecture there is no room for ennui. And what a rare organ must constructiveness be, when even in its mockery it can yield such pleasure! We are very prone to envy the rich man, whose wealth sets no limit to his caprices; but is not a rich fancy, that wondrous imaginative power which unweariedly invents new incidents, new personages, new situations, a very covetable possession? And can we not, in the gratification of the very humblest exercise of this quality, rudely approximate to the ecstasy of him who wields it in all its force? Not that Fred Conyers was one of these; he was a mere tyro in the faculty, and could only carry himself into a region where he saw his Spitz terrier jump between the back rails of a chair, and himself sending bullet after bullet through the very centre of the bull's eye.

Be it so. Perhaps you and I, too, my reader, have our Spitz terrier and bull's-eye days, and, if so, let us be grateful for them.

CHAPTER VI
THE DOCTOR'S DAUGHTER

Whether it was that Dr. Dill expended all the benevolence of his disposition in the course of his practice, and came home utterly exhausted, but so it was, that his family never saw him in those moods of blandness which he invariably appeared in to his patients. In fact, however loaded he went forth with these wares of a morning, he disposed of every item of his stock before he got back at night; and when poor Mrs. Dill heard, as she from time to time did hear, of the doctor's gentleness, his kindness in suffering, his beautiful and touching sympathy with sorrow, she listened with the same sort of semi-stupid astonishment she would have felt on hearing some one eulogizing the climate of Ireland, and going rapturous about the blue sky and the glorious sunshine. Unhappy little woman, she only saw him in his dark days of cloud and rain, and she never came into his presence except in a sort of moral mackintosh made for the worst weather.

The doctor's family consisted of seven children, but our concern is only with the two eldest,—a son and a daughter. Tom was two years younger than his sister, who, at this period of our story, was verging on nineteen. He was an awkward, ungainly youth, large-jointed, but weakly, with a sandy red head and much-freckled face, just such a disparaging counterpart of his sister as a coarse American piracy often presents of one of our well-printed, richly papered English editions. "It was all there," but all unseemly, ungraceful, undignified; for Polly Dill was pretty. Her hair was auburn, her eyes a deep hazel, and her skin a marvel of transparent whiteness. You would never have hesitated to call her a very pretty girl if you had not seen her brother, but, having seen him, all the traits of her good looks suffered in the same way that Grisi's "Norma" does from the horrid recollection of Paul Bedford's.

After all, the resemblance went very little further than this "travestie," for while he was a slow, heavy-witted, loutish creature, with low tastes and low ambitions, she was a clever, intelligent girl, very eagerly intent on making something of her advantages. Though the doctor was a general practitioner, and had a shop, which he called "Surgery," in the village, he was received at the great houses in a sort of half-intimate, half-patronizing fashion; as one, in short, with whom it was not necessary to be formal, but it might become very inconvenient to have a coldness. These were very sorry credentials for acceptance, but he made no objection to them.

A few, however, of the "neighbors" — it would be ungenerous to inquire the motive, for in this world of ours it is just as well to regard one's five-pound note as convertible into five gold sovereigns, and not speculate as to the kind of rags it is made of — were pleased to notice Miss Dill, and occasionally invite her to their larger gatherings, so that she not only gained opportunities of cultivating her social gifts, but, what is often a greater spur to ambition, of comparing them with those of others.

Now this same measuring process, if only conducted without any envy or ungenerous rivalry, is not without its advantage. Polly Dill made it really profitable. I will not presume to say that, in her heart of hearts, she did not envy the social accidents that gave others precedence before her, but into her heart of hearts neither you nor I have any claim to enter. Enough that we know nothing in her outward conduct or bearing revealed such a sentiment. As little did she maintain her position by flattery, which many in her ambiguous station would have relied upon as a stronghold. No; Polly followed a very simple policy, which was all the more successful that it never seemed to be a policy at all. She never in any way attracted towards her the attentions of those men who, in the marriageable market, were looked on as the choice lots; squires in possession, elder sons, and favorite nephews, she regarded as so much forbidden fruit. It was a lottery in which she never took a ticket It is incredible how much kindly notice and favorable recognition accrued to her from this line.

We all know how pleasant it is to be next to the man at a promiscuous dinner who never eats turtle nor cares for "Cliquot;" and in the world at large there are people who represent the calabash and the champagne.

Then Polly played well, but was quite as ready to play as to dance. She sang prettily, too, and had not the slightest objection that one of her simple ballads should be the foil to a grand performance of some young lady, whose artistic agonies rivalled Alboni's. So cleverly did Polly do all this, that even her father could not discover the secret of her success; and though he saw "his little girl" as he called her, more and more sought after and invited, he continued to be persuaded that all this favoritism was only the reflex of his own popularity. How, then, could mere acquaintances ever suspect what to the eye of those nearer and closer was so inscrutable?

Polly Dill rode very well and very fearlessly, and occasionally was assisted to "a mount" by some country gentleman, who combined gallantry with profit, and knew that the horse he lent could never be seen to greater advantage. Yet, even in this, she avoided display, quite satisfied, as it seemed, to enjoy herself thoroughly, and not attract any notice that could be avoided. Indeed, she never tried for "a place," but rather attached herself to some of the older and heavier weights, who grew to believe that they were especially in charge of her, and nothing was more common, at the end of a hard run, than to hear such self-gratulations as, "I think I took great care of you, Miss Dill?" "Eh, Miss Polly! you see I'm not such a bad leader!" and so on.

Such was the doctor's "little girl," whom I am about to present to my readers under another aspect. She is at home, dressed in a neatly fitting but very simple cotton dress, her hair in two plain bands, and she is seated at a table, at the opposite of which lounges her brother Tom with an air of dogged and sleepy indolence, which extends from his ill-trimmed hair to his ill-buttoned waistcoat.

"Never mind it to-day, Polly," said he, with a yawn. "I've been up all night, and have no head for work. There's a good girl, let's have a chat instead."

"Impossible, Tom," said she, calmly, but with decision. "To-day is the third. You have only three weeks now and two days before your examination. We have all the bones and ligaments to go over again, and the whole vascular system. You 've forgotten every word of Harrison."

"It does n't signify, Polly. They never take a fellow on anything but two arteries for the navy. Grove told me so."

"Grove is an ass, and got plucked twice. It is a perfect disgrace to quote him."

"Well, I only wish I may do as well. He's assistant-surgeon to the 'Taurus' gun-brig on the African station; and if I was there, it's little I 'd care for the whole lot of bones and balderdash."

"Come, don't be silly. Let us go on with the scapula. Describe the glenoid cavity."

"If you were the girl you might be, I'd not be bored with all this stupid trash, Polly."

"What do you mean? I don't understand you."

"It's easy enough to understand me. You are as thick as thieves, you and that old Admiral,—that Sir Charles Cobham. I saw you talking to the old fellow at the meet the other morning. You 've only to say, 'There's Tom— my brother Tom—wants a navy appointment; he's not passed yet, but if the fellows at the Board got a hint, just as much as, "Don't be hard on him—"'"

"I 'd not do it to make you a post-captain, sir," said she, severely. "You very much overrate my influence, and very much underrate my integrity, when you ask it."

"Hoity-toity! ain't we dignified! So you'd rather see me plucked, eh?"

"Yes, if that should be the only alternative."

"Thank you, Polly, that's all! thank you," said he; and he drew his sleeve across his eyes.

"My dear Tom," said she, laying her white soft hand on his coarse brown fingers, "can you not see that if I even stooped to anything so unworthy, that it would compromise your whole prospects in life? You'd obtain an assistant-surgeoncy, and never rise above it."

"And do I ask to rise above it? Do I ask anything beyond getting out of this house, and earning bread that is not grudged me?"

"Nay, nay; if you talk that way, I've done."

"Well, I do talk that way. He sent me off to Kilkenny last week—you saw it yourself—to bring out that trash for the shop, and he would n't pay the car hire, and made me carry two stone of carbonate of magnesia and a jar of leeches fourteen miles. You were just taking that post and rail out of Nixon's lawn as I came by. You saw me well enough."

"I am glad to say I did not," said she, sighing.

"I saw you, then, and how that gray carried you! You were waving a handkerchief in your hand; what was that for?"

"It was to show Ambrose Bushe that the ground was good; he was afraid of being staked!"

"That's exactly what I am. I 'm afraid of being 'staked up' at the Hall, and if *you* 'd take as much trouble about your brother as you did for Ambrose Bushe—"

"Tom, Tom, I have taken it for eight weary months. I believe I know Bell on the bones, and Harrison on the arteries, by heart!"

"Who thanks you?" said he, doggedly. "When you read a thing twice, you never forget it; but it's not so with me."

"Try what a little work will do, Tom; be assured there is not half as much disparity between people's brains as there is between their industry."

"I'd rather have luck than either, I know that. It's the only thing, after all."

She gave a very deep sigh, and leaned her head on her hand.

"Work and toil as hard as you may," continued he, with all the fervor of one on a favorite theme, "if you haven't luck you 'll be beaten. Can you deny that, Polly?"

"If you allow me to call merit what you call luck, I'll agree with you. But I 'd much rather go on with our work. What is the insertion of the deltoid? I'm sure you know *that!*"

"The deltoid! the deltoid!" muttered he. "I forget all about the deltoid, but, of course, it's like the rest of them. It's inserted into a ridge or a process, or whatever you call it—"

"Oh, Tom, this is very hopeless. How can you presume to face your examiners with such ignorance as this?"

"I'll tell you what I'll do, Polly; Grove told me he did it,—if I find my pluck failing me, I 'll have a go of brandy before I go in."

She found it very hard not to laugh at the solemn gravity of this speech, and just as hard not to cry as she looked at him who spoke it At the same moment Dr. Dill opened the door, calling out sharply, "Where's that fellow, Tom? Who has seen him this morning?"

"He's here, papa," said Polly. "We are brushing up the anatomy for the last time."

"His head must be in capital order for it, after his night's exploit. I heard of you, sir, and your reputable wager. Noonan was up here this morning with the whole story!"

"I 'd have won if they 'd not put snuff in the punch—"

"You are a shameless hound—"

"Oh, papa! If you knew how he was working,—how eager he is to pass his examination, and be a credit to us all, and owe his independence to himself—"

"I know more of him than you do, miss,—far more, too, than he is aware of,—and I know something of myself also; and I tell him now, that if he's rejected at the examination, he need not come back here with the news."

"And where am I to go, then?" asked the young fellow, half insolently.

"You may go—" Where to, the doctor was not suffered to indicate, for already Polly had thrown herself into his arms and arrested the speech.

"Well, I suppose I can 'list; a fellow need not know much about gallipots for that." As he said this, he snatched up his tattered old cap and made for the door.

"Stay, sir! I have business for you to do," cried Dill, sternly. "There's a young gentleman at the 'Fisherman's Home' laid up with a bad sprain. I have prescribed twenty leeches on the part. Go down and apply them."

"That's what old Molly Day used to do," said Tom, angrily.'

"Yes, sir, and knew more of the occasion that required it than you will ever do. See that you apply them all to the outer ankle, and attend well to the bleeding; the patient is a young man of rank, with whom you had better take no liberties."

"If I go at all—"

"Tom, Tom, none of this!" said Polly, who drew very close to him, and looked up at him with eyes full of tears.

"Am I going as your son this time? or did you tell him—as you told Mr. Nixon—that you 'd send your young man?"

"There! listen to that!" cried the doctor, turning to Polly. "I hope you are proud of your pupil."

She made no answer, but whispering some hurried words in her brother's ear, and pressing at the same time something into his hand, she shuffled him out of the room and closed the door.

The doctor now paced the room, so engrossed by passion that he forgot he was not alone, and uttered threats and mumbled out dark predictions with a fearful energy. Meanwhile Polly put by the books and drawings, and removed everything which might recall the late misadventure.

"What's your letter about, papa?" said she, pointing to a square-shaped envelope which he still held in his hand.

"Oh, by the way," said he, quietly, "this is from Cob-ham. They ask us up there to dinner to-day, and to stop the night." The doctor tried very hard to utter this speech with the unconcern of one alluding to some every-day occurrence. Nay, he did more; he endeavored to throw into it a certain air of fastidious weariness, as though to say, "See how these people will have me; mark how they persecute me with their attentions!"

Polly understood the "situation" perfectly, and it was with actual curiosity in her tone she asked, "Do you mean to go, sir?"

"I suppose we must, dear," he said, with a deep sigh. "A professional man is no more the arbiter of his social hours than of his business ones. Cooper always said dining at home costs a thousand a year."

"So much, papa?" asked she, with much semblance of innocence.

"I don't mean to myself," said he, reddening, "nor to any physician in country practice; but we all lose by it, more or less."

Polly, meanwhile, had taken the letter, and was reading it over. It was very brief. It had been originally begun, "Lady Cobham presents," but a pen was run through the words, and it ran, —

> "*Dear Dr. Dill, — If a short notice will not inconvenience*
> *you, will you and your daughter dine here to-day at seven?*
> *There is no moon, and we shall expect you to stay the night.*
> "*Truly yours,*
> "*Georgiana Cobham.*

"The Admiral hopes Miss D. will not forget to bring her music."

"Then we go, sir?" asked she, with eagerness; for it was a house to which she had never yet been invited, though she had long wished for the entrée.

"I shall go, certainly," said he. "As to you, there will be the old discussion with your mother as to clothes, and the usual declaration that you have really nothing to put on."

"Oh! but I have, papa. My wonderful-worked muslin, that was to have astonished the world at the race ball, but which arrived too late, is now quite ready to captivate all beholders; and I have just learned that new song, 'Where's the slave so lowly?' which I mean to give with a most rebellious fervor; and, in fact, I am dying to assault this same fortress of Cobham, and see what it is like inside the citadel."

"Pretty much like Woodstay, and the Grove, and Mount Kelly, and the other places we go to," said Dill, pompously.

"The same sort of rooms, the same sort of dinner, the same company; nothing different but the liveries."

"Very true, papa; but there is always an interest in seeing how people behave in their own house, whom you have never seen except in strangers'. I have met Lady Cobham at the Beachers', where she scarcely noticed me. I am curious to see what sort of reception she will vouchsafe me at home."

"Well, go and look after your things, for we have eight miles to drive, and Billy has already been at Dangan and over to Mooney's Mills, and he 's not the fresher for it."

"I suppose I 'd better take my hat and habit, papa?"

"What for, child?"

"Just as you always carry your lancets, papa, — you don't know what may turn up." And she was off before he could answer her.

CHAPTER VII
TOM DILL'S FIRST PATIENT

Before Tom Dill had set out on his errand he had learned all about his father and sister's dinner engagement; nor did the contrast with the way in which his own time was to be passed at all improve his temper. Indeed, he took the opportunity of intimating to his mother how few favors fell to her share or his own,—a piece of information she very philosophically received, all her sympathies being far more interested for the sorrows of "Clarissa Harlowe" than for any incident that occurred around her. Poor old lady! she had read that story over and over again, till it might seem that every word and every comma in it had become her own; but she was blessed with a memory that retained nothing, and she could cry over the sorrowful bits, and pant with eagerness at the critical ones, just as passionately, just as fervently, as she had done for years and years before. Dim, vague perceptions she might have retained of the personages, but these only gave them a stronger truthfulness, and made them more like the people of the real world, whom she had seen, passingly, once, and was now to learn more about. I doubt if Mezzofanti ever derived one tenth of the pleasure from all his marvellous memory that she did from the want of one.

Blessed with that one book, she was proof against all the common accidents of life. It was her sanctuary against duns, and difficulties, and the doctor's temper. As the miser feels a sort of ecstasy in the secret of his hoarded wealth, so had she an intense enjoyment in thinking that all dear Clarissa's trials and sufferings were only known to her. Neither the doctor, nor Polly, nor Tom, so much as suspected them. It was like a confidence between Mr. Richardson and herself, and for nothing on earth would she have betrayed it.

Tom had no such resources, and he set out on his mission with no very remarkable good feeling towards the world at large. Still, Polly had pressed into his hand a gold half-guinea,—some very long-treasured keepsake, the birthday gift of a godmother in times remote, and now to be converted into tobacco and beer, and some articles of fishing-gear which he greatly needed.

Seated in one of those light canoe-shaped skiffs,—"cots," as they are called on these rivers,—he suffered himself to be carried lazily along by the stream, while he tied his flies and adjusted his tackle. There is, sometimes, a stronger sense of unhappiness attached to what is called being "hardly used" by the world, than to a direct palpable misfortune; for though the sufferer may not be able, even to his own heart, to set out, with clearness, one single count in the indictment, yet a general sense of hard treatment, unfairness, and so forth, brings with it great depression, and a feeling of desolation.

Like all young fellows of his stamp, Tom only saw his inflictions, not one of his transgressions. He knew that his father made a common drudge of him, employed him in all that was wearisome and even menial in his craft, admitted him to no confidences, gave him no counsels, and treated him in every way like one who was never destined to rise above the meanest cares and lowest duties. Even those little fleeting glances at a brighter future which Polly would now and then open to his ambition, never came from his father, who would actually ridicule the notion of his obtaining a degree, and make the thought of a commission in the service a subject for mockery.

He was low in heart as he thought over these things. "If it were not for Polly," so he said to himself, "he 'd go and enlist;" or, as his boat slowly floated into a dark angle of the stream where the water was still and the shadow deep, he even felt he could do worse. "Poor Polly!" said he, as he moved his hand to and fro in the cold clear water, "you 'd be very, very sorry for me. You, at least, knew that I was not all bad, and that I wanted to be better. It was no fault of mine to have a head that could n't learn. I 'd be clever if I could, and do everything as well as she does; but when they see that I have no talents, that if they put the task before me I cannot master it, sure they ought to pity me, not blame me." And then he bent over the boat and looked down eagerly into the water, till, by long dint of gazing, he saw, or he thought he saw, the gravelly bed beneath; and again he swept his hand through it,—it was cold, and caused a slight shudder. Then, suddenly, with some fresh impulse, he threw off his cap, and kicked his shoes from him. His trembling hands buttoned and unbuttoned his coat with some infirm, uncertain purpose. He stopped and listened; he heard a sound; there was some one near,—quite near. He bent down and peered under the branches that hung over the stream, and there he saw a very old and infirm man, so old and infirm that he could barely creep. He had been carrying a little bundle of fagots for firewood, and the cord had given way, and his burden fallen, scattered, to the ground. This was the noise Tom had heard. For a few minutes the old man seemed overwhelmed with his disaster, and stood motionless, contemplating it; then, as it were, taking courage, he laid down his staff, and bending on his knees, set slowly to work to gather up his fagots.

There are minutes in the lives of all of us when some simple incident will speak to our hearts with a force that human words never carried,— when the most trivial event will teach a lesson that all our wisdom never gave us. "Poor old fellow," said Tom, "he has a stout heart left to him still, and he 'll not leave his load behind him!" And then his own craven spirit flashed across him, and he hid his face in his hand and cried bitterly.

Suddenly rousing himself with a sort of convulsive shake, he sent the skiff with a strong shove in shore, and gave the old fellow what remained to him of Polly's present; and then, with a lighter spirit than he had known for many a day, rowed manfully on his way.

The evening—a soft, mellow, summer evening—was just falling as Tom reached the little boat quay at the "Fisherman's Home,"—a spot it was seldom his fortune to visit, but one for whose woodland beauty and trim comfort he had a deep admiration. He would have liked to have lingered a little to inspect the boat-house, and the little aviary over it, and the small cottage on the island, and the little terrace made to fish from; but Darby had caught sight of him as he landed, and came hurriedly down to say that the young gentleman was growing very impatient for his coming, and was even hinting at sending for another doctor if he should not soon appear.

If Conyers was as impatient as Darby represented, he had, at least, surrounded himself with every appliance to allay the fervor of that spirit He had dined under a spreading sycamore-tree, and now sat with a table richly covered before him. Fruit, flowers, and wine abounded, with a profusion that might have satisfied several guests; for, as he understood that he was to consider himself at an inn, he resolved, by ordering the most costly things, to give the house all the advantage of his presence. The most delicious hothouse fruit had been procured from the gardener of an absent proprietor in the neighborhood, and several kinds of wine figured on the table, over which, and half shadowed by the leaves, a lamp had been suspended, throwing a fitful light over all, that imparted a most picturesque effect to the scene.

And yet, amidst all these luxuries and delights, Bal-shazzar was discontented; his ankle pained him; he had been hobbling about on it all day, and increased the inflammation considerably; and, besides this, he was lonely; he had no one but Darby to talk to, and had grown to feel for that sapient functionary a perfect abhorrence,—his everlasting compliance, his eternal coincidence with everything, being a torment infinitely worse than the most dogged and mulish opposition. When, therefore, he heard at last the doctor's son had come with the leeches, he hailed him as a welcome guest.

"What a time you have kept me waiting!" said he, as the loutish young man came forward, so astounded by the scene before him that he lost all presence of mind. "I have been looking out for you since three o'clock, and pottering down the river and back so often, that I have made the leg twice as thick again."

"Why didn't you sit quiet?" said Tom, in a hoarse, husky tone.

"Sit quiet!" replied Conyers, staring half angrily at him; and then as quickly perceiving that no impertinence had been intended, which the other's changing color and evident confusion attested, he begged him to take a chair and fill his glass. "That next you is some sort of Rhine wine: this is sherry; and here is the very best claret I ever tasted."

"Well, I 'll take that," said Tom, who, accepting the recommendation amidst luxuries all new and strange to him, proceeded to fill his glass, but so tremblingly that he spilled the wine all about the table, and then hurriedly wiped it up with his handkerchief.

Conyers did his utmost to set his guest at his ease. He passed his cigar-case across the table, and led him on, as well as he might, to talk. But Tom was awestruck, not alone by the splendors around him, but by the condescension of his host; and he could not divest himself of the notion that he must have been mistaken for somebody else, to whom all these blandishments might be rightfully due.

"Are you fond of shooting?" asked Conyers, trying to engage a conversation.

"Yes," was the curt reply.

"There must be good sport hereabouts, I should say. Is the game well preserved?"

"Too well for such as me. I never get a shot without the risk of a jail, and it would be cheaper for me to kill a cow than a woodcock!" There was a stern gravity in the way he said this that made it irresistibly comic, and Conyers laughed out in spite of himself.

"Have n't you a game license?" asked he.

"Haven't I a coach-and-six? Where would I get four pounds seven and ten to pay for it?"

The appeal was awkward, and for a moment Conyers was silent At last he said, "You fish, I suppose?"

"Yes; I kill a salmon whenever I get a quiet spot that nobody sees me, and I draw the river now and then with a net at night."

"That's poaching, I take it."

"It 's not the worse for that!" said Tom, whose pluck was by this time considerably assisted by the claret.

"Well, it's an unfair way, at all events, and destroys real sport"

"Real sport is filling your basket."

"No, no; there's no real sport in doing anything that's unfair,—anything that's un——" He stopped short, and swallowed off a glass of wine to cover his confusion.

"That's all mighty fine for you, who can not only pay for a license, but you 're just as sure to be invited here, there, and everywhere there's game to be killed. But think of me, that never snaps a cap, never throws a line, but he knows it's worse than robbing a hen-roost, and often, maybe, just as fond of it as yourself!"

Whether it was that, coming after Darby's mawkish and servile agreement with everything, this rugged nature seemed more palatable, I cannot say; but so it was, Con-yers felt pleasure in talking to this rough unpolished creature, and hearing his opinions in turn. Had there been in Tom Dill's manner the slightest shade of any pretence, was there any element of that which, for want of a better word, we call "snobbery," Conyers would not have endured him for a moment, but Tom was perfectly devoid of this vulgarity. He was often coarse in his remarks, his expressions were rarely measured by any rule of good manners; but it was easy to see that he never intended offence, nor did he so much as suspect that he could give that weight to any opinion which he uttered to make it of moment.

Besides these points in Tom's favor, there was another, which also led Conyers to converse with him. There is some very subtle self-flattery in the condescension of one well to do in all the gifts of fortune associating, in an assumed equality, with some poor fellow to whom fate has assigned the shady side of the highway. Scarcely a subject can be touched without suggesting something for self-gratulation; every comparison, every contrast is in his favor, and Conyers, without being more of a puppy than the majority of his order, constantly felt how immeasurably above all his guest's views of his life and the world were his own,—not alone that he was more moderate in language and less prone to attribute evil, but with a finer sense of honor and a wider feeling of liberality.

When Tom at last, with some shame, remembered that he had forgotten all about the real object of his mission, and had never so much as alluded to the leeches, Conyers only laughed and said, "Never mind them to-night. Come back to-morrow and put them on; and mind,—come to breakfast at ten or eleven o'clock."

"What am I to say to my father?"

"Say it was a whim of mine, which it is. You are quite ready to do this matter now. I see it; but I say no. Is n't that enough?"

"I suppose so!" muttered Tom, with a sort of dogged misgiving.

"It strikes me that you have a very respectable fear of your governor. Am I right?"

"Ain't you afraid of yours?" bluntly asked the other.

"Afraid of mine!" cried Conyers, with a loud laugh; "I should think not. Why, my father and myself are as thick as two thieves. I never was in a scrape that I did n't tell him. I 'd sit down this minute and write to him just as I would to any fellow in the regiment."

"Well, there 's only one in all the world I 'd tell a secret to, and it is n't My father!"

"Who is it, then?"

"My sister Polly!" It was impossible to have uttered these words with a stronger sense of pride. He dwelt slowly upon each of them, and, when he had finished, looked as though he had said something utterly undeniable.

"Here's her health,—in a bumper too!" cried Conyers.

"Hurray, hurray!" shouted out Tom, as he tossed off his full glass, and set it on the table with a bang that smashed it. "Oh, I beg pardon! I didn't mean to break the tumbler."

"Never mind it, Dill; it's a trifle. I half hoped you had done it on purpose, so that the glass should never be drained to a less honored toast. Is she like *you?*"

"Like me,—like me?" asked he, coloring deeply. "Polly like me?"

"I mean is there a family resemblance? Could you be easily known as brother and sister?"

"Not a bit of it. Polly is the prettiest girl in this county, and she 's better than she 's handsome. There's nothing she can't do. I taught her to tie flies, and she can put wings on a green-drake now that would take in any salmon that ever swam. Martin Keene sent her a pound-note for a book of 'brown hackles,' and, by the way, she gave it to *me*. And if you saw her on the back of a horse!—Ambrose Bushe's gray mare, the wickedest devil that ever was bridled, one buck jump after another the length of a field, and the mare trying to get her head between her fore-legs, and Polly handling her so quiet, never out of temper, never hot, but always saying, 'Ain't you ashamed of yourself, Dido? Don't you see them all laughing at us?'"

"I am quite curious to see her. Will you present me one of these days?"

Tom mumbled out something perfectly unintelligible.

"I hope that I may be permitted to make her acquaintance," repeated he, not feeling very certain that his former speech was quite understood.

"Maybe so," grumbled he out at last, and sank back in his chair with a look of sulky ill-humor; for so it was that poor Tom, in his ignorance of life and its ways, deemed the proposal one of those free-and-easy suggestions which might be made to persons of very inferior station, and to whom the fact of acquaintanceship should be accounted as a great honor.

Conyers was provoked at the little willingness shown to meet his offer,—an offer he felt to be a very courteous piece of condescension on his part,—and now both sat in silence. At last Tom Dill, long struggling with some secret impulse, gave way, and in a tone far more decided and firm than heretofore, said, "Maybe you think, from seeing what sort of a fellow I am, that my sister ought to be like me; and because *I* have neither manners nor education, that she 's the same? But listen to me now; she 's just as little like me as you are yourself. You 're not more of a gentleman than she's a lady!"

"I never imagined anything else."

"And what made you talk of bringing her up here to present her to you, as you called it? Was she to be trotted out in a cavasin, like a filly?"

"My dear fellow," said Conyers, good-humoredly, "you never made a greater mistake. I begged that you would present *me* to your sister. I asked the sort of favor which is very common in the world, and in the language usually employed to convey such a request. I observed the recognized etiquette—"

"What do I know about etiquette? If you'd have said, 'Tom Dill, I want to be introduced to your sister,' I 'd have guessed what you were at, and I 'd have said, 'Come back in the boat with me to-morrow, and so you shall.'"

"It's a bargain, then, Dill. I want two or three things in the village, and I accept your offer gladly."

Not only was peace now ratified between them, but a closer feeling of intimacy established; for poor Tom, not much spoiled by any excess of the world's sympathy, was so delighted by the kindly interest shown him, that he launched out freely to tell all about himself and his fortunes, how hardly treated he was at home, and how ill usage had made him despondent, and despondency made him dissolute. "It's all very well to rate a fellow about his taste for low pleasures and low companions; but what if he's not rich enough for better? He takes them just as he smokes cheap tobacco, because he can afford no other. And do you know," continued he, "you are the first real gentleman that ever said a kind word to me, or asked me to sit down in his company. It's even so strange to me yet, that maybe when I 'm rowing home to-night I 'll think it's all a dream,—that it was the wine got into my head."

"Is not some of this your own fault?" broke in Conyers. "What if you had held your head higher—"

"Hold my head higher!" interrupted Tom. "With this on it, eh?" And he took up his ragged and worn cap from the ground, and showed it. "Pride is a very fine thing when you can live up to it; but if you can't it's only ridiculous. I don't say," added he, after a few minutes of silence, "but if I was far away from this, where nobody knew me, where I did n't owe little debts on every side, and was n't obliged to be intimate with every idle vagabond about—I don't say but I'd try to be something better. If, for instance, I could get into the navy—"

"Why not the army? You 'd like it better."

"Ay! but it 's far harder to get into. There's many a rough fellow like myself aboard ship that they would n't take in a regiment. Besides, how could I get in without interest?"

"My father is a Lieutenant-General. I don't know whether he could be of service to you."

"A Lieutenant-General!" repeated Tom, with the reverential awe of one alluding to an actual potentate.

"Yes. He has a command out in India, where I feel full sure he could give you something. Suppose you were to go out there? I 'd write a letter to my father and ask him to befriend you."

"It would take a fortune to pay the journey," said Tom, despondingly.

"Not if you went out on service; the Government would send you free of cost. And even if you were not, I think we might manage it. Speak to your father about it."

"No," said he, slowly. "No; but I 'll talk it over with Polly. Not but I know well she'll say, 'There you are, castle-building and romancing. It's all moonshine! Nobody ever took notice of you,—nobody said he 'd interest himself about you.'"

"That's easily remedied. If you like it, I 'll tell your sister all about it myself. I 'll tell her it's my plan, and I 'll show her what I think are good reasons to believe it will be successful."

"Oh! would you—would you!" cried he, with a choking sensation in the throat; for his gratitude had made him almost hysterical.

"Yes," resumed Conyers. "When you come up here tomorrow, we 'll arrange it all. I 'll turn the matter all over in my mind, too, and I have little doubt of our being able to carry it through."

"You 'll not tell my father, though?"

"Not a word, if you forbid it. At the same time, you must see that he'll have to hear it all later on."

"I suppose so," muttered Tom, moodily, and leaned his head thoughtfully on his hand. But one half-hour back and he would have told Conyers why he desired this concealment; he would have declared that his father, caring more for his services than his future good, would have thrown every obstacle to his promotion, and would even, if need were, have so represented him to Conyers that he would have appeared utterly unworthy of his interest and kindness; but now not one word of all this escaped him. He never hinted another reproach against his father, for already a purer spring had opened in his nature, the rocky heart had been smitten by words of gentleness, and he would have revolted against that which should degrade him in his own esteem.

"Good night," said Conyers, with a hearty shake of the hand, "and don't forget your breakfast engagement tomorrow."

"What 's this?" said Tom, blushing deeply, as he found a crumpled bank-note in his palm.

"It's your fee, my good fellow, that's all," said the other, laughingly.

"But I can't take a fee. I have never done so. I have no right to one. I am not a doctor yet."

"The very first lesson in your profession is not to anger your patient; and if you would not provoke me, say no more on this matter." There was a half-semblance of haughtiness in these words that perhaps the speaker never intended; at all events, he was quick enough to remedy the effect, for he laid his hand good-naturedly on the other's shoulder and said, "For my sake, Dill,—for my sake."

"I wish I knew what I ought to do," said Tom, whose pale cheek actually trembled with agitation. "I mean," said he, in a shaken voice, "I wish I knew what would make *you* think best of me."

"Do you attach so much value to my good opinion, then?"

"Don't you think I might? When did I ever meet any one that treated me this way before?"

The agitation in which he uttered these few words imparted such a semblance of weakness to him that Conyers pressed him down into a chair, and filled up his glass with wine.

"Take that off, and you 'll be all right presently," said he, in a kind tone.

Tom tried to carry the glass to his lips, but his hand trembled so that he had to set it down on the table.

"I don't know how to say it," began he, "and I don't know whether I ought to say it, but somehow I feel as if I could give my heart's blood if everybody would behave to me the way you do. I don't mean, mind you, so generously, but treating me as if—as if—as if—" gulped he out at last, "as if I was a gentleman."

"And why not? As there is nothing in your station that should deny that claim, why should any presume to treat you otherwise?"

"Because I'm not one!" blurted he out; and covering his face with his hands, he sobbed bitterly.

"Come, come, my poor fellow, don't be down-hearted. I 'm not much older than yourself, but I 've seen a good deal of life; and, mark *my* words, the price a man puts on himself is the very highest penny the world will ever bid for him; he 'll not always get *that*, but he 'll never—no, never, get a farthing beyond it!"

Tom stared vacantly at the speaker, not very sure whether he understood the speech, or that it had any special application to him.

"When you come to know life as well as I do," continued Conyers, who had now launched into a very favorite theme, "you'll learn the truth of what I say. Hold your head high; and if the world desires to see you, it must at least look up!"

"Ay, but it might laugh too!" said Tom, with a bitter gravity, which considerably disconcerted the moralist, who pitched away his cigar impatiently, and set about selecting another.

"I suspect I understand *your* nature. For," said he, after a moment or two, "I have rather a knack in reading people. Just answer me frankly a few questions."

"Whatever you like," said the other, in a half-sulky sort of manner.

"Mind," said Conyers, eagerly, "as there can be no offence intended, you'll not feel any by whatever I may say."

"Go on," said Tom, in the same dry tone.

"Ain't you obstinate?"

"I am."

"I knew it. We had not talked half an hour together when I detected it, and I said to myself, 'That fellow is one so rooted in his own convictions, it is scarcely possible to shake him.'"

"What next?" asked Tom.

"You can't readily forgive an injury; you find it very hard to pardon the man who has wronged you."

"I do not; if he did n't go on persecuting me, I would n't think of him at all."

"Ah, that's a mistake. Well, I know you better than you know yourself; you *do* keep up the memory of an old grudge,—you can't help it."

"Maybe so, but I never knew it."

"You have, however, just as strong a sentiment of gratitude."

"I never knew that, either," muttered he; "perhaps because it has had so little provocation!"

"Bear in mind," said Conyers, who was rather disconcerted by the want of concurrence he had met with, "that I am in a great measure referring to latent qualities,—things which probably require time and circumstances to develop."

"Oh, if that's it," said Dili, "I can no more object than I could if you talked to me about what is down a dozen fathoms in the earth under our feet. It may be granite or it may be gold, for what I know; the only thing that *I* see is the gravel before me."

"I 'll tell you a trait of your character you can't gainsay," said Conyers, who was growing more irritated by the opposition so unexpectedly met with, "and it's one you need not dig a dozen fathoms down to discover,— you are very reckless."

"Reckless—reckless,—you call a fellow reckless that throws away his chance, I suppose?"

"Just so."

"But what if he never had one?"

"Every man has a destiny; every man has that in his fate which he may help to make or to mar as he inclines to. I suppose you admit that?"

"I don't know," was the sullen reply.

"Not know? Surely you needn't be told such a fact to recognize it!"

"All I know is this," said Tom, resolutely, "that I scarcely ever did anything in my life that it was n't found out to be wrong, so that at last I 've come to be pretty careless what I do; and if it was n't for Polly,—if it was n't for Polly—" He stopped, drew his sleeve across his eyes, and turned away, unable to finish.

"Come, then," said Conyers, laying his hand affectionately on the other's shoulder, "add my friendship to *her* love for you, and see if the two will not give you encouragement; for I mean to be your friend, Dill."

"Do you?" said Tom, with the tears in his eyes.

"There 's my hand on it."

CHAPTER VIII
FINE ACQUAINTANCES

There is a law of compensation even for the small things of this life, and by the wise enactments of that law, human happiness, on the whole, is pretty equally distributed. The rich man, probably, never felt one tithe of the enjoyment in his noble demesne that it yielded to some poor artisan who strolled through it on a holiday, and tasted at once the charms of a woodland scene with all the rapturous delight of a day of rest.

Arguing from these premises, I greatly doubt if Lady Cobham, at the head of her great household, with her house crowded with distinguished visitors, surrounded by every accessory of luxury and splendor, tasted anything approaching to the delight felt by one, the very humblest of her guests, and who for a brief twenty-four hours partook of her hospitality.

Polly Dill, with all her desire and ambition for notice amongst the great people of the county, had gone to this dinner-party with considerable misgivings. She only knew the Admiral in the hunting-field; of her Ladyship she had no knowledge whatever, save in a few dry sentences uttered to her from a carriage one day at "the meet," when the Admiral, with more sailor-like frankness than politeness, presented her by saying, "This is the heroine of the day's run, Dr. Dill's daughter." And to this was responded a stare through a double eye-glass, and a cold smile and a few still colder words, affecting to be compliment, but sounding far more like a correction and a rebuke.

No wonder, then, if Polly's heart was somewhat faint about approaching as a hostess one who could be so repelling as a mere acquaintance. Indeed, one less resolutely bent on her object would not have encountered all the mortification and misery her anticipation pictured; but Polly fortified herself by the philosophy that said, "There is but one road to this goal; I must either take that one, or abandon the journey." And so she did take it.

Either, however, that she had exaggerated the grievance to her own mind, or that her Ladyship was more courteous at home than abroad; but Polly was charmed with the kindness of her reception. Lady Cobham had shaken hands with her, asked her had she been hunting lately, and was about to speak of her horsemanship to a grim old lady beside her, when the arrival of other guests cut short the compliment, and Polly passed on—her heart lightened of a great load—to mix with the general company.

I have no doubt it was a pleasant country-house; it was called the pleasantest in the county. On the present occasion it counted amongst its guests not only the great families of the neighborhood, but several distinguished visitors from a distance, of whom two, at least, are noteworthy,—one, the great lyric poet; the other, the first tragic actress of her age and country. The occasion which assembled them was a project originally broached at the Admiral's table, and so frequently discussed afterwards that it matured itself into a congress. The plan was to get up theatricals for the winter season at Kilkenny, in which all the native dramatic ability should be aided by the first professional talent. Scarcely a country-house that could not boast of, at least, one promising performer. Ruthven and Campion and Probart had in their several walks been applauded by the great in art, and there were many others who in the estimation of friends were just as certain of a high success.

Some passing remark on Polly's good looks, and the suitability of her face and style for certain small characters in comedy,—the pink ribboned damsels who are made love to by smart valets,—induced Lady Cobham to include her in her list; and thus, on these meagre credentials, was she present. She did not want notice or desire recognition; she was far too happy to be there, to hear and see and mark and observe all around her, to care for any especial attention. If the haughty Arabellas and Georgianas who swept past her without so much as a glance, were not, in her own estimation, superior in personal attractions, she knew well that they were so in all the accidents of station and the advantages of dress; and perhaps— who knows?—the reflection was not such a discouraging one.

No memorable event, no incident worth recording, marked her visit. In the world of such society the machinery moves with regularity and little friction. The comedy of real life is admirably played out by the well-bred, and Polly was charmed to see with what courtesy, what consideration, what deference people behaved to each other; and all without an effort,—perhaps without even a thought.

It was on the following day, when she got home and sat beside her mother's chair, that she related all she had seen. Her heart was filled with joy; for, just as she was taking her leave, Lady Cobham had said, "You have been promised to us for Tuesday next, Miss Dill. Pray don't forget it!" And now she was busily engaged in the cares of toilette; and though it was a mere question of putting bows of a sky-blue ribbon on a muslin dress,— one of those little travesties by which rustic beauty emulates ball-room splendor,—to her eyes it assumed all the importance of a grand preparation, and one which she could not help occasionally rising to contemplate at a little distance.

"Won't it be lovely, mamma," she said, "with a moss-rose—a mere bud—on each of those bows? But I have n't told you of how he sang. He was the smallest little creature in the world, and he tripped across the room with his tiny feet like a bird, and he kissed Lady Cobham's hand with a sort of old-world gallantry, and pressed a little sprig of jasmine she gave him to his heart,—this way,—and then he sat down to the piano. I thought it strange to see a man play!"

"Effeminate,—very," muttered the old lady, as she wiped her spectacles.

"Well, I don't know, mamma,—at least, after a moment, I lost all thought of it, for I never heard anything like his singing before. He had not much voice, nor, perhaps, great skill, but there was an expression in the words, a rippling melody with which the verses ran from his lips, while the accompaniment tinkled on beside them, perfectly rapturous. It all seemed as if words and air were begotten of the moment, as if, inspired on the instant, he poured forth the verses, on which he half dwelt, while thinking over what was to follow, imparting an actual anxiety as you listened, lest he should not be ready with his rhyme; and through all there was a triumphant joy that lighted up his face and made his eyes sparkle with a fearless lustre, as of one who felt the genius that was within him, and could trust it." And then he had been so complimentary to herself, called her that charming little "rebel," after she had sung "Where 's the Slave," and told her that until he had heard the words from her lips he did not know they were half so treasonable. "But, mamma dearest, I have made a conquest; and such a conquest,—the hero of the whole society,—a Captain Stapylton, who did something or captured somebody at Waterloo,—a bold dragoon, with a gorgeous pelisse all slashed with gold, and such a mass of splendor that he was quite dazzling to look upon." She went on, still very rapturously, to picture him. "Not very young; that is to say, he might be thirty-five, or perhaps a little more,—tall, stately, even dignified in appearance, with a beard and moustache almost white,—for he had served much in India, and he was dark-skinned as a native." And this fine soldier, so sought after and so courted, had been markedly attentive to her, danced with her twice, and promised she should have his Arab, "Mahmoud," at her next visit to Cobham. It was very evident that his notice of her had called forth certain jealousies from young ladies of higher social pretensions, nor was she at all indifferent to the peril of such sentiments, though she did not speak of them to her mother, for, in good truth, that worthy woman was not one to investigate a subtle problem, or suggest a wise counsel; not to say that her interests were far more deeply engaged for Miss Harlowe than for her daughter Polly, seeing that in the one case every motive, and the spring to every motive, was familiar to her, while in the other she possessed but some vague and very strange notions of what was told her. Clarissa had made a full confidence to her: she had wept out her sorrows on her bosom, and sat sobbing on her shoulder. Polly came to her with the frivolous narrative of a ball-room flirtation, which threatened no despair nor ruin to any one. Here were no heart-consuming miseries, no agonizing terrors, no dreadful casualties that might darken a whole existence; and so Mrs. Dill scarcely followed Polly's story at all, and never with any interest.

Polly went in search of her brother, but he had left home early that morning with the boat, no one knew whither, and the doctor was in a towering rage at his absence. Tom, indeed, was so full of his success with young Conyers that he never so much as condescended to explain his plans, and simply left a message to say, "It was likely he'd be back by dinner-time." Now Dr. Dill was not in one of his blandest humors. Amongst the company at Cobham, he had found a great physician from Kilkenny, plainly showing him that all his social sacrifices were not to his professional benefit, and that if colds and catarrhs were going, his own services would never be called in. Captain Stapylton, too, to whom Polly had presented him, told him that he "feared a young brother officer of his, Lieutenant Conyers, had fallen into the hands of some small village practitioner, and that he would take immediate measures to get him back to headquarters," and then moved off, without giving him the time for a correction of the mistake.

He took no note of his daughter's little triumphs, the admiration that she excited, or the flatteries that greeted her. It is true he did not possess the same means of measuring these that she had, and in all that dreary leisure which besets an unhonored guest, he had ample time to mope and fret and moralize, as gloomily as might be. If, then, he did not enjoy himself on his visit, he came away from it soured and ill-humored.

He denounced "junketings"—by which unseemly title he designated the late entertainment—as amusements too costly for persons of his means. He made a rough calculation—a very rough one—of all that the "precious tomfoolery" had cost: the turnpike which he had paid, and the perquisites to servants—which he had not; the expense of Polly's finery,—a hazarded guess she would have been charmed to have had confirmed; and, ending the whole with a startling total, declared that a reign of rigid domestic economy must commence from that hour. The edict was something like what one reads from the French Government, when about to protest against some license of the press, and which opens by proclaiming that "the latitude hitherto conceded to public discussion has not been attended with those gratifying results so eagerly anticipated by the Imperial administration." Poor Mrs. Dill—like a mere journalist—never knew she had been enjoying blessings till she was told she had forfeited them forever, and she heard with a confused astonishment that the household charges would be still further reduced, and yet food and fuel and light be not excluded from the supplies. He denounced Polly's equestrianism as a most ruinous and extravagant pursuit. Poor Polly, whose field achievements had always been on a borrowed mount! Tom was a scapegrace, whose debts would have beggared half-a-dozen families,—wretched dog, to whom a guinea was a gold-mine; and Mrs. Dill, unhappy Mrs. Dill, who neither hunted, nor smoked, nor played skittles, after a moment's pause, he told her that his hard-earned pence should not be wasted in maintaining a "circulating library." Was there ever injustice like this? Talk to a man with one meal a day about gluttony, lecture the castaway at sea about not giving way to his appetites, you might just as well do so as to preach to Mrs. Dill—with her one book, and who never wanted another—about the discursive costliness of her readings.

Could it be that, like the cruel jailer, who killed the spider the prisoner had learned to love, he had resolved to rob her of Clarissa? The thought was so overwhelming that it stunned her; and thus stupefied, she saw the doctor issue forth on his daily round, without venturing one word in answer. And he rode on his way,—on that strange mission of mercy, meanness, of honest sympathy, or mock philanthropy, as men's hearts and natures make of it,—and set out for the "Fisherman's Home."

CHAPTER IX
A COUNTRY DOCTOR

In a story, as in a voyage, one must occasionally travel with uncongenial companions. Now I have no reason for hoping that any of my readers care to keep Dr. Dill's company, and yet it is with Dr. Dill we must now for a brief space foregather. He was on his way to visit his patient at the "Fisherman's Home," having started, intentionally very early, to be there before Stapylton could have interposed with any counsels of removing him to Kilkenny.

The world, in its blind confidence in medical skill, and its unbounded belief in certain practitioners of medicine, is but scantily just to the humbler members of the craft in regard to the sensitiveness with which they feel the withdrawal of a patient from their care, and the substitution of another physician. The doctor who has not only heard, but felt Babington's adage, that the difference between a good physician and a bad one is only "the difference between a pound and a guinea," naturally thinks it a hard thing that his interests are to be sacrificed for a mere question of five per cent. He knows, besides, that they can each work on the same materials with the same tools, and it can be only through some defect in his self-confidence that he can bring himself to believe that the patient's chances are not pretty much alike in *his* hands or his rival's. Now Dr. Dill had no feelings of this sort; no undervaluing of himself found a place in his nature. He regarded medical men as tax-gatherers, and naturally thought it mattered but little which received the impost; and, thus reflecting, he bore no good will towards that gallant Captain, who, as we have seen, stood so well in his daughter's favor. Even hardened men of the world—old footsore pilgrims of life—have their prejudices, and one of these is to be pleased at thinking they had augured unfavorably of any one they had afterwards learned to dislike. It smacks so much of acuteness to be able to say, "I was scarcely presented to him; we had not exchanged a dozen sentences when I saw this, that, and t' other." Dill knew this man was overbearing, insolent, and oppressive, that he was meddlesome and interfering, giving advice unasked for, and presuming to direct where no guidance was required. He suspected he was not a man of much fortune; he doubted he was a man of good family. All his airs of pretensions—very high and mighty they were—did not satisfy the doctor.

As he said himself, he was a very old bird, but he forgot to add that he had always lived in an extremely small cage.

The doctor had to leave his horse on the high-road and take a small footpath, which led through some meadows till it reached the little copse of beech and ilex that sheltered the cottage and effectually hid it from all view from the road. The doctor had just gained the last stile, when he suddenly came upon a man repairing a fence, and whose labors were being overlooked by Miss Barrington. He had scarcely uttered his most respectful salutations, when she said, "It is, perhaps, the last time you will take that path through the Lock Meadow, Dr. Dill. We mean to close it up after this week."

"Close it up, dear lady!—a right of way that has existed Heaven knows how long. I remember it as a boy myself."

"Very probably, sir, and what you say vouches for great antiquity; but things may be old and yet not respectable. Besides, it never was what you have called it,—a right of way. If it was, where did it go to?"

"It went to the cottage, dear lady. The 'Home' was a mill in those days."

"Well, sir, it is no longer a mill, and it will soon cease to be an inn."

"Indeed, dear lady! And am I to hope that I may congratulate such kind friends as you have ever been to me on a change of fortune?"

"Yes, sir; we have grown so poor that, to prevent utter destitution, we have determined to keep a private station; and with reference to that, may I ask you when this young gentleman could bear removal without injury?"

"I have not seen him to-day, dear lady; but judging from the inflammatory symptoms I remarked yesterday, and the great nervous depression—"

"I know nothing about medicine, sir; but if the nervous depression be indicated by a great appetite and a most noisy disposition, his case must be critical."

"Noise, dear lady!"

"Yes, sir; assisted by your son, he sat over his wine till past midnight, talking extremely loudly, and occasionally singing. They have now been at breakfast since ten o'clock, and you will very soon be able to judge by your own ears of the well-regulated pitch of the conversation."

"My son, Miss Dinah! Tom Dill at breakfast here?"

"I don't know whether his name be Tom or Harry, sir, nor is it to the purpose; but he is a red-haired youth, with a stoop in the shoulders, and a much-abused cap."

Dill groaned over a portrait which to him was a photograph.

"I 'll see to this, dear lady. This shall be looked into," muttered he, with the purpose of a man who pledged himself to a course of action; and with this he moved on. Nor had he gone many paces from the spot when he heard the sound of voices, at first in some confusion, but afterwards clearly and distinctly.

"I 'll be hanged if I 'd do it, Tom," cried the loud voice of Conyers. "It's all very fine talking about paternal authority and all that, and so long as one is a boy there's no help for it; but you and I are men. We have a right to be treated like men, have n't we?"

"I suppose so," muttered the other, half sulkily, and not exactly seeing what was gained by the admission.

"Well, that being so," resumed Conyers, "I'd say to the governor, 'What allowance are you going to make me?'"

"Did you do that with your father?" asked Tom, earnestly.

"No, not exactly," stammered out the other. "There was not, in fact, any need for it, for my governor is a rare jolly fellow,—such a trump! What he said to me was, 'There's a check-book, George; don't spare it.'"

"Which was as much as to say, 'Draw what you like.'"

"Yes, of course. He knew, in leaving it to my honor, there was no risk of my committing any excess; so you see there was no necessity to make my governor 'book up.' But if I was in your place I 'd do it. I pledge you my word I would."

Tom only shook his head very mournfully, and made no answer. He felt, and felt truly, that there is a worldly wisdom learned only in poverty and in the struggles of narrow fortune, of which the well-to-do know absolutely nothing. Of what avail to talk to him of an unlimited credit, or a credit to be bounded only by a sense of honor? It presupposed so much that was impossible, that he would have laughed if his heart had been but light enough.

"Well, then," said Conyers, "if you have n't courage for this, let me do it; let me speak to your father."

"What could you say to him?" asked Tom, doggedly.

"Say to him?—what could I say to him?" repeated he, as he lighted a fresh cigar, and affected to be eagerly interested in the process. "It's clear enough what I 'd say to him."

"Let us hear it, then," growled out Tom, for he had a sort of coarse enjoyment at the other's embarrassment. "I 'll be the doctor now, and listen to you." And with this he squared his chair full in front of Conyers, and crossed his arms imposingly on his chest "You said you wanted to speak to me about my son Tom, Mr. Conyers; what is it you have to say?"

"Well, I suppose I'd open the matter delicately, and, perhaps, adroitly. I 'd say, 'I have remarked, doctor, that your son is a young fellow of very considerable abilities—'"

"For what?" broke in Tom, huskily.

"Come, you 're not to interrupt in this fashion, or I can't continue. I 'd say something about your natural cleverness; and what a pity it would be if, with very promising talents, you should not have those fair advantages which lead a man to success in life."

"And do you know what *he* 'd say to all that?"

"No."

"Well, I'll tell you. He'd say 'Bother!' Just 'bother.'"

"What do you mean by 'bother'?"

"That what you were saying was all nonsense. That you did n't know, nor you never could know, the struggles of a man like himself, just to make the two ends meet; not to be rich, mind you, or lay by money, or have shares in this, or stocks in that, but just to live, and no more."

"Well, I'd say, 'Give him a few hundred pounds, and start him.'"

"Why don't you say a few thousands? It would sound grander, and be just as likely. Can't you see that everybody hasn't a Lieutenant-General for a father? and that what you 'd give for a horse—that would, maybe, be staked to-morrow—would perhaps be a fortune for a fellow like me? What's that I hear coming up the river? That's the doctor, I 'm sure. I 'll be off till he's gone." And without waiting to hear a word, he sprang from his chair and disappeared in the wood.

Dr. Dill only waited a few seconds to compose his features, somewhat excited by what he had overheard; and then coughing loudly, to announce his approach, moved gravely along the gravel path.

"And how is my respected patient?" asked he, blandly. "Is the inflammation subsiding, and are our pains diminished?"

"My ankle is easier, if you mean that," said Conyers, bluntly.

"Yes, much easier,—much easier," said the doctor, examining the limb; "and our cellular tissue has less effusion, the sheaths of the tendons freer, and we are generally better. I perceive you have had the leeches applied. Did

Tom—my son—give you satisfaction? Was he as attentive and as careful as you wished?"

"Yes, I liked him. I wish he 'd come up every day while I remain. Is there any objection to that arrangement?"

"None, dear sir,—none. His time is fully at your service; he ought to be working hard. It is true he should be reading eight or ten hours a day, for his examination; but it is hard to persuade him to it. Young men will be young men!"

"I hope so, with all my heart. At least, I, for one, don't want to be an old one. Will you do me a favor, doctor? and will you forgive me if I don't know how to ask it with all becoming delicacy? I'd like to give Tom a helping hand. He's a good fellow,—I 'm certain he is. Will you let me send him out to India, to my father? He has lots of places to give away, and he 'd be sure to find something to suit him. You have heard of General Conyers, perhaps, the political resident at Delhi? That's my governor." In the hurry and rapidity with which he spoke, it was easy to see how he struggled with a sense of shame and confusion.

Dr. Dill was profuse of acknowledgments; he was even moved as he expressed his gratitude. "It was true," he remarked, "that his life had been signalled by these sort of graceful services, or rather offers of services; for we are proud if we are poor, sir. 'Dill aut nil' is the legend of our crest, which means that we are ourselves or nothing."

"I conclude everybody else is in the same predicament," broke in Conyers, bluntly.

"Not exactly, young gentleman,—not exactly. I think I could, perhaps, explain—"

"No, no; never mind it. I 'm the stupidest fellow in the world at a nice distinction; besides, I'll take your word for the fact. You have heard of my father, have n't you?"

"I heard of him so late as last night, from a brother officer of yours, Captain Stapylton."

"Where did you meet Stapylton?" asked Conyers, quickly.

"At Sir Charles Cobham's. I was presented to him by my daughter, and he made the most kindly inquiries after you, and said that, if possible, he'd come over here to-day to see you."

"I hope he won't; that's all," muttered Conyers. Then, correcting himself suddenly, he said: "I mean, I scarcely know him; he has only joined us a few months back, and is a stranger to every one in the regiment. I hope you did n't tell him where I was."

"I'm afraid that I did, for I remember his adding, 'Oh! I must carry him off. I must get him back to headquarters.'"

"Indeed! Let us see if he will. That's the style of these 'Company's' officers,—he was in some Native corps or other,—they always fancy they can bully a subaltern; but Black Stapylton will find himself mistaken this time."

"He was afraid that you had not fallen into skilful hands; and, of course, it would not have come well from me to assure him of the opposite."

"Well, but what of Tom, doctor? You have given me no answer."

"It is a case for reflection, my dear young friend, if I may be emboldened to call you so. It is not a matter I can say yes or no to on the instant. I have only two grown-up children: my daughter, the most affectionate, the most thoughtful of girls, educated, too, in a way to grace any sphere—"

"You need n't tell me that Tom is a wild fellow," broke in Conyers,—for he well understood the antithesis that was coming; "he owned it all to me, himself. I have no doubt, too, that he made the worst of it; for, after all, what signifies a dash of extravagance, or a mad freak or two? You can't expect that we should all be as wise and as prudent and as cool-headed as Black Stapylton."

"You plead very ably, young gentleman," said Dill, with his smoothest accent, "but you must give me a little time."

"Well, I'll give you till to-morrow,—to-morrow, at this hour; for it wouldn't be fair to the poor fellow to keep him in a state of uncertainty. His heart is set on the plan; he told me so."

"I 'll do my best to meet your wishes, my dear young gentleman; but please to bear in mind that it is the whole future fate of my son I am about to decide. Your father may not, possibly, prove so deeply interested as you are; he may—not unreasonably, either—take a colder view of this project; he may chance to form a lower estimate of my poor boy than it is your good nature to have done."

"Look here, doctor; I know my governor something better than you do, and if I wrote to him, and said, 'I want this fellow to come home with a lac of rupees,' he 'd start him to-morrow with half the money. If I were to say, 'You are to give him the best thing in your gift,' there's nothing he 'd stop at; he 'd make him a judge, or a receiver, or some one of those fat things that send a man back to England with a fortune. What's that fellow whispering to you about? It's something that concerns me."

This sudden interruption was caused by the approach of Darby, who had come to whisper something in the doctor's ear.

"It is a message he has brought me; a matter of little consequence. I 'll look to it, Darby. Tell your mistress it shall be attended to." Darby lingered for a moment, but the doctor motioned him away, and did not speak again till he had quitted the spot. "How these fellows will wait to pick up what passes between their betters," said Dill, while he continued to follow him with his eyes. "I think I mentioned to you once, already, that the persons who keep this house here are reduced gentry, and it is now my task to add that, either from some change of fortune or from caprice, they are thinking of abandoning the inn, and resuming—so far as may be possible for them— their former standing. This project dates before your arrival here; and now, it would seem, they are growing impatient to effect it; at least, a very fussy old lady—Miss Barrington—has sent me word by Darby to say her brother will be back here tomorrow or next day, with some friends from Kilkenny, and she asks at what time your convalescence is likely to permit removal."

"Turned out, in fact, doctor,—ordered to decamp! You must say, I 'm ready, of course; that is to say, that I 'll go at once. I don't exactly see how I 'm to be moved in this helpless state, as no carriage can come here; but you 'll look to all that for me. At all events, go immediately, and say I shall be off within an hour or so."

"Leave it all to me,—leave it in my hands. I think I see what is to be done," said the doctor, with one of his confident little smiles, and moved away.

There was a spice of irritation in Conyers's manner as he spoke. He was very little accustomed to be thwarted in anything, and scarcely knew the sensation of having a wish opposed, or an obstacle set against him, but simply because there was a reason for his quitting the place, grew all the stronger his desire to remain there. He looked around him, and never before had the foliage seemed so graceful; never had the tints of the copper-beech blended so harmoniously with the stone-pine and the larch; never had the eddies of the river laughed more joyously, nor the blackbirds sung with a more impetuous richness of melody. "And to say that I must leave all this, just when I feel myself actually clinging to it. I could spend my whole life here. I glory in this quiet, unbroken ease; this life, that slips along as waveless as the stream there! Why should n't I buy it; have it all my own, to come down to whenever I was sick and weary of the world and its dissipations? The spot is small; it couldn't be very costly; it would take a mere nothing to maintain. And to have it all one's own!" There was an actual ecstasy in the thought; for in that same sense of possession there is a something that resembles the sense of identity. The little child with his toy, the aged man with his proud demesne, are tasters of the same pleasure.

"You are to use your own discretion, my dear young gentleman, and go when it suits you, and not before," said the doctor, returning triumphantly, for he felt like a successful envoy. "And now I will leave you. To-morrow you shall have my answer about Tom."

Conyers nodded vaguely; for, alas! Tom, and all about him, had completely lapsed from his memory.

CHAPTER X
BEING "BORED"

It is a high testimony to that order of architecture which we call castle-building, that no man ever lived in a house so fine he could not build one more stately still out of his imagination. Nor is it only to grandeur and splendor this superiority extends, but it can invest lowly situations and homely places with a charm which, alas! no reality can rival.

Conyers was a fortunate fellow in a number of ways; he was young, good-looking, healthy, and rich. Fate had made place for him on the very sunniest side of the causeway, and, with all that, he was happier on that day, through the mere play of his fancy, than all his wealth could have made him. He had fashioned out a life for himself in that cottage, very charming, and very enjoyable in its way. He would make it such a spot that it would have resources for him on every hand, and he hugged himself in the thought of coming down here with a friend, or, perhaps, two friends, to pass days of that luxurious indolence so fascinating to those who are, or fancy they are, wearied of life's pomps and vanities.

Now there are no such scoffers at the frivolity and emptiness of human wishes as the well-to-do young fellows of two or three-and-twenty. They know the "whole thing," and its utter rottenness. They smile compassionately at the eagerness of all around them; they look with bland pity at the race, and contemptuously ask, of what value the prize when it is won? They do their very best to be gloomy moralists, but they cannot. They might as well try to shiver when they sit in the sunshine. The vigorous beat of young hearts, and the full tide of young pulses, will tell against all the mock misanthropy that ever was fabricated! It would not be exactly fair to rank Conyers in this school, and yet he was not totally exempt from some of its teachings. Who knows if these little imaginary glooms, these brain-created miseries, are not a kind of moral "alterative" which, though depressing at the instant, render the constitution only more vigorous after?

At all events, he had resolved to have the cottage, and, going practically to work, he called Darby to his counsels to tell him the extent of the place, its boundaries, and whatever information he could afford as to the tenure and its rent.

"You 'd be for buying it, your honor!" said Darby, with the keen quick-sightedness of his order.

"Perhaps I had some thoughts of the kind; and, if so, I should keep you on."

Darby bowed his gratitude very respectfully. It was too long a vista for him to strain his eyes at, and so he made no profuse display of thankfulness. With all their imaginative tendencies, the lower Irish are a very bird-in-the-hand sort of people.

"Not more than seventeen acres!" cried Conyers, in astonishment. "Why, I should have guessed about forty, at least. Isn't that wood there part of it?"

"Yes, but it's only a strip, and the trees that you see yonder is in Carriclough; and them two meadows below the salmon weir is n't ours at all; and the island itself we have only a lease of it."

"It's all in capital repair, well kept, well looked after?"

"Well, it is, and isn't!" said he, with a look of disagreement. "He'd have one thing, and she'd have another; *he* 'd spend every shilling he could get on the place, and *she* 'd grudge a brush of paint, or a coat of whitewash, just to keep things together."

"I see nothing amiss here," said Conyers, looking around him. "Nobody could ask or wish a cottage to be neater, better furnished, or more comfortable. I confess I do not perceive anything wanting."

"Oh, to be sure, it's very nate, as your honor says; but then—" And he scratched his head, and looked confused.

"But then, what—out with it?"

"The earwigs is dreadful; wherever there 's roses and sweetbrier there's no livin' with them. Open the window and the place is full of them."

Mistaking the surprise he saw depicted in his hearer's face for terror, Darby launched forth into a description of insect and reptile tortures that might have suited the tropics; to hear him, all the stories of the white ant of India, or the gallinipper of Demerara, were nothing to the destructive powers of the Irish earwig. The place was known for them all over the country, and it was years and years lying empty, "by rayson of thim plagues."

Now, if Conyers was not intimidated to the full extent Darby intended by this account, he was just as far from guessing the secret cause of this representation, which was simply a long-settled plan of succeeding himself to the ownership of the "Fisherman's Home," when, either from the course of nature or an accident, a vacancy would occur. It was the grand dream of Darby's life, the island of his Government, his seat in the Cabinet, his Judgeship, his Garter, his everything, in short, that makes human ambition like a cup brimful and overflowing; and what a terrible reverse would it be if all these hopes were to be dashed just to gratify the passing caprice of a mere traveller!

"I don't suppose your honor cares for money, and, maybe, you 'd as soon pay twice over the worth of anything; but here, between our two selves, I can tell you, you 'd buy an estate in the county cheaper than this little place. They think, because they planted most of the trees and made the fences themselves, that it's like the King's Park. It's a fancy spot, and a fancy price, they'll ask for it But I know of another worth ten of it,—a real, elegant place; to be sure, it's a trifle out of repair, for the ould naygur that has it won't lay out a sixpence, but there 's every con-vaniency in life about it. There's the finest cup potatoes, the biggest turnips ever I see on it, and fish jumpin' into the parlor-window, and hares runnin' about like rats."

"I don't care for all that; this cottage and these grounds here have taken my fancy."

"And why would n't the other, when you seen it? The ould Major that lives there wants to sell it, and you 'd get it a raal bargain. Let me row your honor up there this evening. It's not two miles off, and the river beautiful all the way."

Conyers rejected the proposal abruptly, haughtily. Darby had dared to throw down a very imposing card-edifice, and for the moment the fellow was odious to him. All the golden visions of his early morning, that poetized life he was to lead, that elegant pastoralism, which was to blend the splendor of Lucullus with the simplicity of a Tityrus, all rent, torn, and scattered by a vile hind, who had not even a conception of the ruin he had caused.

And yet Darby had a misty consciousness of some success. He did not, indeed, know that his shell had exploded in a magazine; but he saw, from the confusion in the garrison, that his shot had told severely somewhere.

"Maybe your honor would rather go to-morrow? or maybe you 'd like the Major to come up here himself, and speak to you?"

"Once for all, I tell you, No! Is that plain? No! And I may add, my good fellow, that if you knew me a little better, you 'd not tender me any advice I did not ask for."

"And why would I? Would n't I be a baste if I did?"

"I think so," said Conyers, dryly, and turned away. He was out of temper with everything and everybody,—the doctor, and his abject manner; Tom, and his roughness; Darby, and his roguish air of self-satisfied craftiness; all, for the moment, displeased and offended him. "I 'll leave the place to-morrow; I 'm not sure I shall not go to-night D'ye hear?"

Darby bowed respectfully.

"I suppose I can reach some spot, by boat, where a carriage can be had?"

"By coorse, your honor. At Hunt's Mills, or Shibna-brack, you 'll get a car easy enough. I won't say it will be an elegant convaniency, but a good horse will rowl you along into Thomastown, where you can change for a shay."

Strange enough, this very facility of escape annoyed him. Had Darby only told him that there were all manner of difficulties to getting away,— that there were shallows in the river, or a landslip across the road,—he would have addressed himself to overcome the obstacles like a man; but to hear that the course was open, that any one might take it, was intolerable.

"I suppose, your honor, I 'd better get the boat ready, at all events?"

"Yes, certainly,—that is, not till I give further orders. I 'm the only stranger here, and I can't imagine there can be much difficulty in having a boat at any hour. Leave me, my good fellow; you only worry me. Go!"

And Darby moved away, revolving within himself the curious problem, that if, having plenty of money enlarged a man's means of enjoyment, it was strange how little effect it produced upon his manners. As for Conyers, he stood moodily gazing on the river, over whose placid surface a few heavy raindrops were just falling; great clouds, too, rolled heavily over the hillsides, and gathered into ominous-looking masses over the stream, while a low moaning sound of very far-off thunder foretold a storm.

Here, at least, was a good tangible grievance, and he hugged it to his heart. He was weather-bound! The tree-tops were already shaking wildly, and dark scuds flying fast over the mottled sky. It was clear that a severe storm was near. "No help for it now," muttered he, "if I must remain here till to-morrow." And hobbling as well as he could into the house, he seated himself at the window to watch the hurricane. Too closely pent up between the steep sides of the river for anything like destructive power, the wind only shook the trees violently, or swept along the stream with tiny waves, which warred against the current; but even these were soon beaten down by the rain,—that heavy, swooping, splashing rain, that seems to come from the overflowing of a lake in the clouds. Darker and darker grew the atmosphere as it fell, till the banks of the opposite side were gradually lost to view, while the river itself became a yellow flood, surging up amongst the willows that lined the banks. It was not one of those storms whose grand effects of lightning, aided by pealing thunder, create a sense of sublime terror, that has its own ecstasy; but it was one of those dreary evenings when the dull sky shows no streak of light, and when the moist earth gives up no perfume, when foliage and hillside and rock and stream are leaden-colored and sad, and one wishes for winter, to close the shutter and draw the curtain, and creep close to the chimney-corner as to a refuge.

Oh, what comfortless things are these summer storms! They come upon us like some dire disaster in a time of festivity. They swoop down upon our days of sunshine like a pestilence, and turn our joy into gloom, and all our gladness to despondency, bringing back to our minds memories of comfortless journeys, weariful ploddings, long nights of suffering.

I am but telling what Conyers felt at this sudden change of weather. You and I, my good reader, know better. We feel how gladly the parched earth drinks up the refreshing draught, how the seared grass bends gratefully to the skimming rain, and the fresh buds open with joy to catch the pearly drops. We know, too, how the atmosphere, long imprisoned, bursts forth into a joyous freedom, and comes back to us fresh from the sea and the mountain rich in odor and redolent of health, making the very air breathe an exquisite luxury. We know all this, and much more that he did not care for.

Now Conyers was only "bored," as if anything could be much worse; that is to say, he was in that state of mind in which resources yield no distraction, and nothing is invested with an interest sufficient to make it even passingly amusing. He wanted to do something, though the precise something did not occur to him. Had he been well, and in full enjoyment of his strength, he 'd have sallied out into the storm and walked off his ennui by a wetting. Even a cold would be a good exchange for the dreary blue-devilism of his depression; but this escape was denied him, and he was left to fret, and chafe, and fever himself, moving from window to chimney-corner, and from chimney-corner to sofa, till at last, baited by self-tormentings, he opened his door and sallied forth to wander through the rooms, taking his chance where his steps might lead him.

Between the gloomy influences of the storm and the shadows of a declining day he could mark but indistinctly the details of the rooms he was exploring. They presented little that was remarkable; they were modestly furnished, nothing costly nor expensive anywhere, but a degree of homely comfort rare to find in an inn. They had, above all, that habitable look which so seldom pertains to a house of entertainment, and, in the loosely scattered books, prints, and maps showed a sort of flattering trustfulness in the stranger who might sojourn there. His wanderings led him, at length, into a somewhat more pretentious room, with a piano and a harp, at one angle of which a little octangular tower opened, with windows in every face, and the spaces between them completely covered by miniatures in oil, or small cabinet pictures. A small table with a chess-board stood here, and an unfinished game yet remained on the board. As Conyers bent over to look, he perceived that a book, whose leaves were held open by a smelling-bottle, lay on the chair next the table. He took this up, and saw that it was a little volume treating of the game, and that the pieces on the board represented a problem. With the eagerness of a man thirsting for some occupation, he seated himself at the table, and set to work at the question. "A Mate in Six Moves" it was headed, but the pieces had been already disturbed by some one attempting the solution. He replaced them by the directions of the volume, and devoted himself earnestly to the task. He was not a good player, and the problem posed him. He tried it again and again, but ever unsuccessfully. He fancied that up to a certain point he had followed the right track, and repeated the same opening moves each time. Meanwhile the evening was fast closing in, and it was only with difficulty he could see the pieces on the board.

Bending low over the table, he was straining his eyes at the game, when a low, gentle voice from behind his chair said, "Would you not wish candles, sir? It is too dark to see here."

Conyers turned hastily, and as hastily recognized that the person who addressed him was a gentlewoman. He arose at once, and made a sort of apology for his intruding.

"Had I known you were a chess-player, sir," said she, with the demure gravity of a composed manner, "I believe I should have sent you a challenge; for my brother, who is my usual adversary, is from home."

"If I should prove a very unworthy enemy, madam, you will find me a very grateful one, for I am sorely tired of my own company."

"In that case, sir, I beg to offer you mine, and a cup of tea along with it."

Conyers accepted the invitation joyfully, and followed Miss Barrington to a small but most comfortable little room, where a tea equipage of exquisite old china was already prepared.

"I see you are in admiration of my teacups; they are the rare Canton blue, for we tea-drinkers have as much epicurism in the form and color of a cup as wine-bibbers profess to have in a hock or a claret glass. Pray take the sofa; you will find it more comfortable than a chair. I am aware you have had an accident."

Very few and simple as were her words, she threw into her manner a degree of courtesy that seemed actual kindness; and coming, as this did, after his late solitude and gloom, no wonder was it that Conyers was charmed with it. There was, besides, a quaint formality—a sort of old-world politeness in her breeding—which relieved the interview of awkwardness by taking it out of the common category of such events.

When tea was over, they sat down to chess, at which Conyers had merely proficiency enough to be worth beating. Perhaps the quality stood him in good stead; perhaps certain others, such as his good looks and his pleasing manners, were even better aids to him; but certain it is, Miss Barrington liked her guest, and when, on arising to say good-night, he made a bungling attempt to apologize for having prolonged his stay at the cottage beyond the period which suited their plans, she stopped him by saying, with much courtesy, "It is true, sir, we are about to relinquish the inn, but pray do not deprive us of the great pleasure we should feel in associating its last day or two with a most agreeable guest. I hope you will remain till my brother comes back and makes your acquaintance."

Conyers very cordially accepted the proposal, and went off to his bed far better pleased with himself and with all the world than he well believed it possible he could be a couple of hours before.

CHAPTER XI
A NOTE TO BE ANSWERED

While Conyers was yet in bed the following morning, a messenger arrived at the house with a note for him, and waited for the answer. It was from Stapylton, and ran thus:—

"Cobham Hall, Tuesday morning.

"Dear Con.,—The world here—and part of it is a very pretty world, with silky tresses and trim ankles—has declared that you have had some sort of slight accident, and are laid up at a miserable wayside inn, to be blue-devilled and doctored à discrétion. I strained my shoulder yesterday hunting,—my horse swerved against a tree,—or I should ascertain all the particulars of your disaster in person; so there is nothing left for it but a note.

"I am here domesticated at a charming country-house, the host an old Admiral, the hostess a ci-devant belle of London,—in times not very recent,—and more lately what is called in newspapers 'one of the ornaments of the Irish Court.' We have abundance of guests,—county dons and native celebrities, clerical, lyrical, and quizzical, several pretty women, a first-rate cellar, and a very tolerable cook. I give you the catalogue of our attractions, for I am commissioned by Sir Charles and my Lady to ask you to partake of them. The invitation is given in all cordiality, and I hope you will not decline it, for it is, amongst other matters, a good opportunity of seeing an Irish 'interior,' a thing of which I have always had my doubts and misgivings, some of which are now solved; others I should like to investigate with your assistance. In a word, the whole is worth seeing, and it is, besides, one of those experiences which can be had on very pleasant terms. There is perfect liberty; always something going on, and always a way to be out of it if you like. The people are, perhaps, not more friendly than in England, but they are far more familiar; and if not more disposed to be pleased, they tell you they are, which amounts to the same. There is a good deal of splendor, a wide hospitality, and, I need scarcely add, a considerable share of bad taste. There is, too, a costly attention to the wishes of a guest, which will remind you of India, though I must own the Irish Brahmin has not the grand, high-bred air of the Bengalee. But again I say, come and see.

"I have been told to explain to you why they don't send their boat. There is something about draught of water, and something about a 'gash,' whatever that is: I opine it to be a rapid. And then I am directed to say, that if you will have yourself paddled up to Brown's Barn, the Cobham barge will be there to meet you.

"I write this with some difficulty, lying on my back on a sofa, while a very pretty girl is impatiently waiting to continue her reading to me of a new novel called 'The Antiquary.' a capital story, but strangely disfigured by whole scenes in a Scottish dialect. You must read it when you come over.

"You have heard of Hunter, of course. I am sure you will be sorry at his leaving us. For myself, I knew him very slightly, and shall not have to regret him like older friends; not to say that I have been so long in the service that I never believe in a Colonel. Would you go with him if he gave you the offer? There is such a row and uproar all around me, that I must leave off. Have I forgotten to say that if you stand upon the 'dignities,' the Admiral will go in person to invite you, though he has a foot in the gout. I conclude you will not exact this, and I *know* they will take your acceptance of this mode of invitation as a great favor. Say the hour and the day, and believe me yours always,

"Horace Stapylton.

"Sir Charles is come to say that if your accident does not interfere with riding, he hopes you will send for your horses. He has ample stabling, and is vainglorious about his beans. That short-legged chestnut you brought from Norris would cut a good figure here, as the fences lie very close, and you must be always 'in hand.' If you saw how the women ride! There is one here now—a 'half-bred 'un'—that pounded us all—a whole field of us—last Saturday. You shall see her. I won't promise you 'll follow her across her country."

The first impression made on the mind of Conyers by this letter was surprise that Stapylton, with whom he had so little acquaintance, should write to him in this tone of intimacy; Stapylton, whose cold, almost stern manner seemed to repel any approach, and now he assumed all the free-and-easy air of a comrade of his own years and standing. Had he mistaken the man, or had he been misled by inferring from his bearing in the regiment what he must be at heart?

This, however, was but a passing thought; the passage which interested him most of all was about Hunter. Where and for what could he have left, then? It was a regiment he had served in since he entered the army. What could have led him to exchange? and why, when he did so, had he not written him one line—even one—to say as much? It was to serve under Hunter, his father's old aide-de-camp in times back, that he had entered that regiment; to be with him, to have his friendship, his counsels, his guidance. Colonel Hunter had treated him like a son in every respect, and Conyers felt in his heart that this same affection and interest it was which formed his strongest tie to the service. The question, "Would you go with him if he gave you the offer?" was like a reflection on him, while no such option had been extended to him. What more natural, after all, than such an offer? so Stapylton thought,—so all the world would think. How he thought over the constantly recurring questions of his brother-officers: "Why didn't you go with Hunter?" "How came it that Hunter did not name you on his staff?" "Was it fair—was it generous in one who owed all his advancement to his father—to treat him in this fashion?" "Were the ties of old friendship so lax as all this?" "Was distance such an enemy to every obligation of affection?" "Would his father believe that such a slight had been passed upon him undeservedly? Would not the ready inference be, 'Hunter knew you to be incapable,—unequal to the duties he required. Hunter must have his reasons for passing you over'?" and such like. These reflections, very bitter in their way, were broken in upon by a request from Miss Barrington for his company at breakfast. Strange enough, he had half forgotten that there was such a person in the world, or that he had spent the preceding evening very pleasantly in her society.

"I hope you have had a pleasant letter," said she, as he entered, with Stapylton's note still in his hand.

"I can scarcely call it so, for it brings me news that our Colonel—a very dear and kind friend to me—is about to leave us."

"Are these not the usual chances of a soldier's life? I used to be very familiar once on a time with such topics."

"I have learned the tidings so vaguely, too, that I can make nothing of them. My correspondent is a mere acquaintance,—a brother officer, who has lately joined us, and cannot feel how deeply his news has affected me; in fact, the chief burden of his letter is to convey an invitation to me, and he is full of country-house people and pleasures. He writes from a place called Cobham."

"Sir Charles Cobham's. One of the best houses in the county."

"Do you know them?" asked Conyers, who did not, till the words were out, remember how awkward they might prove.

She flushed slightly for a moment, but, speedily recovering herself, said: "Yes, we knew them once. They had just come to the country, and purchased that estate, when our misfortunes overtook us. They showed us much attention, and such kindness as strangers could show, and they evinced a disposition to continue it; but, of course, our relative positions made intercourse impossible. I am afraid," said she, hastily, "I am talking in riddles all this time. I ought to have told you that my brother once owned a good estate here. We Barringtons thought a deal of ourselves in those days." She tried to say these words with a playful levity, but her voice shook, and her lip trembled in spite of her.

Conyers muttered something unintelligible about "his having heard before," and his sorrow to have awakened a painful theme; but she stopped him hastily, saying, "These are all such old stories now, one should be able to talk them over unconcernedly; indeed, it is easier to do so than to avoid the subject altogether, for there is no such egotist as your reduced gentleman." She made a pretext of giving him his tea, and helping him to something, to cover the awkward pause that followed, and then asked if he intended to accept the invitation to Cobham.

"Not if you will allow me to remain here. The doctor says three days more will see me able to go back to my quarters."

"I hope you will stay for a week, at least, for I scarcely expect my brother before Saturday. Meanwhile, if you have any fancy to visit Cobham, and make your acquaintance with the family there, remember you have all the privileges of an inn here, to come and go, and stay at your pleasure."

"I do not want to leave this. I wish I was never to leave it," muttered he below his breath.

"Perhaps I guess what it is that attaches you to this place," said she, gently. "Shall I say it? There is something quiet, something domestic here, that recalls 'Home.'"

"But I never knew a home," said Conyers, falteringly. "My mother died when I was a mere infant, and I knew none of that watchful love that first gives the sense of home. You may be right, however, in supposing that I cling to this spot as what should seem to me like a home, for I own to you I feel very happy here."

"Stay then, and be happy," said she, holding out her hand, which he clasped warmly, and then pressed to his lips.

"Tell your friend to come over and dine with you any day that he can tear himself from gay company and a great house, and I will do my best to entertain him suitably."

"No. I don't care to do that; he is a mere acquaintance; there is no friendship between us, and, as he is several years older than me, and far wiser, and more man of the world, I am more chilled than cheered by his company. But you shall read his letter, and I 'm certain you 'll make a better guess at his nature than if I were to give you my own version of him at any length." So saying, he handed Stapyl-ton's note across the table; and Miss Dinah, having deliberately put on her spectacles, began to read it.

"It's a fine manly hand, — very bold and very legible, and says something for the writer's frankness. Eh? 'a miserable wayside inn!' This is less than just to the poor 'Fisherman's Home.' Positively, you must make him come to dinner, if it be only for the sake of our character. This man is not amiable, sir," said she, as she read on, "though I could swear he is pleasant company, and sometimes witty. But there is little of genial in his pleasantry, and less of good nature in his wit."

"Go on," cried Conyers; "I 'm quite with you."

"Is he a person of family?" asked she, as she read on some few lines further.

"We know nothing about him; he joined us from a native corps, in India; but he has a good name and, apparently, ample means. His appearance and manner are equal to any station."

"For all that, I don't like him, nor do I desire that you should like him. There is no wiser caution than that of the Psalmist against 'sitting in the seat of the scornful.' This man is a scoffer."

"And yet it is not his usual tone. He is cold, retiring, almost shy. This letter is not a bit like anything I ever saw in his character."

"Another reason to distrust him. Set my mind at ease by saying 'No' to his invitation, and let me try if I cannot recompense you by homeliness in lieu of splendor. The young lady," added she, as she folded the letter, "whose horsemanship is commemorated at the expense of her breeding, must be our doctor's daughter. She is a very pretty girl, and rides admirably. Her good looks and her courage might have saved her the sarcasm. I have my doubts if the man that uttered it be thorough-bred."

"Well, I 'll go and write my answer," said Conyers, rising. "I have been keeping his messenger waiting all this time. I will show it to you before I send it off."

CHAPTER XII
THE ANSWER

"Will this do?" said Conyers, shortly after, entering the room with a very brief note, but which, let it be owned, cost him fully as much labor as more practised hands occasionally bestow on a more lengthy despatch. "I suppose it's all that's civil and proper, and I don't care to make any needless professions. Pray read it, and give me your opinion." It was so brief that I may quote it:—

"Dear Captain Stapylton,—Don't feel any apprehensions about me. I am in better quarters than I ever fell into in my life, and my accident is not worth speaking of. I wish you had told me more of our Colonel, of whose movements I am entirely ignorant. I am sincerely grateful to your friends for thinking of me, and hope, ere I leave the neighborhood, to express to Sir Charles and Lady Cobham how sensible I am of their kind intentions towards me.

"I am, most faithfully yours,

"F. CONYERS."

"It is very well, and tolerably legible," said Miss Barrington, dryly; "at least I can make out everything but the name at the end."

"I own I do not shine in penmanship; the strange characters at the foot were meant to represent 'Conyers.'"

"Conyers! Conyers! How long is it since I heard that name last, and how familiar I was with it once! My nephew's dearest friend was a Conyers."

"He must have been a relative of mine in some degree; at least, we are in the habit of saying that all of the name are of one family."

Not heeding what he said, the old lady had fallen back in her meditations to a very remote "long ago," and was thinking of a time when every letter from India bore the high-wrought interest of a romance, of which her nephew was the hero,—times of intense anxiety, indeed, but full of hope withal, and glowing with all the coloring with which love and an exalted imagination can invest the incidents of an adventurous life.

"It was a great heart he had, a splendidly generous nature, far too high-souled and too exacting for common friendships, and so it was that he had few friends. I am talking of my nephew," said she, correcting herself suddenly. "What a boon for a young man to have met him, and formed an attachment to him. I wish you could have known him. George would have been a noble example for you!" She paused for some minutes, and then suddenly, as it were remembering herself, said, "Did you tell me just now, or was I only dreaming, that you knew Ormsby Conyers?"

"Ormsby Conyers is my father's name," said he, quickly.

"Captain in the 25th Dragoons?" asked she, eagerly.

"He was so, some eighteen or twenty years ago."

"Oh, then, my heart did not deceive me," cried she, taking his hand with both her own, "when I felt towards you like an old friend. After we parted last night, I asked myself, again and again, how was it that I already felt an interest in you? What subtle instinct was it that whispered this is the son of poor George's dearest friend,—this is the son of that dear Ormsby Conyers of whom every letter is full? Oh, the happiness of seeing you under this roof! And what a surprise for my poor brother, who clings only the closer, with every year, to all that reminds him of his boy!"

"And you knew my father, then?" asked Conyers, proudly.

"Never met him; but I believe I knew him better than many who were his daily intimates: for years my nephew's letters were journals of their joint lives—they seemed never separate. But you shall read them yourself. They go back to the time when they both landed at Calcutta, young and ardent spirits, eager for adventure, and urged by a bold ambition to win distinction. From that day they were inseparable. They hunted, travelled, lived together; and so attached had they become to each other, that George writes in one letter: 'They have offered me an appointment on the staff, but as this would separate me from Ormsby, it is not to be thought of.' It was to me George always wrote, for my brother never liked letter-writing, and thus I was my nephew's confidante, and intrusted with all his secrets. Nor was there one in which your father's name did not figure. It was, how Ormsby got him out of this scrape, or took his duty for him, or made this explanation, or raised that sum of money, that filled all these. At last—I never knew why or how— George ceased to write to me, and addressed all his letters to his father, marked 'Strictly private' too, so that I never saw what they contained. My brother, I believe, suffered deeply from the concealment, and there must have been what to him seemed a sufficient reason for it, or he would never have excluded me from that share in his confidence I had always possessed. At all events, it led to a sort of estrangement between us,—the only one of our lives. He would tell me at intervals that George was on leave; George was at the Hills; he was expecting his troop; he had been sent here or there; but nothing more, till one morning, as if unable to bear the burden longer, he said, 'George has made up his mind to leave his regiment and take service with one of the native princes. It is an arrangement sanctioned by the Government, but it is one I grieve over and regret greatly.' I asked eagerly to hear further about this step, but he said he knew nothing beyond the bare fact. I then said, 'What does his friend Conyers think of it?' and my brother dryly replied, 'I am not aware that he has been consulted.' Our own misfortunes were fast closing around us, so that really we had little time to think of anything but the difficulties that each day brought forth. George's letters grew rarer and rarer; rumors of him reached us; stories of his gorgeous mode of living, his princely state and splendid retinue, of the high favor he enjoyed with the Rajah, and the influence he wielded over neighboring chiefs; and then we heard, still only by rumor, that he had married a native princess, who had some time before been converted to Christianity. The first intimation of the fact from himself came, when, announcing that he had sent his daughter, a child of about five years old, to Europe to be educated—" She paused here, and seemed to have fallen into a revery over the past; when Conyers suddenly asked,—

"And what of my father all this time? Was the old intercourse kept up between them?"

"I cannot tell you. I do not remember that his name occurred till the memorable case came on before the House of Commons—the inquiry, as it was called, into Colonel Barrington's conduct in the case of Edwardes, a British-born subject of his Majesty, serving in the army of the Rajah of Luckerabad. You have, perhaps, heard of it?"

"Was that the celebrated charge of torturing a British subject?"

"The same; the vilest conspiracy that ever was hatched, and the cruellest persecution that ever broke a noble heart. And yet there were men of honor, men of purest fame and most unblemished character, who harkened in to that infamous cry, and actually sent out emissaries to India to collect evidence against my poor nephew. For a while the whole country rang with the case. The low papers, which assailed the Government, made it matter of attack on the nature of the British rule in India, and the ministry only sought to make George the victim to screen themselves from public indignation. It was Admiral Byng's case once more. But I have no temper to speak of it, even after this lapse of years; my blood boils now at the bare memory of that foul and perjured association. If you would follow the story, I will send you the little published narrative to your room, but, I beseech you, do not again revert to it. How I have betrayed myself to speak of it I know not. For many a long year I have prayed to be able to forgive one man, who has been the bitterest enemy of our name and race. I have asked for strength to bear the burden of our calamity, but more earnestly a hundred-fold I have entreated that forgiveness might enter my heart, and that if vengeance for this cruel wrong was at hand, I could be able to say, 'No, the time for such feeling is gone by.' Let me not, then, be tempted by any revival of this theme to recall all the sorrow and all the indignation it once caused me. This infamous book contains the whole story as the world then believed it. You will read it with interest, for it concerned one whom your father dearly loved. But, again. I say, when we meet again let us not return to it. These letters, too, will amuse you; they are the diaries of your father's early life in India as much as George's, but of them we can talk freely."

It was so evident that she was speaking with a forced calm, and that all her self-restraint might at any moment prove unequal to the effort she was making, that Conyers, affecting to have a few words to say to Stapylton's messenger, stole away, and hastened to his room to look over the letters and the volume she had given him.

He had scarcely addressed himself to his task when a knock came to the door, and at the same instant it was opened in a slow, half-hesitating way, and Tom Dill stood before him. Though evidently dressed for the occasion, and intending to present himself in a most favorable guise, Tom looked far more vulgar and unprepossessing than in the worn costume of his every-day life, his bright-buttoned blue coat and yellow waistcoat being only aggravations of the low-bred air that unhappily beset him. Worse even than this, however, was the fact that, being somewhat nervous about the interview before him, Tom had taken what his father would have called a diffusible stimulant, in the shape of "a dandy of punch," and bore the evidences of it in a heightened color and a very lustrous but wandering eye.

"Here I am," said he, entering with a sort of easy swagger, but far more affected than real, notwithstanding the "dandy."

"Well, and what then?" asked Conyers, haughtily, for the vulgar presumption of his manner was but a sorry advocate in his favor. "I don't remember, that I sent for you."

"No; but my father told me what you said to him, and I was to come up and thank you, and say, 'Done!' to it all."

Conyers turned a look—not a very pleased or very flattering look—at the loutish figure before him, and in his changing color might be seen the conflict it cost him to keep down his rising temper. He was, indeed, sorely tried, and his hand shook as he tossed over the books on his table, and endeavored to seem occupied in other matters.

"Maybe you forget all about it," began Tom. "Perhaps you don't remember that you offered to fit me out for India, and send me over with a letter to your father—"

"No, no, I forget nothing of it; I remember it all." He had almost said "only too well," but he coughed down the cruel speech, and went on hurriedly: "You have come, however, when I am engaged,—when I have other things to attend to. These letters here—In fact, this is not a moment when I can attend to you. Do you understand me?"

"I believe I do," said Tom, growing very pale.

"To-morrow, then, or the day after, or next week, will be time enough for all this. I must think over the matter again."

"I see," said Tom, moodily, as he changed from one foot to the other, and cracked the joints of his fingers, till they seemed dislocated. "I see it all."

"What do you mean by that?—what do you see?" asked Conyers, angrily.

"I see that Polly, my sister, was right; that she knew you better than any of us," said Tom, boldly, for a sudden rush of courage had now filled his heart. "She said, 'Don't let him turn your head, Tom, with his fine promises. He was in good humor and good spirits when he made them, and perhaps meant to keep them too; but he little knows what misery disappointment brings, and he'll never fret himself over the heavy heart he's giving you, when he wakes in the morning with a change of mind.' And then, she said another thing," added he, after a pause.

"And what was the other thing?"

"She said, 'If you go up there, Tom,' says she, 'dressed out like a shopboy in his Sunday suit, he'll be actually shocked at his having taken an interest in you. He 'll forget all about your hard lot and your struggling fortune, and only see your vulgarity.' 'Your vulgarity,'—that was the word." As he said this, his lip trembled, and the chair he leaned on shook under his grasp.

"Go back, and tell her, then, that she was mistaken," said Conyers, whose own voice now quavered. "Tell her that when I give my word I keep it; that I will maintain everything I said to you or to your father; and that when she imputed to me an indifference as to the feelings of others, she might have remembered whether she was not unjust to mine. Tell her that also."

"I will," said Tom, gravely. "Is there anything more?" "No, nothing more," said Conyers, who with difficulty suppressed a smile at the words and the manner of his questioner. "Good-bye, then. You 'll send for me when you want me," said Tom; and he was out of the room, and half-way across the lawn, ere Conyers could recover himself to reply.

Conyers, however, flung open the window, and cried to him to come back.

"I was nigh forgetting a most important part of the matter, Tom," said he, as the other entered, somewhat pale and anxious-looking. "You told me, t' other day, that there was some payment to be made,—some sum to be lodged before you could present yourself for examination. What about this? When must it be done?"

"A month before I go in," said Tom, to whom the very thought of the ordeal seemed full of terror and heart-sinking.

"And how soon do you reckon that may be?"

"Polly says not before eight weeks at the earliest. She says we 'll have to go over Bell on the Bones all again, and brush up the Ligaments, besides. If it was the Navy, they 'd not mind the nerves; but they tell me the Army fellows often take a man on the fifth pair, and I know if they do me, it's mighty little of India I 'll see."

"Plucked, eh?"

"I don't know what you mean by 'plucked,' but I 'd be turned back, which is, perhaps, the same. And no great disgrace, either," added he, with more of courage in his voice; "Polly herself says there's days she could n't remember all the branches of the fifth, and the third is almost as bad."

"I suppose if your sister could go up in your place, Tom, you 'd be quite sure of your diploma?"

"It's many and many a day I wished that same," sighed he, heavily. "If you heard her going over the 'Subclavian,' you 'd swear she had the book in her hand."

Conyers could not repress a smile at this strange piece of feminine accomplishment, but he was careful not to let Tom perceive it. Not, indeed, that the poor fellow was in a very observant mood; Polly's perfections, her memory, and her quickness were the themes that filled up his mind.

"What a rare piece of luck for you to have had such a sister, Tom!"

"Don't I say it to myself?—don't I repeat the very same words every morning when I awake? Maybe I 'll never come to any good; maybe my father is right, and that I 'll only be a disgrace as long as I live; but I hope one thing, at least, I 'll never be so bad that I 'll forget Polly, and all she done for me. And I'll tell you more," said he, with a choking fulness in his throat; "if they turn me back at my examination, my heart will be heavier for *her* than for myself."

"Come, cheer up, Tom; don't look on the gloomy side. You 'll pass, I 'm certain, and with credit too. Here 's the thirty pounds you 'll have to lodge—"

"It is only twenty they require. And, besides, I could n't take it; it's my father must pay." He stammered, and hesitated, and grew pale and then crimson, while his lips trembled and his chest heaved and fell almost convulsively.

"Nothing of the kind, Tom," said Conyers, who had to subdue his own emotion by an assumed sternness. "The plan is all my own, and I will stand no interference with it. I mean that you should pass your examination without your father knowing one word about it. You shall come back to him with your diploma, or whatever it is, in your hand, and say, 'There, sir, the men who have signed their names to that do not think so meanly of me as you do.'"

"And he'd say, the more fools they!" said Tom, with a grim smile.

"At all events," resumed Conyers, "I 'll have my own way. Put that note in your pocket, and whenever you are gazetted Surgeon-Major to the Guards, or Inspector-General of all the Hospitals in Great Britain, you can repay me, and with interest, besides, if you like it."

"You 've given me a good long day to be in your debt," said Tom; and he hurried out of the room before his overfull heart should betray his emotion.

It is marvellous how quickly a kind action done to another reconciles a man to himself. Doubtless conscience at such times condescends to play the courtier, and whispers, "What a good fellow you are! and how unjust the world is when it calls you cold and haughty and ungenial!" Not that I would assert higher and better thoughts than these do not reward him who, Samaritan-like, binds up the wounds of misery; but I fear me much that few of us resist self-flattery, or those little delicate adulations one can offer to his own heart when nobody overhears him.

At all events, Conyers was not averse to this pleasure, and grew actually to feel a strong interest for Tom Dill, all because that poor fellow had been the recipient of his bounty; for so is it the waters of our nature must be stirred by some act of charity or kindness, else their healing virtues have small efficacy, and cure not.

And then he wondered and questioned himself whether Polly might not possibly be right, and that his "governor" would maryel where and how he had picked up so strange a specimen as Tom. That poor fellow, too, like many an humble flower, seen not disadvantageously in its native wilds, would look strangely out of place when transplanted and treated as an exotic. Still he could trust to the wide and generous nature of his father to overlook small defects of manner and breeding, and take the humble fellow kindly.

Must I own that a considerable share of his hopefulness was derived from thinking that the odious blue coat and brass buttons could scarcely make part of Tom's kit for India, and that in no other costume known to civilized man could his *protégé* look so unprepossessingly?

CHAPTER XIII
A FEW LEAVES FROM A BLUE-BOOK

The journal which Miss Barrington had placed in Conyers's hands was little else than the record of the sporting adventures of two young and very dashing fellows. There were lion and tiger hunts, so little varied in detail that one might serve for all, though doubtless to the narrator each was marked with its own especial interest. There were travelling incidents and accidents, and straits for money, and mishaps and arrests, and stories of steeple-chases and balls all mixed up together, and recounted so very much in the same spirit as to show how very little shadow mere misadventure could throw across the sunshine of their every-day life. But every now and then Conyers came upon some entry which closely touched his heart. It was how nobly Ormsby behaved. What a splendid fellow he was! so frank, so generous, such a horseman! "I wish you saw the astonishment of the Mahratta fellows as Ormsby lifted the tent-pegs in full career; he never missed one. Ormsby won the rifle-match; we all knew he would. Sir Peregrine invited Ormsby to go with him to the Hills, but he refused, mainly because I was not asked." Ormsby has been offered this, that, or t'other; in fact, that one name recurred in every second sentence, and always with the same marks of affection. How proud, too, did Barrington seem of his friend. "They have found out that no country-house is perfect without Ormsby, and he is positively persecuted with invitations. I hear the 'G.-G.' is provoked at Ormsby's refusal of a staff appointment. I'm in rare luck; the old Rajah of Tannanoohr has asked Ormsby to a grand elephant-hunt next week, and I 'm to go with him. I 'm to have a leave in October. Ormsby managed it somehow; he never fails, whatever he takes in hand. Such a fright as I got yesterday! There was a report in the camp Ormsby was going to England with despatches; it's all a mistake, however, he says. He believes he might have had the opportunity, had he cared for it."

If there was not much in these passing notices of his father, there was quite enough to impart to them an intense degree of interest. There is a wondrous charm, besides, in reading of the young days of those we have only known in maturer life, in hearing of them when they were fresh, ardent, and impetuous; in knowing, besides, how they were regarded by contemporaries, how loved and valued. It was not merely that Ormsby recurred in almost every page of this journal, but the record bore testimony to his superiority and the undisputed sway he exercised over his companions. This same power of dominating and directing had been the distinguishing feature of his after-life, and many an unruly and turbulent spirit had been reclaimed under Ormsby Conyers's hands.

As he read on, he grew also to feel a strong interest for the writer himself; the very heartiness of the affection he bestowed on his father, and the noble generosity with which he welcomed every success of that "dear fellow Ormsby," were more than enough to secure his interest for him. There was a bold, almost reckless dash, too, about Barrington which has a great charm occasionally for very young men. He adventured upon life pretty much as he would try to cross a river; he never looked for a shallow nor inquired for a ford, but plunged boldly in, and trusted to his brave heart and his strong arms for the rest. No one, indeed, reading even these rough notes, could hesitate to pronounce which of the two would "make the spoon," and which "spoil the horn." Young Conyers was eager to find some mention of the incident to which Miss Barrington had vaguely alluded. He wanted to read George Barrington's own account before he opened the little pamphlet she gave him, but the journal closed years before this event; and although some of the letters came down to a later date, none approached the period he wanted.

It was not till after some time that he remarked how much more unfrequently his father's name occurred in the latter portion of the correspondence. Entire pages would contain no reference to him, and in the last letter of all there was this towards the end: "After all, I am almost sorry that I am first for purchase, for I believe Ormsby is most anxious for his troop. I say 'I believe,' for he has not told me so, and when I offered to give way to him, he seemed half offended with me. You know what a bungler I am where a matter of any delicacy is to be treated, and you may easily fancy either that I mismanage the affair grossly, or that I am as grossly mistaken. One thing is certain, I 'd see promotion far enough, rather than let it make a coldness beween us, which could never occur if he were as frank as he used to be. My dear aunt, I wish I had your wise head to counsel me, for I have a scheme in my mind which I have scarcely courage for without some advice, and for many reasons I cannot ask O.'s opinion. Between this and the next mail I 'll think it over carefully, and tell you what I intend.

"I told you that Ormsby was going to marry one of the Gpvernor-General's daughters. It is all off,—at least, I hear so,—and O. has asked for leave to go home. I suspect he is sorely cut up about this, but he is too proud a fellow to let the world see it. Report says that Sir Peregrine heard that he played. So he does, because he does everything, and everything well. If he does go to England, he will certainly pay you a visit. Make much of him for my sake; you could not make too much for his own."

This was the last mention of his father, and he pondered long and thoughtfully over it. He saw, or fancied he saw, the first faint glimmerings of a coldness between them, and he hastily turned to the printed report of the House of Commons inquiry, to see what part his father had taken. His name occurred but once; it was appended to an extract of a letter, addressed to him by the Governor-General. It was a confidential report, and much of it omitted in publication. It was throughout, however, a warm and generous testimony to Barrington's character. "I never knew a man," said he, "less capable of anything mean or unworthy; nor am I able to imagine any temptation strong enough to warp him from what he believed to be right. That on a question of policy his judgment might be wrong, I am quite ready to admit, but I will maintain that, on a point of honor, he would, and must, be infallible." Underneath this passage there was written, in Miss Barrington's hand, "Poor George never saw this; it was not published till after his death." So interested did young Conyers feel as to the friendship between these two men, and what it could have been that made a breach between them, — if breach there were, — that he sat a long time without opening the little volume that related to the charge against Colonel Barrington. He had but to open it, however, to guess the spirit in which it was written. Its title was, "The Story of Samuel Ed-wardes, with an Account of the Persecutions and Tortures inflicted on him by Colonel George Barrington, when serving in command of the Forces of the Meer Nagheer Assahr, Rajah of Luckerabad, based on the documents produced before the Committee of the House, and private authentic information." Opposite to this lengthy title was an ill-executed wood-cut of a young fellow tied up to a tree, and being flogged by two native Indians, with the inscription at foot: "Mode of celebrating His Majesty's Birthday, 4th of June, 18—, at the Residence of Luckerabad."

In the writhing figure of the youth, and the ferocious glee of his executioners, the artist had displayed all his skill in expression, and very unmistakably shown, besides, the spirit of the publication. I have no intention to inflict this upon my reader. I will simply give him—and as briefly as I am able—its substance.

The Rajah of Luckerabad, an independent sovereign, living on the best of terms with the Government of the Company, had obtained permission to employ an English officer in the chief command of his army, a force of some twenty-odd thousand, of all arms. It was essential that he should be one not only well acquainted with the details of command, but fully equal to the charge of organization of a force; a man of energy and decision, well versed in Hindostanee, and not altogether ignorant of Persian, in which, occasionally, correspondence was carried on. Amongst the many candidates for an employment so certain to insure the fortune of its possessor, Major Barrington, then a brevet Lieutenant-Colonel, was chosen.

It is not improbable that, in mere technical details of his art, he might have had many equal and some superior to him; it was well known that his personal requisites were above all rivalry. He was a man of great size and strength, of a most commanding presence, an accomplished linguist in the various dialects of Central India and a great master of all manly exercises. To these qualities he added an Oriental taste for splendor and pomp. It had always been his habit to live in a style of costly extravagance, with the retinue of a petty prince, and when he travelled it was with the following of a native chief.

Though, naturally enough, such a station as a separate command gave might be regarded as a great object of ambition by many, there was a good deal of surprise felt at the time that Barrington, reputedly a man of large fortune, should have accepted it; the more so since, by his contract, he bound himself for ten years to the Rajah, and thus forever extinguished all prospect of advancement in his own service. There were all manner of guesses afloat as to his reasons. Some said that he was already so embarrassed by his extravagance that it was his only exit out of difficulty; others pretended that he was captivated by the gorgeous splendor of that Eastern life he loved so well; that pomp, display, and magnificence were bribes he could not resist; and a few, who affected to see more nearly, whispered that he was unhappy of late, had grown peevish and uncompanionable, and sought any change, so that it took him out of his regiment. Whatever the cause, he bade his brother-officers farewell without revealing it, and set out for his new destination. He had never anticipated a life of ease or inaction, but he was equally far from imagining anything like what now awaited him. Corruption, falsehood, robbery, on every hand! The army was little else than a brigand establishment, living on the peasants, and exacting, at the sword point, whatever they wanted. There was no obedience to discipline. The Rajah troubled himself about nothing but his pleasures, and, indeed, passed his days so drugged with opium as to be almost insensible to all around him. In the tribunals there was nothing but bribery, and the object of every one seemed to be to amass fortunes as rapidly as possible, and then hasten away from a country so insecure and dangerous.

For some days after his arrival, Barrington hesitated whether he would accept a charge so apparently hopeless; his bold heart, however, decided the doubt, and he resolved to remain. His first care was to look about him for one or two more trustworthy than the masses, if such there should be, to assist him, and the Rajah referred him to his secretary for that purpose. It was with sincere pleasure Barring-ton discovered that this man was English,—that is, his father had been an Englishman, and his mother was a Malabar slave in the Rajah's household: his name was Edwardes, but called by the natives Ali Edwardes. He looked about sixty, but his real age was about forty-six when Barrington came to the Residence. He was a man of considerable ability, uniting all the craft and subtlety of the Oriental with the dogged perseverance of the Briton. He had enjoyed the full favor of the Rajah for nigh twenty years, and was strongly averse to the appointment of an English officer to the command of the army, knowing full well the influence it would have over his own fortunes. He represented to the Rajah that the Company was only intriguing to absorb his dominions with their own; that the new Commander-in-chief would be their servant and not his; that it was by such machinery as this they secretly possessed themselves of all knowledge of the native sovereigns, learned their weakness and their strength, and through such agencies hatched those plots and schemes by which many a chief had been despoiled of his state.

The Rajah, however, saw that if he had a grasping Government on one side, he had an insolent and rebellious army on the other. There was not much to choose between them, but he took the side that he thought the least bad, and left the rest to Fate.

Having failed with the Rajah, Edwardes tried what he could do with Barrington; and certainly, if but a tithe of what he told him were true, the most natural thing in the world would have been that he should give up his appointment, and quit forever a land so hopelessly sunk in vice and corruption. Cunning and crafty as he was, however, he made one mistake, and that an irreparable one. When dilating on the insubordination of the army, its lawless ways and libertine habits, he declared that nothing short of a superior force in the field could have any chance of enforcing discipline. "As to a command," said he, "it is simply ludicrous. Let any man try it and they will cut him down in the very midst of his staff."

That unlucky speech decided the question; and Barring-ton simply said,—

"I have heard plenty of this sort of thing in India; I never saw it,—I 'll stay."

Stay he did; and he did more: he reformed that rabble, and made of them a splendid force, able, disciplined, and obedient. With the influence of his success, added to that derived from the confidence reposed in him by the Rajah, he introduced many and beneficial changes into the administration; he punished peculators by military law, and brought knavish sutlers to the drum-head. In fact, by the exercise of a salutary despotism, he rescued the state from an impending bankruptcy and ruin, placed its finances in a healthy condition, and rendered the country a model of prosperity and contentment. The Rajah had, like most of his rank and class, been in litigation, occasionally in armed contention, with some of his neighbors,—one especially, an uncle, whom he accused of having robbed him, when his guardian, of a large share of his heritage. This suit had gone on for years, varied at times by little raids into each other's territories, to burn villages and carry away cattle. Though with a force more than sufficient to have carried the question with a strong hand, Barrington preferred the more civilized mode of leaving the matter in dispute to others, and suggested the Company as arbitrator. The negotiations led to a lengthy correspondence, in which Edwardes and his son, a youth of seventeen or eighteen, were actively occupied; and although Barrington was not without certain misgivings as to their trustworthiness and honesty, he knew their capacity, and had not, besides, any one at all capable of replacing them. While these affairs were yet pending, Barrington married the daughter of the Meer, a young girl whose mother had been a convert to Christianity, and who had herself been educated by a Catholic missionary. She died in the second year of her marriage, giving birth to a daughter; but Barrington had now become so completely the centre of all action in the state, that the Rajah interfered in nothing, leaving in his hands the undisputed control of the Government; nay, more, he made him his son by adoption, leaving to him not alone all his immense personal property, but the inheritance to his throne. Though Barrington was advised by all the great legal authorities he consulted in England that such a bequest could not be good in law, nor a British subject be permitted to succeed to the rights of an Eastern sovereignty, he obstinately declared that the point was yet untried; that, however theoretically the opinion might be correct, practically the question had not been determined, nor had any case yet occurred to rule as a precedent on it. If he was not much of a lawyer, he was of a temperament that could not brook opposition. In fact, to make him take any particular road in life, you had only to erect a barricade on it. When, therefore, he was told the matter could not be, his answer was, "It shall!" Calcutta lawyers, men deep in knowledge of Oriental law and custom, learned Moonshees and Pundits, were despatched by him at enormous cost, to England, to confer with the great authorities at home. Agents were sent over to procure the influence of great Parliamentary speakers and the leaders in the press to the cause. For a matter which, in the beginning, he cared scarcely anything, if at all, he had now grown to feel the most intense and absorbing interest. Half persuading himself that the personal question was less to him than the great privilege and right of an Englishman, he declared that he would rather die a beggar in the defence of the cause than abandon it. So possessed was he, indeed, of his rights, and so resolved to maintain them, supported by a firm belief that they would and must be ultimately conceded to him, that in the correspondence with the other chiefs every reference which spoke of the future sovereignty of Luckerabad included his own name and title, and this with an ostentation quite Oriental.

Whether Edwardes had been less warm and energetic in the cause than Barrington expected, or whether his counsels were less palatable, certain it is he grew daily more and more distrustful of him; but an event soon occurred to make this suspicion a certainty.

The negotiations between the Meer and his uncle had been so successfully conducted by Barrington, that the latter agreed to give up three "Pegunnahs," or villages he had unrightfully seized upon, and to pay a heavy mulct, besides, for the unjust occupation of them. This settlement had been, as may be imagined, a work of much time and labor, and requiring not only immense forbearance and patience, but intense watchfulness and unceasing skill and craft. Edwardes, of course, was constantly engaged in the affair, with the details of which he had been for years familiar. Now, although Barrington was satisfied with the zeal he displayed, he was less so with his counsels, Edwardes always insisting that in every dealing with an Oriental you must inevitably be beaten if you would not make use of all the stratagem and deceit he is sure to employ against you. There was not a day on which the wily secretary did not suggest some cunning expedient, some clever trick; and Barrington's abrupt rejection of them only impressed him with a notion of his weakness and deficiency.

One morning—it was after many defeats—Edwardes appeared with the draft of a document he had been ordered to draw out, and in which, of his own accord, he had made a large use of threats to the neighboring chief, should he continue to protract these proceedings. These threats very unmistakably pointed to the dire consequences of opposing the great Government of the Company; for, as the writer argued, the succession to the Ameer being already vested in an Englishman, it is perfectly clear the powerful nation he belongs to will take a very summary mode of dealing with this question, if not settled before he comes to the throne. He pressed, therefore, for an immediate settlement, as the best possible escape from difficulty.

Barrington scouted the suggestion indignantly; he would not hear of it.

"What," said he, "is it while these very rights are in litigation that I am to employ them as a menace? Who is to secure me being one day Rajah of Luckerabad? Not you, certainly, who have never ceased to speak coldly of my claims. Throw that draft into the fire, and never propose a like one to me again!"

The rebuke was not forgotten. Another draft was, however, prepared, and in due time the long-pending negotiations were concluded, the Meer's uncle having himself come to Luckerabad to ratify the contract, which, being engrossed on a leaf of the Rajah's Koran, was duly signed and sealed by both.

It was during the festivities incidental to this visit that Edwardes, who had of late made a display of wealth and splendor quite unaccountable, made a proposal to the Rajah for the hand of his only unmarried daughter, sister to Barrington's wife. The Rajah, long enervated by excess and opium, probably cared little about the matter; there were, indeed, but a few moments in each day when he could be fairly pronounced awake. He referred the question to Barrington. Not satisfied with an insulting rejection of the proposal, Barrington, whose passionate moments were almost madness, tauntingly asked by what means Edwardes had so suddenly acquired the wealth which had prompted this demand. He hinted that the sources of his fortune were more than suspected, and at last, carried away by anger, for the discussion grew violent, he drew from his desk a slip of paper, and held it up. "When your father was drummed out of the 4th Bengal Fusiliers for theft, of which this is the record, the family was scarcely so ambitious." For an instant Edwardes seemed overcome almost to fainting; but he rallied, and, with a menace of his clenched hand, but without one word, he hurried away before Barrington could resent the insult. It was said that he did not return to his house, but, taking the horse of an orderly that he found at the door, rode away from the palace, and on the same night crossed the frontier into a neighboring state.

It was on the following morning, as Barrington was passing a cavalry regiment in review, that young Edwardes, forcing his way through the staff, insolently asked, "What had become of his father?" and at the same instant levelling a pistol, he fired. The ball passed through Barrington's shako, and so close to the head that it grazed it. It was only with a loud shout to abstain that Barrington arrested the gleaming sabres that now flourished over his head. "Your father has fled, youngster!" cried he. "When you show him *that*," —and he struck him across the face with his horsewhip, —"tell him how near you were to have been an assassin!" With this savage taunt, he gave orders that the young fellow should be conducted to the nearest frontier, and turned adrift. Neither father nor son ever were seen there again.

Little did George Barrington suspect what was to come of that morning's work. Through what channel Edwardes worked at first was not known, but that he succeeded in raising up for himself friends in England is certain; by their means the very gravest charges were made against Barrington. One allegation was that by a forged document, claiming to be the assent of the English Government to his succession, he had obtained the submission of several native chiefs to his rule and a cession of territory to the Rajah of Luckerabad; and another charged him with having cruelly tortured a British subject named Samuel Edwardes,—an investigation entered into by a Committee of the House, and becoming, while it lasted, one of the most exciting subjects of public interest. Nor was the anxiety lessened by the death of the elder Edwardes, which occurred during the inquiry, and which Barrington's enemies declared to be caused by a broken heart; and the martyred or murdered Edwardes was no uncommon heading to a paragraph of the time.

Conyers turned to the massive Blue-book that contained the proceedings "in Committee," but only to glance at the examination of witnesses, whose very names were unfamiliar to him. He could perceive, however, that the inquiry was a long one, and, from the tone of the member at whose motion it was instituted, angry and vindictive.

Edwardes appeared to have preferred charges of long continued persecution and oppression, and there was native testimony in abundance to sustain the allegation; while the British Commissioner sent to Luckerabad came back so prejudiced against Barrington, from his proud and haughty bearing, that his report was unfavorable to him in all respects. There was, it is true, letters from various high quarters, all speaking of Barrington's early career as both honorable and distinguished; and, lastly, there was one signed Ormsby Conyers, a warm-hearted testimony "to the most straightforward gentleman and truest friend I have ever known." These were words the young man read and re-read a dozen times.

Conyers turned eagerly to read what decision had been come to by the Committee, but the proceedings had come abruptly to an end by George Barrington's death. A few lines at the close of the pamphlet mentioned that, being summoned to appear before the Governor-General in Council at Calcutta, Barrington refused. An armed force was despatched to occupy Luckerabad, on the approach of which Barrington rode forth to meet them, attended by a brilliant staff,—with what precise object none knew; but the sight of a considerable force, drawn up at a distance in what seemed order of battle, implied at least an intention to resist. Coming on towards the advanced pickets at a fast gallop, and not slackening speed when challenged, the men, who were Bengal infantry, fired, and Barrington fell, pierced by four bullets. He never uttered a word after, though he lingered on till evening. The force was commanded by Lieutenant-General Conyers.

There was little more to tell. The Rajah, implicated in the charges brought against Barrington, and totally unable to defend himself, despatched a confidential minister, Meer Mozarjah, to Europe to do what he might by bribery. This unhappy blunder filled the measure of his ruin, and after a very brief inquiry the Rajah was declared to have forfeited his throne and all his rights of succession. The Company took possession of Luckerabad, as a portion of British India, but from a generous compassion towards the deposed chief, graciously accorded him a pension of ten thousand rupees a month during his life.

My reader will bear in mind that I have given him this recital, not as it came before Conyers, distorted by falsehood and disfigured by misstatements, but have presented the facts as nearly as they might be derived from a candid examination of all the testimony adduced. Ere I return to my own tale, I ought to add that Edwardes, discredited and despised by some, upheld and maintained by others, left Calcutta with the proceeds of a handsome subscription raised in his behalf. Whether he went to reside in Europe, or retired to some other part of India, is not known. He was heard of no more.

As for the Rajah, his efforts still continued to obtain a revision of the sentence pronounced upon him, and his case was one of those which newspapers slur over and privy councils try to escape from, leaving to Time to solve what Justice has no taste for.

But every now and then a Blue-book would appear, headed "East India (the deposed Rajah of Luckerabad)," while a line in an evening paper would intimate that the Envoy of Meer Nagheer Assahr had arrived at a certain West-end hotel to prosecute the suit of his Highness before the Judicial Committee of the Lords. How pleasantly does a paragraph dispose of a whole life-load of sorrows and of wrongs that, perhaps, are breaking the hearts that carry them!

While I once more apologize to my reader for the length to which this narrative has run, I owe it to myself to state that, had I presented it in the garbled and incorrect version which came before Conyers, and had I interpolated all the misconceptions he incurred, the mistakes he first fell into and then corrected, I should have been far more tedious and intolerable still; and now I am again under weigh, with easy canvas, but over a calm sea, and under a sky but slightly clouded.

CHAPTER XIV
BARRINGTON'S FORD

Conyers had scarcely finished his reading when he was startled by the galloping of horses under his window; so close, indeed, did they come that they seemed to shake the little cottage with their tramp. He looked out, but they had already swept past, and were hidden from his view by the copse that shut out the river. At the same instant he heard the confused sound of many voices, and what sounded to him like the plash of horses in the stream.

Urged by a strong curiosity, he hurried downstairs and made straight for the river by a path that led through the trees; but before he could emerge from the cover he heard cries of "Not there! not there! Lower down!" "No, no! up higher! up higher! Head up the stream, or you 'll be caught in the gash!" "Don't hurry; you've time enough!"

When he gained the bank, it was to see three horsemen, who seemed to be cheering, or, as it might be, warning a young girl who, mounted on a powerful black horse, was deep in the stream, and evidently endeavoring to cross it. Her hat hung on the back of her neck by its ribbon, and her hair had also fallen down; but one glance was enough to show that she was a consummate horsewoman, and whose courage was equal to her skill; for while steadily keeping her horse's head to the swift current, she was careful not to control him overmuch, or impede the free action of his powers. Heeding, as it seemed, very little the counsels or warnings showered on her by the bystanders, not one of whom, to Conyers's intense amazement, had ventured to accompany her, she urged her horse steadily forward.

"Don't hurry,—take it easy!" called out one of the horsemen, as he looked at his watch. "You have fifty-three minutes left, and it's all turf."

"She 'll do it,—I know she will!" "She 'll lose,—she must lose!" "It's ten miles to Foynes Gap!" "It's more!" "It's less!" "There!—see!—she's in, by Jove! she's in!" These varying comments were now arrested by the intense interest of the moment, the horse having impatiently plunged into a deep pool, and struck out to swim with all the violent exertion of an affrighted animal. "Keep his head up!" "Let him free, quite free!" "Get your foot clear of the stirrup!" cried out the bystanders, while in lower tones they muttered, "She would cross here!" "It's all her own fault!" Just at this instant she turned in her saddle, and called out something which, drowned in the rush of the river, did not reach them.

"Don't you see," cried Conyers, passionately, for his temper could no longer endure the impassive attitude of this on-looking, "one of the reins is broken, her bridle is smashed?"

And, without another word, he sprang into the river, partly wading, partly swimming, and soon reached the place where the horse, restrained by one rein alone, swam in a small circle, fretted by restraint and maddened by inability to resist.

"Leave him to me,—let go your rein," said Conyers, as he grasped the bridle close to the bit; and the animal, accepting the guidance, suffered himself to be led quietly till he reached the shallow. Once there, he bounded wildly forward, and, splashing through the current, leaped up the bank, where he was immediately caught by the others.

By the time Conyers had gained the land, the girl had quitted her saddle and entered the cottage, never so much as once turning a look on him who had rescued her. If he could not help feeling mortified at this show of indifference, he was not less puzzled by the manner of the others, who, perfectly careless of his dripping condition, discussed amongst themselves how the bridle broke, and what might have happened if the leather had proved tougher.

"It's always the way with her," muttered one, sulkily.

"I told her to ride the match in a ring-snaffle, but she's a mule in obstinacy! She 'd have won easily—ay, with five minutes to spare—if she'd have crossed at Nunsford. I passed there last week without wetting a girth."

"She 'll not thank you young gentleman, whoever you are," said the oldest of the party, turning to Conyers, "for your gallantry. She 'll only remember you as having helped her to lose a wager!"

"That's true!" cried another. "I never got as much as thank you for catching her horse one day at Lyrath, though it threw me out of the whole run afterwards."

"And this was a wager, then?" said Conyers.

"Yes. An English officer that is stopping at Sir Charles's said yesterday that nobody could ride from Lowe's Folly to Foynes as the crow flies; and four of us took him up—twenty-five pounds apiece—that Polly Dill would do it,—and against time, too,—an hour and forty."

"On a horse of mine," chimed in another,—"Bayther-shini"

"I must say it does not tell very well for your chivalry in these parts," said Conyers, angrily. "Could no one be found to do the match without risking a young girl's life on it?"

A very hearty burst of merriment met this speech, and the elder of the party rejoined,—

"You must be very new to this country, or you'd not have said that, sir. There's not a man in the hunt could get as much out of a horse as that girl."

"Not to say," added another, with a sly laugh, "that the Englishman gave five to one against her when he heard she was going to ride."

Disgusted by what he could not but regard as a most disgraceful wager, Conyers turned away, and walked into the house.

"Go and change your clothes as fast as you can," said Miss Barrington, as she met him in the porch. "I am quite provoked you should have wetted your feet in such a cause."

It was no time to ask for explanations; and Conyers hurried away to his room, marvelling much at what he had heard, but even more astonished by the attitude of cool and easy indifference as to what might have imperilled a human life. He had often heard of the reckless habits and absurd extravagances of Irish life, but he fancied that they appertained to a time long past, and that society had gradually assumed the tone and the temper of the English. Then he began to wonder to what class in life these persons belonged. The girl, so well as he could see, was certainly handsome, and appeared ladylike; and yet, why had she not even by a word acknowledged the service he rendered her? And lastly, what could old Miss Barrington mean by that scornful speech? These were all great puzzles to him, and like many great puzzles only the more embarrassing the more they were thought over.

The sound of voices drew him now to the window, and he saw one of the riding-party in converse with Darby at the door. They talked in a low tone together, and laughed; and then the horseman, chucking a half-crown towards Darby, said aloud,—

"And tell her that we'll send the boat down for her as soon as we get back."

Darby touched his hat gratefully, and was about to retire within the house when he caught sight of Conyers at the window. He waited till the rider had turned the angle of the road, and then said,—

"That's Mr. St. George. They used to call him the Slasher, he killed so many in duels long ago; but he 's like a lamb now."

"And the young lady?"

"The young lady is it!" said Darby, with the air of one not exactly concurring in the designation. "She's old Dill's daughter, the doctor that attends you."

"What was it all about?"

"It was a bet they made with an English captain this morning that she 'd ride from Lowe's Folly to the Gap in an hour and a half. The Captain took a hundred on it, because he thought she 'd have to go round by the bridge; and they pretinded the same, for they gave all kinds of directions about clearing the carts out of the road, for it's market-day at Thomastown; and away went the Captain as hard as he could, to be at the bridge first, to 'time her,' as she passed. But he has won the money!" sighed he, for the thought of so much Irish coin going into a Saxon pocket completely overcame him; "and what's more," added he, "the gentleman says it was all your fault!"

"All my fault!" cried Conyers, indignantly. "All my fault! Do they imagine that I either knew or cared for their trumpery wager! I saw a girl struggling in a danger from which not one of them had the manliness to rescue her!"

"Oh, take my word for it," burst in Darby, "it's not courage they want!"

"Then it is something far better than even courage, and I'd like to tell them so."

And he turned away as much disgusted with Darby as with the rest of his countrymen. Now, all the anger that filled his breast was not in reality provoked by the want of gallantry that he condemned; a portion, at least, was owing to the marvellous indifference the young lady had manifested to her preserver. Was peril such an every-day incident of Irish life that no one cared for it, or was gratitude a quality not cultivated in this strange land? Such were the puzzles that tormented him as he descended to the drawing-room.

As he opened the door, he heard Miss Barrington's voice, in a tone which he rightly guessed to be reproof, and caught the words, "Just as unwise as it is unbecoming," when he entered.

"Mr. Conyers, Miss Dill," said the old lady, stiffly; "the young gentleman who saved you, the heroine you rescued!" The two allocutions were delivered with a gesture towards each. To cover a moment of extreme awkwardness, Conyers blundered out something about being too happy, and a slight service, and a hope of no ill consequences to herself.

"Have no fears on that score, sir," broke in Miss Dinah. "Manly young ladies are the hardiest things in nature. They are as insensible to danger as they are to—" She stopped, and grew crimson, partly from anger and partly from the unspoken word that had almost escaped her.

"Nay, madam," said Polly, quietly, "I am really very much 'ashamed.'" And, simple as the words were, Miss Barrington felt the poignancy of their application to herself, and her hand trembled over the embroidery she was working.

She tried to appear calm, but in vain; her color came and went, and the stitches, in spite of her, grew irregular; so that, after a moment's struggle, she pushed the frame away, and left the room. While this very brief and painful incident was passing, Conyers was wondering to himself how the dashing horsewoman, with flushed cheek, flashing eye, and dishevelled hair, could possibly be the quiet, demure girl, with a downcast look, and almost Quaker-like simplicity of demeanor. It is but fair to add, though he himself did not discover it, that the contributions of Miss Dinah's wardrobe, to which poor Polly was reduced for dress, were not exactly of a nature to heighten her personal attractions; nor did a sort of short jacket, and a very much beflounced petticoat, set off the girl's figure to advantage. Polly never raised her eyes from the work she was sewing as Miss Barrington withdrew, but, in a low, gentle voice, said, "It was very good of you, sir, to come to my rescue, but you mustn't think ill of my countrymen for not having done so; they had given their word of honor not to lead a fence, nor open a gate, nor, in fact, aid me in any way."

"So that, if they could win their wager, your peril was of little matter," broke he in.

She gave a little low, quiet laugh, perhaps as much at the energy as at the words of his speech. "After all," said she, "a wetting is no great misfortune; the worst punishment of my offence was one that I never contemplated."

"What do you mean?" asked he.

"Doing penance for it in this costume," said she, drawing out the stiff folds of an old brocaded silk, and displaying a splendor of flowers that might have graced a peacock's tail; "I never so much as dreamed of this!"

There was something so comic in the way she conveyed her distress that he laughed outright. She joined him; and they were at once at their ease together.

"I think Miss Barrington called you Mr. Conyers," said she; "and if so, I have the happiness of feeling that my gratitude is bestowed where already there has been a large instalment of the sentiment. It is you who have been so generous and so kind to my poor brother."

"Has he told you, then, what we have been planning together?"

"He has told me all that *you* had planned out for him," said she, with a very gracious smile, which very slightly colored her cheek, and gave great softness to her expression. "My only fear was that the poor boy should have lost his head completely, and perhaps exaggerated to himself your intentions towards him; for, after all, I can scarcely think—"

"What is it that you can scarcely think?" asked he, after a long pause.

"Not to say," resumed she, unheeding his question, "that I cannot imagine how this came about. What could have led him to tell *you*—a perfect stranger to him—his hopes and fears, his struggles and his sorrows? How could you—by what magic did you inspire him with that trustful confidence which made him open his whole heart before you? Poor Tom, who never before had any confessor than myself!"

"Shall I tell you how it came about? It was talking of *you!*"

"Of me! talking of me!" and her cheek now flushed more deeply.

"Yes, we had rambled on over fifty themes, not one of which seemed to attach him strongly, till, in some passing allusion to his own cares and difficulties, he mentioned one who has never ceased to guide and comfort him; who shared not alone his sorrows, but his hard hours of labor, and turned away from her own pleasant paths to tread the dreary road of toil beside him."

"I think he might have kept all this to himself," said she, with a tone of almost severity.

"How could he? How was it possible to tell me his story, and not touch upon what imparted the few tints of better fortune that lighted it? I'm certain, besides, that there is a sort of pride in revealing how much of sympathy and affection we have derived from those better than ourselves, and I could see that he was actually vain of what you had done for him."

"I repeat, he might have kept this to himself. But let us leave this matter; and now tell me,—for I own I can hardly trust my poor brother's triumphant tale,—tell me seriously what the plan is?"

Conyers hesitated for a few seconds, embarrassed how to avoid mention of himself, or to allude but passingly to his own share in the project. At last, as though deciding to dash boldly into the question, he said, "I told him, if he 'd go out to India, I 'd give him such a letter to my father that his fortune would be secure. My governor is something of a swell out there,"—and he reddened, partly in shame, partly in pride, as he tried to disguise his feeling by an affectation of ease,—"and that with *him* for a friend, Tom would be certain of success. You smile at my confidence, but you don't know India, and what scores of fine things are—so to say—to be had for asking; and although doctoring is all very well, there are fifty other ways to make a fortune faster. Tom could be a Receiver of Revenue; he might be a Political Resident. You don't know what they get. There's a fellow at Baroda has four thousand rupees a month, and I don't know how much more for dâk-money."

"I can't help smiling," said she, "at the notion of poor Tom in a palanquin. But, seriously, sir, is all this possible? or might it not be feared that your father, when he came to see my brother—who, with many a worthy quality, has not much to prepossess in his favor,—when, I say, he came to see your *protégé* is it not likely that he might—might—hold him more cheaply than you do?"

"Not when he presents a letter from me; not when it's I that have taken him up. You 'll believe me, perhaps, when I tell you what happened when I was but ten years old. We were up at Rangoon, in the Hills, when a dreadful hurricane swept over the country, destroying everything before it; rice, paddy, the indigo-crop, all were carried away, and the poor people left totally destitute. A subscription-list was handed about amongst the British residents, to afford some aid in the calamity, and it was my tutor, a native Moonshee, who went about to collect the sums. One morning he came back somewhat disconsolate at his want of success. A payment of eight thousand rupees had to be made for grain on that day, and he had not, as he hoped and expected, the money ready. He talked freely to me of his disappointment, so that, at last, my feelings being worked upon, I took up my pen and wrote down my name on the list, with the sum of eight thousand rupees to it Shocked at what he regarded as an act of levity, he carried the paper to my father, who at once said, 'Fred wrote it; his name shall not be dishonored;' and the money was paid. I ask you, now, am I reckoning too much on one who could do that, and for a mere child too?"

"That was nobly done," said she, with enthusiasm; and though Conyers went on, with warmth, to tell more of his father's generous nature, she seemed less to listen than to follow out some thread of her own reflections. Was it some speculation as to the temperament the son of such a father might possess? or was it some pleasurable revery regarding one who might do any extravagance and yet be forgiven? My reader may guess this, perhaps,—I cannot. Whatever her speculation, it lent a very charming expression to her features,—that air of gentle, tranquil happiness we like to believe the lot of guileless, simple natures.

Conyers, like many young men of his order, was very fond of talking of himself, of his ways, his habits, and his temper, and she listened to him very prettily,—so prettily, indeed, that when Darby, slyly peeping in at the half-opened door, announced that the boat had come, he felt well inclined to pitch the messenger into the stream.

"I must go and say good-bye to Miss Barrington," said Polly, rising. "I hope that this rustling finery will impart some dignity to my demeanor." And drawing wide the massive folds, she made a very deep courtesy, throwing back her head haughtily as she resumed her height in admirable imitation of a bygone school of manners.

"Very well,—very well, indeed! Quite as like what it is meant for as is Miss Polly Dill for the station she counterfeits!" said Miss Dinah, as, throwing wide the door, she stood before them.

"I am overwhelmed by your flattery, madam," said Polly, who, though very red, lost none of her self-possession; "but I feel that, like the traveller who tried on Charlemagne's armor, I am far more equal to combat in my every-day clothes."

"Do not enter the lists with me in either," said Miss Dinah, with a look of the haughtiest insolence. "Mr. Conyers, will you let me show you my flower-garden?"

"Delighted! But I will first see Miss Dill to her boat." "As you please, sir," said the old lady; and she withdrew with a proud toss of her head that was very unmistakable in its import.

"What a severe correction that was!" said Polly, half gayly, as she went along, leaning on his arm. "And *you* know that, whatever my offending, there was no mimicry in it. I was simply thinking of some great-grandmother who had, perhaps, captivated the heroes of Dettingen; and, talking of heroes, how courageous of you to come to my rescue!"

Was it that her arm only trembled slightly, or did it really press gently on his own as she said this? Certainly Conyers inclined to the latter hypothesis, for he drew her more closely to his side, and said, "Of course I stood by you. She was all in the wrong, and I mean to tell her so."

"Not if you would serve me," said she, eagerly. "I have paid the penalty, and I strongly object to be sentenced again. Oh, here's the boat!"

"Why it's a mere skiff. Are you safe to trust yourself in such a thing?" asked he, for the canoe-shaped "cot" was new to him.

"Of course!" said she, lightly stepping in. "There is even room for another." Then, hastily changing her theme, she asked, "May I tell poor Tom what you have said to me, or is it just possible that you will come up one of these days and see us?"

"If I might be permitted —"

"Too much honor for us!" said she, with such a capital imitation of his voice and manner that he burst into a laugh in spite of himself.

"Mayhap Miss Bamngton was not so far wrong: after all, you *are* a terrible mimic."

"Is it a promise, then? Am I to say to my brother you will come?" said she, seriously.

"Faithfully!" said he, waving his hand, for the boatmen had already got the skiff under weigh, and were sending her along like an arrow from a bow.

Polly turned and kissed her hand to him, and Conyers muttered something over his own stupidity for not being beside her, and then turned sulkily back towards the cottage. A few hours ago and he had thought he could have passed his life here; there was a charm in the unbroken tranquillity that seemed to satisfy the longings of his heart, and now, all of a sudden, the place appeared desolate. Have you never, dear reader, felt, in gazing on some fair landscape, with mountain and stream and forest before you, that the scene was perfect, wanting nothing in form or tone or color, till suddenly a flash of strong sunlight from behind a cloud lit up some spot with a glorious lustre, to fade away as quickly into the cold tint it had worn before? Have you not felt then, I say, that the picture had lost its marvellous attraction, and that the very soul of its beauty had departed? In vain you try to recall the past impression; your memory will mourn over the lost, and refuse to be comforted. And so it is often in life: the momentary charm that came unexpectedly can become all in all to our imaginations, and its departure leave a blank, like a death, behind it.

Nor was he altogether satisfied with Miss Barrington. The "old woman" — alas! for his gallantry, it was so that he called her to himself — was needlessly severe. Why should a mere piece of harmless levity be so visited? At all events, he felt certain that he himself would have shown a more generous spirit. Indeed, when Polly had quizzed him, he took it all good-naturedly, and by thus turning his thoughts to his natural goodness and the merits of his character, he at length grew somewhat more well-disposed to the world at large. He knew he was naturally forgiving, and he felt he was very generous. Scores of fellows, bred up as he was, would have been perfectly unendurable; they would have presumed on their position, and done this, that, and t' other. Not one of them would have dreamed of taking up a poor ungainly bumpkin, a country doctor's cub, and making a man of him; not one of them would have had the heart to conceive or the energy to carry out such a project. And yet this he would do. Polly herself, sceptical as she was, should be brought to admit that he had kept his word. Selfish fellows would limit their plans to their own engagements, and weak fellows could be laughed out of their intentions; but *he* flattered himself that he was neither of these, and it was really fortunate that the world should see how little spoiled a fine nature could be, though surrounded with all the temptations that are supposed to be dangerous.

In this happy frame—for he was now happy—he reentered the cottage. "What a coxcomb!" will say my reader. Be it so. But it was a coxcomb who wanted to be something better.

Miss Barrington met him in the porch, not a trace of her late displeasure on her face, but with a pleasant smile she said, "I have just got a few lines from my brother. He writes in excellent spirits, for he has gained a lawsuit; not a very important case, but it puts us in a position to carry out a little project we are full of. He will be here by Saturday, and hopes to bring with him an old and valued friend, the Attorney-General, to spend a few days with us. I am, therefore, able to promise you an ample recompense for all the loneliness of your present life. I have cautiously abstained from telling my brother who you are; I keep the delightful surprise for the moment of your meeting. Your name, though associated with some sad memories, will bring him back to the happiest period of his life."

Conyers made some not very intelligible reply about his reluctance to impose himself on them at such a time, but she stopped him with a good-humored smile, and said,—

"Your father's son should know that where a Barrington lived he had a home,—not to say you have already paid some of the tribute of this homeliness, and seen me very cross and ill-tempered. Well, let us not speak of that now. I have your word to remain here." And she left him to attend to her household cares, while he strolled into the garden, half amused, half embarrassed by all the strange and new interests that had grown up so suddenly around him.

CHAPTER XV
AN EXPLORING EXPEDITION

Whether from simple caprice, or that Lady Cobham desired to mark her disapprobation of Polly Dill's share in the late wager, is not open to me to say, but the festivities at Cob-ham were not, on that day, graced or enlivened by her presence. If the comments on her absence were brief, they were pungent, and some wise reflections, too, were uttered as to the dangers that must inevitably attend all attempts to lift people into a sphere above their own. Poor human nature! that unlucky culprit who is flogged for everything and for everybody, bore the brunt of these severities, and it was declared that Polly had done what any other girl "in her rank of life" might have done; and this being settled, the company went to luncheon, their appetites none the worse for the small *auto-da-fé* they had just celebrated.

"You'd have lost your money, Captain," whispered Ambrose Bushe to Stapylton, as they stood talking together in a window recess, "if that girl had only taken the river three hundred yards higher up. Even as it was, she 'd have breasted her horse at the bank if the bridle had not given way. I suppose you have seen the place?"

"I regret to say I have not. They tell me it's one of the strongest rapids in the river."

"Let me describe it to you," replied he; and at once set about a picture in which certainly no elements of peril were forgotten, and all the dangers of rocks and rapids were given with due emphasis. Stapylton seemed to listen with fitting attention, throwing out the suitable "Indeed! is it possible!" and such-like interjections, his mind, however, by no means absorbed by the narrative, but dwelling solely on a chance name that had dropped from the narrator.

"You called the place 'Barrington's Ford,'" said he, at last. "Who is Barrington?"

"As good a gentleman by blood and descent as any in this room, but now reduced to keep a little wayside inn,—the 'Fisherman's Home,' it is called. All come of a spendthrift son, who went out to India, and ran through every acre of the property before he died."

"What a strange vicissitude! And is the old man much broken by it?"

"Some would say he was; my opinion is, that he bears up wonderfully. Of course, to me, he never makes any mention of the past; but while my father lived, he would frequently talk to him over bygones, and liked nothing better than to speak of his son, Mad George as they called him, and tell all his wildest exploits and most harebrained achievements. But you have served yourself in India. Have you never heard of George Barrington?"

Stapylton shook his head, and dryly added that India was very large, and that even in one Presidency a man might never hear what went on in another.

"Well, this fellow made noise enough to be heard even over here. He married a native woman, and he either shook off his English allegiance, or was suspected of doing so. At all events, he got himself into trouble that finished him. It's a long complicated story, that I have never heard correctly. The upshot was, however, old Barrington was sold out stick and stone, and if it was n't for the ale-house he might starve."

"And his former friends and associates, do they rally round him and cheer him?"

"Not a great deal. Perhaps, however, that's as much his fault as theirs. He is very proud, and very quick to resent anything like consideration for his changed condition. Sir Charles would have him up here,—he has tried it scores of times, but all in vain; and now he is left to two or three of his neighbors, the doctor and an old half-pay major, who lives on the river, and I believe really he never sees any one else. Old M'Cormick knew George Barrington well; not that they were friends,—two men less alike never lived; but that's enough to make poor Peter fond of talking to him, and telling all about some lawsuits George left him for a legacy."

"This Major that you speak of, does he visit here? I don't remember to have seen him."

"M'Cormick!" said the other, laughing. "No, he 's a miserly old fellow that has n't a coat fit to go out in, and he's no loss to any one. It's as much as old Peter Barrington can do to bear his shabby ways, and his cranky temper, but he puts up with everything because he knew his son George. That's quite enough for old Peter; and if you were to go over to the cottage, and say, 'I met your son up in Bombay or Madras; we were quartered together at Ram-something-or-other,' he 'd tell you the place was your own, to stop at as long as you liked, and your home for life."

"Indeed!" said Stapylton, affecting to feel interested, while he followed out the course of his own thoughts.

"Not that the Major could do even that much!" continued Bushe, who now believed that he had found an eager listener. "There was only one thing in this world he'd like to talk about,—Walcheren. Go how or when you liked, or where or for what,—no matter, it was Walcheren you 'd get, and nothing else."

"Somewhat tiresome this, I take it!"

"Tiresome is no name for it! And I don't know a stronger proof of old Peter's love for his son's memory, than that, for the sake of hearing about him, he can sit and listen to the 'expedition.'"

There was a half-unconscious mimicry in the way he gave the last word that showed how the Major's accents had eaten their way into his sensibilities.

"Your portrait of this Major is not tempting," said Stapylton, smiling.

"Why would it? He's eighteen or twenty years in the neighborhood, and I never heard that he said a kind word or did a generous act by any one. But I get cross if I talk of him. Where are you going this morning? Will you come up to the Long Callows and look at the yearlings? The Admiral is very proud of his young stock, and he thinks he has some of the best bone and blood in Ireland there at this moment."

"Thanks, no; I have some notion of a long walk this morning. I take shame to myself for having seen so little of the country here since I came that I mean to repair my fault and go off on a sort of voyage of discovery."

"Follow the river from Brown's Barn down to Inistioge, and if you ever saw anything prettier I'm a Scotchman." And with this appalling alternative, Mr. Bushe walked away, and left the other to his own guidance.

Perhaps Stapylton is not the companion my reader would care to stroll with, even along the grassy path beside that laughing river, with spray-like larches bending overhead, and tender water-lilies streaming, like pennants, in the fast-running current. It may be that he or she would prefer some one more impressionable to the woodland beauty of the spot, and more disposed to enjoy the tranquil loveliness around him; for it is true the swarthy soldier strode on, little heeding the picturesque effects which made every succeeding reach of the river a subject for a painter. He was bent on finding out where M'Cormick lived, and on making the acquaintance of that bland individual.

"That's the Major's, and there's himself," said a countryman, as he pointed to a very shabbily dressed old man hoeing his cabbages in a dilapidated bit of garden-ground, but who was so absorbed in his occupation as not to notice the approach of a stranger.

"Am I taking too great a liberty," said Stapylton, as he raised his hat, "if I ask leave to follow the river path through this lovely spot?"

"Eh—what?—how did you come? You didn't pass round by the young wheat, eh?" asked M'Cormick, in his most querulous voice.

"I came along by the margin of the river."

"That's just it!" broke in the other. "There's no keeping them out that way. But I 'll have a dog as sure as my name is Dan. I'll have a bull-terrier that'll tackle the first of you that's trespassing there."

"I fancy I'm addressing Major M'Cormick," said Stapylton, never noticing this rude speech; "and if so, I will ask him to accord me the privilege of a brother-soldier, and let me make myself known to him,—Captain Stapylton, of the Prince's Hussars."

"By the wars!" muttered old Dan; the exclamation being a favorite one with him to express astonishment at any startling event. Then recovering himself, he added, "I think I heard there were three or four of ye stopping up there at Cobham; but I never go out myself anywhere. I live very retired down here."

"I am not surprised at that. When an old soldier can nestle down in a lovely nook like this, he has very little to regret of what the world is busy about outside it."

"And they are all ruining themselves, besides," said M'Cormick, with one of his malicious grins. "There's not a man in this county is n't mortgaged over head and ears. I can count them all on my fingers for you, and tell what they have to live on."

"You amaze me," said Stapylton, with a show of interest

"And the women are as bad as the men: nothing fine enough for them to wear; no jewels rich enough to put on! Did you ever hear them mention *me?*" asked he, suddenly, as though the thought flashed upon him that he had himself been exposed to comment of a very different kind.

"They told me of an old retired officer, who owned a most picturesque cottage, and said, if I remember aright, that the view from one of the windows was accounted one of the most perfect bits of river landscape in the kingdom."

"Just the same as where you 're standing,—no difference in life," said M'Cormick, who was not to be seduced by the flattery into any demonstration of hospitality.

"I cannot imagine anything finer," said Stapylton, as he threw himself at the foot of a tree, and seemed really to revel in enjoyment of the scene.

"One might, perhaps, if disposed to be critical, ask for a little opening in that copse yonder. I suspect we should get a peep at the bold cliff whose summit peers above the tree-tops."

"You'd see the quarry, to be sure," croaked out the Major, "if that's what you mean."

"May I offer you a cigar?" said Stapylton, whose self-possession was pushed somewhat hard by the other. "An old campaigner is sure to be a smoker."

"I am not. I never had a pipe in my mouth since Walcheren."

"Since Walcheren! You don't say that you are an old Walcheren man?"

"I am, indeed. I was in the second battalion of the 103d,—the Duke's Fusiliers, if ever you heard of them."

"Heard of them! The whole world has heard of them; but I did n't know there was a man of that splendid corps surviving. Why, they lost—let me see—they lost every officer but—" Here a vigorous effort to keep his cigar alight interposed, and kept him occupied for a few seconds. "How many did you bring out of action,—four was it, or five? I'm certain you had n't six!"

"We were the same as the Buffs, man for man," said M'Cormick.

"The poor Buffs!—very gallant fellows too!" sighed Stapylton. "I have always maintained, and I always will maintain, that the Walcheren expedition, though not a success, was the proudest achievement of the British arms."

"The shakes always began after sunrise, and in less than ten minutes you 'd see your nails growing blue."

"How dreadful!"

"And if you felt your nose, you would n't know it was your nose; you 'd think it was a bit of a cold carrot."

"Why was that?"

"Because there was no circulation; the blood would stop going round; and you 'd be that way for four hours,—till the sweating took you,—just the same as dead."

"There, don't go on,—I can't stand it,—my nerves are all ajar already."

"And then the cramps came on," continued M'Cormick, in an ecstasy over a listener whose feelings he could harrow; "first in the calves of the legs, and then all along the spine, so that you 'd be bent like a fish."

"For Heaven's sake, spare me! I've seen some rough work, but that description of yours is perfectly horrifying! And when one thinks it was the glorious old 105th—"

"No, the 103d; the 105th was at Barbadoes," broke in the Major, testily.

"So they were, and got their share of the yellow fever at that very time too," said Stapylton, hazarding a not very rash conjecture.

"Maybe they did, and maybe they didn't," was the dry rejoinder.

It required all Stapylton's nice tact to get the Major once more full swing at the expedition, but he at last accomplished the feat, and with such success that M'Cormick suggested an adjournment within doors, and faintly hinted at a possible something to drink. The wily guest, however, declined this. "He liked," he said, "that nice breezy spot under those fine old trees, and with that glorious reach of the river before them. Could a man but join to these enjoyments," he continued, "just a neighbor or two,—an old friend or so that he really liked,—one not alone agreeable from his tastes, but to whom the link of early companionship also attached us, with this addition I could call this a paradise."

"Well, I have the village doctor," croaked out M'Cor-mick, "and there's Barrington—old Peter—up at the 'Fisherman's Home.' I have *them* by way of society. I might have better, and I might have worse."

"They told me at Cobham that there was no getting you to 'go out;' that, like a regular old soldier, you liked your own chimney-corner, and could not be tempted away from it."

"They didn't try very hard, anyhow," said he, harshly. "I'll be nineteen years here if I live till November, and I think I got two invitations, and one of them to a 'dancing tea,' whatever that is; so that you may observe they did n't push the temptation as far as St. Anthony's!"

Stapylton joined in the laugh with which M'Cormick welcomed his own drollery.

"Your doctor," resumed he, "is, I presume, the father of the pretty girl who rides so cleverly?"

"So they tell me. I never saw her mounted but once, and she smashed a melon-frame for me, and not so much as 'I ask your pardon!' afterwards."

"And Barrington," resumed Stapylton, "is the ruined gentleman I have heard of, who has turned innkeeper. An extravagant son, I believe, finished him?"

"His own taste for law cost him just as much," muttered M'Cormick. "He had a trunk full of old title-deeds and bonds and settlements, and he was always poring over them, discovering, by the way, flaws in this and omissions in that, and then he 'd draw up a case for counsel, and get consultations on it, and before you could turn round, there he was, trying to break a will or get out of a covenant, with a special jury and the strongest Bar in Ireland. That's what ruined him."

"I gather from what you tell me that he is a bold, determined, and perhaps a vindictive man. Am I right?"

"You are not; he's an easy-tempered fellow, and careless, like every one of his name and race. If you said he hadn't a wise head on his shoulders, you 'd be nearer the mark. Look what he 's going to do now!" cried he, warming with his theme: "he 's going to give up the inn—"

"Give it up! And why?"

"Ay, that's the question would puzzle him to answer; but it's the haughty old sister persuades him that he ought to take this black girl—George Barrington's daughter—home to live with him, and that a shebeen is n't the place to bring her to, and she a negress. That's more of the family wisdom!"

"There may be affection in it."

"Affection! For what,—for a black! Ay, and a black that they never set eyes on! If it was old Withering had the affection for her, I wouldn't be surprised."

"What do you mean? Who is he?"

"The Attorney-General, who has been fighting the East India Company for her these sixteen years, and making more money out of the case than she 'll ever get back again. Did you ever hear of Barrington and Lot Rammadahn Mohr against the India Company? That's the case. Twelve millions of rupees and the interest on them! And I believe in my heart and soul old Peter would be well out of it for a thousand pounds."

"That is, you suspect he must be beaten in the end?"

"I mean that I am sure of it! We have a saying in Ireland, 'It's not fair for one man to fall on twenty,' and it's just the same thing to go to law with a great rich Company. You 're sure to have the worst of it."

"Did it never occur to them to make some sort of compromise?"

"Not a bit of it. Old Peter always thinks he has the game in his hand, and nothing would make him throw up the cards. No; I believe if you offered to pay the stakes, he 'd say, 'Play the game out, and let the winner take the money!'"

"His lawyer may, possibly, have something to say to this spirit."

"Of course he has; they are always bolstering each other up. It is, 'Barrington, my boy, you 'll turn the corner yet. You 'll drive up that old avenue to the house you were born in, Barrington, of Barrington Hall;' or, 'Withering, I never heard you greater than on that point before the twelve Judges;' or, 'Your last speech at Bar was finer than Curran.' They'd pass the evening that way, and call me a cantankerous old hound when my back was turned, just because I did n't hark in to the cry. Maybe I have the laugh at them, after all." And he broke out into one of his most discordant cackles to corroborate his boast.

"The sound sense and experience of an old Walcheren man might have its weight with them. I know it would with me."

"Ay," muttered the Major, half aloud, for he was thinking to himself whether this piece of flattery was a bait for a little whiskey-and-water.

"I 'd rather have the unbought judgment of a shrewd man of the world than a score of opinions based upon the quips and cranks of an attorney's instructions."

"Ay!" responded the other, as he mumbled to himself, "he's mighty thirsty."

"And what's more," said Stapylton, starting to his legs, "I 'd follow the one as implicitly as I'd reject the other. I 'd say, 'M'Cormick is an old friend; we have known each other since boyhood.'"

"No, we haven't I never saw Peter Barrington till I came to live here."

"Well, after a close friendship of years with his son—"

"Nor that, either," broke in the implacable Major. "He was always cutting his jokes on me, and I never could abide him, so that the close friendship you speak of is a mistake."

"At all events," said Stapylton, sharply, "it could be no interest of yours to see an old—an old acquaintance lavishing his money on lawyers and in the pursuit of the most improbable of all results. *You* have no design upon him. *You* don't want to marry his sister!"

"No, by Gemini! "—a favorite expletive of the Major's in urgent moments.

"Nor the Meer's daughter, either, I suppose?"

"The black! I think not. Not if she won the lawsuit, and was as rich as—she never will be."

"I agree with you there, Major, though I know nothing of the case or its merits; but it is enough to hear that a beggared squire is on one side, and Leadenhall Street on the other, to predict the upshot, and, for my own part, I wonder they go on with it."

"I'll tell you how it is," said M'Cormick, closing one eye so as to impart a look of intense cunning to his face. "It's the same with law as at a fox-hunt: when you 're tired out beating a cover, and ready to go off home, one dog—very often the worst in the whole pack—will yelp out. You know well enough he's a bad hound, and never found in his life. What does that signify? When you 're wishing a thing, whatever flatters your hopes is all right,—is n't that true?—and away you dash after the yelper as if he was a good hound."

"You have put the matter most convincingly before me."

"How thirsty he is now!" thought the Major; and grinned maliciously at his reflection.

"And the upshot of all," said Stapylton, like one summing up a case,—"the upshot of all is, that this old man is not satisfied with his ruin if it be not complete; he must see the last timbers of the wreck carried away ere he leaves the scene of his disaster. Strange, sad infatuation!"

"Ay," muttered the Major, who really had but few sympathies with merely moral abstractions.

"Not what I should have done in a like case; nor you either, Major, eh?"

"Very likely not"

"But so it is. There are men who cannot be practical, do what they will. This is above them."

A sort of grunt gave assent to this proposition; and Stapylton, who began to feel it was a drawn game, arose to take his leave.

"I owe you a very delightful morning, Major," said he. "I wish I could think it was not to be the last time I was to have this pleasure. Do you ever come up to Kilkenny? Does it ever occur to you to refresh your old mess recollections?"

Had M'Cormick been asked whether he did not occasionally drop in at Holland House, and brush up his faculties by intercourse with the bright spirits who resorted there, he could scarcely have been more astounded. That he, old Dan M'Cormick, should figure at a mess-table,—he, whose wardrobe, a mere skeleton battalion thirty years ago, had never since been recruited,—he should mingle with the gay and splendid young fellows of a "crack" regiment!

"I'd just as soon think of—of—" he hesitated how to measure an unlikelihood— "of marrying a young wife, and taking her off to Paris!"

"And I don't see any absurdity in the project There is certainly a great deal of brilliancy about it!"

"And something bitter too!" croaked out M'Cormick, with a fearful grin.

"Well, if you'll not come to see me, the chances are I'll come over and make *you* another visit before I leave the neighborhood." He waited a second or two, not more, for some recognition of this offer; but none came, and he con-tinned: "I'll get you to stroll down with me, and show me this 'Fisherman's Home,' and its strange proprietor."

"Oh, I 'll do *that!*" said the Major, who had no objection to a plan which by no possibility could involve himself in any cost.

"As it is an inn, perhaps they 'd let us have a bit of dinner. What would you say to being my guest there tomorrow? Would that suit you?"

"It would suit *me* well enough!" was the strongly marked reply.

"Well, we 'll do it this wise. You 'll send one of your people over to order dinner for two at—shall we say five o'clock?—yes, five—to-morrow. That will give us a longer evening, and I 'll call here for you about four. Is that agreed?"

"Yes, that might do," was M'Cormick's half-reluctant assent, for, in reality, there were details in the matter that he scarcely fancied. First of all, he had never hitherto crossed that threshold except as an invited guest, and he had his misgivings about the prudence of appearing in any other character, and secondly, there was a responsibility in ordering the dinner, which he liked just as little, and, as he muttered to himself, "Maybe I 'll have to order the bill too!"

Some unlucky experiences of casualties of this sort had, perhaps, shadowed his early life; for so it was, that long after Stapylton had taken his leave and gone off, the Major stood there ruminating over this unpleasant contingency, and ingeniously imagining all the pleas he could put in, should his apprehension prove correct, against his own indebtedness.

"Tell Miss Dinah," said he to his messenger,—"tell her 't is an officer by the name of Captain Staples, or something like that, that 's up at Cobham, that wants a dinner for two to-morrow at five o'clock; and mind that you don't say who the other is, for it's nothing to her. And if she asks you what sort of a dinner, say the best in the house, for the Captain—mind you say the Captain—is to pay for it, and the other man only dines with him. There, now, you have your orders, and take care that you follow them!"

There was a shrewd twinkle in the messenger's eye as he listened, which, if not exactly complimentary, guaranteed how thoroughly he comprehended the instructions that were given to him; and the Major saw him set forth on his mission, well assured that he could trust his envoy.

In that nothing-for-nothing world Major M'Cormick had so long lived in, and to whose practice and ways he had adapted all his thoughts, there was something puzzling in the fact of a dashing Captain of Hussars of "the Prince's Own," seeking him out, to form his acquaintance and invite him to dinner. Now, though the selfishness of an unimaginative man is the most complete of all, it yet exposes him to fewer delusions than the same quality when found allied with a hopeful or fanciful temperament. M'Cormick had no "distractions" from such sources. He thought very ill of the world at large; he expected extremely little from its generosity, and he resolved to be "quits" with it. To his often put question, "What brought him here?— what did he come for?" he could find no satisfactory reply. He scouted the notion of "love of scenery, solitude, and so forth," and as fully he ridiculed to himself the idea of a stranger caring to hear the gossip and small-talk of a mere country neighborhood. "I have it!" cried he at last, as a bright thought darted through his brain,—"I have it at last! He wants to pump me about the 'expedition.' It's for that he's come. He affected surprise, to be sure, when I said I was a Walcheren man, and pretended to be amazed, besides; but that was all make-believe. He knew well enough who and what I was before he came. And he was so cunning, leading the conversation away in another direction, getting me to talk of old Peter and his son George. Wasn't it deep?—was n't it sly? Well, maybe we are not so innocent as we look, ourselves; maybe we have a trick in our sleeves too! 'With a good dinner and a bottle of port wine,' says he, 'I 'll have the whole story, and be able to write it with the signature "One who was there."' But you 're mistaken this time, Captain; the sorrow bit of Walcheren you 'll hear out of my mouth to-morrow, be as pleasant and congenial as you like. I 'll give you the Barringtons, father and son,—ay, and old Dinah, too, if you fancy her,—but not a syllable about the expedition. It's the Scheldt you want, but you 'll have to 'take it out' in the Ganges." And his uncouth joke so tickled him that he laughed till his eyes ran over; and in the thought that he was going to obtain a dinner under false pretences, he felt something as nearly like happiness as he had tasted for many a long day before.

CHAPTER XVI
COMING HOME

Miss Barrtngton waited with impatience for Conyers's appearance at the breakfast-table,—she had received such a pleasant note from her brother, and she was so eager to read it. That notion of imparting some conception of a dear friend by reading his own words to a stranger is a very natural one. It serves so readily to corroborate all we have already said, to fill up that picture of which wo have but given the mere outline, not to speak of the inexplicable charm there is in being able to say, "Here is the man without reserve or disguise; here he is in all the freshness and warmth of genuine feeling; no tricks of style, no turning of phrases to mar the honest expression of his nature. You see him as we see him."

"My brother is coming home, Mr. Conyers; he will be here to-day. Here is his note," said Miss Dinah, as she shook hands with her guest "I must read it for you:—

"'At last, my dear Dinah—at last I am free, and, with all my love of law and lawyers, right glad to turn my steps homeward. Not but I have had a most brilliant week of it; dined with my old schoolfellow Longmore, now Chief Baron, and was the honored guest of the "Home Circuit," not to speak of one glorious evening with a club called the "Unbriefed," the pleasantest dogs that ever made good speeches for nothing!—an amount of dissipation upon which I can well retire and live for the next twelve months. How strange it seems to me to be once more in the "world," and listening to scores of things in which I have no personal interest; how small it makes my own daily life appear, but how secure and how homelike, Dinah! You have often heard me grumbling over the decline of social agreeability, and the dearth of those pleasant speeches that could set the table in a roar. You shall never hear the same complaint from me again. These fellows are just as good as their fathers. If I missed anything, it was that glitter of scholarship, that classical turn which in the olden day elevated table-talk, and made it racy with the smart aphorisms and happy conceits of those who, even over their wine, were poets and orators. But perhaps I am not quite fair even in this. At all events, I am not going to disparage those who have brought back to my old age some of the pleasant memories of my youth, and satisfied me that even yet I have a heart for those social joys I once loved so dearly!

"'And we have won our suit, Dinah,—at least, a juror was withdrawn by consent,—and Brazier agrees to an arbitration as to the Moyalty lands, the whole of Clanebrach and Barrymaquilty property being released from the sequestration.'

"This is all personal matter, and technical besides," said Miss Barrington; "so I skip it."

"'Withering was finer than ever I heard him in the speech to evidence. We have been taunted with our defensive attitude so suddenly converted into an attack, and he compared our position to Wellington's at Torres Vedras. The Chief Justice said Curran, at his best, never excelled it, and they have called me nothing but Lord Wellington ever since. And now, Dinah, to answer the question your impatience has been putting these ten minutes: "What of the money part of all this triumph?" I fear much, my dear sister, we are to take little by our motion. The costs of the campaign cut up all but the glory! Hogan's bill extends to thirty-eight folio pages, and there's a codicil to it of eleven more, headed "Confidential between Client and Attorney," and though I have not in a rapid survey seen anything above five pounds, the gross total is two thousand seven hundred and forty-three pounds three and fourpence. I must and will say, however, it was a great suit, and admirably prepared. There was not an instruction Withering did not find substantiated, and Hogan is equally delighted with *him*, With all my taste for field sports and manly games, Dinah, I am firmly convinced that a good trial at bar is a far finer spectacle than the grandest tournament that ever was tilted. There was a skirmish yesterday that I 'd rather have witnessed than I 'd have seen Brian de Bois himself at Ashby-de-la-Zouch. And, considering that my own share for this passage at arms will come to a trifle above two thousand pounds, the confession may be taken as an honest one.

"'And who is your young guest whom I shall be so delighted to see? This gives no clew to him, Dinah, for you know well how I would welcome any one who has impressed you so favorably. Entreat of him to prolong his stay for a week at least, and if I can persuade Withering to come down with me, we 'll try and make his sojourn more agreeable. Look out for me—at least, about five o'clock—and have the green-room ready for W., and let Darby be at Holt's stile to take the trunks, for Withering likes that walk through the woods, and says that he leaves his wig and gown on the holly-bushes there till he goes back.'"

The next paragraph she skimmed over to herself. It was one about an advance that Hogan had let him have of two hundred pounds. "Quite ample," W. says, "for our excursion to fetch over Josephine." Some details as to the route followed, and some wise hints about travelling on the Continent, and a hearty concurrence on the old lawyer's part with the whole scheme.

"These are little home details," said she, hurriedly, "but you have heard enough to guess what my brother is like. Here is the conclusion:—

"'I hope your young friend is a fisherman, which will give me more chance of his company than walking up the partridges, for which I am getting too old. Let him however understand that we mean him to enjoy himself in his own way, to have the most perfect liberty, and that the only despotism we insist upon is, not to be late for dinner.

"'Your loving brother,

"'Peter Barrington.

"'There is no fatted calf to feast our return, Dinah, but Withering has an old weakness for a roast sucking-pig. Don't you think we could satisfy it?'"

Conyers readily caught the contagion of the joy Miss Barrington felt at the thought of her brother's return. Short as the distance was that separated him from home, his absences were so rare, it seemed as though he had gone miles and miles away, for few people ever lived more dependent on each other, with interests more concentrated, and all of whose hopes and fears took exactly the same direction, than this brother and sister, and this, too, with some strong differences on the score of temperament, of which the reader already has an inkling.

What a pleasant bustle that is of a household that prepares for the return of a well-loved master! What feeling pervades twenty little offices of every-day routine! And how dignified by affection are the smallest cares and the very humblest attentions! "He likes this!" "He is so fond of that!" are heard at every moment It is then that one marks how the observant eye of love has followed the most ordinary tricks of habit, and treasured them as things to be remembered. It is not the key of the street door in your pocket, nor the lease of the premises in your drawer, that make a home. Let us be grateful when we remember that, in this attribute, the humblest shealing on the hillside is not inferior to the palace of the king!

Conyers, I have said, partook heartily of Miss Barring-ton's delight, and gave a willing help to the preparations that went forward. All were soon busy within doors and without. Some were raking the gravel before the door; while others were disposing the flower-pots in little pyramids through the grass plats; and then there were trees to be nailed up, and windows cleaned, and furniture changed in various ways. What superhuman efforts did not Conyers make to get an old jet d'eau to play which had not spouted for nigh twenty years; and how reluctantly he resigned himself to failure and assisted Betty to shake a carpet!

And when all was completed, and the soft and balmy air sent the odor of the rose and the jessamine through the open windows, within which every appearance of ease and comfort prevailed, Miss Barrington sat down at the piano and began to refresh her memory of some Irish airs, old favorites of Withering's, which he was sure to ask for. There was that in their plaintive wildness which strongly interested Conyers; while, at the same time, he was astonished at the skill of one at whose touch, once on a time, tears had trembled in the eyes of those who listened, and whose fingers had not yet forgot their cunning.

"Who is that standing without there?" said Miss Barrington, suddenly, as she saw a very poor-looking countryman who had drawn close to the window to listen. "Who are you? and what do you want here?" asked she, approaching him.

"I 'm Terry, ma'am,—Terry Delany, the Major's man," said he, taking off his hat.

"Never heard of you; and what 's your business?"

"'T is how I was sent, your honor's reverence," began he, faltering at every word, and evidently terrified by her imperious style of address. "'Tis how I came here with the master's compliments,—not indeed his own but the other man's,—to say, that if it was plazing to you, or, indeed, anyhow at all, they 'd be here at five o'clock to dinner; and though it was yesterday I got it, I stopped with my sister's husband at Foynes Gap, and misremembered it all till this morning, and I hope your honor's reverence won't tell it on me, but have the best in the house all the same, for he's rich enough and can well afford it."

"What can the creature mean?" cried Miss Barrington. "Who sent you here?"

"The Major himself; but not for him, but for the other that's up at Cobham."

"And who is this other? What is he called?"

"'Twas something like Hooks, or Nails; but I can't remember," said he, scratching his head in sign of utter and complete bewilderment.

"Did any one ever hear the like! Is the fellow an idiot?" exclaimed she, angrily.

"No, my lady; but many a one might be that lived with ould M'Cormick!" burst out the man, in a rush of unguardedness.

"Try and collect yourself, my good fellow," said Miss Barrington, smiling, in spite of herself, at his confession, "and say, if you can, what brought you here?"

"It's just, then, what I said before," said he, gaining a little more courage. "It's dinner for two ye're to have; and it's to be ready at five o'clock; but ye 're not to look to ould Dan for the money, for he as good as said he would never pay sixpence of it, but 't is all to come out of the other chap's pocket, and well affordin' it. There it is now, and I defy the Pope o' Rome to say that I did n't give the message right!"

"Mr. Conyers," began Miss Barrington, in a voice shaking with agitation, "it is nigh twenty years since a series of misfortunes brought us so low in the world that—" She stopped, partly overcome by indignation, partly by shame; and then, suddenly turning towards the man, she continued, in a firm and resolute tone, "Go back to your master and say, 'Miss Barrington hopes he has sent a fool on his errand, otherwise his message is so insolent it will be far safer he should never present himself here again!' Do you hear me? Do you understand me?"

"If you mane you'd make them throw him in the river, the divil a straw I 'd care, and I would n't wet my feet to pick him out of it!"

"Take the message as I have given it you, and do not dare to mix up anything of your own with it."

"Faix, I won't. It's trouble enough I have without that! I 'll tell him there's no dinner for him here to-day, and that, if he 's wise, he won't come over to look for it."

"There, go—be off," cried Conyers, impatiently, for he saw that Miss Barrington's temper was being too sorely tried.

She conquered, however, the indignation that at one moment had threatened to master her, and in a voice of tolerable calm said,—

"May I ask you to see if Darby or any other of the workmen are in the garden? It is high time to take down these insignia of our traffic, and tell our friends how we would be regarded in future."

"Will you let me do it? I ask as a favor that I may be permitted to do it," cried Conyers, eagerly; and without waiting for her answer, hurried away to fetch a ladder. He was soon back again and at work.

"Take care how you remove that board, Mr. Conyers," said she. "If there be the tiniest sprig of jessamine broken, my brother will miss it. He has been watching anxiously for the time when the white bells would shut out every letter of his name, and I like him not to notice the change immediately. There, you are doing it very handily indeed. There is another holdfast at this corner. Ah, be careful; that is a branch of the passion-tree, and though it looks dead, you will see it covered with flowers in spring. Nothing could be better. Now for the last emblem of our craft,—can you reach it?"

"Oh, easily," said Conyers, as he raised his eyes to where the little tin fish hung glittering above him. The ladder, however, was too short, and, standing on one of the highest rungs, still he could not reach the little iron stanchion. "I must have it, though," cried he; "I mean to claim that as my prize. It will be the only fish I ever took with my own hands." He now cautiously crept up another step of the ladder, supporting himself by the frail creepers which covered the walls. "Help me now with a crooked stick, and I shall catch it."

"I'll fetch you one," said she, disappearing within the porch.

Still wistfully looking at the object of his pursuit, Conyers never turned his eyes downwards as the sound of steps apprised him some one was near, and, concluding it to be Miss Barrington, he said, "I'm half afraid that I have torn some of this jessamine-tree from the wall; but see here's the prize!" A slight air of wind had wafted it towards him, and he suatched the fish from its slender chain and held it up in triumph.

"A poacher caught in the fact, Barrington!" said a deep voice from below; and Conyers, looking down, saw two men, both advanced in life, very gravely watching his proceedings.

Not a little ashamed of a situation to which he never expected an audience, he hastily descended the ladder; but before he reached the ground Miss Barrington was in her brother's arms, and welcoming him home with all the warmth of true affection. This over, she next shook hands cordially with his companion, whom she called Mr. Withering.

"And now, Peter," said she, "to present one I have been longing to make known to you. You, who never forget a well-known face, will recognize him."

"My eyes are not what they used to be," said Barrington, holding out his hand to Conyers, "but they are good enough to see the young gentleman I left here when I went away."

"Yes, Peter," said she, hastily; "but does the sight of him bring back to you no memory of poor George?"

"George was dark as a Spaniard, and this gentleman—But pray, sir, forgive this rudeness of ours, and let us make ourselves better acquainted within doors. You mean to stay some time here, I hope."

"I only wish I could; but I have already overstayed my leave, and waited here only to shake your hand before I left."

"Peter, Peter," said Miss Dinah, impatiently, "must I then tell whom you are speaking to?"

Barrington seemed pazzled. He looked from the stranger to his sister, and back again.

She drew near and whispered in his ear: "The son of poor George's dearest friend on earth,—the son of Ormsby Conyers."

"Of whom?" said Barrington, in a startled and half-angry voice.

"Of Ormsby Conyers."

Barrington trembled from head to foot; his face, for an instant crimson, became suddenly of an ashy paleness, and his voice shook as he said,—

"I was not—I am not—prepared for this honor. I mean, I could not have expected that Mr. Conyers would have desired—Say this—do this for me, Withering, for I am not equal to it," said the old man, as, with his hands pressed over his face, he hurried within the house, followed by his sister.

"I cannot make a guess at the explanation my friend has left me to make," cried Withering, courteously; "but it is plain to see that your name has revived some sorrow connected with the great calamity of his life. You have heard of his son, Colonel Barrington?"

"Yes, and it was because my father had been his dearest friend that Miss Barrington insisted on my remaining here. She told me, over and over again, of the joy her brother would feel on meeting me—"

"Where are you going,—what's the matter?" asked Withering, as a man hurriedly passed out of the house and made for the river.

"The master is taken bad, sir, and I 'm going to Inistioge for the doctor."

"Let me go with you," said Conyers; and, only returning by a nod the good-bye of Withering, he moved past and stepped into the boat.

"What an afternoon to such a morning!" muttered he to himself, as the tears started from his eyes and stole heavily along his cheeks.

CHAPTER XVII
A SHOCK

If Conyers had been in the frame of mind to notice it, the contrast between the neat propriety of the "Fisherman's Home," and the disorder and slovenliness of the little inn at Inistioge could not have failed to impress itself upon him. The "Spotted Duck" was certainly, in all its details, the very reverse of that quiet and picturesque cottage he had just quitted. But what did he care at that moment for the roof that sheltered him, or the table that was spread before him? For days back he had been indulging in thoughts of that welcome which Miss Barrington had promised him. He fancied how, on the mere mention of his father's name, the old man's affection would have poured forth in a flood of kindest words; he had even prepared himself for a scene of such emotion as a father might have felt on seeing one who brought back to mind his own son's earlier years; and instead of all this, he found himself shunned, avoided, repulsed. If there was a thing on earth in which his pride was greatest, it was his name; and yet it was on the utterance of that word, "Conyers," old Barrington turned away and left him.

Over and over again had he found the spell of his father's name and title opening to him society, securing him attentions, and obtaining for him that recognition and acceptance which go so far to make life pleasurable; and now that word, which would have had its magic at a palace, fell powerless and cold at the porch of a humble cottage.

To say that it was part of his creed to believe his father could do no wrong is weak. It was his whole belief,—his entire and complete conviction. To his mind his father embodied all that was noble, high-hearted, and chivalrous. It was not alone the testimony of those who served under him could be appealed to. All India, the Government at home, his own sovereign knew it. From his earliest infancy he had listened to this theme, and to doubt it seemed like to dispute the fact of his existence. How was it, then, that this old man refused to accept what the whole world had stamped with its value? Was it that he impugned the services which had made his father's name famous throughout the entire East?

He endeavored to recall the exact words Barrington had used towards him, but he could not succeed. There was something, he thought, about intruding, unwarrantably intruding; or it might be a mistaken impression of the welcome that awaited him. Which was it? or was it either of them? At all events, he saw himself rejected and repulsed, and the indignity was too great to be borne.

While he thus chafed and fretted, hours went by; and Mr. M'Cabe, the landlord, had made more than one excursion into the room, under pretence of looking after the fire, or seeing that the windows were duly closed, but, in reality, very impatient to learn his guest's intentions regarding dinner.

"Was it your honor said that you'd rather have the chickens roast than biled?" said he at last, in a very submissive tone.

"I said nothing of the kind."

"Ah, it was No. 5 then, and I mistook; I crave your honor's pardon." Hoping that the chord he had thus touched might vibrate, he stooped down to arrange the turf, and give time for the response, but none came. Mr. M'Cabe gave a faint sigh, but returned to the charge. "When there's the laste taste of south in the wind, there 's no making this chimney draw."

Not a word of notice acknowledged this remark.

"But it will do finely yet; it's just the outside of the turf is a little wet, and no wonder; seven weeks of rain—glory be to Him that sent it—has nearly desthroyed us."

Still Conyers vouchsafed no reply.

"And when it begins to rain here, it never laves off. It isn't like in your honor's country. Your honor is English?"

A grunt,—it might be assent, it sounded like malediction.

"'T is azy seen. When your honor came out of the boat, I said, 'Shusy,' says I, 'he's English; and there's a coat they could n't make in Ireland for a king's ransom.'"

"What conveyances leave this for Kilkenny?" asked Conyers, sternly.

"Just none at all, not to mislead you," said M'Cabe, in a voice quite devoid of its late whining intonation.

"Is there not a chaise or a car to be had?"

"Sorrow one. Dr. Dill has a car, to be sure, but not for hire."

"Oh, Dr. Dill lives here. I forgot that. Go and tell him I wish to see him."

The landlord withdrew in dogged silence, but returned in about ten minutes, to say that the doctor had been sent for to the "Fisherman's Home," and Mr. Barrington was so ill it was not likely he would be back that night.

"So ill, did you say?" cried Conyers. "What was the attack,—what did they call it?"

"'T is some kind of a 'plexy, they said. He's a full man, and advanced in years, besides."

"Go and tell young Mr. Dill to come over here."

"He's just gone off with the cuppin' instruments. I saw him steppin' into the boat."

"Let me have a messenger; I want a man to take a note up to Miss Barrington, and fetch my writing-desk here."

In his eager anxiety to learn how Mr. Barrington was, Conyers hastily scratched off a few lines; but on reading them over, he tore them up: they implied a degree of interest on his part which, considering the late treatment extended to him, was scarcely dignified. He tried again; the error was as marked on the other side. It was a cold and formal inquiry. "And yet," said he, as he tore this in fragments, "one thing is quite clear,—this illness is owing to *me!* But for *my* presence there, that old man had now been hale and hearty; the impressions, rightfully or wrongfully, which the sight of *me* and the announcement of *my* name produced are the cause of this malady. I cannot deny it." With this revulsion of feeling he wrote a short but kindly worded note to Miss Barrington, in which, with the very faintest allusion to himself, he begged for a few lines to say how her brother was. He would have added something about the sorrow he experienced in requiting all her kindness by this calamitous return, but he felt that if the case should be a serious one, all reference to himself would be misplaced and impertinent.

The messenger despatched, he sat down beside his fire, the only light now in the room, which the shade of coming night had darkened. He was sad and dispirited, and ill at ease with his own heart. Mr. M'Cabe, indeed, appeared with a suggestion about candles, and a shadowy hint that if his guest speculated of dining at all, it was full time to intimate it; but Conyers dismissed him with a peremptory command not to dare to enter the room again until he was summoned to it. So odious to him was the place, the landlord, and all about him, that he would have set out on foot had his ankle been only strong enough to bear him. "What if he were to write to Stapylton to come and fetch him away? He never liked the man; he liked him less since the remark Miss Barrrington had made upon him from mere reading of his letter, but what was he to do?" While he was yet doubting what course to take, he heard the voices of some new arrivals outside, and, strange enough, one seemed to be Stapylton's. A minute or two after, the travellers had entered the room adjoining his own, and from which a very frail partition of lath and plaster alone separated him.

"Well, Barney," said a harsh, grating voice, addressing the landlord, "what have you got in the larder? We mean to dine with you."

"To dine here, Major!" exclaimed M'Cabe. "Well, well, wondhers will never cease." And then hurriedly seeking to cover a speech not very flattering to the Major's habits of hospitality, "Sure, I 've a loin of pork, and there 's two chickens and a trout fresh out of the water, and there's a cheese; it isn't mine, to be sure, but Father Cody's, but he 'll not miss a slice out of it; and barrin' you dined at the 'Fisherman's Home,' you 'd not get better."

"That 's where we were to have dined by right," said the Major, crankily,—"myself and my friend here,—but we're disappointed, and so we stepped in here, to do the best we can."

"Well, by all accounts, there won't be many dinners up there for some time."

"Why so?"

"Ould Barrington was took with a fit this afternoon, and they say he won't get over it."

"How was it?—what brought it on?"

"Here's the way I had it. Ould Peter was just come home from Kilkenny, and had brought the Attorney-General with him to stay a few days at the cottage, and what was the first thing he seen but a man that come all the way from India with a writ out against him for some of mad George Barrington's debts; and he was so overcome by the shock, that he fainted away, and never came rightly to himself since."

"This is simply impossible," said a voice Conyers well knew to be Stapylton's.

"Be that as it may, I had it from the man that came for the doctor, and what's more, he was just outside the window, and could hear ould Barrington cursin' and swearin' about the man that ruined his son, and brought his poor boy to the grave; but I 'll go and look after your honor's dinner, for I know more about that."

"I have a strange half-curiosity to know the correct version of this story," said Stapylton, as the host left the room. "The doctor is a friend of yours, I think. Would he step over here, and let us hear the matter accurately?"

"He's up at the cottage now, but I 'll get him to come in here when he returns."

If Conyers was shocked to hear how even this loose version of what had occurred served to heighten the anxiety his own fears created, he was also angry with himself at having learned the matter as he did. It was not in his nature to play the eavesdropper, and he had, in reality, heard what fell between his neighbors, almost ere he was aware of it. To apprise them, therefore, of the vicinity of a stranger, he coughed and sneezed, poked the fire noisily, and moved the chairs about; but though the disturbance served to prevent him from hearing, it did not tend to impress any greater caution upon them, for they talked away as before, and more than once above the din of his own tumult, he heard the name of Barrington, and even his own, uttered.

Unable any longer to suffer the irritation of a position so painful, he took his hat, and left the house. It was now night, and so dark that he had to stand some minutes on the door-sill ere he could accustom his sight to the obscurity. By degrees, however, he was enabled to guide his steps, and, passing through the little square, he gained the bridge; and here he resolved to walk backwards and forwards till such time as he hoped his neighbors might have concluded their convivialities, and turned homeward.

A thin cold rain was falling, and the night was cheerless, and without a star; but his heart was heavy, and the dreariness without best suited that within him. For more than an hour he continued his lonely walk, tormented by all the miseries his active ingenuity could muster. To have brought sorrow and mourning beneath the roof where you have been sheltered with kindness is sad enough, but far sadder is it to connect the calamity you have caused with one dearer to you than yourself, and whose innocence, while assured of, you cannot vindicate. "My father never wronged this man, for the simple reason that he has never been unjust to any one. It is a gross injustice to accuse him! If Colonel Barrington forfeited my father's friendship, who could doubt where the fault lay? But I will not leave the matter questionable. I will write to my father and ask him to send me such a reply as may set the issue at rest forever; and then I will come down here, and, with my father's letter in my hand, say, 'The mention of my name was enough, once on a time, to make you turn away from me on the very threshold of your own door—'" When he had got thus far in his intended appeal, his ear was suddenly struck by the word "Conyers," uttered by one of two men who had passed him the moment before, and now stood still in one of the projections of the bridge to talk. He as hastily recognized Dr. Dill as the speaker. He went on thus: "Of course it was mere raving, but one must bear in mind that memory very often is the prompter of these wanderings; and it was strange how persistently he held to the one theme, and continued to call out, 'It was not fair, sir! It was not manly! You know it yourself, Conyers; you cannot deny it!'"

"But you attach no importance to such wanderings, doctor?" asked one whose deep-toned voice betrayed him to be Stapylton.

"I do; that is, to the extent I have mentioned. They are incoherencies, but they are not without some foundation. This Conyers may have had his share in that famous accusation against Colonel Barrington,—that well-known charge I told you of; and if so, it is easy to connect the name with these ravings."

"And the old man will die of this attack," said Stapylton, half musingly.

"I hope not. He has great vigor of constitution; and old as he is, I think he will rub through it."

"Young Conyers left for Kilkenny, then, immediately?" asked he.

"No; he came down here, to the village. He is now at the inn."

"At the inn, here? I never knew that. I am sorry I was not aware of it, doctor; but since it is so, I will ask of you not to speak of having seen me here. He would naturally take it ill, as his brother officer, that I did not make him out, while, as you see, I was totally ignorant of his vicinity."

"I will say nothing on the subject, Captain," said the doctor. "And now one word of advice from you on a personal matter. This young gentleman has offered to be of service to my son—"

Conyers, hitherto spellbound while the interest attached to his father, now turned hastily from the spot and walked away, his mind not alone charged with a heavy care, but full of an eager anxiety as to wherefore Stapylton should have felt so deeply interested in Barrington's illness, and the causes that led to it,—Stapylton, the most selfish of men, and the very last in the world to busy himself in the sorrows or misfortunes of a stranger. Again, too, why had he desired the doctor to preserve his presence there as a secret? Conyers was exactly in the frame of mind to exaggerate a suspicion, or make a mere doubt a grave question. While be thus mused, Stapylton and the doctor passed him on their way towards the village, deep in converse, and, to all seeming, in closest confidence.

"Shall I follow him to the inn, and declare that I overheard a few words on the bridge which give me a claim to explanation? Shall I say, 'Captain Stapylton, you spoke of my father, just now, sufficiently aloud to be overheard by me as I passed, and in your tone there was that which entitles me to question you? Then if he should say, 'Go on; what is it you ask for?' shall I not be sorely puzzled to continue? Perhaps, too, he might remind me that the mode in which I obtained my information precludes even a reference to it. He is one of those fellows not to throw away such an advantage, and I must prepare myself for a quarrel. Oh, if I only had Hunter by me! What would I not give for the brave Colonel's counsel at such a moment as this?"

Of this sort were his thoughts as he strolled up and down for hours, wearing away the long "night watches," till a faint grayish tinge above the horizon showed that morning was not very distant. The whole landscape was wrapped in that cold mysterious tint in which tower and hill-top and spire are scarcely distinguishable from each other, while out of the low-lying meadows already arose the bluish vapor that proclaims the coming day. The village itself, overshadowed by the mountain behind it, lay a black, unbroken mass.

Not a light twinkled from a window, save close to the river's bank, where a faint gleam stole forth and flickered on the water.

Who has not felt the strange interest that attaches to a solitary light seen thus in the tranquil depth of a silent night? How readily do we associate it with some incident of sorrow! The watcher beside the sick-bed rises to the mind, or the patient sufferer himself trying to cheat the dull hours by a book, or perhaps some poor son of toil arising to his daily round of labor, and seated at that solitary meal which no kind word enlivens, no companionship beguiles. And as I write, in what corner of earth are not such scenes passing,—such dark shadows moving over the battlefield of life?

In such a feeling did Conyers watch this light as, leaving the high-road, he took a path that led along the river towards it. As he drew nigher, he saw that the light came from the open window of a room which gave upon a little garden,—a mere strip of ground fenced off from the path by a low paling. With a curiosity he could not master, he stopped and looked in. At a large table, covered with books and papers, and on which a skull also stood, a young man was seated, his head leaning on his hand, apparently in deep thought, while a girl was slowly pacing the little chamber as she talked to him.

"It does not require," said she, in a firm voice, "any great effort of memory to bear in mind that a nerve, an artery, and a vein always go in company."

"Not for you, perhaps,—not for you, Polly."

"Not for any one, I 'm sure. Your fine dragoon friend with the sprained ankle might be brought to that amount of instruction by one telling of it."

"Oh, he 's no fool, I promise you, Polly. Don't despise him because he has plenty of money and can lead a life of idleness."

"I neither despise nor esteem him, nor do I mean that he should divert our minds from what we are at. Now for the popliteal space. Can you describe it? Do you know where it is, or anything about it?"

"I do," said he, doggedly, as he pushed his long hair back from his eyes, and tried to think,—"I do, but I must have time. You must n't hurry me."

She made no reply, but continued her walk in silence.

"I know all about it, Polly, but I can't describe it. I can't describe anything; but ask me a question about it."

"Where is it,—where does it lie?"

"Isn't it at the lower third of the humerus, where the flexors divide?"

"You are too bad,—too stupid!" cried she, angrily. "I cannot believe that anything short of a purpose, a determination to be ignorant, could make a person so unteach-able. If we have gone over this once, we have done so fifty times. It haunts me in my sleep, from very iteration."

"I wish it would haunt me a little when I 'm awake," said he, sulkily.

"And when may that be, I'd like to know? Do you fancy, sir, that your present state of intelligence is a very vigilant one?"

"I know one thing. I hope there won't be the like of you on the Court of Examiners, for I would n't bear the half of what *you've* said to me from another."

"Rejection will be harder to bear, Tom. To be sent back as ignorant and incapable will be far heavier as a punishment than any words of mine. What are you laughing at, sir? Is it a matter of mirth to you?"

"Look at the skull, Polly,—look at the skull." And he pointed to where he had stuck his short, black pipe, between the grinning teeth of the skeleton.

She snatched it angrily away, and threw it out of the window, saying, "You may be ignorant, and not be able to help it. I will take care you shall not be irreverent, sir."

"There's my short clay gone, anyhow," said Tom, submissively, "and I think I 'll go to bed." And he yawned drearily as he spoke.

"Not till you have done this, if we sit here till breakfast-time," said she, resolutely. "There's the plate, and there's the reference. Read it till you know it!"

"What a slave-driver you 'd make, Polly!" said he, with a half-bitter smile.

"What a slave I am!" said she, turning away her head.

"That's true," cried he, in a voice thick with emotion; "and when I 'm thousands of miles away, I 'll be longing to hear the bitterest words you ever said to me, rather than never see you any more."

"My poor brother," said she, laying her hand softly on his rough head, "I never doubted your heart, and I ought to be better tempered with you, and I will. Come, now, Tom,"—and she seated herself at the table next him,—"see, now, if I cannot make this easy to you." And then the two heads were bent together over the table, and the soft brown hair of the girl half mingled with the rough wool of the graceless numskull beside her.

"I will stand by him, if it were only for her sake," said Conyers to himself. And he stole slowly away, and gained the inn.

So intent upon his purpose was he that he at once set about its fulfilment. He began a long letter to his father, and, touching slightly on the accident by which he made Dr. Dill's acquaintance, professed to be deeply his debtor for kindness and attention. With this prelude he introduced Tom. Hitherto his pen had glided along flippantly enough. In that easy mixture of fact and fancy by which he opened his case, no grave difficulty presented itself; but Tom was now to be presented, and the task was about as puzzling as it would have been to have conducted him bodily into society.

"I was ungenerous enough to be prejudiced against this poor fellow when I first met him," wrote he. "Neither his figure nor his manners are in his favor, and in his very diffidence there is an apparent rudeness and forwardness which are not really in his nature. These, however, are not mistakes you, my dear father, will fall into. With your own quickness you will see what sterling qualities exist beneath this rugged outside, and you will befriend him at first for my sake. Later on, I trust he will open his own account in your heart. Bear in mind, too, that it was all my scheme,— the whole plan mine. It was I persuaded him to try his luck in India; it was through me he made the venture; and if the poor fellow fail, all the fault will fall back upon *me*." From this he went into little details of Tom's circumstances, and the narrow means by which he was surrounded, adding how humble he was, and how ready to be satisfied with the most moderate livelihood. "In that great wide world of the East, what scores of things there must be for such a fellow to do; and even should he not turn out to be a Sydenham or a Harvey, he might administer justice, or collect revenue, or assist in some other way the process of that system which we call the British rule in India. In a word, get him something he may live by, and be able, in due time, to help those he has left behind here, in a land whose 'Paddy-fields' are to the full as pauperized as those of Bengal."

He had intended, having disposed of Tom Dill's case, to have addressed some lines to his father about the Barring-tons, sufficiently vague to be easily answered if the subject were one distasteful or unpleasing to him; but just as he reached the place to open this, he was startled by the arrival of a jaunting-car at the inn-door, whose driver stopped to take a drink. It was a chance conveyance, returning to Kilkenny, and Conyers at once engaged it; and, leaving an order to send on the reply when it arrived from the cottage, he wrote a hasty note to Tom Dill and departed. This note was simply to say that he had already fulfilled his promise of interesting his father in his behalf, and that whenever Tom had passed his examination, and was in readiness for his voyage, he should come or write to him, and he would find him fully disposed to serve and befriend him. "Meanwhile," wrote he, "let me hear of you. I am really anxious to learn how you acquit yourself at the ordeal, for which you have the cordial good wishes of your friend, F. Conyers."

Oh, if the great men of our acquaintance—and we all of us, no matter how hermit-like we may live, have our "great men"—could only know and feel what ineffable pleasure will sometimes be derived from the chance expressions they employ towards us,—words which, little significant in themselves, perhaps have some touch of good fellowship or good feeling, now reviving a "bygone," now far-seeing a future, tenderly thrilling through us by some little allusion to a trick of our temperament, noted and observed by one in whose interest we never till then knew we had a share,—if, I say, they were but aware of this, how delightful they might make themselves!— what charming friends!—and, it is but fair to own, what dangerous patrons!

I leave my reader to apply the reflection to the case before him, and then follow me to the pleasant quarters of a well-maintained country-house, full of guests and abounding in gayety.

CHAPTER XVIII
COBHAM

My reader is already aware that I am telling of some forty years ago, and therefore I have no apologies to make for habits and ways which our more polished age has pronounced barbarous. Now, at Cobham, the men sat after dinner over their wine when the ladies had withdrawn, and, I grieve to say, fulfilled this usage with a zest and enjoyment that unequivocally declared it to be the best hour of the whole twenty-four.

Friends could now get together, conversation could range over personalities, egotisms have their day, and bygones be disinterred without need of an explanation. Few, indeed, who did not unbend at such a moment, and relax in that genial atmosphere begotten of closed curtains, and comfort, and good claret. I am not so certain that we are wise in our utter abandonment of what must have often conciliated a difference or reconciled a grudge. How many a lurking discontent, too subtle for intervention, must have been dissipated in the general burst of a common laugh, or the racy enjoyment of a good story! Decidedly the decanter has often played peacemaker, though popular prejudice inclines to give it a different mission.

On the occasion to which I would now invite my reader, the party were seated—by means of that genial discovery, a horseshoe-table—around the fire at Cobham. It was a true country-house society of neighbors who knew each other well, sprinkled with guests,—strangers to every one. There were all ages and all temperaments, from the hardy old squire, whose mellow cheer was known at the fox-cover, to the young heir fresh from Oxford and loud about Leicestershire; gentlemen-farmers and sportsmen, and parsons and soldiers, blended together with just enough disparity of pursuit to season talk and freshen experiences.

The conversation, which for a while was partly on sporting matters, varied with little episodes of personal achievement, and those little boastings which end in a bet, was suddenly interrupted by a hasty call for Dr. Dill, who was wanted at the "Fisherman's Home."

"Can't you stay to finish this bottle, Dill?" said the Admiral, who had not heard for whom he had been sent.

"I fear not, sir. It is a long row down to the cottage."

"So it 's poor Barrington again! I 'm sincerely sorry for it! And now I 'll not ask you to delay. By the way, take my boat. Elwes," said he to the servant, "tell the men to get the boat ready at once for Dr. Dill, and come and say when it is so."

The doctor's gratitude was profuse, though probably a dim vista of the "tip" that might be expected from him detracted from the fulness of the enjoyment.

"Find out if I could be of any use, Dill," whispered the Admiral, as the doctor arose. "Your own tact will show if there be anything I could do. You understand me; I have the deepest regard for old Barrington, and his sister too."

Dill promised to give his most delicate attention to the point, and departed.

While this little incident was occurring, Stapylton, who sat at an angle of the fireplace, was amusing two or three listeners by an account of his intended dinner at the "Home," and the haughty refusal of Miss Barrington to receive him.

"You must tell Sir Charles the story!" cried out Mr. Bushe. "He'll soon recognize the old Major from your imitation of him."

"Hang the old villain! he shot a dog-fox the other morning, and he knows well how scarce they are getting in the country," said another.

"I 'll never forgive myself for letting him have a lease of that place," said a third; "he's a disgrace to the neighborhood."

"You're not talking of Barrington, surely," called out Sir Charles.

"Of course not. I was speaking of M'Cormick. Harrington is another stamp of man, and here's his good health!"

"He'll need all your best wishes, Jack," said the host, "for Dr. Dill has just been called away to see him."

"To see old Peter! Why, I never knew him to have a day's illness!"

"He's dangerously ill now," said the Admiral, gravely. "Dill tells me that he came home from the Assizes hale and hearty, in high spirits at some verdict in his favor, and brought back the Attorney-General to spend a day or two with him; but that, on arriving, he found a young fellow whose father or grandfather—for I have n't it correctly—had been concerned in some way against George Barrington, and that high words passed between old Peter and this youth, who was turned out on the spot, while poor Barrington, overcome by emotion, was struck down with a sort of paralysis. As I have said, I don't know the story accurately, for even Dill himself only picked it up from the servants at the cottage, neither Miss Barrington nor Withering having told him one word on the subject."

"That is the very same story I heard at the village where we dined," broke in Stapylton, "and M'Cormick added that he remembered the name. Conyers—the young man is called Conyers—did occur in a certain famous accusation against Colonel Barrington."

"Well, but," interposed Bushe, "isn't all that an old story now? Is n't the whole thing a matter of twenty years ago?"

"Not so much as that," said Sir Charles. "I remember reading it all when I was in command of the 'Madagascar,'—I forget the exact year, but I was at Corfu."

"At all events," said Bushe, "it's long enough past to be forgotten or forgiven; and old Peter was the very last man I could ever have supposed likely to carry on an ancient grudge against any one."

"Not where his son was concerned. Wherever George's name entered, forgiveness of the man that wronged him was impossible," said another.

"You are scarcely just to my old friend," interposed the Admiral. "First of all, we have not the facts before us. Many of us here have never seen, some have never heard of the great Barrington Inquiry, and of such as have, if their memories be not better than mine, they can't discuss the matter with much profit."

"I followed the case when it occurred," chimed in the former speaker, "but I own, with Sir Charles, that it has gone clean out of my head since that time."

"You talk of injustice, Cobham, injustice to old Peter Barrington," said an old man from the end of the table; "but I would ask, are we quite just to poor George? I knew him well. My son served in the same regiment with him before he went out to India, and no finer nor nobler-hearted fellow than George Barrington ever lived. Talk of him ruining his father by his extravagance! Why, he'd have cut off his right hand rather than caused him one pang, one moment of displeasure. Barrington ruined himself; that insane passion for law has cost him far more than half what he was worth in the world. Ask Withering; he 'll tell you something about it. Why, Withering's own fees in that case before 'the Lords' amount to upwards of two thousand guineas."

"I won't dispute the question with you, Fowndes," said the Admiral. "Scandal says you have a taste for a trial at bar yourself."

The hit told, and called for a hearty laugh, in which Fowndes himself joined freely.

"*I* 'm a burned child, however, and keep away from the fire," said he, good-humoredly; "but old Peter seems rather to like being singed. There he is again with his Privy Council case for next term, and with, I suppose, as much chance of success as I should have in a suit to recover a Greek estate of some of my Phoenician ancestors."

It was not a company to sympathize deeply with such a litigious spirit. The hearty and vigorous tone of squiredom, young and old, could not understand it as a passion or a pursuit, and they mainly agreed that nothing but some strange perversion could have made the generous nature of old Barrington so fond of law. Gradually the younger members of the party slipped away to the drawing-room, till, in the changes that ensued, Stapylton found himself next to Mr. Fowndes.

"I'm glad to see, Captain," said the old squire, "that modern fashion of deserting the claret-jug has not invaded your mess. I own I like a man who lingers over his wine."

"We have no pretext for leaving it, remember that," said Stapylton, smiling.

"Very true. The *placeus uxor* is sadly out of place in a soldier's life. Your married officer is but a sorry comrade; besides, how is a fellow to be a hero to the enemy who is daily bullied by his wife?"

"I think you said that you had served?" interposed Stapylton.

"No. My son was in the army; he is so still, but holds a Governorship in the West Indies. He it was who knew this Barrington we were speaking of."

"Just so," said Stapylton, drawing his chair closer, so as to converse more confidentially.

"You may imagine what very uneventful lives we country gentlemen live," said the old squire, "when we can continue to talk over one memorable case for something like twenty years, just because one of the parties to it was our neighbor."

"You appear to have taken a lively interest in it," said Stapylton, who rightly conjectured it was a favorite theme with the old squire.

"Yes. Barrington and my son were friends; they came down to my house together to shoot; and with all his eccentricities—and they were many—I liked Mad George, as they called him."

"He was a good fellow, then?"

"A thoroughly good fellow, but the shyest that ever lived; to all outward seeming rough and careless, but sensitive as a woman all the while. He would have walked up to a cannon's mouth with a calm step, but an affecting story would bring tears to his eyes; and then, to cover this weakness, which he was well ashamed of, he 'd rush into fifty follies and extravagances. As he said himself to me one day, alluding to some feat of rash absurdity, 'I have been taking another inch off the dog's tail,'—he referred to the story of Alcibiades, who docked his dog to take off public attention from his heavier transgressions."

"There was no truth in these accusations against him?"

"Who knows? George was a passionate fellow, and he 'd have made short work of the man that angered him. I myself never so entirely acquitted him as many who loved him less. At all events, he was hardly treated; he was regularly hunted down. I imagine he must have made many enemies, for witnesses sprung up against him on all sides, and he was too proud a fellow to ask for one single testimony in his favor! If ever a man met death broken-hearted, he did!"

A pause of several minutes occurred, after which the old squire resumed,—

"My son told me that after Barrington's death there was a strong revulsion in his favor, and a great feeling that he had been hardly dealt by. Some of the Supreme Council, it is said, too, were disposed to behave generously towards his child, but old Peter, in an evil hour, would hear of nothing short of restitution of all the territory, and a regular rehabilitation of George's memory, besides; in fact, he made the most extravagant demands, and disgusted the two or three who were kindly and well disposed towards his cause. Had they, indeed,—as he said,—driven his son to desperation, he could scarcely ask them to declare it to the world; and yet nothing short of this would satisfy him! 'Come forth,' wrote he,—I read the letter myself,— 'come forth and confess that your evidence was forged and your witnesses suborned; that you wanted to annex the territory, and the only road to your object was to impute treason to the most loyal heart that ever served the King!' Imagine what chance of favorable consideration remained to the man who penned such words as these."

"And he prosecutes the case still?"

"Ay, and will do to the day of his death. Withering—who was an old schoolfellow of mine—has got me to try what I could do to persuade him to come to some terms; and, indeed, to do old Peter justice, it is not the money part of the matter he is so obstinate about; it is the question of what he calls George's fair fame and honor; and one cannot exactly say to him, 'Who on earth cares a brass button whether George Barrington was a rebel or a true man? Whether he deserved to die an independent Rajah of some place with a hard name, or the loyal subject of his Majesty George the Third?' I own I, one day, did go so close to the wind, on that subject, that the old man started up and said, 'I hope I misapprehend you, Harry Fowndes. I hope sincerely that I do so, for if not, I 'll have a shot at you, as sure as my name is Peter Barrington.' Of course I 'tried back' at once, and assured him it was a pure misconception of my meaning, and that until the East India folk fairly acknowledged that they had wronged his son, *he* could not, with honor, approach the question of a compromise in the money matter."

"That day, it may be presumed, is very far off," said Stapylton, half languidly.

"Well, Withering opines not. He says that they are weary of the whole case. They have had, perhaps, some misgivings as to the entire justice of what they did. Perhaps they have learned something during the course of the proceedings which may have influenced their judgment; and not impossible is it that they pity the old man fighting out his life; and perhaps, too, Barrington himself may have softened a little, since he has begun to feel that his granddaughter—for George left a child—had interests which his own indignation could not rightfully sacrifice; so that amongst all these perhapses, who knows but some happy issue may come at last?"

"That Barrington race is not a very pliant one," said Stapylton, half dreamily; and then, in some haste, added, "at least, such is the character they give them here."

"Some truth there may be in that. Men of a strong temperament and with a large share of self-dependence generally get credit from the world for obstinacy, just because the road *they* see out of difficulties is not the popular one. But even with all this, I 'd not call old Peter self-willed; at least, Withering tells me that from time to time, as he has conveyed to him the opinions and experiences of old Indian officers, some of whom had either met with or heard of George, he has listened with much and even respectful attention. And as all their counsels have gone against his own convictions, it is something to give them a patient hearing."

"He has thus permitted strangers to come and speak with him on these topics?" asked Stapylton, eagerly.

"No, no,—not he. These men had called on Withering,—met him, perhaps, in society,—heard of his interest in George Barrington's case, and came good-naturedly to volunteer a word of counsel in favor of an old comrade. Nothing more natural, I think."

"Nothing. I quite agree with you; so much so, indeed, that having served some years in India, and in close proximity, too, to one of the native courts, I was going to ask you to present me to your friend Mr. Withering, as one not altogether incapable of affording him some information."

"With a heart and a half. I 'll do it."

"I say, Harry," cried out the host, "if you and Captain Stapylton will neither fill your glasses nor pass the wine, I think we had better join the ladies."

And now there was a general move to the drawing-room, where several evening guests had already assembled, making a somewhat numerous company. Polly Dill was there, too,—not the wearied-looking, careworn figure we last saw her, when her talk was of "dead anatomies," but the lively, sparkling, bright-eyed Polly, who sang the Melodies to the accompaniment of him who could make every note thrill with the sentiment his own genius had linked to it. I half wish I had not a story to tell,—that is, that I had not a certain road to take,—that I might wander at will through by-path and lane, and linger on the memories thus by a chance awakened! Ah, it was no small triumph to lift out of obscure companionship and vulgar associations the music of our land, and wed it to words immortal, to show us that the pebble at our feet was a gem to be worn on the neck of beauty, and to prove to us, besides, that our language could be as lyrical as Anacreon's own!

"I am enchanted with your singing," whispered Stapylton, in Polly's ear; "but I 'd forego all the enjoyment not to see you so pleased with your companion. I begin to detest the little Poet."

"I 'll tell him so," said she, half gravely; "and he 'll know well that it is the coarse hate of the Saxon."

"I'm no Saxon!" said he, flushing and darkening at the same time. And then, recovering his calm, he added, "There are no Saxons left amongst us, nor any Celts for us to honor with our contempt; but come away from the piano, and don't let him fancy he has bound you by a spell."

"But he has," said she, eagerly,—"he has, and I don't care to break it."

But the little Poet, running his fingers lightly over the keys, warbled out, in a half-plaintive whisper,—

> "Oh, tell me, dear Polly, why is it thine eyes
> Through their brightness have something of sorrow?
> I cannot suppose that the glow of such skies
> Should ever mean gloom for the morrow;

"Or must I believe that your heart is afar,

And you only make semblance to hear me,

While your thoughts are away to that splendid hussar,

And 't is only your image is near me?"

"An unpublished melody, I fancy," said Stapylton, with a malicious twinkle of his eye.

"Not even corrected as yet," said the Poet, with a glance at Polly.

What a triumph it was for a mere village beauty to be thus tilted for by such gallant knights; but Polly was practical as well as vain, and a certain unmistakable something in Lady Cobham's eye told her that two of the most valued guests of the house were not to be thus withdrawn from circulation; and with this wise impression on her mind, she slipped hastily away, on the pretext of something to say to her father. And although it was a mere pretence on her part, there was that in her look as they talked together that betokened their conversation to be serious.

"I tell you again," said he, in a sharp but low whisper, "she will not suffer it. You used not to make mistakes of this kind formerly, and I cannot conceive why you should do so now."

"But, dear papa," said she, with a strange half-smile, "don't you remember your own story of the gentleman who got tipsy because he foresaw he would never be invited again?"

But the doctor was in no jesting mood, and would not accept of the illustration. He spoke now even more angrily than before.

"You have only to see how much they make of him to know well that he is out of our reach," said he, bitterly.

"A long shot, Sir Lucius; there is such honor in a long shot," said she, with infinite drollery; and then with a sudden gravity, added, "I have never forgotten the man you cured, just because your hand shook and you gave him a double dose of laudanum."

This was too much for his patience, and he turned away in disgust at her frivolity. In doing so, however, he came in front of Lady Cobham, who had come up to request Miss Dill to play a certain Spanish dance for two young ladies of the company.

"Of course, your Ladyship,—too much honor for her,—she will be charmed; my little girl is overjoyed when she can contribute even thus humbly to the pleasure of your delightful house."

Never did a misdemeanist take his "six weeks" with a more complete consciousness of penalty than did Polly sit down to that piano. She well understood it as a sentence, and, let me own, submitted well and gracefully to her fate. Nor was it, after all, such a slight trial, for the fandango was her own speciality; she had herself brought the dance and the music to Cobham. They who were about to dance it were her own pupils, and not very proficient ones, either. And with all this she did her part well and loyally. Never had she played with more spirit; never marked the time with a firmer precision; never threw more tenderness into the graceful parts, nor more of triumphant daring into the proud ones. Amid the shower of "Bravos!" that closed the performance,—for none thought of the dancers,—the little Poet drew nigh and whispered, "How naughty!"

"Why so?" asked she, innocently.

"What a blaze of light to throw over a sorry picture!" said he, dangling his eyeglass, and playing that part of middle-aged Cupid he was so fond of assuming.

"Do you know, sir," said Lady Cobham, coming hastily towards him, "that I will not permit you to turn the heads of my young ladies? Dr. Dill is already so afraid of your fascinations that he has ordered his carriage,—is it not so?" she went on appealing to the doctor, with increased rapidity. "But you will certainly keep your promise to us. We shall expect you on Thursday at dinner."

Overwhelmed with confusion, Dill answered—he knew not what—about pleasure, punctuality, and so forth; and then turned away to ring for that carriage he had not ordered before.

"And so you tell me Barrington is better?" said the Admiral, taking him by the arm and leading him away. "The danger is over, then?"

"I believe so; his mind is calm, and he is only suffering now from debility. What with the Assizes, and a week's dissipation at Kilkenny, and this shock,—for it was a shock,—the whole thing was far more of a mental than a bodily ailment."

"You gave him my message? You said how anxious I felt to know if I could be of any use to him?"

"Yes; and he charged Mr. Withering to come and thank you, for he is passing by Cobham to-morrow on his way to Kilkenny."

"Indeed! Georgiana, don't forget that. Withering will call here to-morrow; try and keep him to dine, at least, if we cannot secure him for longer. He's one of those fellows I am always delighted to meet Where are you going, Dill? Not taking your daughter away at this hour, are you?"

The doctor sighed, and muttered something about dissipations that were only too fascinating, too engrossing. He did not exactly like to say that his passports had been sent him, and the authorities duly instructed to give him "every aid and assistance possible." For a moment, indeed, Polly looked as though she would make some explanation of the matter; but it was only for a moment, and the slight flush on her cheek gave way quickly, and she looked somewhat paler than her wont. Meanwhile, the little Poet had fetched her shawl, and led her away, humming, "Buona notte,—buona sera!" as he went, in that half-caressing, half-quizzing way he could assume so jauntily. Stapylton walked behind with the doctor, and whispered as he went, "If not inconvenient, might I ask the favor of a few minutes with you to-morrow?"

Dill assured him he was devotedly his servant; and having fixed the interview for two o'clock, away they drove. The night was calm and starlight, and they had long passed beyond the grounds of Cobham, and were full two miles on their road before a word was uttered by either.

"What was it her Ladyship said about Thursday next, at dinner?" asked the doctor, half pettishly.

"Nothing to me, papa."

"If I remember, it was that we had accepted the invitation already, and begging me not to forget it."

"Perhaps so," said she, dryly.

"You are usually more mindful about these matters," said he, tartly, "and not so likely to forget promised festivities."

"They certainly were not promised to me," said she, "nor, if they had been, should I accept of them."

"What do you mean?" said he, angrily.

"Simply, papa, that it is a house I will not re-enter, that's all."

"Why, your head is turned, your brains are destroyed by flattery, girl. You seem totally to forget that we go to these places merely by courtesy,— we are received only on sufferance; we are not *their* equals."

"The more reason to treat us with deference, and not render our position more painful than it need be."

"Folly and nonsense! Deference, indeed! How much deference is due from eight thousand a year to a dispensary doctor, or his daughter? I'll have none of these absurd notions. If they made any mistake towards you, it was by over-attention,—too much notice."

"That is very possible, papa; and it was not always very flattering for that reason."

"Why, what is your head full of? Do you fancy you are one of Lord Carricklough's daughters, eh?"

"No, papa; for they are shockingly freckled, and very plain."

"Do you know your real station?" cried he, more angrily, "and that if, by the courtesy of society, my position secures acceptance anywhere, it entails nothing—positively nothing—to those belonging to me?"

"Such being the case, is it not wise of us not to want anything,—not to look for it,—not to pine after it? You shall see, papa, whether I fret over my exclusion from Cobham."

The doctor was not in a mood to approve of such philosophy, and he drove on, only showing—by an extra cut of his whip—the tone and temper that beset him.

"You are to have a visit from Captain Stapylton tomorrow, papa?" said she, in the manner of a half question.

"Who told you so?" said he, with a touch of eagerness in his voice; for suddenly it occurred to him if Polly knew of this appointment, she herself might be interested in its object.

"He asked me what was the most likely time to find you at home, and also if he might venture to hope he should be presented to mamma."

That was, as the doctor thought, a very significant speech; it might mean a great deal,—a very great deal, indeed; and so he turned it over and over in his mind for some time before he spoke again. At last he said,—

"I haven't a notion what he's coming about, Polly,—have you?"

"No, sir; except, perhaps, it be to consult you. He told me he had sprained his arm, or his shoulder, the other day, when his horse swerved."

"Oh no, it can't be that, Polly; it can't be that."

"Why not the pleasure of a morning call, then? He is an idle man, and finds time heavy on his hands."

A short "humph" showed that this explanation was not more successful than the former, and the doctor, rather irritated with this game of fence, for so he deemed it, said bluntly,—

"Has he been showing you any marked attentions of late? Have you noticed anything peculiar in his manner towards you?"

"Nothing whatever, sir," said she, with a frank boldness. "He has chatted and flirted with me, just as every one else presumes he has a right to do with a girl in a station below their own; but he has never been more impertinent in this way than any other young man of fashion."

"But there have been"—he was sorely puzzled for the word he wanted, and it was only as a resource, not out of choice, he said—"attentions?"

"Of course, papa, what many would call in the cognate phrase, marked attentions; but girls who go into the world as I do no more mistake what these mean than would you yourself, papa, if passingly asked what was good for a sore-throat fancy that the inquirer intended to fee you."

"I see, Polly, I see," muttered he, as the illustration came home to him. Still, after ruminating for some time, a change seemed to come over his thoughts, for he said,—

"But you might be wrong this time, Polly: it is by no means impossible that you might be wrong."

"My dear papa," said she, gravely, "when a man of his rank is disposed to think seriously of a girl in mine, he does not begin by flattery; he rather takes the line of correction and warning, telling her fifty little platitudes about trifles in manner, and so forth, by her docile acceptance of which he conceives a high notion of *himself*, and a half liking for *her*. But I have no need to go into these things; enough if I assure you Captain Stapylton's visit has no concern for me; he either comes out of pure idleness, or he wants to make use of *you*."

The last words opened a new channel to Dill's thoughts, and he drove on in silent meditation over them.

CHAPTER XIX
THE HOUR OF LUNCHEON

If there be a special agreeability about all the meal-times of a pleasant country-house, there is not one of them which, in the charm of an easy, unconstrained gayety, can rival the hour of luncheon. At breakfast, one is too fresh; at dinner, too formal; but luncheon, like an opening manhood, is full of its own bright projects. The plans of the day have already reached a certain maturity, and fixtures have been made for riding-parties, or phaeton drives, or flirtations in the garden. The very strangers who looked coldly at each other over their morning papers have shaken into a semi-intimacy, and little traits of character and temperament, which would have been studiously shrouded in the more solemn festivals of the day, are now displayed with a frank and fearless confidence. The half-toilette and the tweed coat, mutton broth and "Balmorals," seem infinitely more congenial to acquaintanceship than the full-blown splendor of evening dress and the grander discipline of dinner.

Irish social life permits of a practice of which I do not, while recording, constitute myself the advocate or the apologist,—a sort of good-tempered banter called quizzing,—a habit I scarcely believe practicable in other lands; that is, I know of no country where it could be carried on as harmlessly and as gracefully, where as much wit could be expended innocuously, as little good feeling jeopardized in the display. The happiest hour of the day for such passages as these was that of luncheon, and it was in the very clash and clatter of the combat that a servant announced the Attorney-General!

What a damper did the name prove! Short of a bishop himself, no announcement could have spread more terror over the younger members of the company, embodying as it seemed to do all that could be inquisitorial, intolerant, and overbearing. Great, however, was the astonishment to see, instead of the stern incarnation of Crown prosecutions and arbitrary commitments, a tall, thin, slightly stooped man, dressed in a gray shooting-jacket, and with a hat plentifully garnished with fishing-flies. He came lightly into the room, and kissed the hand of his hostess with a mixture of cordiality and old-fashioned gallantry that became him well.

"My old luck, Cobham!" said he, as he seated himself at table. "I have fished the stream all the way from the Red House to this, and never so much as a rise to reward me.

"They knew you,—they knew you, Withering," chirped out the Poet, "and they took good care not to put in an appearance, with the certainty of a 'detainer.'"

"Ah! you here! That decanter of sherry screened you completely from my view," said Withering, whose sarcasm on his size touched the very sorest of the other's susceptibilities. "And talking of recognizances, how comes it you are here, and a large party at Lord Dunraney's all assembled to meet you?"

The Poet, as not infrequent with him, had forgotten everything of this prior engagement, and was now overwhelmed with his forgetfulness. The ladies, however, pressed eagerly around him with consolation so like caresses, that he was speedily himself again.

"How natural a mistake, after all!" said the lawyer. "The old song says,—

> 'Tell me where beauty and wit and wine
> Are met, and I 'll say where I 'm asked to dine.'

Ah! Tommy, yours *is* the profession, after all; always sure of your retainer, and never but one brief to sustain—'T. M. *versus* the Heart of Woman.'"

"One is occasionally nonsuited, however," said the other, half pettishly. "By the way, how was it you got that verdict for old Barrington t'other day? Was it true that Plowden got hold of *your* bag by mistake?"

"Not only that, but he made a point for us none of us had discovered."

"How historical the blunder:—

> 'The case is classical, as I and you know;
> He came from Venus, but made love to Juno.'"

"If Peter Barrington gained his cause by it I 'm heartily rejoiced, and I wish him health and years to enjoy it." The Admiral said this with a cordial good will as he drank off his glass.

"He's all right again," said Withering. "I left him working away with a hoe and a rake this morning, looking as hale and hearty as he did a dozen years ago."

"A man must have really high deserts in whose good fortune so many are well-wishers," said Stapylton; and by the courteous tone of the remark Withering's attention was attracted, and he speedily begged the Admiral to present him to his guest. They continued to converse together as they arose from table, and with such common pleasure that when Withering expressed a hope the acquaintance might not end there, Stapylton replied by a request that he would allow him to be his fellow-traveller to Kilkenny, whither he was about to go on a regimental affair. The arrangement was quickly made, to the satisfaction of each; and as they drove away, while many bewailed the departure of such pleasant members of the party, the little Poet simperingly said, —

> "Shall I own that my heart is relieved of a care? —
> Though you 'll think the confession is petty —
> I cannot but feel, as I look on the pair,
> It is 'Peebles' gone off with 'Dalgetty.'"

As for the fellow-travellers, they jogged along very pleasantly on their way, as two consummate men of the world are sure to do when they meet. For what Freemasonry equals that of two shrewd students of life? How flippantly do they discuss each theme! how easily read each character, and unravel each motive that presents itself! What the lawyer gained by the technical subtlety of his profession, the soldier made up for by his wider experience of mankind. There were, besides, a variety of experiences to exchange. Toga could tell of much that interested the "man of war," and he, in turn, made himself extremely agreeable by his Eastern information, not to say, that he was able to give a correct version of many Hindostanee phrases and words which the old lawyer eagerly desired to acquire.

"All you have been telling me has a strong interest for me, Captain Stapylton," said he, as they drove into Kilkenny. "I have a case which has engaged my attention for years, and is likely to occupy what remains to me of life, — a suit of which India is the scene, and Orientals figure as some of the chief actors, — so that I can scarcely say how fortunate I feel this chance meeting with you."

"I shall deem myself greatly honored if the acquaintance does not end here."

"It shall not, if it depend upon me," said Withering, cordially. "You said something of a visit you were about to make to Dublin. Will you do me a great—a very great—favor, and make my house your home while you stay? This is my address: '18 Merrion Square.' It is a bachelor's hall; and you can come and go without ceremony."

"The plan is too tempting to hesitate about. I accept your invitation with all the frankness you have given it. Meanwhile you will be my guest here."

"'That is impossible. I must start for Cork this evening." And now they parted,—not like men who had been strangers a few hours back, but like old acquaintances, only needing the occasion to feel as old friends.

CHAPTER XX
AN INTERIOR AT THE DOCTOR'S

When Captain Stapylton made his appointment to wait on Dr. Dill, he was not aware that the Attorney-General was expected at Cobham. No sooner, however, had he learned that fact than he changed his purpose, and intimated his intention of running up for a day to Kilkenny, to hear what was going on in the regiment. No regret for any disappointment he might be giving to the village doctor, no self-reproach for the breach of an engagement—all of his own making—crossed his mind. It is, indeed, a theme for a moralist to explore, the ease with which a certain superiority in station can divest its possessor of all care for the sensibilities of those below him; and yet in the little household of the doctor that promised visit was the source of no small discomfort and trouble. The doctor's study— the sanctum in which the interview should be held—had to be dusted and smartened up. Old boots, and overcoats, and smashed driving-whips, and odd stirrup-leathers, and stable-lanterns, and garden implements had all to be banished. The great table in front of the doctor's chair had also to be professionally littered with notes and cards and periodicals, not forgetting an ingenious admixture of strange instruments of torture, quaint screws, and inscrutable-looking scissors, destined, doubtless, to make many a faint heart the fainter in their dread presence. All these details had to be carried out in various ways through the rest of the establishment,—in the drawing-room, wherein the great man was to be ushered; in the dining-room, where he was to lunch. Upon Polly did the greater part of these cares devolve; not alone attending to the due disposal of chairs and sofas and tables, but to the preparation of certain culinary delicacies, which were to make the Captain forget the dainty luxuries of Cobham. And, in truth, there is a marvellous *esprit du corps* in the way a woman will fag and slave herself to make the humble household she belongs to look its best, even to the very guest she has least at heart; for Polly did not like Stapylton. Flattered at first by his notice, she was offended afterwards at the sort of conscious condescension of his manner,—a something which seemed to say, I can be charming, positively fascinating, but don't imagine for a moment that there is anything especial in it. I captivate—just as I fish, hunt, sketch, or shoot—to amuse myself.

And with all this, how was it he was really not a coxcomb? Was it the grave dignity of his address, or the quiet state-liness of his person, or was it a certain uniformity, a keeping, that pervaded all he said or did? I am not quite sure whether all three did not contribute to this end, and make him what the world confessed,—a most well-bred gentleman.

Polly was, in her way, a shrewd observer, and she felt that Stapylton's manner towards her was that species of urbane condescension with which a great master of a game deigns to play with a very humble proficient. He moved about the board with an assumption that said, I can checkmate you when I will! Now this is hard enough to bear when the pieces at stake are stained ivory, but it is less endurable: still when they are our emotions and our wishes. And yet with all this before her, Polly ordered and arranged and superintended and directed with an energy that never tired, and an activity that never relaxed.

As for Mrs. Dill, no similar incident in the life of Clarissa had prepared her for the bustle and preparation she saw on every side, and she was fairly perplexed between the thought of a seizure for rent and a fire,—casualties which, grave as they were, she felt she could meet with Mr. Richardson beside her. The doctor himself was unusually fidgety and anxious. Perhaps he ascribed considerable importance to this visit; perhaps he thought Polly had not been candid with him, and that, in reality, she knew more of its object than she had avowed; and so he walked hurriedly from room to room, and out into the garden, and across the road to the river's side, and once as far as the bridge, consulting his watch, and calculating that as it now only wanted eight minutes of two o'clock, the arrival could scarcely be long delayed.

It was on his return he entered the drawing-room and found Polly, now plainly but becomingly dressed, seated at her work, with a seeming quietude and repose about her, strangely at variance with her late display of activity. "I've had a look down the Graigue Road," said he, "but can see nothing. You are certain he said two o'clock?"

"Quite certain, sir."

"To be sure he might come by the river; there's water enough now for the Cobham barge."

She made no answer, though she half suspected some reply was expected.

"And of course," continued the doctor, "they'd have offered him the use of it. They seem to make a great deal of him up there."

"A great deal, indeed, sir," said she; but in a voice that was a mere echo of his own.

"And I suspect they know why. I 'm sure they know why. People in their condition make no mistakes about each other; and if he receives much attention, it is because it's his due."

No answer followed this speech, and he walked feverishly up and down the room, holding his watch in his closed hand. "I have a notion you must have mistaken him. It was not two he said."

"I 'm positive it was two, sir. But it can scarcely be much past that hour now."

"It is seventeen minutes past two," said he, solemnly. And then, as if some fresh thought had just occurred to him, asked, "Where 's Tom? I never saw him this morning."

"He 's gone out to take a walk, sir. The poor fellow is dead beat by work, and had such a headache that I told him to go as far as the Red House or Snow's Mill."

"And I 'll wager he did not want to be told twice. Anything for idleness with *him!*"

"Well, papa, he is really doing his very best now. He is not naturally quick, and he has a bad memory, so that labor is no common toil; but his heart is in it, and I never saw him really anxious for success before."

"To go out to India, I suppose," said Dill, sneeringly, "that notable project of the other good-for-nothing; for, except in the matter of fortune, there's not much to choose between them. There 's the half-hour striking now!"

"The project has done this for him, at least," said she, firmly,—"it has given him hope!"

"How I like to hear about hope!" said he, with a peculiarly sarcastic bitterness. "I never knew a fellow worth sixpence that had that cant of 'hope' in his mouth! How much hope had I when I began the world! How much have I now?"

"Don't you hope Captain Stapylton may not have forgotten his appointment, papa?" said she, with a quick drollery, which sparkled in her eye, but brought no smile to her lips.

"Well, here he is at last," said Dill, as he heard the sharp click made by the wicket of the little garden; and he started up, and rushed to the window. "May I never!" cried he, in horror, "if it isn't M'Cormick! Say we're out,— that I'm at Graigue,—that I won't be home till evening!"

But while he was multiplying these excuses, the old Major had caught sight of him, and was waving his hand in salutation from below. "It's too late,—it's too late!" sighed Dill, bitterly; "he sees me now,—there's no help for it!"

What benevolent and benedictory expressions were muttered below his breath, it is not for this history to record; but so vexed and irritated was he, that the Major had already entered the room ere he could compose his features into even a faint show of welcome.

"I was down at the Dispensary," croaked out M'Cormick, "and they told me you were not expected there to-day, and so I said, maybe he's ill, or maybe,"—and here he looked shrewdly around him,—"maybe there 's something going on up at the house."

"What should there be going on, as you call it?" responded Dill, angrily, for he was now at home, in presence of the family, and could not compound for that tone of servile acquiescence he employed on foreign service.

"And, faix, I believe I was right; Miss Polly isn't so smart this morning for nothing, no more than the saving cover is off the sofa, and the piece of gauze taken down from before the looking-glass, and the 'Times' newspaper away from the rug!"

"Are there any other domestic changes you 'd like to remark upon, Major M'Cormick?" said Dill, pale with rage.

"Indeed, yes," rejoined the other; "there 's yourself, in the elegant black coat that I never saw since Lord Kilraney's funeral, and looking pretty much as lively and pleasant as you did at the ceremony."

"A gentleman has made an appointment with papa," broke in Polly, "and may be here at any moment."

"I know who it is," said M'Cormick, with a finger on the side of his nose to imply intense cunning. "I know all about it."

"What do you know?—what do you mean by all about it?" said Dill, with an eagerness he could not repress.

"Just as much as yourselves,—there now! Just as much as yourselves!" said he, sententiously.

"But apparently, Major, you know far more," said Polly.

"Maybe I do, maybe I don't; but I 'll tell you one thing, Dill, for your edification, and mind me if I 'm not right: you 're all mistaken about him, every one of ye!"

"Whom are you talking of?" asked the doctor, sternly.

"Just the very man you mean yourself, and no other! Oh, you need n't fuss and fume, I don't want to pry into your family secrets. Not that they 'll be such secrets tomorrow or next day,—the whole town will be talking of them,—but as an old friend that could, maybe, give a word of advice—"

"Advice about what? Will you just tell me about what?" cried Dill, now bursting with anger.

"I 've done now. Not another word passes my lips about it from this minute. Follow your own road, and see where it will lead ye?"

"Cannot you understand, Major M'Cormick, that we are totally unable to guess what you allude to? Neither papa nor I have the very faintest clew to your meaning, and if you really desire to serve us, you will speak out plainly."

"Not another syllable, if I sat here for two years!"

The possibility of such an infliction seemed so terrible to poor Polly that she actually shuddered as she heard it.

"Is n't that your mother I see sitting up there, with all the fine ribbons in her cap?" whispered M'Cormick, as he pointed to a small room which opened off an angle of the larger one. "That 's 'the boodoo,' is n't it?" said he, with a grin. This, I must inform my reader, was the M'Cormick for "boudoir." "Well, I'll go and pay my respects to her."

So little interest did Mrs. Dill take in the stir and movement around her that the Major utterly failed in his endeavors to torture her by all his covert allusions and ingeniously drawn inferences. No matter what hints he dropped or doubts he suggested, *she* knew "Clarissa" would come well out of her trials; and beyond a little unmeaning simper, and a muttered "To be sure," "No doubt of it," and, "Why not?" M'Cormick could obtain nothing from her.

Meanwhile, in the outer room the doctor continued to stride up and down with impatience, while Polly sat quietly working on, not the less anxious, perhaps, though her peaceful air betokened a mind at rest.

"That must be a boat, papa," said she, without lifting her head, "that has just come up to the landing-place. I heard the plash of the oars, and now all is still again."

"You 're right; so it is!" cried he, as he stopped before the window. "But how is this! That 's a lady I see yonder, and a gentleman along with her. That's not Stapylton, surely!"

"He is scarcely so tall," said she, rising to look out, "but not very unlike him. But the lady, papa,—the lady is Miss Barrington."

Bad as M'Cormick's visit was, it was nothing to the possibility of such an advent as this, and Dill's expressions of anger were now neither measured nor muttered.

"This is to be a day of disasters. I see it well, and no help for it," exclaimed he, passionately. "If there was one human being I 'd hate to come here this morning, it's that old woman! She's never civil. She's not commonly decent in her manner towards me in her own house, and what she 'll be in mine, is clean beyond me to guess. That's herself! There she goes! Look at her remarking,—I see, she's remarking on the weeds over the beds, and the smashed paling. She's laughing too! Oh, to be sure, it's fine laughing at people that's poor; and she might know something of that same herself. I know who the man is now. That 's the Colonel, who came to the 'Fisherman's Home' on the night of the accident."

"It would seem we are to hold a levee to-day," said Polly, giving a very fleeting glance at herself in the glass. And now a knock came to the door, and the man who acted gardener and car-driver and valet to the doctor announced that Miss Barrington and Colonel Hunter were below.

"Show them up," said Dill, with the peremptory voice of one ordering a very usual event, and intentionally loud enough to be heard below stairs.

If Polly's last parting with Miss Barrington gave little promise of pleasure to their next meeting, the first look she caught of the old lady on entering the room dispelled all uneasiness on that score. Miss Dinah entered with a pleasing smile, and presented her friend, Colonel Hunter, as one come to thank the doctor for much kindness to his young subaltern. "Whom, by the way," added he, "we thought to find here. It is only since we landed that we learned he had left the inn for Kilkenny."

While the Colonel continued to talk to the doctor, Miss Dinah had seated herself On the sofa, with Polly at her side.

"My visit this morning is to you," said she. "I have come to ask your forgiveness. Don't interrupt me, child; your forgiveness was the very word I used. I was very rude to you t' other morning, and being all in the wrong,— like most people in such circumstances,—I was very angry with the person who placed me so."

"But, my dear madam," said Polly, "you had such good reason to suppose you were in the right that this *amende* on your part is far too generous."

"It is not at all generous,—it is simply just. I was sorely vexed with you about that stupid wager, which you were very wrong to have had any share in; vexed with your father, vexed with your brother,—not that I believed his counsel would have been absolute wisdom,—and I was even vexed with my young friend Conyers, because he had not the bad taste to be as angry with you as I was. When I was a young lady," said she, bridling up, and looking at once haughty and defiant, "no man would have dared to approach me with such a proposal as complicity in a wager. But I am told that my ideas are antiquated, and the world has grown much wiser since that day."

"Nay, madam," said Polly, "but there is another difference that your politeness has prevented you from appreciating. I mean the difference in station between Miss Barrington and Polly Dill."

It was a well-directed shot, and told powerfully, for Miss Barrington's eyes became clouded, and she turned her head away, while she pressed Polly's hand within her own with a cordial warmth. "Ah!" said she, feelingly, "I hope there are many points of resemblance between us. I have always tried to be a good sister. I know well what you have been to your brother."

A very jolly burst of laughter from the inner room, where Hunter had already penetrated, broke in upon them, and the merry tones of his voice were heard saying, "Take my word for it, madam, nobody could spare time nowadays to make love in nine volumes. Life 's too short for it. Ask my old brother-officer here if he could endure such a thirty years' war; or rather let me turn here for an opinion. What does your daughter say on the subject?"

"Ay, ay," croaked out M'Cormick. "Marry in haste—"

"Or repent that you did n't. That 's the true reading of the adage."

"The Major would rather apply leisure to the marriage, and make the repentance come—"

"As soon as possible afterwards," said Miss Dinah, tartly.

"Faix, I 'll do better still; I won't provoke the repentance at all."

"Oh, Major, is it thus you treat me?" said Polly, affecting to wipe her eyes. "Are my hopes to be dashed thus cruelly?"

But the doctor, who knew how savagely M'Cormick could resent even the most harmless jesting, quickly interposed, with a question whether Polly had thought of ordering luncheon.

It is but fair to Dr. Dill to record the bland but careless way he ordered some entertainment for his visitors. He did it like the lord of a well-appointed household, who, when he said "serve," they served. It was in the easy confidence of one whose knowledge told him that the train was laid, and only waited for the match to explode it.

"May I have the honor, dear lady?" said he, offering his arm to Miss Barrington.

Now, Miss Dinah had just observed that she had various small matters to transact in the village, and was about to issue forth for their performance; but such is the force of a speciality, that she could not tear herself away without a peep into the dining-room, and a glance, at least, at arrangements that appeared so magically conjured up. Nor was Dill insensible to the astonishment expressed in her face as her eyes ranged over the table.

"If your daughter be your housekeeper, Dr. Dill," said she, in a whisper, "I must give her my very heartiest approbation. These are matters I can speak of with authority, and I pronounce her worthy of high commendation."

"What admirable salmon cutlets!" cried the Colonel. "Why, doctor, these tell of a French cook."

"There she is beside you, the French cook!" said the Major, with a malicious twinkle.

"Yes," said Polly, smiling, though with a slight flush on her face, "if Major M'Cormick will be indiscreet enough to tell tales, let us hope they will never be more damaging in their import."

"And do you say—do you mean to tell me that this curry is your handiwork? Why, this is high art."

"Oh, she 's artful enough, if it 's that ye 're wanting," muttered the Major.

Miss Barrington, having apparently satisfied the curiosity she felt about the details of the doctor's housekeeping, now took her leave, not, however, without Dr. Dill offering his arm on one side, while Polly, with polite observance, walked on the other.

"Look at that now," whispered the Major. "They 're as much afraid of that old woman as if she were the Queen of Sheba! And all because she was once a fine lady living at Barrington Hall."

"Here's their health for it," said the Colonel, filling his glass,—"and in a bumper too! By the way," added he, looking around, "does not Mrs. Dill lunch with us?"

"Oh, she seldom comes to her meals! She's a little touched here." And he laid his finger on the centre of his forehead. "And, indeed, no wonder if she is." The benevolent Major was about to give some details of secret family history, when the doctor and his daughter returned to the room.

The Colonel ate and talked untiringly. He was delighted with everything, and charmed with himself for his good luck in chancing upon such agreeable people. He liked the scenery, the village, the beetroot salad, the bridge, the pickled oysters, the evergreen oaks before the door. He was not astonished Conyers should linger on such a spot; and then it suddenly occurred to him to ask when he had left the village, and how.

The doctor could give no information on the point, and while he was surmising one thing and guessing another, M'Cormick whispered in the Colonel's ear, "Maybe it's a delicate point. How do you know what went on with—" And a significant nod towards Polly finished the remark.

"I wish I heard what Major M'Cormick has just said," said Polly.

"And it is exactly what I cannot repeat to you."

"I suspected as much. So that my only request will be that you never remember it."

"Isn't she sharp!—sharp as a needle!" chimed in the Major.

Checking, and not without some effort, a smart reprimand on the last speaker, the Colonel looked hastily at his watch, and arose from table.

"Past three o'clock, and to be in Kilkenny by six."

"Do you want a car? There's one of Rice's men now in the village; shall I get him for you?"

"Would you really do me the kindness?" While the Major bustled off on his errand, the Colonel withdrew the doctor inside the recess of a window. "I had a word I wished to say to you in private, Dr. Dill; but it must really be in private,—you understand me?"

"Strictly confidential, Colonel Hunter," said Dill, bowing.

"It is this: a young officer of mine, Lieutenant Conyers, has written to me a letter mentioning a plan he had conceived for the future advancement of your son, a young gentleman for whom, it would appear, he had formed a sudden but strong attachment. His project was, as I understand it, to accredit him to his father with such a letter as must secure the General's powerful influence in his behalf. Just the sort of thing a warm-hearted young fellow would think of doing for a friend he determined to serve, but exactly the kind of proceeding that might have a very unfortunate ending. I can very well imagine, from my own short experience here, that your son's claims to notice and distinction may be the very highest; I can believe readily what very little extraneous aid he would require to secure his success; but you and I are old men of the world, and are bound to look at things cautiously, and to ask, 'Is this scheme a very safe one?' 'Will General Conyers enter as heartily into it as his son?' 'Will the young surgeon be as sure to captivate the old soldier as the young one?' In a word, would it be quite wise to set a man's whole venture in life on such a cast, and is it the sort of risk that, with your experience of the world, you would sanction?"

It was evident, from the pause the Colonel left after these words, that he expected Dill to say something; but, with the sage reserve of his order, the doctor stood still, and never uttered a syllable. Let us be just to his acuteness, he never did take to the project from the first; he thought ill of it, in every way, but yet he did not relinquish the idea of making the surrender of it "conditional;" and so he slowly shook his head with an air of doubt, and smoothly rolled his hands one over the other, as though to imply a moment of hesitation and indecision.

"Yes, yes," muttered he, talking only to himself, — "disappointment, to be sure! — very great disappointment too! And his heart so set upon it, that's the hardship."

"Naturally enough," broke in Hunter, hastily. "Who would n't be disappointed under such circumstances? Better even that, however, than utter failure later on." The doctor sighed, but over what precise calamity was not so clear; and Hunter continued, —

"Now, as I have made this communication to you in strictest confidence, and not in any concert with Conyers, I only ask you to accept the view as a mere matter of opinion. I think you would be wrong to suffer your son to engage in such a venture. That's all I mean by my interference, and I have done."

Dill was, perhaps, scarcely prepared for the sudden summing up of the Colonel, and looked strangely puzzled and embarrassed.

"Might I talk the matter over with my daughter Polly? She has a good head for one so little versed in the world."

"By all means. It is exactly what I would have proposed. Or, better still, shall I repeat what I have just told you?"

"Do so," said the doctor, "for I just remember Miss Barrington will call here in a few moments for that medicine I have ordered for her brother, and which is not yet made up."

"Give me five minutes of your time and attention, Miss Dill," said Hunter, "on a point for which your father has referred me to your counsel."

"To mine?"

"Yes," said he, smiling at her astonishment. "We want your quick faculties to come to the aid of our slow ones. And here's the case." And in a few sentences he put the matter before her, as he had done to her father.

While he thus talked, they had strolled out into the garden, and walked slowly side by side down one of the alleys.

"Poor Tom!—poor fellow!" was all that Polly said, as she listened; but once or twice her handkerchief was raised to her eyes, and her chest heaved heavily.

"I am heartily sorry for him—that is, if his heart be bent on it—if he really should have built upon the scheme already."

"Of course he has, sir. You don't suppose that in such lives as ours these are common incidents? If we chance upon a treasure, or fancy that we have, once in a whole existence, it is great fortune."

"It was a brief, a very brief acquaintance,—a few hours, I believe. The— What was that? Did you hear any one cough there?"

"No, sir; we are quite alone. There is no one in the garden but ourselves."

"So that, as I was saying, the project could scarcely have taken a very deep root, and—and—in fact, better the first annoyance than a mistake that should give its color to a whole lifetime. I'm certain I heard a step in that walk yonder."

"No, sir; we are all alone."

"I half wish I had never come on this same errand. I have done an ungracious thing, evidently very ill, and with the usual fate of those who say disagreeable things, I am involved in the disgrace I came to avert."

"But I accept your view."

"There! I knew there was some one there!" said Hunter, springing across a bed and coming suddenly to the side of M'Cormick, who was affecting to be making a nosegay.

"The car is ready at the door, Colonel," said he, in some confusion. "Maybe you 'd oblige me with a seat as far as Lyrath?"

"Yes, yes; of course. And how late it is!" cried he, looking at his watch. "Time does fly fast in these regions, no doubt of it."

"You see, Miss Polly, you have made the Colonel forget himself," said M'Cormick, maliciously.

"Don't be severe on an error so often your own, Major M'Cormick," said she, fiercely, and turned away into the house.

The Colonel, however, was speedily at her side, and in an earnest voice said: "I could hate myself for the impression I am leaving behind me here. I came with those excellent intentions which so often make a man odious, and I am going away with those regrets which follow all failures; but I mean to come back again one of these days, and erase, if I can, the ill impression."

"One who has come out of his way to befriend those who had no claim upon his kindness can have no fear for the estimation he will be held in; for my part, I thank you heartily, even though I do not exactly see the direct road out of this difficulty."

"Let me write to you. One letter—only one," said Hunter.

But M'Cormick had heard the request, and she flushed up with anger at the malicious glee his face exhibited.

"You 'll have to say my good-byes for me to your father, for I am sorely pressed for time; and, even as it is, shall be late for my appointment in Kilkenny." And before Polly could do more than exchange his cordial shake hands, he was gone.

CHAPTER XXI
DARK TIDINGS

If I am not wholly without self-reproach when I bring my reader into uncongenial company, and make him pass time with Major M'Cormick he had far rather bestow upon a pleasanter companion, I am sustained by the fact—unpalatable fact though it be—that the highway of life is not always smooth, nor its banks flowery, and that, as an old Derry woman once remarked to me, "It takes a' kind o' folk to mak' a world."

Now, although Colonel Hunter did drive twelve weary miles of road with the Major for a fellow-traveller,—thanks to that unsocial conveniency called an Irish jaunting-car,—they rode back to back, and conversed but little. One might actually believe that unpopular men grow to feel a sort of liking for their unpopularity, and become at length delighted with the snubbings they meet with, as though an evidence of the amount of that discomfort they can scatter over the world at large; just, in fact, as a wasp or a scorpion might have a sort of triumphant joy in the consciousness of its power for mischief, and exult in the terror caused by its vicinity.

"Splendid road—one of the best I ever travelled on," said the Colonel, after about ten miles, during which he smoked on without a word.

"Why wouldn't it be, when they can assess the county for it? They're on the Grand Jury, and high up, all about here," croaked out the Major.

"It is a fine country, and abounds in handsome places." "And well mortgaged, too, the most of them." "You 'd not see better farming than that in Norfolk, cleaner wheat or neater drills; in fact, one might imagine himself in England."

"So he might, for the matter of taxes. I don't see much difference."

"Why don't you smoke? Things look pleasanter through the blue haze of a good Havannah," said Hunter, smiling.

"I don't want them to look pleasanter than they are," was the dry rejoinder.

Whether Hunter did or did not, he scarcely liked his counsellor, and, re-lighting a cigar, he turned his back once more on him.

"I'm one of those old-fashioned fellows," continued the Major, leaning over towards his companion, "who would rather see things as they are, not as they might be; and when I remarked you awhile ago so pleased with the elegant luncheon and Miss Polly's talents for housekeeping, I was laughing to myself over it all."

"How do you mean? What did you laugh at?" said Hunter, half fiercely.

"Just at the way you were taken in, that's all."

"Taken in?—taken in? A very strange expression for an hospitable reception and a most agreeable visit."

"Well, it's the very word for it, after all; for as to the hospitable reception, it was n't meant for us, but for that tall Captain,—the dark-complexioned fellow,—Staples, I think they call him."

"Captain Stapylton?"

"Yes, that's the man. He ordered Healey's car to take him over here; and I knew when the Dills sent over to Mrs. Brierley for a loan of the two cut decanters and the silver cruet-stand, something was up; and so I strolled down, by way of—to reconnoitre the premises, and see what old Dill was after."

"Well, and then?"

"Just that I saw it all,—the elegant luncheon, and the two bottles of wine, and the ginger cordials, all laid out for the man that never came; for it would seem he changed his mind about it, and went back to head-quarters."

"You puzzle me more and more at every word. What change of mind do you allude to? What purpose do you infer he had in coming over here to-day?"

The only answer M'Cormick vouchsafed to this was by closing one eye and putting his finger significantly to the tip of his nose, while he said, "Catch a weasel asleep!"

"I more than suspect," said Hunter, sternly, "that this half-pay life works badly for a man's habits, and throws him upon very petty and contemptible modes of getting through his time. What possible business could it be of yours to inquire why Stapylton came, or did not come here to-day, no more than for the reason of *my* visit?"

"Maybe I could guess that, too, if I was hard pushed," said M'Cormick, whose tone showed no unusual irritation from the late rebuke. "I was in the garden all the time, and heard everything."

"Listened to what I was saying to Miss Dill!" cried Hunter, whose voice of indignation could not now be mistaken.

"Every word of it," replied the unabashed Major. "I heard all you said about a short acquaintance—a few hours you called it—but that your heart was bent upon it, all the same. And then you went on about India; what an elegant place it was, and the fine pay and the great allowances. And ready enough she was to believe it all, for I suppose she was sworn at Highgate, and would n't take the Captain if she could get the Colonel."

By this time, and not an instant earlier, it flashed upon Hunter's mind that M'Cormick imagined he had overheard a proposal of marriage; and so amused was he by the blunder, that he totally drowned his anger in a hearty burst of laughter.

"I hope that, as an old brother-officer, you 'll be discreet, at all events," said he, at last. "You have not come by the secret quite legitimately, and I trust you will preserve it."

"My hearing is good, and my eyesight too, and I mean to use them both as long as they 're spared to me."

"It was your tongue that I referred to," said Hunter, more gravely.

"Ay, I know it was," said the Major, crankily. "My tongue will take care of itself also."

"In order to make its task the easier, then," said Hunter, speaking in a slow and serious voice, "let me tell you that your eaves-dropping has, for once at least, misled you. I made no proposal, such as you suspected, to Miss Dill. Nor did she give me the slightest encouragement to do so. The conversation you so unwarrantably and imperfectly overheard had a totally different object, and I am not at all sorry you should not have guessed it. So much for the past. Now one word for the future. Omit my name, and all that concerns me, from the narrative with which you amuse your friends, or, take my word for it, you 'll have to record more than you have any fancy for. This is strictly between ourselves; but if you have a desire to impart it, bear in mind that I shall be at my quarters in Kilkenny till Tuesday next."

"You may spend your life there, for anything I care," said the Major. "Stop, Billy; pull up. I'll get down here." And shuffling off the car, he muttered a "Good-day" without turning his head, and bent his steps towards a narrow lane that led from the high-road.

"Is this the place they call Lyrath?" asked the Colonel of the driver.

"No, your honor. We're a good four miles from it yet."

The answer showed Hunter that his fellow-traveller had departed in anger; and such was the generosity of his nature, he found it hard not to overtake him and make his peace with him.

"After all," thought he, "he 's a crusty old fellow, and has hugged his ill-temper so long, it may be more congenial to him now than a pleasanter humor." And he turned his mind to other interests that more closely touched him. Nor was he without cares, —heavier ones, too, than his happy nature had ever yet been called to deal with. There are few more painful situations in life than to find our advancement—the long-wished and strived-for promotion—achieved at the cost of some dearly loved friend; to know that our road to fortune had led us across the fallen figure of an old comrade, and that he who would have been the first to hail our success is already bewailing his own defeat. This was Hunter's lot at the present moment. He had been sent for to hear of a marvellous piece of good-fortune. His name and character, well known in India, had recommended him for an office of high trust,—the Political Resident of a great native court; a position not alone of power and influence, but as certain to secure, and within a very few years, a considerable fortune. It was the Governor-General who had made choice of him; and the Prince of Wales, in the brief interview he accorded him, was delighted with his frank and soldierlike manner, his natural cheerfulness, and high spirit. "We 're not going to unfrock you, Hunter," said he, gayly, in dismissing him. "You shall have your military rank, and all the steps of your promotion. We only make you a civilian till you have saved some lacs of rupees, which is what I hear your predecessor has forgotten to do."

It was some time before Hunter, overjoyed as he was, even bethought him of asking who that predecessor was. What was his misery when he heard the name of Ormsby Conyers, his oldest, best friend; the man at whose table he had sat for years, whose confidence he had shared, whose heart was open to him to its last secret! "No," said he, "this is impossible. Advancement at such a price has no temptation for me. I will not accept it" He wrote his refusal at once, not assigning any definite reasons, but declaring that, after much thought and consideration, he had decided the post was one he could not accept of. The Secretary, in whose province the affairs of India lay, sent for him, and, after much pressing and some ingenious cross-questioning, got at his reasons. "These may be all reasonable scruples on your part," said he, "but they will avail your friend nothing. Conyers must go; for his own interest and character's sake, he must come home and meet the charges made against him, and which, from their very contradictions, we all hope to see him treat triumphantly: some alleging that he has amassed untold wealth; others that it is, as a ruined man, he has involved himself in the intrigues of the native rulers. All who know him say that at the first whisper of a charge against him he will throw up his post and come to England to meet his accusers. And now let me own to you that it is the friendship in which he held you lay one of the suggestions for your choice. We all felt that if a man ill-disposed or ungenerously minded to Conyers should go out to Agra, numerous petty and vexatious accusations might be forthcoming; the little local injuries and pressure, so sure to beget grudges, would all rise up as charges, and enemies to the fallen man spring up in every quarter. It is as a successor, then, you can best serve your friend." I need not dwell on the force and ingenuity with which this view was presented; enough that I say it was successful, and Hunter returned to Ireland to take leave of his regiment, and prepare for a speedy departure to India.

Having heard, in a brief note from young Conyers, his intentions respecting Tom Dill, Hunter had hastened off to prevent the possibility of such a scheme being carried out. Not wishing, however, to divulge the circumstances of his friend's fortune, he had in his interview with the doctor confined himself to arguments on the score of prudence. His next charge was to break to Fred the tidings of his father's troubles, and it was an office he shrunk from with a coward's fear. With every mile he went his heart grew heavier. The more he thought over the matter the more difficult it appeared. To treat the case lightly, might savor of heartlessness and levity; to approach it more seriously, might seem a needless severity. Perhaps, too, Conyers might have written to his son; he almost hoped he had, and that the first news of disaster should not come from him.

That combination of high-heartedness and bashfulness, a blended temerity and timidity,—by no means an uncommon temperament,—renders a man's position in the embarrassments of life one of downright suffering. There are operators who feel the knife more sensitively than the patients. Few know what torments such men conceal under a manner of seeming slap-dash and carelessness. Hunter was of this order, and would, any day of his life, far rather have confronted a real peril than met a contingency that demanded such an address. It was, then, with a sense of relief he learned, on arrival at the barracks, that Conyers had gone out for a walk, so that there was a reprieve at least of a few hours of the penalty that overhung him.

The trumpet-call for the mess had just sounded as Conyers gained the door of the Colonel's quarters, and Hunter taking Fred's arm, they crossed the barrack-square together.

"I have a great deal to say to you, Conyers," said he, hurriedly; "part of it unpleasant,—none of it, indeed, very gratifying—"

"I know you are going to leave us, sir," said Fred, who perceived the more than common emotion in the other's manner. "And for myself, I own I have no longer any desire to remain in the regiment. I might go further, and say no more zest for the service. It was through your friendship for me

I learned to curb many and many promptings to resistance, and when *you* go—"

"I am very sorry,—very, very sorry to leave you all," said Hunter, with a broken voice. "It is not every man that proudly can point to seven-and-twenty-years' service in a regiment without one incident to break the hearty cordiality that bound us. We had no bickerings, no petty jealousies amongst us. If a man joined us who wanted partisanship and a set, he soon found it better to exchange. I never expect again to lead the happy life I have here, and I 'd rather have led our bold squadrons in the field than have been a General of Division." Who could have believed that he, whose eyes ran over, as he spoke these broken words, was, five minutes after, the gay and rattling Colonel his officers always saw him, full of life, spirit, and animation, jocularly alluding to his speedy departure, and gayly speculating on the comparisons that would be formed between himself and his successor? "I'm leaving him the horses in good condition," said he; "and when Hargrave learns to give the word of command above a whisper, and Eyreton can ride without a backboard, he 'll scarcely report you for inefficiency." It is fair to add, that the first-mentioned officer had a voice like a bassoon, and the second was the beau-ideal of dragoon horsemanship.

It would not have consisted with military etiquette to have asked the Colonel the nature of his promotion, nor as to what new sphere of service he was called. Even the old Major, his contemporary, dared not have come directly to the question; and while all were eager to hear it, the utmost approach was by an insinuation or an innuendo. Hunter was known for no quality more remarkably than for his outspoken frankness, and some surprise was felt that in his returning thanks for his health being drank, not a word should escape him on this point; but the anxiety was not lessened by the last words he spoke. "It may be, it is more than likely, I shall never see the regiment again; but the sight of a hussar jacket or a scarlet busby will bring you all back to my memory, and you may rely on it, that whether around the mess-table or the bivouac fire my heart will be with you."

Scarcely had the cheer that greeted the words subsided, when a deep voice from the extreme end of the table said,—

"If only a new-comer in the regiment, Colonel Hunter, I am too proud of my good fortune not to associate myself with the feelings of my comrades, and, while partaking of their deep regrets, I feel it a duty to contribute, if in my power, by whatever may lighten the grief of our loss. Am I at liberty to do so? Have I your free permission, I mean?"

"I am fairly puzzled by your question, Captain Stapylton. I have not the very vaguest clew to your meaning, but, of course, you have my permission to mention whatever you deem proper."

"It is a toast I would propose, sir."

"By all means. The thing is not very regular, perhaps, but we are not exactly remarkable for regularity this evening. Fill, gentlemen, for Captain Stapylton's toast!"

"Few words will propose it," said Stapylton. "We have just drank Colonel Hunter's health with all the enthusiasm that befits the toast, but in doing so our tribute has been paid to the past; of the present and the future we have taken no note whatever, and it is to these I would now recall you. I say, therefore, bumpers to the health, happiness, and success of Major-General Hunter, Political Resident and Minister at the Court of Agra!"

"No, no!" cried young Conyers, loudly, "this is a mistake. It is my father—it is Lieutenant-General Conyers—who resides at Agra. Am I not right, sir?" cried he, turning to the Colonel.

But Hunter's face, pale as death even to the lips, and the agitation with which he grasped Fred's hand, so overcame the youth that with a sudden cry he sprang from his seat, and rushed out of the room. Hunter as quickly followed him; and now all were grouped around Stapylton, eagerly questioning and inquiring what his tidings might mean.

"The old story, gentlemen,—the old story, with which we are all more or less familiar in this best of all possible worlds: General Hunter goes out in honor, and General Conyers comes home in—well, under a cloud,— of course one that he is sure and certain to dispel. I conclude the Colonel would rather have had his advancement under other circumstances; but in this game of leap-frog that we call life, we must occasionally jump over our friends as well as our enemies."

"How and where did you get the news?"

"It came to me from town. I heard it this morning, and of course I imagined that the Colonel had told it to Conyers, whom it so intimately concerned. I hope I may not have been indiscreet in what I meant as a compliment."

None cared to offer their consolings to one so fully capable of supplying the commodity to himself, and the party broke up in twos or threes, moodily seeking their own quarters, and brooding gloomily over what they had just witnessed.

CHAPTER XXII
LEAVING HOME

I will ask my reader now to turn for a brief space to the "Fisherman's Home," which is a scene of somewhat unusual bustle. The Barringtons are preparing for a journey, and old Peter's wardrobe has been displayed for inspection along a hedge of sweet-brier in the garden,—an arrangement devised by the genius of Darby, who passes up and down, with an expression of admiration on his face, the sincerity of which could not be questioned. A more reflective mind than his might have been carried away, at the sight to thoughts of the strange passages in the late history of Ireland, so curiously typified in that motley display. There, was the bright green dress-coat of Daly's club, recalling days of political excitement, and all the plottings and cabals of a once famous opposition. There was, in somewhat faded splendor it must be owned, a court suit of the Duke of Portland's day, when Irish gentlemen were as gorgeous as the courtiers of Versailles. Here came a grand colonel's uniform, when Barrington commanded a regiment of Volunteers; and yonder lay a friar's frock and cowl, relics of those "attic nights" with the Monks of the Screw, and recalling memories of Avonmore and Curran, and Day and Parsons; and with them were mixed hunting-coats, and shooting-jackets, and masonic robes, and "friendly brother" emblems, and long-waisted garments, and swallow-tailed affectations of all shades and tints,—reminders of a time when Buck Whalley was the eccentric, and Lord Llandaff the beau of Irish society. I am not certain that Monmouth Street would have endorsed Darby's sentiment as he said, "There was clothes there for a king on his throne!" but it was an honestly uttered speech, and came out of the fulness of an admiring heart, and although in truth he was nothing less than an historian, he was forcibly struck by the thought that Ireland must have been a grand country to live in, in those old days when men went about their ordinary avocations in such splendor as he saw there.

Nor was Peter Barrington himself an unmoved spectator of these old remnants of the past Old garments, like old letters, bring oftentimes very forcible memories of a long ago; and as he turned over the purple-stained flap of a waistcoat, he bethought him of a night at Daly's, when, in returning thanks for his health, his shaking hand had spilled that identical glass of

Burgundy; and in the dun-colored tinge of a hunting-coat he remembered the day he had plunged into the Nore at Corrig O'Neal, himself and the huntsman, alone of all the field, to follow the dogs!

"Take them away, Darby, take them away; they only set me a-thinking about the pleasant companions of my early life. It was in that suit there I moved the amendment in '82, when Henry Grattan crossed over and said, 'Barrington will lead us here, as he does in the hunting-field.' Do you see that peach-colored waistcoat? It was Lady Caher embroidered every stitch of it with her own hands, for me."

"Them 's elegant black satin breeches," said Darby, whose eyes of covetousness were actually rooted on the object of his desire.

"I never wore them," said Barrington, with a sigh. "I got them for a duel with Mat Fortescue, but Sir Toby Blake shot him that morning. Poor Mat!"

"And I suppose you'll never wear them now. You couldn't bear the sight then," said Darby, insinuatingly.

"Most likely not," said Barrington, as he turned away with a heavy sigh. Darby sighed also, but not precisely in the same spirit.

Let me passingly remark that the total unsuitability to his condition of any object seems rather to enhance its virtue in the eyes of a lower Irishman, and a hat or a coat which he could not, by any possibility, wear in public, might still be to him things to covet and desire.

"What is the meaning of all this rag fair?" cried Miss Barrington, as she suddenly came in front of the exposed wardrobe. "You are not surely making any selections from these tawdry absurdities, brother, for your journey?"

"Well, indeed," said Barrington, with a droll twinkle of his eye, "it was a point that Darby and I were discussing as you came up. Darby opines that to make a suitable impression upon the Continent, I must not despise the assistance of dress, and he inclines much to that Corbeau coat with the cherry-colored lining."

"If Darby 's an ass, brother, I don't imagine it is a good reason to consult him," said she, angrily. "Put all that trash where you found it. Lay out your master's black clothes and the gray shooting-coat, see that his strong boots are in good repair, and get a serviceable lock on that valise."

It was little short of magic the spell these few and distinctly uttered words seemed to work on Darby, who at once descended from a realm of speculation and scheming to the commonplace world of duty and obedience. "I really wonder how you let yourself be imposed on, brother, by the assumed simplicity of that shrewd fellow."

"I like it, Dinah, I positively like it," said he, with a smile. "I watch him playing the game with a pleasure almost as great as his own; and as I know that the stakes are small, I 'm never vexed at his winning."

"But you seem to forget the encouragement this impunity suggests."

"Perhaps it does, Dinah; and very likely his little rogueries are as much triumphs to him as are all the great political intrigues the glories of some grand statesman."

"Which means that you rather like to be cheated," said she, scoffingly.

"When the loss is a mere trifle, I don't always think it ill laid out."

"And I," said she, resolutely, "so far from participating in your sentiment, feel it to be an insult and an outrage. There is a sense of inferiority attached to the position of a dupe that would drive me to any reprisals."

"I always said it; I always said it," cried he, laughing. "The women of our family monopolized all the com-bativeness."

Miss Barrington's eyes sparkled, and her cheek glowed, and she looked like one stung to the point of a very angry rejoinder, when by an effort she controlled her passion, and, taking a letter from her pocket, she opened it, and said, "This is from Withering. He has managed to obtain all the information we need for our journey. We are to sail for Ostend by the regular packet, two of which go every week from Dover. From thence there are stages or canal-boats to Bruges and Brussels, cheap and commodious, he says. He gives us the names of two hotels, one of which—the 'Lamb,' at Brussels—he recommends highly; and the Pension of a certain Madame Ochteroogen, at Namur, will, he opines, suit us better than an inn. In fact, this letter is a little road book, with the expenses marked down, and we can quietly count the cost of our venture before we make it."

"I 'd rather not, Dinah. The very thought of a limit is torture to me. Give me bread and water every day, if you like, but don't rob me of the notion that some fine day I am to be regaled with beef and pudding."

"I don't wonder that we have come to beggary," said she, passionately. "I don't know what fortune and what wealth could compensate for a temperament like yours."

"You may be right, Dinah. It may go far to make a man squander his substance, but take my word for it, it will help him to bear up under the loss."

If Barrington could have seen the gleam of affection that filled his sister's eyes, he would have felt what love her heart bore him; but he had stooped down to take a caterpillar off a flower, and did not mark it.

"Withering has seen young Conyers," she continued, as her eyes ran over the letter "He called upon him." Barrington made no rejoinder, though she waited for one. "The poor lad was in great affliction; some distressing news from India—of what kind Withering could not guess—had just reached him, and he appeared overwhelmed by it."

"He is very young for sorrow," said Barrington, feelingly.

"Just what Withering said;" and she read out, "'When I told him that I had come to make an *amende* for the reception he had met with at the cottage, he stopped me at once, and said, "Great grief s are the cure of small ones, and you find me under a very heavy affliction. Tell Miss Barrington that I have no other memories of the 'Fisherman's Home' than of all her kindness towards me."'"

"Poor boy!" said Barrington, with emotion. "And how did Withering leave him?"

"Still sad and suffering. Struggling too, Withering thought, between a proud attempt to conceal his grief and an ardent impulse to tell all about it 'Had *you* been there,' he writes, 'you'd have had the whole story; but I saw that he could n't stoop to open his heart to a man.'"

"Write to him, Dinah. Write and ask him down here for a couple of days."

"You forget that we are to leave this the day after tomorrow, brother."

"So I did. I forgot it completely. Well, what if he were to come for one day? What if you were to say come over and wish us good-bye?"

"It is so like a man and a man's selfishness never to consider a domestic difficulty," said she, tartly. "So long as a house has a roof over it, you fancy it may be available for hospitalities. You never take into account the carpets to be taken up, and the beds that are taken down, the plate-chest that is packed, and the cellar that is walled up. You forget, in a word, that to make that life you find so very easy, some one else must pass an existence full of cares and duties."

"There 's not a doubt of it, Dinah. There 's truth and reason in every word you 've said."

"I will write to him if you like, and say that we mean to be at home by an early day in October, and that if he is disposed to see how our woods look in autumn, we will be well pleased to have him for our guest."

"Nothing could be better. Do so, Dinah. I owe the young fellow a reparation, and I shall not have an easy conscience till I make it."

"Ah, brother Peter, if your moneyed debts had only given you one-half the torment of your moral ones, what a rich man you might have been to-day!"

Long after his sister had gone away and left him, Peter Barrington continued to muse over this speech. He felt it, felt it keenly too, but in no bitterness of spirit.

Like most men of a lax and easy temper, he could mete out to himself the same merciful measure he accorded to others, and be as forgiving to his own faults as to theirs. "I suppose Dinah is right, though," said he to himself. "I never did know that sensitive irritability under debt which insures solvency. And whenever a man can laugh at a dun, he is pretty sure to be on the high-road to bankruptcy! Well, well, it is somewhat late to try and reform, but I'll do my best!" And thus comforted, he set about tying up fallen rose-trees and removing noxious insects with all his usual zeal.

"I half wish the place did not look in such beauty, just as I must leave it for a while. I don't think that japonica ever had as many flowers before; and what a season for tulips! Not to speak of the fruit There are peaches enough to stock a market. I wonder what Dinah means to do with them? She 'll be sorely grieved to make them over as perquisites to Darby, and I know she 'll never consent to have them sold. No, that is the one concession she cannot stoop to. Oh, here she comes! What a grand year for the wall fruit, Dinah!" cried he, aloud.

"The apricots have all failed, and fully one-half of the peaches are worm-eaten," said she, dryly.

Peter sighed as he thought, how she does dispel an illusion, what a terrible realist is this same sister! "Still, my dear Dinah, one-half of such a crop is a goodly yield."

"Out with it, Peter Barrington. Out with the question that is burning for utterance. What's to be done with them? I have thought of that already. I have told Polly Dill to preserve a quantity for us, and to take as much more as she pleases for her own use, and make presents to her friends of the remainder. She is to be mistress here while we are away, and has promised to come up two or three times a week, and see after everything, for I neither desire to have the flower-roots sold, nor the pigeons eaten before our return."

"That is an admirable arrangement, sister. I don't know a better girl than Polly!"

"She is better than I gave her credit for," said Miss Barrington, who was not fully pleased at any praise not bestowed by herself. A man's estimate of a young woman's goodness is not so certain of finding acceptance from her own sex! "And as for that girl, the wonder is that with a fool for a mother, and a crafty old knave for a father, she really should possess one good trait or one amiable quality." Barrington muttered what sounded like concurrence, and she went on: "And it is for this reason I have taken an interest in her, and hope, by occupying her mind with useful cares and filling her hours with commendable duties, she will estrange herself from that going about to fine houses, and frequenting society where she is exposed to innumerable humiliations, and worse."

"Worse, Dinah!—what could be worse?"

"Temptations are worse, Peter Barrington, even when not yielded to; for like a noxious climate, which, though it fails to kill, it is certain to injure the constitution during a lifetime. Take my word for it, she 'll not be the better wife to the Curate for the memory of all the fine speeches she once heard from the Captain. Very old and ascetic notions I am quite aware, Peter; but please to bear in mind all the trouble we take that the roots of a favorite tree should not strike into a sour soil, and bethink you how very indifferent we are as to the daily associates of our children!"

"There you are right, Dinah, there you are right,—at least, as regards girls."

"And the rule applies fully as much to boys. All those manly accomplishments and out-of-door habits you lay such store by, could be acquired without the intimacy of the groom or the friendship of the gamekeeper. What are you muttering there about old-maids' children? Say it out, sir, and defend it, if you have the courage!"

But either that he had not said it, or failed in the requisite boldness to maintain it, he blundered out a very confused assurance of agreement on every point.

A woman is seldom merciful in argument; the consciousness that she owes victory to her violence far more than to her logic, prompts persistence in the course she has followed so successfully, and so was it that Miss Dinah contrived to gallop over the battlefield long after the enemy was routed! But Barrington was not in a mood to be vexed; the thought of the journey filled him with so many pleasant anticipations, the brightest of all being the sight of poor George's child! Not that this thought had not its dark side, in contrition for the long, long years he had left her unnoticed and neglected. Of course he had his own excuses and apologies for all this: he could refer to his overwhelming embarrassments, and the heavy cares that surrounded him; but then she—that poor friendless girl, that orphan—could have known nothing of these things; and what opinion might she not have formed of those relatives who had so coldly and heartlessly abandoned her! Barrington took down her miniature, painted when she was a mere infant, and scanned it well, as though to divine what nature might possess her! There was little for speculation there,—perhaps even less for hope! The eyes were large and lustrous, it is true, but the brow was heavy, and the mouth, even in infancy, had something that seemed like firmness and decision,— strangely at variance with the lips of childhood.

Now, old Barrington's heart was deeply set on that lawsuit—that great cause against the Indian Government—that had formed the grand campaign of his life. It was his first waking thought of a morning, his last at night. All his faculties were engaged in revolving the various points of evidence, and imagining how this and that missing link might be supplied; and yet, with all these objects of desire before him, he would have given them up, each and all, to be sure of one thing,—that his granddaughter might be handsome! It was not that he did not value far above the graces of person a number of other gifts; he would not, for an instant, have hesitated, had he to choose between mere beauty and a good disposition. If he knew anything of himself, it was his thorough appreciation of a kindly nature, a temper to bear well, and a spirit to soar nobly; but somehow he imagined these were gifts she was likely enough to possess. George's child would resemble him; she would have his light-heartedness and his happy nature, but would she be handsome? It is, trust me, no superficial view of life that attaches a great price to personal atractions, and Barrington was one to give these their full value. Had she been brought up from childhood under his roof, he had probably long since ceased to think of such a point; he would have attached himself to her by the ties of that daily domesticity which grow into a nature. The hundred little cares and offices that would have fallen to her lot to meet, would have served as links to bind their hearts; but she was coming to them a perfect stranger, and he wished ardently that his first impression should be all in her favor.

Now, while such were Barrington's reveries, his sister took a different turn. She had already pictured to herself the dark-orbed, heavy-browed child, expanded into a sallow-complexioned, heavy-featured girl, ungainly and ungraceful, her figure neglected, her very feet spoiled by the uncouth shoes of the convent, her great red hands untrained to all occupation save the coarse cares of that half-menial existence. "As my brother would say," muttered she, "a most unpromising filly, if it were not for the breeding."

Both brother and sister, however, kept their impressions to themselves, and of all the subjects discussed between them not one word betrayed what each forecast about Josephine. I am half sorry it is no part of my task to follow them on the road, and yet I feel I could not impart to my reader the almost boylike enjoyment old Peter felt at every stage of the journey. He had made the grand tour of Europe more than half a century before, and he was in ecstasy to find so much that was unchanged around him. There were the long-eared caps, and the monstrous earrings, and the sabots, and the heavily tasselled team horses, and the chiming church-bells, and the old-world equipages, and the strangely undersized soldiers,—all just as he saw them last! And every one was so polite and ceremonious, and so idle and so unoccupied, and the theatres were so large and the newspapers so small, and the current coin so defaced, and the order of the meats at dinner so inscrutable, and every one seemed contented just because he had nothing to do.

"Isn't it all I have told you, Dinah dear? Don't you perceive how accurate my picture has been? And is it not very charming and enjoyable?"

"They are the greatest cheats I ever met in my life, brother Peter; and when I think that every grin that greets us is a matter of five francs, it mars considerably the pleasure I derive from the hilarity."

It was in this spirit they journeyed till they arrived at Brussels.

CHAPTER XXIII
THE COLONEL'S COUNSELS

When Conyers had learned from Colonel Hunter all that he knew of his father's involvement, it went no further than this, that the Lieutenant-General had either resigned or been deprived of his civil appointments, and Hunter was called upon to replace him. With all his habit of hasty and impetuous action, there was no injustice in Fred's nature, and he frankly recognized that, however painful to him personally, Hunter could not refuse to accede to what the Prince had distinctly pressed him to accept.

Young Conyers had heard over and over again the astonishment expressed by old Indian officials how his father's treatment of the Company's orders had been so long endured. Some prescriptive immunity seemed to attach to him, or some great patronage to protect him, for he appeared to do exactly as he pleased, and the despotic sway of his rule was known far and near. With the changes in the constitution of the Board, some members might have succeeded less disposed to recognize the General's former services, or endure so tolerantly his present encroachments, and Fred well could estimate the resistance his father would oppose to the very mildest remonstrance, and how indignantly he would reject whatever came in the shape of a command. Great as was the blow to the young man, it was not heavier in anything than the doubt and uncertainty about it, and he waited with a restless impatience for his father's letter, which should explain it all. Nor was his position less painful from the estrangement in which he lived, and the little intercourse he maintained with his brother-officers. When Hunter left, he knew that he had not one he could call friend amongst them, and Hunter was to go in a very few days, and even of these he could scarcely spare him more than a few chance moments!

It was in one of these flitting visits that Hunter bethought him of young Dill, of whom, it is only truth to confess, young Conyers had forgotten everything. "I took time by the forelock, Fred, about that affair," said he, "and I trust I have freed you from all embarrassment about it."

"As how, sir?" asked Conyers, half in pique.

"When I missed you at the 'Fisherman's Home,' I set off to pay the doctor a visit, and a very charming visit it turned out; a better pigeon-pie I never ate, nor a prettier girl than the maker of it would I ask to meet with. We became great friends, talked of everything, from love at first sight to bone spavins, and found that we agreed to a miracle. I don't think I ever saw a girl before who suited me so perfectly in all her notions. She gave me a hint about what they call 'mouth lameness' our Vet would give his eye for. Well, to come back to her brother,—a dull dog, I take it, though I have not seen him,—I said, 'Don't let him go to India, they 've lots of clever fellows out there; pack him off to Australia; send him to New Zealand.' And when she interrupted me, 'But young Mr. Conyers insisted,—he would have it so; his father is to make Tom's fortune, and to send him back as rich as a Begum,' I said, 'He has fallen in love with you, Miss Polly, that's the fact, and lost his head altogether; and I don't wonder at it, for here am I, close upon forty-eight,—I might have said forty-nine, but no matter,—close upon forty-eight, and I 'm in the same book!' Yes, if it was the sister, *vice* the brother, who wanted to make a fortune in India, I almost think I could say, 'Come and share mine!'"

"But I don't exactly understand. Am I to believe that they wish Tom to be off—to refuse my offer—and that the rejection comes from them?"

"No, not exactly. I said it was a bad spec, that you had taken a far too sanguine view of the whole thing, and that as I was an old soldier, and knew more of the world,—that is to say, had met a great many more hard rubs and disappointments,—my advice was, not to risk it. 'Young Conyers,' said I, 'will do all that he has promised to the letter. You may rely upon every word that he has ever uttered. But bear in mind that he's only a mortal man; he's not one of those heathen gods who used to make fellows invincible in a battle, or smuggle them off in a cloud, out of the way of demons, or duns, or whatever difficulties beset them. He might die, his father might die, any of us might die.' Yes, by Jove! there's nothing so uncertain as life, except the Horse Guards.' And putting one thing with another, Miss Polly,' said I, 'tell him to stay where he is,'—open a shop at home, or go to one of the colonies,—Heligoland, for instance, a charming spot for the bathing-season."

"And she, what did she say?"

"May I be cashiered if I remember! I never do remember very clearly what any one says. Where I am much interested on my own side, I have no time for the other fellow's arguments. But I know if she was n't convinced she ought to have been. I put the thing beyond a question, and I made her cry."

"Made her cry!"

"Not cry,—that is, she did not blubber; but she looked glassy about the lids, and turned away her head. But to be sure we were parting,—a rather soft bit of parting, too,—and I said something about my coming back with a wooden leg, and she said, 'No! have it of cork, they make them so cleverly now.' And I was going to say something more, when a confounded old half-pay Major came up and interrupted us, and—and, in fact, there it rests."

"I 'm not at all easy in mind as to this affair. I mean, I don't like how I stand in it."

"But you stand out of it,—out of it altogether! Can't you imagine that your father may have quite enough cares of his own to occupy him without needing the embarrassment of looking after this bumpkin, who, for aught you know, might repay very badly all the interest taken in him? If it had been the girl,—if it had been Polly—" "I own frankly," said Conyers, tartly, "it did not occur to me to make such an offer to *her!*"

"Faith! then, Master Fred, I was deuced near doing it,—so near, that when I came away I scarcely knew whether I had or had not done so."

"Well, sir, there is only an hour's drive on a good road required to repair the omission."

"That's true, Fred,—that's true; but have you never, by an accident, chanced to come up with a stunning fence,—a regular rasper that you took in a fly a few days before with the dogs, and as you looked at the place, have you not said, 'What on earth persuaded me to ride at *that?*'"

"Which means, sir, that your cold-blooded reflections are against the project?"

"Not exactly that, either," said he, in a sort of confusion; "but when a man speculates on doing something for which the first step must be an explanation to this fellow, a half apology to that,—with a whimpering kind of entreaty not to be judged hastily, not to be condemned unheard, not to be set down as an old fool who couldn't stand the fire of a pair of bright eyes,—I say when it comes to this, he ought to feel that his best safeguard is his own misgiving!"

"If I do not agree with you, sir, it is because I incline to follow my own lead, and care very little for what the world says of it."

"Don't believe a word of that, Fred; it's all brag,—all nonsense! The very effrontery with which you fancy you are braving public opinion is only Dutch courage. What each of us in his heart thinks of himself is only the reflex of the world's estimate of him; at least, what he imagines it to be. Now, for my own part, I 'd rather ride up to a battery in full fire than I'd sit down and write to my old aunt Dorothy Hunter a formal letter announcing my approaching marriage, telling her that the lady of my choice was twenty or thereabouts, not to add that her family name was Dill. Believe me, Fred, that if you want the concentrated essence of public opinion, you have only to do something which shall irritate and astonish the half-dozen people with whom you live in intimacy. Won't they remind you about the mortgages on your lands and the gray in your whiskers, that last loan you raised from Solomon Hymans, and that front tooth you got replaced by Cartwright, though it was the week before they told you you were a miracle of order and good management, and actually looking younger than you did five years ago! You're not minding me, Fred,—not following me; you 're thinking of your *protégé*, Tom Dill, and what he 'll think and say of your desertion of him."

"You have hit it, sir. It was exactly what I was asking myself."

"Well, if nothing better offers, tell him to get himself in readiness, and come out with me. I cannot make him a Rajah, nor even a Zemindar; but I 'll stick him into a regimental surgeoncy, and leave him to fashion out his own future. He must look sharp, however, and lose no time. The 'Ganges' is getting ready in all haste, and will be round at Portsmouth by the 8th, and we expect to sail on the 12th or 13th at furthest."

"I 'll write to him to-day. I 'll write this moment."

"Add a word of remembrance on my part to the sister, and tell bumpkin to supply himself with no end of letters, recommendatory and laudatory, to muzzle our Medical Board at Calcutta, and lots of light clothing, and all the torturing instruments he 'll need, and a large stock of good humor, for he'll be chaffed unmercifully all the voyage." And, with these comprehensive directions, the Colonel concluded his counsels, and bustled away to look after his own personal interests.

Fred Conyers was not over-pleased with the task assigned him. The part he liked to fill in life, and, indeed, that which he had usually performed, was the Benefactor and the Patron, and it was but an ungracious office for him to have to cut the wings and disfigure the plumage of his generosity. He made two, three, four attempts at conveying his intentions, but with none was he satisfied; so he ended by simply saying, "I have something of importance to tell you, and which, not being altogether pleasant, it will be better to say than to write; so I have to beg you will come up here at once, and see me." Scarcely was this letter sealed and addressed than he bethought him of the awkwardness of presenting Tom to his brother-officers, or the still greater indecorum of not presenting him. "How shall I ask him to the mess, with the certainty of all the impertinences he will be exposed to?—and what pretext have I for not offering him the ordinary attention shown to every stranger?" He was, in fact, wincing under that public opinion he had only a few moments before declared he could afford to despise. "No," said he, "I have no right to expose poor Tom to this. I 'll drive over myself to the village, and if any advice or counsel be needed, he will be amongst those who can aid him."

He ordered his servant to harness his handsome roan, a thoroughbred of surpassing style and action, to the dog-cart,—not over-sorry to astonish his friend Tom by the splendor of a turn-out that had won the suffrages of Tattersall's,—and prepared for his mission to Inistioge.

Was it with the same intention of "astonishing" Tom Dill that Conyers bestowed such unusual attention upon his dress? At his first visit to the "Fisherman's Home" he had worn the homely shooting-jacket and felt hat which, however comfortable and conventional, do not always redound to the advantage of the wearer, or, if they do, it is by something, perhaps, in the contrast presented to his ordinary appearance, and the impression ingeniously insinuated that he is one so unmistakably a gentleman, no travesty of costume can efface the stamp.

It was in this garb Polly had seen him, and if Polly Dill had been a duchess it was in some such garb she would have been accustomed to see her brother or her cousin some six out of every seven mornings of the week; but Polly was not a duchess: she was the daughter of a village doctor, and might, not impossibly, have acquired a very erroneous estimate of his real pretensions from having beheld him thus attired. It was, therefore, entirely by a consideration for her ignorance of the world and its ways that he determined to enlighten her.

At the time of which I am writing, the dress of the British army was a favorite study with that Prince whose taste, however questionable, never exposed him to censure on grounds of over-simplicity and plainness. As the Colonel of the regiment Conyers belonged to, he had bestowed upon his own especial corps an unusual degree of splendor in equipment, and amongst other extravagances had given them an almost boundless liberty of combining different details of dress. Availing himself of this privilege, our young Lieutenant invented a costume which, however unmilitary and irregular, was not deficient in becomingness. Under a plain blue jacket very sparingly braided he wore the rich scarlet waistcoat, all slashed with gold, they had introduced at their mess. A simple foraging-cap and overalls, seamed with a thin gold line, made up a dress that might have passed for the easy costume of the barrack-yard, while, in reality, it was eminently suited to set off the wearer.

Am I to confess that he looked at himself in the glass with very considerable satisfaction, and muttered, as he turned away, "Yes, Miss Polly, this is in better style than that Quakerish drab livery you saw me last in, and I have little doubt that you 'll think so!"

"Is this our best harness, Holt?"

"Yes, sir."

"All right!"

CHAPTER XXIV
CONYERS MAKES A MORNING CALL

When Conyers, to the astonishment and wonder of an admiring village public, drove his seventeen-hand-high roan into the market square of Inistioge, he learned that all of the doctor's family were from home except Mrs. Dill. Indeed, he saw the respectable lady at the window with a book in her hand, from which not all the noise and clatter of his arrival for one moment diverted her. Though not especially anxious to attract her attention, he was half piqued at her show of indifference. A dog-cart by Adams and a thoroughbred like Boanerges were, after all, worth a glance at. Little did he know what a competitor be had in that much-thumbed old volume, whose quaintly told miseries were to her as her own sorrows. Could he have assembled underneath that window all the glories of a Derby Day, Mr. Richardson's "Clarissa" would have beaten the field. While he occupied himself in dexterously tapping the flies from his horse with the fine extremity of his whip, and thus necessitating that amount of impatience which made the spirited animal stamp and champ his bit, the old lady read on undisturbed.

"Ask at what hour the doctor will be at home, Holt," cried he, peevishly.

"Not till to-morrow, sir; he has gone to Castle Durrow."

"And Miss Dill, is she not in the house?"

"No, sir; she has gone down to the 'Fisherman's Home' to look after the garden,—the family having left that place this morning."

After a few minutes' reflection, Conyers ordered his servant to put up the horse at the inn, and wait for him there; and then engaging a "cot," he set out for the "Fisherman's Home." "After having come so far, it would be absurd to go back without doing something in this business," thought he. "Polly, besides, is the brains carrier of these people. The matter would be referred to her; and why should I not go at once, and directly address her myself? With her womanly tact, too, she will see that for any reserve in my manner there must be a corresponding reason, and she'll not press me with awkward questions or painful inquiries, as the underbred brother might do. It will be enough when I intimate to her that my plan is not so practicable as when I first projected it." He reassured himself with a variety of reasonings of this stamp, which had the double effect of convincing his own mind and elevating Miss Polly in his estimation. There is a very subtle self-flattery in believing that the true order of person to deal with us—to understand and appreciate us—is one possessed of considerable ability united with the very finest sensibility. Thus dreaming and "mooning," he reached the "Fisherman's Home." The air of desertion struck him even as he landed; and is there not some secret magic in the vicinity of life, of living people, which gives the soul to the dwelling-place? Have we to more than cross the threshold of the forsaken house to feel its desertion,—to know that our echoing step will track us along stair and corridor, and that through the thin streaks of light between the shutters phantoms of the absent will flit or hover, while the dimly descried objects of the room will bring memories of bright mornings and of happy eves? It is strange to measure the sadness of this effect upon us when caused even by the aspect of houses which we frequented not as friends but mere visitors; just as the sight of death thrills us, even though we had not loved the departed in his lifetime. But so it is: there is unutterable bitterness attached to the past, and there is no such sorrow as over the bygone!

All about the little cottage was silent and desolate; even the shrill peacock, so wont to announce the coming stranger with his cry, sat voiceless and brooding on a branch; and except the dull flow of the river, not a sound was heard. After tapping lightly at the door and peering through the partially closed shutters, Conyers turned towards the garden at the back, passing as he went his favorite seat under the great sycamore-tree. It was not a widely separated "long ago" since he had sat there, and yet how different had life become to him in the interval! With what a protective air he had talked to poor Tom on that spot,—how princely were the promises of his patronage, yet not exaggerated beyond his conscious power of performance! He hurried on, and came to the little wicket of the garden; it was open, and he passed in. A spade in some fresh-turned earth showed where some one had recently been at work, but still, as he went, he could find none. Alley after alley did he traverse, but to no purpose; and at last, in his ramblings, he came to a little copse which separated the main garden from a small flower-plat, known as Miss Dinah's, and on which the windows of her own little sitting-room opened. He had but seen this spot from the windows, and never entered it; indeed, it was a sort of sacred enclosure, within which the profane step of man was not often permitted to intrude. Nor was Conyers without a sting of self-reproach as he now passed in. He had not gone many steps when the reason of the seclusion seemed revealed to him. It was a small obelisk of white marble under a large willow-tree, bearing for inscription on its side,

"To the Memory of George Barrington, the Truehearted, the Truthful, and the Brave, killed on the 19th February, 18—, at Agra, in the East Indies."

How strange that he should be standing there beside the tomb of his father's dearest friend, his more than brother! That George who shared his joys and perils, the comrade of his heart! No two men had ever lived in closer bonds of affection, and yet somehow of all that love he had never heard his father speak, nor of the terrible fate that befell his friend had one syllable escaped him. "Who knows if friendships ever survive early manhood?" said Fred, bitterly, as he sat himself down at the base of the monument: "and yet might not this same George Barrington, had he lived, been of priceless value to my father now? Is it not some such manly affection, such generous devotion as his, that he may stand in need of?" Thus thinking, his imagination led him over the wide sea to that far-distant land of his childhood, and scenes of vast arid plains and far-away mountains, and wild ghauts, and barren-looking nullahs, intersected with yellow, sluggish streams, on whose muddy shore the alligator basked, rose before him, contrasted with the gorgeous splendors of retinue and the glittering host of gold-adorned followers. It was in a vision of grand but dreary despotism, power almost limitless, but without one ray of enjoyment, that he lost himself and let the hours glide by. At length, as though dreamily, he thought he was listening to some faint but delicious music; sounds seemed to come floating towards him through the leaves, as if meant to steep him in a continued languor, and imparted a strange half-fear that he was under a spell. With an effort he aroused himself and sprang to his legs; and now he could plainly perceive that the sounds came through an open window, where a low but exquisitely sweet voice was singing to the accompaniment of a piano. The melody was sad and plaintive; the very words came dropping slowly, like the drops of a distilled grief; and they sank into his heart with a feeling of actual poignancy, for they were as though steeped in sorrow. When of a sudden the singer ceased, the hands ran boldly, almost wildly, over the keys; one, two, three great massive chords were struck, and then, in a strain joyous as the skylark, the clear voice carolled forth with,—

> "But why should we mourn for the grief of the morrow?
> Who knows in what frame it may find us?
> Meeker, perhaps, to bend under our sorrow,
> Or more boldly to fling it behind us."

And then, with a loud bang, the piano was closed, and Polly Dill, swinging her garden hat by its ribbon, bounded forth into the walk, calling for her terrier, Scratch, to follow.

"Mr. Conyers here!" cried she, in astonishment. "What miracle could have led you to this spot?"

"To meet you."

"To meet me!"

"With no other object. I came from Kilkenny this morning expressly to see you, and learning at your house that you had come on here, I followed. You still look astonished,—incredulous—"

"Oh, no; not incredulous, but very much astonished. I am, it is true, sufficiently accustomed to find myself in request in my own narrow home circle, but that any one out of it should come three yards—not to say three miles—to speak to me, is, I own, very new and very strange."

"Is not this profession of humility a little—a very little—bit of exaggeration, Miss Dill?"

"Is not the remark you have made on it a little—a very little—bit of a liberty, Mr. Conyers?"

So little was he prepared for this retort that he flushed up to his forehead, and for an instant was unable to recover himself: meanwhile, she was busy in rescuing Scratch from a long bramble that had most uncomfortably associated itself with his tail, in gratitude for which service the beast jumped up on her with all the uncouth activity of his race.

"He at least, Miss Dill, can take liberties unrebuked," said Conyers, with irritation.

"We are very old friends, sir, and understand each other's humors, not to say that Scratch knows well he 'd be tied up if he were to transgress."

Conyers smiled; an almost irresistible desire to utter a smartness crossed his mind, and he found it all but impossible to resist saying something about accepting the bonds if he could but accomplish the transgression; but he bethought in time how unequal the war of banter would be between them, and it was with a quiet gravity he began: "I came to speak to you about Tom—"

"Why, is that not all off? Colonel Hunter represented the matter so forcibly to my father, put all the difficulties so clearly before him, that I actually wrote to my brother, who had started for Dublin, begging him on no account to hasten the day of his examination, but to come home and devote himself carefully to the task of preparation."

"It is true, the Colonel never regarded the project as I did, and saw obstacles to its success which never occurred to me; with all that, however, he never convinced me I was wrong."

"Perhaps not always an easy thing to do," said she, dryly.

"Indeed! You seem to have formed a strong opinion on the score of my firmness."

"I was expecting you to say obstinacy," said she, laughing, "and was half prepared with a most abject retractation. At all events, I was aware that you did not give way."

"And is the quality such a bad one?"

"Just as a wind may be said to be a good or a bad one; due west, for instance, would be very unfavorable if you were bound to New York."

It was the second time he had angled for a compliment, and failed; and he walked along at her side, fretful and discontented. "I begin to suspect," said he, at last, "that the Colonel was far more eager to make himself agreeable here than to give fair play to my reasons."

"He was delightful, if you mean that; he possesses the inestimable boon of good spirits, which is the next thing to a good heart."

"You don't like depressed people, then?"

"I won't say I dislike, but I dread them. The dear friends who go about with such histories of misfortune and gloomy reflections on every one's conduct always give me the idea of a person who should carry with him a watering-pot to sprinkle his friends in this Irish climate, where it rains ten months out of the twelve. There is a deal to like in life,—a deal to enjoy, as well as a deal to see and to do; and the spirit which we bring to it is even of more moment than the incidents that befall us."

"That was the burden of your song awhile ago," said he, smiling; "could I persuade you to sing it again?"

"What are you dreaming of, Mr. Conyers? Is not this meeting here—this strolling about a garden with a young gentleman, a Hussar!—compromising enough, not to ask me to sit down at a piano and sing for him? Indeed, the only relief my conscience gives me for the imprudence of this interview is the seeing how miserable it makes *you*."

"Miserable!—makes *me* miserable!"

"Well, embarrassed,—uncomfortable,—ill at ease; I don't care for the word. You came here to say a variety of things, and you don't like to say them. You are balked in certain very kind intentions towards us, and you don't know how very little of even intended good nature has befallen us in life to make us deeply your debtor for the mere project. Why, your very notice of poor Tom has done more to raise him in his own esteem and disgust him with low associates than all the wise arguments of all his family. There, now, if you have not done us all the good you meant, be satisfied with what you really have done."

"This is very far short of what I intended."

"Of course it is; but do not dwell upon that. I have a great stock of very fine intentions, too, but I shall not be in the least discouraged if I find them take wing and leave me."

"What would you do then?"

"Raise another brood. They tell us that if one seed of every million of acorns should grow to be a tree, all Europe would be a dense forest within a century. Take heart, therefore, about scattered projects; fully their share of them come to maturity. Oh dear! what a dreary sigh you gave! Don't you imagine yourself very unhappy?"

"If I did, I'd scarcely come to you for sympathy, certainly," said he, with a half-bitter smile.

"You are quite right there; not but that I could really condole with some of what I opine are your great afflictions: for instance, I could bestow very honest grief on that splint that your charger has just thrown out on his back tendon; I could even cry over the threatened blindness of that splendid steeple-chaser; but I 'd not fret about the way your pelisse was braided, nor because your new phaeton made so much noise with the axles."

"By the way," said Conyers, "I have such a horse to show you! He is in the village. Might I drive him up here? Would you allow me to take you back?"

"Not on any account, sir! I have grave misgivings about talking to you so long here, and I am mainly reconciled by remembering how disagreeable I have proved myself."

"How I wish I had your good spirits!"

"Why don't you rather wish for my fortunate lot in life,—so secure from casualties, so surrounded with life's comforts, so certain to attach to it consideration and respect? Take my word for it, Mr. Conyers, your own position is not utterly wretched; it is rather a nice thing to be a Lieutenant of Hussars, with good health, a good fortune, and a fair promise of mustachios. There, now, enough of impertinence for one day. I have a deal to do, and you 'll not help me to do it. I have a whole tulip-bed to transplant, and several trees to remove, and a new walk to plan through the beech shrubbery, not to speak of a change of domicile for the pigs,—if such creatures can be spoken of in your presence. Only think, three o'clock, and that weary Darby not got back from his dinner! has it ever occurred to you to wonder at the interminable time people can devote to a meal of potatoes?"

"I cannot say that I have thought upon the matter."

"Pray do so, then; divide the matter, as a German would, into all its 'Bearbeitungen,' and consider it ethnologically, esculently, and aesthetically, and you'll be surprised how puzzled you 'll be! Meanwhile, would you do me a favor?—I mean a great favor."

"Of course I will; only say what it is."

"Well; but I 'm about to ask more than you suspect."

"I do not retract. I am ready."

"What I want, then, is that you should wheel that barrow-ful of mould as far as the melon-bed. I 'd have done it myself if you had not been here."

With a seriousness which cost him no small effort to maintain, Conyers addressed himself at once to the task; and she walked along at his side, with a rake over her shoulder, talking with the same cool unconcern she would have bestowed on Darby.

"I have often told Miss Barrington," said she, "that our rock melons were finer than hers, because we used a peculiar composite earth, into which ash bark and soot entered,—what you are wheeling now, in fact, however hurtful it may be to your feelings. There! upset it exactly on that spot; and now let me see if you are equally handy with a spade."

"I should like to know what my wages are to be after all this," said he, as he spread the mould over the bed.

"We give boys about eightpence a day."

"Boys! what do you mean by boys?"

"Everything that is not married is boy in Ireland; so don't be angry, or I 'll send you off. Pick up those stones, and throw these dock-weeds to one side."

"You 'll send me a melon, at least, of my own raising, won't you?"

"I won't promise; Heaven knows where you'll be—where I 'll be, by that time! Would *you* like to pledge yourself to anything on the day the ripe fruit shall glow between those pale leaves?"

"Perhaps I might," said he, stealing a half-tender glance towards her.

"Well, I would not," said she, looking him full and steadfastly in the face.

"Then that means you never cared very much for any one?"

"If I remember aright, you were engaged as a gardener, not as father confessor. Now, you are really not very expert at the former; but you 'll make sad work of the latter."

"You have not a very exalted notion of my tact, Miss Dill."

"I don't know,—I'm not sure; I suspect you have at least what the French call 'good dispositions.' You took to your wheelbarrow very nicely, and you tried to dig—as little like a gentleman as need be."

"Well, if this does not bate Banagher, my name is n't Darby!" exclaimed a rough voice, and a hearty laugh followed his words. "By my conscience, Miss Polly, it's only yerself could do it; and it's truth they say of you, you 'd get fun out of an archdaycon!"

Conyers flung away his spade, and shook the mould from his boots in irritation.

"Come, don't be cross," said she, slipping her arm within his, and leading him away; "don't spoil a very pleasant little adventure by ill humor. If these melons come to good, they shall be called after you. You know that a Duke of Montmartre gave his name to a gooseberry; so be good, and, like him, you shall be immortal."

"I should like very much to know one thing," said he, thoughtfully.

"And what may that be?"

"I 'd like to know,—are you ever serious?"

"Not what you would call serious, perhaps; but I 'm very much in earnest, if that will do. That delightful Saxon habit of treating all trifles with solemnity I have no taste for. I'm aware it constitutes that great idol of English veneration, Respectability; but we have not got that sort of thing here. Perhaps the climate is too moist for it."

"I 'm not a bit surprised that the Colonel fell in love with you," blurted he out, with a frank abruptness.

"And did he,—oh, really did he?"

"Is the news so very agreeable, then?"

"Of course it is. I 'd give anything for such a conquest. There 's no glory in capturing one of those calf elephants who walk into the snare out of pure stupidity; but to catch an old experienced creature who has been hunted scores of times, and knows every scheme and artifice, every bait and every pitfall, there is a real triumph in that."

"Do I represent one of the calf elephants, then?"

"I cannot think so. I have seen no evidence of your capture—not to add, nor any presumption of my own—to engage in such a pursuit. My dear Mr. Conyers," said she, seriously, "you have shown so much real kindness to the brother, you would not, I am certain, detract from it by one word which could offend the sister. We have been the best of friends up to this; let us part so."

The sudden assumption of gravity in this speech seemed to disconcert him so much that he made no answer, but strolled along at her side, thoughtful and silent.

"What are you thinking of?" said she, at last.

"I was just thinking," said he, "that by the time I have reached my quarters, and begin to con over what I have accomplished by this same visit of mine, I 'll be not a little puzzled to say what it is."

"Perhaps I can help you. First of all, tell me what was your object in coming."

"Chiefly to talk about Tom."

"Well, we have done so. We have discussed the matter, and are fully agreed it is better he should not go to India, but stay at home here and follow his profession, like his father."

"But have I said nothing about Hunter's offer?"

"Not a word; what is it?"

"How stupid of me; what could I have been thinking of all this time?"

"Heaven knows; but what was the offer you allude to?"

"It was this: that if Tom would make haste and get his diploma or his license, or whatever it is, at once, and collect all sorts of testimonials as to his abilities and what not, that he'd take him out with him and get him an assistant-surgeoncy in a regiment, and in time, perhaps, a staff-appointment."

"I 'm not very certain that Tom could obtain his diploma at once. I 'm quite sure he could n't get any of those certificates you speak of. First of all, because he does not possess these same abilities you mention, nor, if he did, is there any to vouch for them. We are very humble people, Mr. Conyers, with a village for our world; and we contemplate a far-away country— India, for instance—pretty much as we should do Mars or the Pole-star."

"As to that, Bengal is more come-at-able than the Great Bear," said he, laughing.

"For you, perhaps, not for us. There is nothing more common in people's mouths than go to New Zealand or Swan River, or some far-away island in the Pacific, and make your fortune!—just as if every new and barbarous land was a sort of Aladdin's cave, where each might fill his pockets with gems and come out rich for life. But reflect a little. First, there is an outfit; next, there is a voyage; thirdly, there is need of a certain subsistence in the new country before plans can be matured to render it profitable. After all these come a host of requirements,—of courage, and energy, and patience, and ingenuity, and personal strength, and endurance, not to speak of the constitution of a horse, and some have said, the heartlessness of an ogre. *My* counsel to Tom would be, get the 'Arabian Nights' out of your head, forget the great Caliph Conyers and all his promises, stay where you are, and be a village apothecary."

These words were uttered in a very quiet and matter-of-fact way, but they wounded Conyers more than the accents of passion. He was angry at the cold realistic turn of a mind so devoid of all heroism; he was annoyed at the half-implied superiority a keener view of life than his own seemed to assert; and he was vexed at being treated as a well-meaning but very inconsiderate and inexperienced young gentleman.

"Am I to take this as a refusal," said he, stiffly; "am I to tell Colonel Hunter that your brother does not accept his offer?"

"If it depended on me,—yes; but it does not. I 'll write to-night and tell Tom the generous project that awaits him; he shall decide for himself."

"I know Hunter will be annoyed; he'll think it was through some bungling mismanagement of mine his plan has failed; he 'll be certain to say, If it was I myself bad spoken toner—"

"Well, there's no harm in letting him think so," said she, laughing. "Tell him I think him charming, that I hope he 'll have a delightful voyage and a most prosperous career after it, that I intend to read the Indian columns in the newspaper from this day out, and will always picture him to my mind as seated in the grandest of howdabs on the very tallest of elephants, humming 'Rule Britannia' up the slopes of the Himalaya, and as the penny-a-liners say, extending the blessings of the English rule in India." She gave her hand to him, made a little salutation,—half bow, half courtesy,—and, saying "Good-bye," turned back into the shrubbery and left him.

He hesitated,—almost turned to follow her; waited a second or two more, and then, with an impatient toss of his head, walked briskly to the river-side and jumped into his boat. It was a sulky face that he wore, and a sulky spirit was at work within him. There is no greater discontent than that of him who cannot define the chagrin that consumes him. In reality, he was angry with himself, but he turned the whole force of his displeasure upon her.

"I suppose she is clever. I 'm no judge of that sort of thing; but, for my own part, I'd rather see her more womanly, more delicate. She has not a bit of heart, that's quite clear; nor, with all her affectations, does she pretend it." These were his first meditations, and after them he lit a cigar and smoked it. The weed was a good one; the evening was beautifully calm and soft, and the river scenery looked its very best. He tried to think of a dozen things: he imagined, for instance, what a picturesque thing a boat-race would be in such a spot; he fancied he saw a swift gig sweep round the point and head up the stream; he caught sight of a little open in the trees with a background of dark rock, and he thought what a place for a cottage. But whether it was the "match" or the "chalet" that occupied him, Polly Dill was a figure in the picture; and he muttered unconsciously, "How pretty she is, what a deal of expression those gray-blue eyes possess! She's as active as a fawn, and to the full as graceful. Fancy her an Earl's daughter; give her station and all the advantages station will bring with it,—what a girl it would be! Not that she'd ever have a heart; I'm certain of that. She's as worldly—as worldly as—" The exact similitude did not occur; but he flung the end of his cigar into the river instead, and sat brooding mournfully for the rest of the way.

CHAPTER XXV
DUBLIN REVISITED

The first stage of the Barringtons' journey was Dublin. They alighted at Reynolds's Hotel, in Old Dominick Street, the once favorite resort of country celebrities. The house, it is true, was there, but Reynolds had long left for a land where there is but one summons and one reckoning; even the old waiter, Foster, whom people believed immortal, was gone; and save some cumbrous old pieces of furniture,—barbarous relics of bad taste in mahogany,—nothing recalled the past. The bar, where once on a time the "Beaux" and "Bloods" had gathered to exchange the smart things of the House or the hunting-field, was now a dingy little receptacle for umbrellas and overcoats, with a rickety case crammed full of unacknowledged and unclaimed letters, announcements of cattle fairs, and bills of houses to let. Decay and neglect were on everything, and the grim little waiter who ushered them upstairs seemed as much astonished at their coming as were they themselves with all they saw. It was not for some time, nor without searching inquiry, that Miss Dinah discovered that the tide of popular favor had long since retired from this quarter, and left it a mere barren strand, wreck-strewn and deserted. The house where formerly the great squire held his revels had now fallen to be the resort of the traveller by canal-boat, the cattle salesman, or the priest. While she by an ingenious cross-examination was eliciting these details, Barrington had taken a walk through the city to revisit old scenes and revive old memories. One needs not to be as old as Peter Barrington to have gone through this process and experienced all its pain. Unquestionably, every city of Europe has made within such a period as five-and-thirty or forty years immense strides of improvement. Wider and finer streets, more commodious thoroughfares, better bridges, lighter areas, more brilliant shops, strike one on every hand; while the more permanent monuments of architecture are more cleanly, more orderly, and more cared for than of old. We see these things with astonishment and admiration at first, and then there comes a pang of painful regret,—not for the old dark alley and the crooked street, or the tumbling arch of long ago,—but for the time when they were there, for the time when they entered into our daily life, when with them were associated friends long lost sight of, and scenes dimly fading away from memory. It is for our youth, for the glorious spring and elasticity of our once high-hearted spirit, of our lives so free of care, of our days undarkened by a serious sorrow,—it is for these we mourn, and to our eyes at such moments the spacious street is but a desert, and the splendid monument but a whitened sepulchre!

"I don't think I ever had a sadder walk in my life, Dinah," said Peter Barrington, with a weary sigh. "'Till I got into the courts of the College, I never chanced upon a spot that looked as I had left it. There, indeed, was the quaint old square as of old, and the great bell—bless it for its kind voice!—was ringing out a solemn call to something, that shook the window-frames, and made the very air tremulous; and a pale-faced student or two hurried past, and those centurions in the helmets,—ancient porters or Senior Fellows,—I forget which,—stood in a little knot to stare at me. That, indeed, was like old times, Dinah, and my heart grew very full with the memory. After that I strolled down to the Four Courts. I knew you'd laugh, Dinah. I knew well you'd say, 'Was there nothing going on in the King's Bench or the Common Pleas?' Well, there was only a Revenue case, my dear, but it was interesting, very interesting; and there was my old friend Harry Bushe sitting as the Judge. He saw me, and sent round the tipstaff to have me come up and sit on the bench with him, and we had many a pleasant remembrance of old times—as the cross-examination went on—between us, and I promised to dine with him on Saturday."

"And on Saturday we will dine at Antwerp, brother, if I know anything of myself."

"Sure enough, sister, I forgot all about it Well, well, where could my head have been?"

"Pretty much where you have worn it of late years, Peter Barrington. And what of Withering? Did you see him?"

"No, Dinah, he was attending a Privy Council; but I got his address, and I mean to go over to see him after dinner."

"Please to bear in mind that you are not to form any engagements, Peter,—we leave this to-morrow evening by the packet,—if it was the Viceroy himself that wanted your company."

"Of course, dear, I never thought of such a thing. It was only when Harry said, 'You'll be glad to meet Casey and Burrowes, and a few others of the old set,' I clean forgot everything of the present, and only lived in the long-past time, when life really was a very jolly thing."

"How did you find your friend looking?"

"Old, Dinah, very old! That vile wig has, perhaps, something to say to it; and being a judge, too, gives a sternness to the mouth and a haughty imperiousness to the brow. It spoils Harry; utterly spoils that laughing blue eye, and that fine rich humor that used to play about his lips."

"Which *did*, you ought to say,—which did some forty years ago. What are you laughing at, Peter? What is it amuses you so highly?"

"It was a charge of O'Grady's, that Harry told me,—a charge to one of those petty juries that, he says, never will go right, do what you may. The case was a young student of Trinity, tried for a theft, and whose defence was only by witnesses to character, and O'Grady said, 'Gentlemen of the jury, the issue before you is easy enough. This is a young gentleman of pleasing manners and the very best connections, who stole a pair of silk stockings, and you will find accordingly.' And what d'ye think, Dinah? They acquitted him, just out of compliment to the Bench."

"I declare, brother Peter, such a story inspires any other sentiment than mirth to me."

"I laughed at it till my sides ached," said he, wiping his eyes. "I took a peep into the Chancery Court and saw O'Connell, who has plenty of business, they tell me. He was in some altercation with the Court. Lord Manners was scowling at him, as if he hated him. I hear that no day passes without some angry passage between them."

"And is it of these jangling, quarrelsome, irritable, and insolent men your ideal of agreeable society is made up, brother Peter?"

"Not a doubt of it, Dinah. All these displays are briefed to them. They cannot help investing in their client's cause the fervor of their natures, simply because they are human; but they know how to leave all the acrimony of the contest in the wig-box, when they undress and come back to their homes,— the most genial, hearty, and frank fellows in all the world. If human nature were all bad, sister, he who saw it closest would be, I own, most like to catch its corruption, but it is not so, far from it. Every day and every hour reveals something to make a man right proud of his fellow-men."

Miss Barrington curtly recalled her brother from these speculations to the practical details of their journey, reminding him of much that he had to consult Withering upon, and many questions of importance to put to him. Thoroughly impressed with the perils of a journey abroad, she conjured up a vast array of imaginary difficulties, and demanded special instructions how each of them was to be met. Had poor Peter been—what he certainly was not—a most accomplished casuist, he might have been puzzled by the ingenious complexity of some of those embarrassments. As it was, like a man in the labyrinth, too much bewildered to attempt escape, he sat down in a dogged insensibility, and actually heard nothing.

"Are you minding me, Peter?" asked she, fretfully, at last; "are you paying attention to what I am saying?"

"Of course I am, Dinah dear; I'm listening with all ears."

"What was it, then, that I last remarked? What was the subject to which I asked your attention?"

Thus suddenly called on, poor Peter started and rubbed his forehead. Vague shadows of passport people, and custom-house folk, and waiters, and money-changers, and brigands; insolent postilions, importunate beggars, cheating innkeepers, and insinuating swindlers were passing through his head, with innumerable incidents of the road; and, trying to catch a clew at random, he said, "It was to ask the Envoy, her Majesty's Minister at Brussels, about a washerwoman who would not tear off my shirt buttons—eh, Dinah? wasn't that it?"

"You are insupportable, Peter Barrington," said she, rising in anger. "I believe that insensibility like this is not to be paralleled!" and she left the room in wrath.

Peter looked at his watch, and was glad to see it was past eight o'clock, and about the hour he meant for his visit to Withering. He set out accordingly, not, indeed, quite satisfied with the way he had lately acquitted himself, but consoled by thinking that Dinah rarely went back of a morning on the dereliction of the evening before, so that they should meet good friends as ever at the breakfast-table. Withering was at home, but a most discreet-looking butler intimated that he had dined that day tête-à-tête with a gentleman, and had left orders not to be disturbed on any pretext "Could you not at least, send in my name?" said Barrington; "I am a very old friend of your master's, whom he would regret not having seen." A little persuasion aided by an argument that butlers usually succumb to succeeded, and before Peter believed that his card could have reached its destination, his friend was warmly shaking him by both hands, as he hurried him into the dinner-room.

"You don't know what an opportune visit you have made me, Barrington," said he; "but first, to present you to my friend, Captain Stapylton—or Major—which is it?"

"Captain. This day week, the 'Gazette,' perhaps, may call me Major."

"Always a pleasure to me to meet a soldier, sir," said Barrington; "and I own to the weakness of saying, all the greater when a Dragoon. My own boy was a cavalryman."

"It was exactly of him we were talking," said Withering; "my friend here has had a long experience of India, and has frankly told me much I was totally ignorant of. From one thing to another we rambled on till we came to discuss our great suit with the Company, and Captain Stapylton assures me that we have never taken the right road in the case."

"Nay, I could hardly have had such presumption; I merely remarked, that without knowing India and its habits, you could scarcely be prepared to encounter the sort of testimony that would be opposed to you, or to benefit by what might tend greatly in your favor."

"Just so—continue," said Withering, who looked as though he had got an admirable witness on the table.

"I'm astonished to hear from the Attorney-General," resumed Stapylton, "that in a case of such magnitude as this you have never thought of sending out an efficient agent to India to collect evidence, sift testimony, and make personal inquiry as to the degree of credit to be accorded to many of the witnesses. This inquisitorial process is the very first step in every Oriental suit; you start at once, in fact, by sapping all the enemy's works,—countermining him everywhere."

"Listen, Barrington,—listen to this; it is all new to us."

"Everything being done by documentary evidence, there is a wide field for all the subtlety of the linguist; and Hindostanee has complexities enough to gratify the most inordinate appetite for quibble. A learned scholar—a Moonshee of erudition—is, therefore, the very first requisite, great care being taken to ascertain that he is not in the pay of the enemy."

"What rascals!" muttered Barrington.

"Very deep—very astute dogs, certainly, but perhaps not much more unprincipled than some fellows nearer home," continued the Captain, sipping his wine; "the great peculiarity of this class is, that while employing them in the most palpably knavish manner, and obtaining from them services bought at every sacrifice of honor, they expect all the deference due to the most umblemished integrity."

"I'd see them—I won't say where—first," broke out Barrington; "and I 'd see my lawsuit after them, if only to be won by their intervention."

"Remember, sir," said Stapylton, calmly, "that such are the weapons employed against you. That great Company does not, nor can it afford to, despise such auxiliaries. The East has its customs, and the natures of men are not light things to be smoothed down by conventionalities. Were you, for instance, to measure a testimony at Calcutta by the standard of Westminster Hall, you would probably do a great and grievous injustice."

"Just so," said Withering; "you are quite right there, and I have frequently found myself posed by evidence that I felt must be assailable. Go on, and tell my friend what you were mentioning to me before he came in."

"I am reluctant, sir," said Stapylton, modestly, "to obtrude upon you, in a matter of such grand importance as this, the mere gossip of a mess-table, but, as allusion has been made to it, I can scarcely refrain. It was when serving in another Presidency an officer of ours, who had been long in Bengal, one night entered upon the question of Colonel Barrington's claims. He quoted the words of an uncle—I think he said his uncle—who was a member of the Supreme Council, and said, 'Barrington ought to have known we never could have conceded this right of sovereignty, but he ought also to have known that we would rather have given ten lacs of rupees than have it litigated.'"

"Have you that gentleman's name?" asked Barrington, eagerly.

"I have; but the poor fellow is no more,—he was of that fatal expedition to Beloochistan eight years ago."

"You know our case, then, and what we claim?" asked Barrington.

"Just as every man who has served in India knows it,—popularly, vaguely. I know that Colonel Barrington was, as the adopted son of a Rajah, invested with supreme power, and only needed the ratification of Great Britain to establish a sovereignty; and I have heard"—he laid stress on the word "heard"—"that if it had not been for some allegation of plotting against the Company's government, he really might ultimately have obtained that sanction."

"Just what I have said over and over again?" burst in Barrington. "It was the worst of treachery that mined my poor boy."

"I have heard that also," said Stapylton, and with a degree of feeling and sympathy that made the old man's heart yearn towards him.

"How I wish you had known him!" said he, as he drew his hand over his eyes. "And do you know, sir," said he, warming, "that if I still follow up this suit, devoting to it the little that is left to me of life or fortune, that I do so less for any hope of gain than to place my poor boy before the world with his honor and fame unstained."

"My old friend does himself no more than justice there!" cried Withering.

"A noble object,—may you have all success in it!" said Stapylton. He paused, and then, in a tone of deeper feeling, added: "It will, perhaps, seem a great liberty, the favor I'm about to ask; but remember that, as a brother soldier with your son I have some slight claim to approach you. Will you allow me to offer you such knowledge as I possess of India, to aid your suit? Will you associate me, in fact, with your cause? No higher one could there be than the vindication of a brave man's honor."

"I thank you with all my heart and soul!" cried the old man, grasping his hand. "In my own name, and in that of my poor dear granddaughter, I thank you."

"Oh, then, Colonel Barrington has left a daughter? I was not aware of that," said Stapylton, with a certain coldness.

"And a daughter who knows no more of this suit than of our present discussion of it," said Withering.

In the frankness of a nature never happier than when indulging its own candor, Barrington told how it was to see and fetch back with him the same granddaughter he had left a spot he had not quitted for years. "She's coming back to a very humble home, it is true; but if you, sir," said he, addressing Stapylton, "will not despise such lowly fare as a cottage can afford you, and would condescend to come and see us, you shall have the welcome that is due to one who wishes well to my boy's memory."

"And if you do," broke in Withering, "you'll see the prettiest cottage and the first hostess in Europe; and here's to her health,—Miss Dinah Barrington!"

"I'm not going to refuse that toast, though I have just passed the decanter," said Peter. "Here's to the best of sisters!"

"Miss Barrington!" said Stapylton, with a courteous bow; and he drained his glass to the bottom.

"And that reminds me I promised to be back to tea with her," said Barrington; and renewing with all warmth his invitation to Stapylton, and cordially taking leave of his old friend, he left the house and hastened to his hotel.

"What a delightful evening I have passed, Dinah!" said he, cheerfully, as he entered.

"Which means that the Attorney-General gave you a grand review and sham fight of all the legal achievements of the term; but bear in mind, brother, there is no professional slang so odious to me as the lawyer's, and I positively hate a joke which cost six-and-eightpence, or even three-and-fourpence."

"Nothing of this kind was there at all, Dinah! Withering had a friend with him, a very distinguished soldier, who had seen much Indian service, and entered with a most cordial warmth into poor George's case. He knew it,—as all India knows it, by report,—and frankly told us where our chief difficulties lay, and the important things we were neglecting."

"How generous! of a perfect stranger too!" said she, with a scarcely detectable tone of scorn.

"Not—so to say—an utter stranger, for George was known to him by reputation and character."

"And who is, I suppose I am to say, your friend, Peter?"

"Captain or Major Stapylton, of the Regent's Hussars?"

"Oh! I know him,—or, rather, I know of him."

"What and how, Dinah? I am very curious to hear this."

"Simply, that while young Conyers was at the cottage he showed me a letter from that gentleman, asking him in the Admiral's name, to Cobham, and containing, at the same time, a running criticism on the house and his guests far more flippant than creditable."

"Men do these things every day, Dinah, and there is no harm in it."

"That all depends upon whom the man is. The volatile gayety of a high-spirited nature, eager for effect and fond of a sensation, will lead to many an indiscretion; but very different from this is the well-weighed sarcasm of a more serious mind, who not only shots his gun home, but takes time to sight ere he fires it. I hear that Captain Stapylton is a grand, cold, thoughtful man, of five or six-and-thirty. Is that so?"

"Perhaps he may be. He 's a splendid fellow to look at, and all the soldier. But you shall see for yourself, and I 'll warrant you 'll not harbor a prejudice against him."

"Which means, you have asked him on a visit, brother Peter?"

"Scarcely fair to call it on a visit, Dinah," blundered he out, in confusion; "but I have said with what pleasure we should see him under our roof when we returned."

"I solemnly declare my belief, that if you went to a cattle-show you 'd invite every one you met there, from the squire to the pig-jobber, never thinking the while that nothing is so valueless as indiscriminate hospitality, even if it were not costly. Nobody thanks you,—no one is grateful for it."

"And who wants them to be grateful, Dinah? The pleasure is in the giving, not in receiving. You see your friends with their holiday faces on, when they sit round the table. The slowest and dreariest of them tries to look cheery; and the stupid dog who has never a jest in him has at least a ready laugh for the wit of his neighbor."

"Does it not spoil some of your zest for this pleasantry to think how it is paid for, brother?"

"It might, perhaps, if I were to think of it; but, thank Heaven! it's about one of the last things would come into my head. My dear sister, there's no use in always treating human nature as if it was sick, for if you do, it will end by being hypochondriac!"

"I protest, brother Peter, I don't know where you meet all the good and excellent people you rave about, and I feel it very churlish of you that you never present any of them to *me!*" And so saying, she gathered her knitting materials hastily together, and reminding him that it was past eleven o'clock, she uttered a hurried good-night, and departed.

CHAPTER XXVI
A VERY SAD GOOD-BYE

Conyers sat alone in his barrack-room, very sad and dispirited. Hunter had left that same morning, and the young soldier felt utterly friendless. He had obtained some weeks' leave of absence, and already two days of the leave had gone over, and he had not energy to set out if he had even a thought as to the whither. A variety of plans passed vaguely through his head. He would go down to Portsmouth and see Hunter off; or he would nestle down in the little village of Inistioge and dream away the days in quiet forgetfulness; or he would go over to Paris, which he had never seen, and try whether the gay dissipations of that brilliant city might not distract and amuse him. The mail from India had arrived and brought no letter from his father, and this, too, rendered him irritable and unhappy. Not that his father was a good correspondent; he wrote but rarely, and always like one who snatched a hurried moment to catch a post. Still, if this were a case of emergency, any great or critical event in his life, he was sure his father would have informed him; and thus was it that he sat balancing doubt against doubt, and setting probability against probability, till his very head grew addled with the labor of speculation.

It was already late; all the usual sounds of barrack life had subsided, and although on the opposite side of the square the brilliant lights of the mess-room windows showed where the convivial spirits of the regiment were assembled, all around was silent and still. Suddenly there came a dull heavy knock to the door, quickly followed by two or three others.

Not caring to admit a visitor, whom, of course, he surmised would be some young brother-officer full of the plans and projects of the mess, he made no reply to the summons, nor gave any token of his presence. The sounds, however, were redoubled, and with an energy that seemed to vouch for perseverance; and Conyers, partly in anger, and partly in curiosity, went to the door and opened it. It was not till after a minute or two that he was able to recognize the figure before him. It was Tom Dill, but without a hat or neckcloth, his hair dishevelled, his face colorless, and his clothes torn, while from a recent wound in one hand the blood flowed fast, and dropped on the floor. The whole air and appearance of the young fellow so resembled drunkenness that Conyers turned a stern stare upon him as he stood in the centre of the room, and in a voice of severity said, "By what presumption, sir, do you dare to present yourself in this state before me?"

"You think I'm drunk, sir, but I am not," said he, with a faltering accent and a look of almost imploring misery.

"What is the meaning of this state, then? What disgraceful row have you been in?"

"None, sir. I have cut my hand with the glass on the barrack-wall, and torn my trousers too; but it's no matter, I 'll not want them long."

"What do you mean by all this? Explain yourself."

"May I sit down, sir, for I feel very weak?" but before the permission could be granted, his knees tottered, and he fell in a faint on the floor. Conyers knelt down beside him, bathed his temples with water, and as soon as signs of animation returned, took him up in his arms and laid him at full length on a sofa.

In the vacant, meaningless glance of the poor fellow as he looked first around him, Conyers could mark how he was struggling to find out where he was.

"You are with me, Tom,—with your friend Conyers," said he, holding the cold clammy hand between his own.

"Thank you, sir. It is very good of you. I do not deserve it," said he, in a faint whisper.

"My poor boy, you mustn't say that; I am your friend. I told you already I would be so."

"But you 'll not be my friend when I tell you—when I tell you—all;" and as the last word dropped, he covered his face with both his hands, and burst into a heavy passion of tears.

"Come, come, Tom, this is not manly; bear up bravely, bear up with courage, man. You used to say you had plenty of pluck if it were to be tried."

"So I thought I had, sir, but it has all left me;" and he sobbed as if his heart was breaking. "But I believe I could bear anything but this," said he, in a voice shaken by convulsive throes. "It is the disgrace,—that 's what unmans me."

"Take a glass of wine, collect yourself, and tell me all about it."

"No, sir. No wine, thank you; give me a glass of water. There, I am better now; my brain is not so hot. You are very good to me, Mr. Conyers, but it 's the last time I'll ever ask it,—the very last time, sir; but I 'll remember it all my life."

"If you give way in this fashion, Tom, I 'll not think you the stout-hearted fellow I once did."

"No, sir, nor am I. I 'll never be the same again. I feel it here. I feel as if something gave, something broke." And he laid his hand over his heart and sighed heavily.

"Well, take your own time about it, Tom, and let me hear if I cannot be of use to you."

"No, sir, not now. Neither you nor any one else can help me now. It's all over, Mr. Conyers,—it's all finished."

"What is over,—what is finished?"

"And so, as I thought it would n't do for one like me to be seen speaking to you before people, I stole away and climbed over the barrack-wall. I cut my hand on the glass, too, but it's nothing. And here I am, and here's the money you gave me; I've no need of it now." And as he laid some crumpled bank-notes on the table, his overcharged heart again betrayed him, and he burst into tears. "Yes, sir, that's what you gave me for the College, but I was rejected."

"Rejected, Tom! How was that? Be calm, my poor fellow, and tell me all about it quietly."

"I'll try, sir, I will, indeed; and I'll tell you nothing but the truth, that you may depend upon." He took a great drink of water, and went on. "If there was one man I was afraid of in the world, it was Surgeon Asken, of Mercer's Hospital. I used to be a dresser there, and he was always angry with me, exposing me before the other students, and ridiculing me, so that if anything was done badly in the wards, he 'd say, 'This is some of Master Dill's work, is n't it?' Well, sir, would you believe it, on the morning I went up for my examination, Dr. Coles takes ill, and Surgeon Asken is called on to replace him. I did n't know it till I was sent for to go in, and my head went round, and I could n't see, and a cold sweat came over me, and I was so confused that when I got into the room I went and sat down beside the examiners, and never knew what they were laughing at.

"'I have no doubt, Mr. Dill, you 'll occupy one of these places at some future day,' says Dr. Willes, 'but for the present your seat is yonder.' I don't remember much more after that, till Mr. Porter said, 'Don't be so nervous, Mr. Dill; collect yourself; I am persuaded you know what I am asking you, if you will not be flurried.' And all I could say was, 'God bless you for that speech, no matter how it goes with me' and they all laughed out.

"It was Asken's turn now, and he began. 'You are destined for the navy, I understand, sir?'

"'No, sir; for the army,' said I.

"'From what we have seen to-day, you 'll prove an ornament to either service. Meanwhile, sir, it will be satisfactory to the court to have your opinion on gun-shot wounds. Describe to us the case of a man laboring under the worst form of concussion of the brain, and by what indications you would distinguish it from fracture of the base of the skull, and what circumstances might occur to render the distinction more difficult, and what impossible?' That was his question, and if I was to live a hundred years I 'll never forget a word in it,—it's written on my heart, I believe, for life.

"'Go on, sir,' said he, 'the court is waiting for you.'

"'Take the case of concussion first,' said Dr. Willes.

"'I hope I may be permitted to conduct my own examination in my own manner,' said Asken.

"That finished me, and I gave a groan that set them all laughing again.

"'Well, sir, I 'm waiting,' said Asken. 'You can have no difficulty to describe concussion, if you only give us your present sensations.'

"'That's as true as if you swore it,' said I. 'I 'm just as if I had a fall on the crown of my head. There's a haze over my eyes, and a ringing of bells in my ears, and a feeling as if my brain was too big.'

"'Take my word for it, Mr. Dill,' said he, sneeringly, 'the latter is a purely deceptive sensation; the fault lies in the opposite direction. Let us, however, take something more simple;' and with that he described a splinter wound of the scalp, with the whole integuments torn in fragments, and gunpowder and sticks and sand all mixed up with the flap that hung down over the patient's face. 'Now,' said he, after ten minutes' detail of this,—'now,' said he, 'when you found the man in this case, you 'd take out your scalpel, perhaps, and neatly cut away all these bruised and torn integuments?'

"'I would, sir,' cried I, eagerly.

"'I knew it,' said he, with a cry of triumph,—'I knew it. I 've no more to ask you. You may retire.'

"I got up to leave the room, but a sudden flash went through me, and I said out boldly,—

"'Am I passed? Tell me at once. Put me out of pain, for I can't bear any more!'

"'If you'll retire for a few minutes,' said the President—

"'My heart will break, sir,' said I, 'if I'm to be in suspense any more. Tell me the worst at once.'

"And I suppose they did tell me, for I knew no more till I found myself in the housekeeper's room, with wet cloths on my head, and the money you see there in the palm of my hand. *That* told everything. Many were very kind to me, telling how it happened to this and to that man, the first time; and that Asken was thought very unfair, and so on; but I just washed my face with cold water, and put on my hat and went away home, that is, to where I lodged, and I wrote to Polly just this one line: 'Rejected; I'm not coming back.' And then I shut the shutters and went to bed in my clothes as I was, and I slept sixteen hours without ever waking. When I awoke, I was all right. I could n't remember everything that happened for some time, but I knew it all at last, and so I went off straight to the Royal Barracks and 'listed."

"Enlisted?—enlisted?"

"Yes, sir, in the Forty-ninth Regiment of Foot, now in India, and sending off drafts from Cork to join them on Tuesday. It was out of the dépôt at the bridge I made my escape to-night to come and see you once more, and to give you this with my hearty blessing, for you were the only one ever stood to me in the world,—the only one that let me think for a moment I *could* be a gentleman!"

"Come, come, this is all wrong and hasty and passionate, Tom. You have no right to repay your family in this sort; this is not the way to treat that fine-hearted girl who has done so much for you; this is but an outbreak of angry selfishness."

"These are hard words, sir, very hard words, and I wish you had not said them."

"Hard or not, you deserve them; and it is their justice that wounds you."

"I won't say that it is *not*, sir. But it isn't justice I'm asking for, but forgiveness. Just one word out of your mouth to say, 'I'm sorry for you, Tom;' or, 'I wish you well.'"

"So I do, my poor fellow, with all my heart," cried Con-yers, grasping his hand and pressing it cordially, "and I'll get you out of this scrape, cost what it may."

"If you mean, sir, that I am to get my discharge, it's better to tell the truth at once. I would n't take it. No, sir, I'll stand by what I've done. I see I never could be a doctor, and I have my doubts, too, if I ever could be a gentleman; but there's something tells me I could be a soldier, and I'll try."

Conyers turned from him with an impatient gesture, and walked the room in moody silence.

"I know well enough, sir," continued Tom, "what every one will say; perhaps you yourself are thinking it this very minute: 'It's all out of his love of low company he's gone and done this; he's more at home with those poor ignorant boys there than he would be with men of education and good manners.' Perhaps it's true, perhaps it is 'n't! But there's one thing certain, which is, that I'll never try again to be anything that I feel is clean above me, and I'll not ask the world to give me credit for what I have not the least pretension to."

"Have you reflected," said Conyers, slowly, "that if you reject my assistance now, it will be too late to ask for it a few weeks, or even a few days hence?"

"I *have* thought of all that, sir. I'll never trouble you about myself again."

"My dear Tom," said Conyers, as he laid his arm on the other's shoulder, "just think for one moment of all the misery this step will cause your sister,— that kind, true-hearted sister, who has behaved so nobly by you."

"I have thought of that, too, sir; and in my heart I believe, though she 'll fret herself at first greatly, it will all turn out best in the end. What could I ever be but a disgrace to her? Who 'd ever think the same of Polly after seeing *me*? Don't I bring her down in spite of herself; and is n't it a hard trial for her to be a lady when I am in the same room with her? No, sir, I'll not go back; and though I haven't much hope in me, I feel I'm doing right."

"I know well," said Conyers, pettishly, "that your sister will throw the whole blame on me. She 'll say, naturally enough, *You* could have obtained his discharge,—*you* should have insisted on his leaving."

"That's what you could not, sir," said Tom, sturdily. "It's a poor heart hasn't some pride in it; and I would not go back and meet my father, after my disgrace, if it was to cost me my right hand,—so don't say another word about it. Good-bye, sir, and my blessing go with you wherever you are. I 'll never forget how you stood to me."

"That money there is yours, Dill," said Conyers, half haughtily. "You may refuse my advice and reject my counsel, but I scarcely suppose you 'll ask me to take back what I once have given."

Tom tried to speak, but he faltered and moved from one foot to the other, in an embarrassed and hesitating way. He wanted to say how the sum originally intended for one object could not honestly be claimed for another; he wanted to say, also, that he had no longer the need of so much money, and that the only obligation he liked to submit to was gratitude for the past; but a consciousness that in attempting to say these things some unhappy word, some ill-advised or ungracious expression might escape him, stopped him, and he was silent.

"You do not wish that we should part coldly, Tom?"

"No, sir,—oh, no!" cried he, eagerly.

"Then let not that paltry gift stand in the way of our esteem. Now, another thing. Will you write to me? Will you tell me how the world fares with you, and honestly declare whether the step you have taken to-day brings with it regret or satisfaction?"

"I'm not over-much of a letter-writer," said he, falter-ingly, "but I'll try. I must be going, Mr. Conyers," said he, after a moment's silence; "I must get back before I'm missed."

"Not as you came, Tom, however. I'll pass you out of the barrack-gate."

As they walked along side by side, neither spoke till they came close to the gate; then Conyers halted and said, "Can you think of nothing I can do for you, or is there nothing you would leave to my charge after you have gone?"

"No, sir, nothing." He paused, and then, as if with a struggle, said, "Except you 'd write one line to my sister Polly, to tell her that I went away in good heart, that I did n't give in one bit, and that if it was n't for thinking that maybe I 'd never see her again—" He faltered, his voice grew thick, he tried to cough down the rising emotion, but the feeling overcame him, and he burst out into tears. Ashamed at the weakness he was endeavoring to deny, he sprang through the gate and disappeared.

Conyers slowly returned to his quarters, very thoughtful and very sad.

CHAPTER XXVII
THE CONVENT ON THE MEUSE

While poor Tom Dill, just entering upon life, went forth in gloom and disappointment to his first venture, old Peter Barrington, broken by years and many a sorrow, set out on his journey with a high heart and a spirit well disposed to see everything in its best light and be pleased with all around him. Much of this is, doubtless, matter of temperament; but I suspect, too, that all of us have more in our power in this way than we practise. Barrington had possibly less merit than his neighbors, for nature had given him one of those happy dispositions upon which the passing vexations of life produce scarcely any other effect than a stimulus to humor, or a tendency to make them the matter of amusing memory.

He had lived, besides, so long estranged from the world, that life had for him all the interests of a drama, and he could no more have felt angry with the obtrusive waiter or the roguish landlord than he would with their fictitious representatives on the stage. They were, in his eyes, parts admirably played, and no more; he watched them with a sense of humorous curiosity, and laughed heartily at successes of which he was himself the victim. Miss Barrington was no disciple of this school; rogues to her were simply rogues, and no histrionic sympathies dulled the vexation they gave her. The world, out of which she had lived so long, had, to her thinking, far from improved in the mean while. People were less deferential, less courteous than of old. There was an indecent haste and bustle about everything, and a selfish disregard of one's neighbor was the marked feature of all travel. While her brother repaid himself for many an inconvenience by thinking over some strange caprice, or some curious inconsistency in human nature, — texts for amusing afterthought, — she only winced under the infliction, and chafed at every instance of cheating or impertinence that befell them.

The wonderful things she saw, the splendid galleries rich in art, the gorgeous palaces, the grand old cathedrals, were all marred to her by the presence of the loquacious lackey whose glib tongue had to be retained at the salary of the "vicar of our parish," and who never descanted on a saint's tibia without costing the price of a dinner; so that old Peter at last said to himself, "I believe my sister Dinah would n't enjoy the garden of Eden if Adam had to go about and show her its beauties."

The first moment of real enjoyment of her tour was on that morning when they left Namur to drive to the Convent of Bramaigne, about three miles off, on the banks of the Meuse. A lovelier day never shone upon a lovelier scene. The river, one side guarded by lofty cliffs, was on the other bounded by a succession of rich meadows, dotted with picturesque homesteads half hidden in trees. Little patches of cultivation, labored to the perfection of a garden, varied the scene, and beautiful cattle lay lazily under the giant trees, solemn voluptuaries of the peaceful happiness of their lot.

Hitherto Miss Dinah had stoutly denied that anything they had seen could compare with their own "vale and winding river," but now she frankly owned that the stream was wider, the cliffs higher, the trees taller and better grown, while the variety of tint in the foliage far exceeded all she had any notion of; but above all these were the evidences of abundance, the irresistible charm that gives the poetry to peasant life; and the picturesque cottage, the costume, the well-stored granary, bespeak the condition with which we associate our ideas of rural happiness. The giant oxen as they marched proudly to their toil, the gay-caparisoned pony who jingled his bells as he trotted by, the peasant girls as they sat at their lace cushions before the door, the rosy urchins who gambolled in the deep grass, all told of plenty,—that blessing which to man is as the sunlight to a landscape, making the fertile spots more beautiful, and giving even to ruggedness an aspect of stern grandeur.

"Oh, brother Peter, that we could see something like this at home," cried she. "See that girl yonder watering the flowers in her little garden,—how prettily that old vine is trained over the balcony,—mark the scarlet tassels in the snow-white team,—are not these signs of an existence not linked to daily drudgery? I wish our people could be like these."

"Here we are, Dinah: there is the convent!" cried Barrington, as a tall massive roof appeared over the tree-tops, and the little carriage now turned from the high-road into a shady avenue of tall elms. "What a grand old place it is! some great seigniorial château once on a time."

As they drew nigh, nothing bespoke the cloister. The massive old building, broken by many a projection and varied by many a gable, stood, like the mansion of some rich proprietor, in a vast wooded lawn. The windows lay open, the terrace was covered with orange and lemon trees and flowering plants, amid which seats were scattered; and in the rooms within, the furniture indicated habits of comfort and even of luxury. With all this, no living thing was to be seen; and when Barrington got down and entered the hall, he neither found a servant nor any means to summon one.

"You'll have to move that little slide you see in the door there," said the driver of the carriage, "and some one will come to you."

He did so; and after waiting a few moments, a somewhat ruddy, cheerful face, surmounted by a sort of widow's cap, appeared, and asked his business.

"They are at dinner, but if you will enter the drawing-room she will come to you presently."

They waited for some time; to them it seemed very long, for they never spoke, but sat there in still thoughtfulness, their hearts very full, for there was much in that expectancy, and all the visions of many a wakeful night or dreary day might now receive their shock or their support. Their patience was to be further tested; for, when the door opened, there entered a grim-looking little woman in a nun's costume, who, without previous salutation, announced herself as Sister Lydia. Whether the opportunity for expansiveness was rare, or that her especial gift was fluency, never did a little old woman hold forth more volubly. As though anticipating all the worldly objections to a conventual existence, or rather seeming to suppose that every possible thing had been actually said on that ground, she assumed the defence the very moment she sat down. Nothing short of long practice with this argument could have stored her mind with all her instances, her quotations, and her references. Nor could anything short of a firm conviction have made her so courageously indifferent to the feelings she was outraging, for she never scrupled to arraign the two strangers before her for ignorance, apathy, worldliness, sordid and poor ambitions, and, last of all, a levity unbecoming their time of life.

"I 'm not quite sure that I understand her aright," whispered Peter, whose familiarity with French was not what it had once been; "but if I do, Dinah, she 's giving us a rare lesson."

"She's the most insolent old woman I ever met in my life," said his sister, whose violent use of her fan seemed either likely to provoke or to prevent a fit of apoplexy.

"It is usual," resumed Sister Lydia, "to give persons who are about to exercise the awful responsibility now devolving upon you the opportunity of well weighing and reflecting over the arguments I have somewhat faintly shadowed forth."

"Oh, not faintly!" groaned Barrington.

But she minded nothing the interruption, and went on,—

"And for this purpose a little tract has been composed, entitled 'A Word to the Worldling.' This, with your permission, I will place in your hands. You will there find at more length than I could bestow—But I fear I impose upon this lady's patience?"

"It has left me long since, madam," said Miss Dinah, as she actually gasped for breath.

In the grim half-smile of the old nun might be seen the triumphant consciousness that placed her above the "mundane;" but she did not resent the speech, simply saying that, as it was the hour of recreation, perhaps she would like to see her young ward in the garden with her companions.

"By all means. We thank you heartily for the offer," cried Barrington, rising hastily.

With another smile, still more meaningly a reproof, Sister Lydia reminded him that the profane foot of a man had never transgressed the sacred precincts of the convent garden, and that he must remain where he was.

"For Heaven's sake! Dinah, don't keep me a prisoner here a moment longer than you can help it," cried he, "or I'll not answer for my good behavior."

As Barrington paced up and down the room with impatient steps, he could not escape the self-accusation that all his present anxiety was scarcely compatible with the long, long years of neglect and oblivion he had suffered to glide over.

The years in which he had never heard of Josephine—never asked for her—was a charge there was no rebutting. Of course he could fall back upon all that special pleading ingenuity and self-love will supply about his own misfortunes, the crushing embarrassments that befell him, and such like. But it was no use, it was desertion, call it how he would; and poor as he was he had never been without a roof to shelter her, and if it had not been for false pride he would have offered her that refuge long ago. He was actually startled as he thought over all this. Your generous people, who forgive injuries with little effort, who bear no malice nor cherish any resentment, would be angels—downright angels—if we did not find that they are just as indulgent, just as merciful to themselves as to the world at large. They become perfect adepts in apologies, and with one cast of the net draw in a whole shoal of attenuating circumstances. To be sure, there will now and then break in upon them a startling suspicion that all is not right, and that conscience has been "cooking" the account; and when such a moment does come, it is a very painful one.

"Egad!" muttered he to himself, "we have been very heartless all this time, there's no denying it; and if poor George's girl be a disciple of that grim old woman with the rosary and the wrinkles, it is nobody's fault but our own." He looked at his watch; Dinah had been gone more than half an hour. What a time to keep him in suspense! Of course there were formalities,—the Sister Lydia described innumerable ones,—jail delivery was nothing to it, but surely five-and-thirty minutes would suffice to sign a score of documents. The place was becoming hateful to him. The grand old park, with its aged oaks, seemed sad as a graveyard, and the great silent house, where not a footfall sounded, appeared a tomb. "Poor child! what a dreary spot you have spent your brightest years in,—what a shadow to throw over the whole of a lifetime!"

He had just arrived at that point wherein his granddaughter arose before his mind a pale, careworn, sorrow-struck girl, crushed beneath the dreary monotony of a joyless life, and seeming only to move in a sort of dreamy melancholy, when the door opened, and Miss Barrington entered with her arm around a young girl tall as herself, and from whose commanding figure even the ungainly dress she wore could not take away the dignity.

"This is Josephine, Peter," said Miss Dinah; and though Barrington rushed forward to clasp her in his arms, she merely crossed hers demurely on her breast and courtesied deeply.

"It is your grandpapa, Josephine," said Miss Dinah, half tartly.

The young girl opened her large, full, lustrous eyes, and stared steadfastly at him, and then, with infinite grace, she took his hand and kissed it.

"My own dear child," cried the old man, throwing his arms around her, "it is not homage, it is your love we want."

"Take care, Peter, take care," whispered his sister; "she is very timid and very strange."

"You speak English, I hope, dear?" said the old man.

"Yes, sir, I like it best," said she. And there was the very faintest possible foreign accent in the words.

"Is n't that George's own voice, Dinah? Don't you think you heard himself there?"

"The voice is certainly like him," said Miss Dinah, with a marked emphasis.

"And so are—no, not her eyes, but her brow, Dinah. Yes, darling, you have his own frank look, and I feel sure you have his own generous nature."

"They say I'm like my mother's picture," said she, unfastening a locket she wore from its chain and handing it. And both Peter and his sister gazed eagerly at the miniature. It was of a very dark but handsome woman in a rich turban, and who, though profusely ornamented with costly gems, did, in reality, present a resemblance to the cloistered figure before them.

"Am I like her?" asked the girl, with a shade more of earnestness in her voice.

"You are, darling; but like your father, too, and every word you utter brings back his memory; and see, Dinah, if that is n't George's old trick,—to lay one hand in the palm of the other."

As if corrected, the young girl dropped her arms to her sides and stood like a statue.

"Be like him in everything, dearest child," said the old man, "if you would have my heart all your own."

"I must be what I am," said she, solemnly.

"Just so, Josephine; well said, my good girl. Be natural," said Miss Dinah, kissing her, "and our love will never fail you."

There was the faintest little smile of acknowledgment to this speech; but faint as it was, it dimpled her cheek, and seemed to have left a pleasant expression on her face, for old Peter gazed on her with increased delight as he said, "That was George's own smile; just the way he used to look, half grave, half merry. Oh, how you bring him back tome!"

"You see, my dear child, that you are one of us; let us hope you will share in the happiness this gives us."

The girl listened attentively to Miss Dinah's words, and after a pause of apparent thought over them, said, "I will hope so."

"May we leave this, Dinah? Are we free to get away?" whispered Barrington to his sister, for an unaccountable oppression seemed to weigh on him, both from the place and its belongings.

"Yes; Josephine has only one good-bye to say; her trunks are already on the carriage, and there is nothing more to detain us."

"Go and say that farewell, dear child," said he, affectionately; "and be speedy, for there are longing hearts here to wish for your return."

With a grave and quiet mien she walked away, and as she gained the door turned round and made a deep, respectful courtesy,—a movement so ceremonious that the old man involuntarily replied to it by a bow as deep and reverential.

CHAPTER XXVIII
GEORGE'S DAUGHTER

I suppose, nay, I am certain, that the memory of our happiest moments ought ever to be of the very faintest and weakest, since, could we recall them in all their fulness and freshness, the recollection would only serve to deepen the gloom of age, and imbitter all its daily trials. Nor is it, altogether, a question of memory! It is in the very essence of happiness to be indescribable. Who could impart in words the simple pleasure he has felt as he lay day-dreaming in the deep grass, lulled by the humming insect, or the splash of falling water, with teeming fancy peopling the space around, and blending the possible with the actual? The more exquisite the sense of enjoyment, the more will it defy delineation. And so, when we come to describe the happiness of others, do we find our words weak, and our attempt mere failure.

It is in this difficulty that I now find myself. I would tell, if I could, how enjoyably the Barringtons sauntered about through the old villages on the Rhine and up the Moselle, less travelling than strolling along in purposeless indolence, resting here, and halting there, always interested, always pleased. It was strange into what perfect harmony these three natures—unlike as they were—blended!

Old Peter's sympathies went with all things human, and he loved to watch the village life and catch what he could of its ways and instincts. His sister, to whom the love of scenery was a passion, never wearied of the picturesque land they travelled; and as for Josephine, she was no longer the demure pensionnaire of the convent,—thoughtful and reserved, even to secrecy,—but a happy child, revelling in a thousand senses of enjoyment, and actually exulting in the beauty of all she saw around her. What depression must come of captivity, when even its faintest image, the cloister, could have weighed down a heart like hers! Such was Barrington's thought as he beheld her at play with the peasant children, weaving garlands for a village *fête*, or joyously joining the chorus of a peasant song. There was, besides, something singularly touching in the half-consciousness of her freedom, when recalled for an instant to the past by the tinkling bell of a church. She would seem to stop in her play, and bethink her how and why she was there, and then, with a cry of joy, bound away after her companions in wild delight.

"Dearest aunt," said she, one day, as they sat on a rocky ledge over the little river that traverses the Lahnech, "shall I always find the same enjoyment in life that I feel now, for it seems to me this is a measure of happiness that could not endure?"

"Some share of this is owing to contrast, Fifine. Your convent life had not too many pleasures."

"It was, or rather it seems to me now, as I look back, a long and weary dream; but, at the same time, it appears more real than this; for do what I may I cannot imagine this to be the world of misery and sorrow I have heard so much of. Can any one fancy a scene more beautiful than this before us? Where is the perfume more exquisite than these violets I now crush in my hand? The peasants, as they salute us, look happy and contented. Is it, then, only in great cities that men make each other miserable?"

Dinah shook her head, but did not speak.

"I am so glad grandpapa does not live in a city. Aunt, I am never wearied of hearing you talk of that dear cottage beside the river; and through all my present delight I feel a sense of impatience to be there, to be at 'home.'"

"So that you will not hold us to our pledge to bring you back to Bramaigne, Fifine," said Miss Dinah, smiling.

"Oh no, no! Not if you will let me live with you. Never!"

"But you have been happy up to this, Fifine? You have said over and over again that your convent life was dear to you, and all its ways pleasant."

"It is just the same change to me to live as I now do, as in my heart I feel changed after reading out one of those delightful stories to grandpapa,— Rob Roy, for instance. It all tells of a world so much more bright and beautiful than I know of, that it seems as though new senses were given to me. It is so strange and so captivating, too, to hear of generous impulses, noble devotion,—of faith that never swerved, and love that never faltered.

"In novels, child; these were in novels."

"True, aunt; but they had found no place there had they been incredible; at least, it is clear that he who tells the tale would have us believe it to be true."

Miss Dinah had not been a convert to her brother's notions as to Fifine's readings; and she was now more disposed to doubt than ever. To overthrow of a sudden, as though by a great shock, all the stem realism of a cloister existence, and supply its place with fictitious incidents and people, seemed rash and perilous; but old Peter only thought of giving a full liberty to the imprisoned spirit,—striking off chain and fetter, and setting the captive free,—free in all the glorious liberty of a young imagination.

"Well, here comes grandpapa," said Miss Dinah, "and, if I don't mistake, with a book in his hand for one of your morning readings."

Josephine ran eagerly to meet him, and, fondly drawing her arm within his own, came back at his side.

"The third volume, Fifine, the third volume," said he, holding the book aloft. "Only think, child, what fates are enclosed within a third volume! What a deal of happiness or long-living misery are here included!"

She straggled to take the book from his hand, but he evaded her grasp, and placed it in his pocket, saying,—

"Not till evening, Fifine. I am bent on a long ramble up the Glen this morning, and you shall tell me all about the sisterhood, and sing me one of those little Latin canticles I'm so fond of."

"Meanwhile, I 'll go and finish my letter to Polly Dill. I told her, Peter, that by Thursday next, or Friday, she might expect us."

"I hope so, with all my heart; for, beautiful as all this is, it wants the greatest charm,—it's not home! Then I want, besides, to see Fifine full of household cares."

"Feeding the chickens instead of chasing the butterflies, Fifine. Totting up the house-bills, in lieu of sighing over 'Waverley.'"

"And, if I know Fifine, she will be able to do one without relinquishing the other," said Peter, gravely. "Our daily life is all the more beautiful when it has its landscape reliefs of light and shadow."

"I think I could, too," cried Fifine, eagerly. "I feel as though I could work in the fields and be happy, just in the conscious sense of doing what it was good to do, and what others would praise me for."

"There's a paymaster will never fail you in such hire," said Miss Dinah, pointing to her brother; and then, turning away, she walked back to the little inn. As she drew nigh, the landlord came to tell her that a young gentleman, on seeing her name in the list of strangers, had made many inquiries after her, and begged he might be informed of her return. On learning that he was in the garden, she went thither at once.

"I felt it was you. I knew who had been asking for me, Mr. Conyers," said she, advancing towards Fred with her hand out. "But what strange chance could have led you here?"

"You have just said it, Miss Barrington; a chance,—a mere chance. I had got a short leave fron I my regiment, and came abroad to wander about with no very definite object; but, growing impatient of the wearisome hordes of our countrymen on the Rhine, I turned aside yesterday from that great high-road and reached this spot, whose greatest charm—shall I own it?—was a fancied resemblance to a scene I loved far better."

"You are right. It was only this morning my brother said it was so like our own cottage."

"And he is here also?" said the young man, with a half-constraint.

"Yes, and very eager to see you, and ask your forgive ness for his ungracious manner to you; not that I saw it, or understand what it could mean, but he says that he has a pardon to crave at your hands."

So confused was Conyers for an instant that he made no answer, and when he did speak it was falteringly and with embarrassment, "I never could have anticipated meeting you here. It is more good fortune than I ever looked for."

"We came over to the Continent to fetch away my grand-niece, the daughter of that Colonel Barrington you have heard so much of."

"And is she—" He stopped, and grew scarlet with confusion; but she broke in, laughingly,—

"No, not black, only dark-complexioned; in fact, a brunette, and no more."

"Oh, I don't mean,—I surely could not have said—"

"No matter what you meant or said. Your unuttered question was one that kept occurring to my brother and myself every morning as we journeyed here, though neither of us had the courage to speak it. But our wonders are over; she is a dear good, girl, and we love her better every day we see her. But now a little about yourself. Why do I find you so low and depressed?"

"I have had much to fret me, Miss Barrington. Some were things that could give but passing unhappiness; others were of graver import."

"Tell me so much as you may of them, and I will try to help you to bear up against them."

"I will tell you all,—everything!" cried he. "It is the very moment I have been longing for, when I could pour out all my cares before you and ask, What shall I do?"

Miss Barrington silently drew her arm within his, and they strolled along the shady alley without a word.

"I must begin with my great grief,—it absorbs all the rest," said he, suddenly. "My father is coming home; he has lost, or thrown up, I can't tell which, his high employment. I have heard both versions of the story; and his own few words, in the only letter he has written me, do not confirm either. His tone is indignant; but far more it is sad and depressed,—he who never wrote a line but in the joyousness of his high-hearted nature; who met each accident of life with an undaunted spirit, and spurned the very thought of being cast down by fortune. See what he says here." And he took a much crumpled letter from his pocket, and folded down a part of it "Read that. 'The time for men of my stamp is gone by in India. We are as much bygones as the old flint musket or the matchlock. Soldiers of a different temperament are the fashion now; and the sooner we are pensioned or die off the better. For my own part, I am sick of it. I have lost my liver and have not made my fortune, and like men who have missed their opportunities, I come away too discontented with myself to think well of any one. They fancied that by coldness and neglect they might get rid of me, as they did once before of a far worthier and better fellow; but though I never had the courage that he had, they shall not break *my* heart.' Does it strike you to whom he alludes there?" asked Conyers, suddenly; "for each time that I read the words I am more disposed to believe that they refer to Colonel Barrington."

"I am sure of it!" cried she. "It is the testimony of a sorrow-stricken heart to an old friend's memory; but I hear my brother's voice; let me go and tell him you are here." But Barrington was already coming towards them.

"Ah, Mr. Conyers!" cried he. "If you knew how I have longed for this moment! I believe you are the only man in the world I ever ill treated on my own threshold; but the very thought of it gave me a fit of illness, and now the best thing I know on my recovery is, that I am here to ask your pardon."

"I have really nothing to forgive. I met under your roof with a kindness that never befell me before; nor do I know the spot on earth where I could look for the like to-morrow."

"Come back to it, then, and see if the charm should not be there still."

"Where 's Josephine, brother?" asked Miss Barrington, who, seeing the young man's agitation, wished to change the theme.

"She's gone to put some ferns in water; but here she comes now."

Bounding wildly along, like a child in joyous freedom, Josephine came towards them, and, suddenly halting at sight of a stranger, she stopped and courtesied deeply, while Conyers, half ashamed at his own unhappy blunder about her, blushed deeply as he saluted her. Indeed, their meeting was more like that of two awkward timid children than of two young persons of their age; and they eyed each other with the distrust school boys and girls exchange on a first acquaintance.

"Brother, I have something to tell you," said Miss Barrington, who was eager to communicate the news she had just heard of General Conyers; and while she drew him to one side, the young people still stood there, each seeming to expect the other would make some advance towards acquaintanceship. Conyers tried to say some commonplace,—some one of the fifty things that would have occurred so naturally in presence of a young lady to whom he had been just presented; but he could think of none, or else those that *he* thought of seemed inappropriate. How talk, for instance, of the world and its pleasures to one who had been estranged from it! While he thus struggled and contended with himself, she suddenly started as if with a flash of memory, and said, "How forgetful!"

"Forgetful!—and of what?" asked he.

"I have left the book I was reading to grandpapa on the rock where we were sitting. I must go and fetch it."

"May I go with you?" asked he, half timidly.

"Yes, if you like."

"And your book,—what was it?"

"Oh, a charming book,—such a delightful story! So many people one would have loved to know!—such scenes one would have loved to visit!—incidents, too, that keep the heart in intense anxiety, that you wonder how he who imagined them could have sustained the thrilling interest, and held his own heart so long in terrible suspense!"

"And the name of this wonderful book is—"

"'Waverley.'"

"I have read it," said he, coldly.

"And have you not longed to be a soldier? Has not your heart bounded with eagerness for a life of adventure and peril?"

"I am a soldier," said he, quietly.

"Indeed!" replied she, slowly, while her steadfast glance scanned him calmly and deliberately.

"You find it hard to recognize as a soldier one dressed as I am, and probably wonder how such a life as this consorts with enterprise and danger. Is not that what is passing in your mind?"

"Mayhap," said she, in a low voice.

"It is all because the world has changed a good deal since Waverley's time."

"How sorry I am to hear it!"

"Nay, for your sake it is all the better. Young ladies have a pleasanter existence now than they had sixty years since. They lived then lives of household drudgery or utter weariness."

"And what have they now?" asked she, eagerly.

"What have they not! All that can embellish life is around them; they are taught in a hundred ways to employ the faculties which give to existence its highest charm. They draw, sing, dance, ride, dress becomingly, read what may give to their conversation an added elegance and make their presence felt as an added lustre."

"How unlike all this was our convent life!" said she, slowly. "The beads in my rosary were not more alike than the days that followed each other, and but for the change of season I should have thought life a dreary sleep. Oh, if you but knew what a charm there is in the changeful year to one who lives in any bondage!"

"And yet I remember to have heard how you hoped you might not be taken away from that convent life, and be compelled to enter the world," said he, with a malicious twinkle of the eye.

"True; and had I lived there still I had not asked for other. But how came it that you should have heard of me? I never heard of *you!*"

"That is easily told. I was your aunt's guest at the time she resolved to come abroad to see you and fetch you home. I used to hear all her plans about you, so that at last—I blush to own—I talked of Josephine as though she were my sister."

"How strangely cold you were, then, when we met!" said she, quietly. "Was it that you found me so unlike what you expected?"

"Unlike, indeed!"

"Tell me how—tell me, I pray you, what you had pictured me."

"It was not mere fancy I drew from. There was a miniature of you as a child at the cottage, and I have looked at it till I could recall every line of it."

"Go on!" cried she, as he hesitated.

"The child's face was very serious,—actually grave for childhood,—and had something almost stern in its expression; and yet I see nothing of this in yours."

"So that, like grandpapa," said she, laughing, "you were disappointed in not finding me a young tiger from Bengal; but be patient, and remember how long it is since I left the jungle."

Sportively as the words were uttered, her eyes flashed and her cheek colored, and Conyers saw for the first time how she resembled her portrait in infancy.

"Yes," added she, as though answering what was passing in his mind, "you are thinking just like the sisters, 'What years and years it would take to discipline one of such a race!' I have heard that given as a reason for numberless inflictions. And now, all of a sudden, comes grandpapa to say, 'We love you so because you are one of us.' Can you understand this?"

"I think I can,—that is, I think I can understand why—" he was going to add, "why they should love you;" but he stopped, ashamed of his own eagerness.

She waited a moment for him to continue, and then, herself blushing, as though she had guessed his embarrassment, she turned away.

"And this book that we have been forgetting,—let us go and search for it," said she, walking on rapidly in front of him; but he was speedily at her side again.

"Look there, brother Peter,—look there!" said Miss Dinah, as she pointed after them, "and see how well fitted we are to be guardians to a young lady!"

"I see no harm in it, Dinah,—I protest, I see no harm in it."

"Possibly not, brother Peter, and it may only be a part of your system for making her—as you phrase it—feel a holy horror of the convent."

"Well," said he, meditatively, "he seems a fine, frank-hearted young fellow, and in this world she is about to enter, her first experiences might easily be worse."

"I vow and declare," cried she, warmly, "I believe it is your slipshod philosophy that makes me as severe as a holy inquisitor!"

"Every evil calls forth its own correction, Dinah," said he, laughing. "If there were no fools to skate on the Serpentine, there had been no Humane Society."

"One might grow tired of the task of resuscitating, Peter Barrington," said she, hardly.

"Not you, not you, Dinah,—at least, if I was the drowned man," said he, drawing her affectionately to his side; "and as for those young creatures yonder, it's like gathering dog-roses, and they 'll stop when they have pricked their fingers."

"I'll go and look after the nosegay myself," said she, turning hastily away, and following them.

A real liking for Conyers, and a sincere interest in him were the great correctives to the part of Dragon which Miss Dinah declared she foresaw to be her future lot in life. For years and years had she believed that the cares of a household and the rule of servants were the last trials of human patience. The larder, the dairy, and the garden were each of them departments with special opportunities for deception and embezzlement, and it seemed to her that new discoveries in roguery kept pace with the inventions of science; but she was energetic and active, and kept herself at what the French would call "the level of the situation;" and neither the cook nor the dairymaid nor Darby could be vainglorious over their battles with her. And now, all of a sudden, a new part was assigned her, with new duties, functions, and requirements; and she was called on to exercise qualities which had lain long dormant and in disuse, and renew a knowledge she had not employed for many a year. And what a strange blending of pleasure and pain must have come of that memory of long ago! Old conquests revived, old rivalries and jealousies and triumphs; glorious little glimpses of brilliant delight, and some dark hours, too, of disappointment,—almost despair!

"Once a bishop, always a bishop," says the canon; but might we not with almost as much truth say, "Once a beauty, always a beauty"?—not in lineament and feature, in downy cheek or silky tresses, but in the heartfelt consciousness of a once sovereign power, in that sense of having been able to exact a homage and enforce a tribute. And as we see in the deposed monarch how the dignity of kingcraft clings to him, how through all he does and says there runs a vein of royal graciousness as from one the fount of honor, so it is with beauty. There lives through all its wreck the splendid memory of a despotism the most absolute, the most fascinating of all!

"I am so glad that young Conyers has no plans, Dinah," said Barrington; "he says he will join us if we permit him."

"Humph!" said Miss Barrington, as she went on with her knitting.

"I see nothing against it, sister."

"Of course not, Peter," said she, snappishly; "it would surprise me much if you did."

"Do *you*, Dinah?" asked he, with a true simplicity of voice and look.

"I see great danger in it, if that be what you mean. And what answer did you make him, Peter?"

"The same answer that I make to every one,—I would consult my sister Dinah. 'Le Roi s'avisera' meant, I take it, that he 'd be led by a wiser head than his own."

"He was wise when he knew it," said she, sententiously, and continued her work.

And from that day forth they all journeyed together, and one of them was very happy, and some were far more than happy; and Aunt Dinah was anxious even beyond her wont.

CHAPTER XXIX
THE RAMBLE

Day after day, week after week rolled on, and they still rambled about among the picturesque old villages on the Moselle, almost losing themselves in quaint unvisited spots, whose very names were new to them. To Barrington and his sister this picture of a primitive peasant life, with its own types of costume and custom, had an indescribable charm. Though debarred, from his ignorance of their dialect, of anything like intercourse with the people, he followed them in their ways with intense interest, and he would pass hours in the market-place, or stroll through the fields watching the strange culture, and wondering at the very implements of their labor. And the young people all this while? They were never separate. They read, and walked, and sat together from dawn to dark. They called each other Fifine and Freddy. Sometimes she sang, and he was there to listen; sometimes he drew, and she was as sure to be leaning over him in silent wonder at his skill; but with all this there was no love-making between them,—that is, no vows were uttered, no pledges asked for. Confidences, indeed, they interchanged, and without end. She told the story of her friendless infancy, and the long dreary years of convent life passed in a dull routine that had almost barred the heart against a wish for change; and he gave her the story of his more splendid existence, charming her imagination with a picture of that glorious Eastern life, which seemed to possess an instinctive captivation for her. And at last he told her, but as a great secret never to be revealed, how his father and her own had been the dearest, closest friends; that for years and years they had lived together like brothers, till separated by the accidents of life. *Her* father went away to a long distant station, and *his* remained to hold a high military charge, from which he was now relieved and on his way back to Europe. "What happiness for you, Freddy," cried she, as her eyes ran over, "to see him come home in honor! What had I given that such a fate were mine!"

For an instant he accepted her words in all their flattery, but the hypocrisy was brief; her over-full heart was bursting for sympathy, and he was eager to declare that his sorrows were scarcely less than her own. "No, Fifine," said he, "my father is coming back to demand satisfaction of a Government that has wronged him, and treated him with the worst ingratitude. In that Indian life men of station wield an almost boundless power; but if they are irresponsible as to the means, they are tested by the results, and whenever an adverse issue succeeds they fall irrevocably. What my father may have done, or have left undone, I know not. I have not the vaguest clew to his present difficulty, but, with his high spirit and his proud heart, that he would resent the very shadow of a reproof I can answer for, and so I believe, what many tell me, that it is a mere question of personal feeling,—some small matter in which the Council have not shown him the deference he felt his due, but which his haughty nature would not forego."

Now these confidences were not love-making, nor anything approaching to it, and yet Josephine felt a strange half-pride in thinking that she had been told a secret which Conyers had never revealed to any other; that to her he had poured forth the darkest sorrow of his heart, and actually confided to her the terrors that beset him, for he owned that his father was rash and headstrong, and if he deemed himself wronged would be reckless in his attempt at justification.

"You do not come of a very patient stock, then," said she, smiling.

"Not very, Fifine."

"Nor I," said she, as her eyes flashed brightly. "My poor Ayah, who died when I was but five years old, used to tell me such tales of my father's proud spirit and the lofty way he bore himself, so that I often fancy I have seen him and heard him speak. You have heard he was a Rajah?" asked she, with a touch of pride.

The youth colored deeply as he muttered an assent, for he knew that she was ignorant of the details of her father's fate, and he dreaded any discussion of her story.

"And these Rajahs," resumed she, "are really great princes, with power of life and death, vast retinues, and splendid armies. To my mind, they present a more gorgeous picture than a small European sovereignty with some vast Protectorate looming over it. And now it is my uncle," said she, suddenly, "who rules there."

"I have heard that your own claims, Fifine, are in litigation," said he, with a faint smile.

"Not as to the sovereignty," said she, with a grave look, half rebukeful of his levity. "The suit grandpapa prosecutes in my behalf is for my mother's jewels and her fortune; a woman cannot reign in the Tannanoohr."

There was a haughty defiance in her voice as she spoke, that seemed to say, "This is a theme I will not suffer to be treated lightly,—beware how you transgress here."

"And yet it is a dignity would become you well," said he, seriously.

"It is one I would glory to possess," said she, as proudly.

"Would you give me a high post, Fifine, if you were on the throne?—would you make me Commander-in-Chief of your army?"

"More likely that I would banish you from the realm," said she, with a haughty laugh; "at least, until you learned to treat the head of the state more respectfully."

"Have I ever been wanting in a proper deference?" said he, bowing, with a mock humility.

"If you had been, sir, it is not now that you had first heard of it," said she, with a proud look, and for a few seconds it seemed as though their jesting was to have a serious ending. She was, however, the earliest to make terms, and in a tone of hearty kindliness said: "Don't be angry, Freddy, and I 'll tell you a secret. If that theme be touched on, I lose my head: whether it be in the blood that circles in my veins, or in some early teachings that imbued my childhood, or long dreaming over what can never be, I cannot tell, but it is enough to speak of these things, and at once my imagination becomes exalted and my reason is routed."

"I have no doubt your Ayah was to blame for this; she must have filled your head with ambitions, and hopes of a grand hereafter. Even I myself have some experiences of this sort; for as my father held a high post and was surrounded with great state and pomp, I grew at a very early age to believe myself a very mighty personage, and gave my orders with despotic insolence, and suffered none to gainsay me."

"How silly!" said she, with a supercilious toss of her head that made Conyers flush up; and once again was peace endangered between them.

"You mean that what was only a fair and reasonable assumption in *you* was an absurd pretension in me, Miss Barrington; is it not so?" asked he, in a voice tremulous with passion.

"I mean that we must both have been very naughty children, and the less we remember of that childhood the better for us. Are we friends, Freddy?" and she held out her hand.

"Yes, if you wish it," said he, taking her hand half coldly in his own.

"Not that way, sir. It is *I* who have condescended; not *you*."

"As you please, Fifine,—will this do?" and kneeling with well-assumed reverence, he lifted her hand to his lips.

"If my opinion were to be asked, Mr. Conyers, I would say it would *not* do at all," said Miss Dinah, coming suddenly up, her cheeks crimson, and her eyes flashing.

"It was a little comedy we were acting, Aunt Dinah," said the girl, calmly.

"I beg, then, that the piece may not be repeated," said she, stiffly.

"Considering how ill Freddy played his part, aunt, he will scarcely regret its withdrawal."

Conyers, however, could not get over his confusion, and looked perfectly miserable for very shame.

"My brother has just had a letter which will call us homeward, Mr. Conyers," said Miss Dinah, turning to him, and now using a tone devoid of all irritation. "Mr. Withering has obtained some information which may turn out of great consequence in our suit, and he wishes to consult with my brother upon it."

"I hope—I sincerely hope—you do not think—" he began, in a low voice.

"I do not think anything to your disadvantage, and I hope I never may," replied she, in a whisper low as his own; "but bear in mind, Josephine is no finished coquette like Polly Dill, nor must she be the mark of little gallantries, however harmless. Josephine, grandpapa has some news for you; go to him."

"Poor Freddy," whispered the girl in the youth's ear as she passed, "what a lecture you are in for!" "You mustn't be angry with me if I play Duenna a little harshly, Mr. Conyers," said Miss Dinah; "and I am far more angry with myself than you can be. I never concurred with my brother that romance reading and a young dragoon for a companion were the most suitable educational means for a young lady fresh from a convent, and I have only myself to blame for permitting it."

Poor Conyers was so overwhelmed that he could say nothing; for though he might, and with a safe conscience, have answered a direct charge, yet against a general allegation he was powerless. He could not say that he was the best possible companion for a young lady, though he felt, honestly felt, that he was not a bad one. He had never trifled with her feelings, nor sought to influence her in his favor. Of all flirtation, such as he would have adventured with Polly Dill, for instance, he was guiltless. He respected her youth and ignorance of life too deeply to take advantage of either. He thought, perhaps, how ungenerous it would have been for a man of the world like himself to entrap the affections of a young, artless creature, almost a child in her innocence. He was rather fond of imagining himself "a man of the world," old soldier, and what not,—a delusion which somehow very rarely befalls any but very young men, and of which the experience of life from thirty to forty is the sovereign remedy. And so overwhelmed and confused and addled was he with a variety of sensations, he heard very little of what Miss Dinah said to him, though that worthy lady talked very fluently and very well, concluding at last with words which awoke Conyers from his half-trance with a sort of shock. "It is for these reasons, my dear Mr. Conyers,—reasons whose force and nature you will not dispute,—that I am forced to do what, were the occasion less important, would be a most ungenerous task. I mean, I am forced to relinquish all the pleasure that I had promised ourselves from seeing you our guest at the cottage. If you but knew the pain I feel to speak these words—"

"There is no occasion to say more, madam," said he; for, unfortunately, so unprepared was he for the announcement, its chief effect was to wound his pride. "It is the second time within a few months destiny has stopped my step on your threshold. It only remains for me to submit to my fate, and not adventure upon an enterprise above my means."

"You are offended with me, and yet you ought not," said she, sorrowfully; "you ought to feel that I am consulting *your* interests fully as much as ours."

"I own, madam," said he, coldly, "I am unable to take the view you have placed before me."

"Must I speak out, then?—must I declare my meaning in all its matter-of-fact harshness, and say that your family and your friends would have little scruple in estimating the discretion which encouraged your intimacy with my niece,—the son of the distinguished and highly favored General Conyers with the daughter of the ruined George Barring-ton? These are hard words to say, but I have said them."

"It is to my father you are unjust now, Miss Harrington."

"No, Mr. Conyers; there is no injustice in believing that a father loves his son with a love so large that it cannot exclude even worldliness. There is no injustice in believing that a proud and successful man would desire to see his son successful too; and we all know what we call success. I see you are very angry with me. You think me very worldly and very small-minded; perhaps, too, you would like to say that all the perils I talk of are of my own inventing; that Fifine and you could be the best of friends, and never think of more than friendship; and that I might spare my anxieties, and not fret for sorrows that have no existence;—and to all this I would answer, I 'll not risk the chance. No, Mr. Conyers, I 'll be no party to a game where the stakes are so unequal. What might give *you* a month's sorrow might cost *her* the misery of a life long."

"I have no choice left me. I will go,—I will go to-night, Miss Barrington."

"Perhaps it would be better," said she, gravely, and walked slowly away.

I will not tell the reader what harsh and cruel things Conyers said of every one and everything, nor how severely he railed at the world and its ways. Lord Byron had taught the youth of that age a very hearty and wholesome contempt for all manner of conventionalities, into which category a vast number of excellent customs were included, and Conyers could spout "Manfred" by heart, and imagine himself, on very small provocation, almost as great a man-hater; and so he set off on a long walk into the forest, determined not to appear at dinner, and equally determined to be the cause of much inquiry, and, if possible, of some uneasiness. "I wonder what that old-maid,"—alas for his gallantry, it was so he called her,—"what she would say if her harsh, ungenerous words had driven me to—" what he did not precisely define, though it was doubtless associated with snow peaks and avalanches, eternal solitudes and demoniac possessions. It might, indeed, have been some solace to him had he known how miserable and anxious old Peter became at his absence, and how incessantly he questioned every one about him.

"I hope that no mishap has befallen that boy, Dinah; he was always punctual. I never knew him stray away in this fashion before."

"It would be rather a severe durance, brother Peter, if a young gentleman could not prolong his evening walk without permission."

"What says Fifine? I suspect she agrees with me."

"If that means that he ought to be here, grandpapa, I do."

"I must read over Withering's letter again, brother," said Miss Dinah, by way of changing the subject "He writes, you say, from the Home?"

"Yes; he was obliged to go down there to search for some papers he wanted, and he took Stapylton with him; and he says they had two capital days at the partridges. They bagged,—egad! I think it was eight or ten brace before two o'clock, the Captain or Major, I forget which, being a first-rate shot."

"What does he say of the place,—how is it looking?"

"In perfect beauty. Your deputy, Polly, would seem to have fulfilled her part admirably. The garden in prime order; and that little spot next your own sitting-room, he says, is positively a better flower-show than one he paid a shilling to see in Dublin. Polly herself, too, comes in for a very warm share of his admiration."

"How did he see her, and where?"

"At the Home. She was there the evening they arrived, and Withering insisted on her presiding at the tea-table for them."

"It did not require very extraordinary entreaty, I will make bold to say, Peter."

"He does not mention that; he only speaks of her good looks, and what he calls her very pretty manners. In a situation not devoid of a certain awkwardness he says she displayed the most perfect tact; and although doing the honors of the house, she, with some very nice ingenuity, insinuated that she was herself but a visitor."

"She could scarce have forgotten herself so far as to think anything else, Peter," said Miss Dinah, bridling up. "I suspect her very pretty manners were successfully exercised. That old gentleman is exactly of the age to be fascinated by her."

"What! Withering, Dinah,—do you mean Withering?" cried he, laughing.

"I do, brother; and I say that he is quite capable of making her the offer of his hand. You may laugh, Peter Barrington, but my observation of young ladies has been closer and finer than yours." And the glance she gave at Josephine seemed to say that her gun had been double-shotted.

"But your remark, sister Dinah, rather addresses itself to old gentlemen than to young ladies."

"Who are much the more easily read of the two," said she, tartly. "But really, Peter, I will own that I am more deeply concerned to know what Mr. Withering has to say of our lawsuit than about Polly Dill's attractions."

"He speaks very hopefully,—very hopefully, indeed. In turning over George's papers some Hindoo documents have come to light, which Stapylton has translated, and it appears that there is a certain Moonshee, called Jokeeram, who was, or is, in the service of Meer Rustum, whose testimony would avail us much. Stapylton inclines to think he could trace this man for us. His own relations are principally in Madras, but he says he could manage to institute inquiries in Bengal."

"What is our claim to this gentleman's interest for us, Peter?"

"Mere kindness on his part; he never knew George, except from hearsay. Indeed, they could not have been contemporaries. Stapylton is not, I should say, above five-and-thirty."

"The search after this creature with the horrid name will be, of course, costly, brother Peter. It means, I take it, sending some one out to India; that is to say, sending one fool after another. Are you prepared for this expense?"

"Withering opines it would be money well spent. What he says is this: The Company will not willingly risk another inquiry before Parliament, and if we show fight and a firm resolve to give the case publicity, they will probably propose terms. This Moonshee had been in his service, but was dismissed, and his appearance as a witness on our side would occasion great uneasiness."

"You are going to play a game of brag, then, brother Peter, well aware that the stronger purse is with your antagonist?"

"Not exactly, Dinah; not exactly. We are strengthening our position so far that we may say, 'You see our order of battle; would it not be as well to make peace?' Listen to what Withering says." And Peter opened a letter of several sheets, and sought out the place he wanted.

"Here it is, Dinah. 'From one of these Hindoo papers we learn that Ram Shamsoolah Sing was not at the Meer's residence during the feast of the Rhamadan, and could not possibly have signed the document to which his name and seal are appended. Jokeeram, who was himself the Moon-shee interpreter in Luckerabad, writes to his friend Cossien Aga, and says—'"

"Brother Peter, this is like the Arabian Nights in all but the entertainment to me, and the jumble of these abominable names only drives me mad. If you flatter yourself that you can understand one particle of the matter, it must be that age has sharpened your faculties, that's all."

"I'm not quite sure of that, Dinah," said he, laughing. "I'm half disposed to believe that years are not more merciful to our brains than to our ankles; but I'll go and take a stroll in the shady alleys under the linden-trees, and who knows how bright it will make me!"

"Am I to go with you, grandpapa?" said the young girl, rising.

"No, Fifine; I have something to say to you here," said Miss Dinah; and there was a significance in the tone that was anything but reassuring.

CHAPTER XXX
UNDER THE LINDEN

That shady alley under the linden-trees was a very favorite walk with Peter Barrington. It was a nice cool lane, with a brawling little rivulet close beside it, with here and there a dark silent pool for the dragon-fly to skim over and see his bronzed wings reflected in the still water; and there was a rustic bench or two, where Peter used to sit and fancy he was meditating, while, in reality, he was only watching a speckled lizard in the grass, or listening to the mellow blackbird over his head. I have had occasion once before to remark on the resources of the man of imagination, but I really suspect that for the true luxury of idleness there is nothing like the temperament devoid of fancy. There is a grand breadth about those quiet, peaceful minds over which no shadows flit, and which can find sufficient occupation through the senses, and never have to go "within" for their resources. These men can sit the livelong day and watch the tide break over a rock, or see the sparrow teach her young to fly, or gaze on the bee as he dives into the deep cup of the foxglove, and actually need no more to fill the hours. For them there is no memory with its dark bygones, there is no looming future with its possible misfortunes; there is simply a half-sleepy present, with soft sounds and sweet odors through it,—a balmy kind of stupor, from which the awaking comes without a shock.

When Barrington reached his favorite seat, and lighted his cigar,—it is painting the lily for such men to smoke,—he intended to have thought over the details of Withering's letter, which were both curious and interesting; he intended to consider attentively certain points which, as Withering said, "he must master before he could adopt a final resolve;" but they were knotty points, made knottier, too, by hard Hindoo words for things unknown, and names totally unpronounceable. He used to think that he understood "George's claim" pretty well; he had fancied it was a clear and very intelligible case, that half a dozen honest men might have come to a decision on in an hour's time; but now he began to have a glimmering perception that George must have been egregiously duped and basely betrayed, and that the Company were not altogether unreasonable in assuming their distrust of him. Now, all these considerations coming down upon him at once were overwhelming, and they almost stunned him. Even his late attempt to enlighten his sister Dinah on a matter he so imperfectly understood now recoiled upon him, and added to his own mystification.

"Well, well," muttered he, at last, "I hope Tom sees his way through it," — Tom was Withering, — "and if *he* does, there's no need of my bothering *my* head about it. What use would there be in lawyers if they hadn't got faculties sharper than other folk? and as to 'making up my mind,' my mind is made up already, that I want to win the cause if he'll only show me how." From these musings he was drawn off by watching a large pike, — the largest pike, he thought, he had ever seen, — which would from time to time dart out from beneath a bank, and after lying motionless in the middle of the pool for a minute or so, would, with one whisk of its tail, skim back again to its hiding-place. "That fellow has instincts of its own to warn him," thought he; "he knows he was n't safe out there. He sees some peril that *I* cannot see; and that ought to be the way with Tom, for, after all, the lawyers are just pikes, neither more nor less." At this instant a man leaped across the stream, and hurriedly passed into the copse. "What! Mr. Conyers — Conyers, is that you?" cried Barrington; and the young man turned and came towards him. "I am glad to see you all safe and sound again," said Peter; "we waited dinner half an hour for you, and have passed all the time since in conjecturing what might have befallen you."

"Did n't Miss Barrington say — did not Miss Barrington know — " He stopped in deep confusion, and could not finish his speech.

"My sister knew nothing, — at least, she did not tell me any reason for your absence."

"No, not for my absence," began he once more, in the same embarrassment; "but as I had explained to her that I was obliged to leave this suddenly, — to start this evening — "

"To start this evening! and whither?"

"I cannot tell; I don't know, — that is, I have no plans."

"My dear boy," said the old man, affectionately, as he laid his hand on the other's arm, "if you don't know where you are going, take my word for it there is no such great necessity to go."

"Yes, but there is," replied he, quickly; "at least Miss Barrington thinks so, and at the time we spoke together she made me believe she was in the right."

"And are you of the same opinion *now?*" asked Peter, with a humorous drollery in his eye.

"I am,—that is, I was a few moments back. I mean, that whenever I recall the words she spoke to me, I feel their full conviction."

"Come, now, sit down here beside me! It can scarcely be anything I may not be a party to. Just let me hear the case like a judge in chamber"—and he smiled at an illustration that recalled his favorite passion, "I won't pretend to say my sister has not a wiser head—as I well know she has a far better heart—than myself, but now and then she lets a prejudice or a caprice or even a mere apprehension run away with her, and it's just possible it is some whim of this kind is now uppermost."

Conyers only shook his head dissentingly, and said nothing.

"Maybe I guess it,—I suspect that I guess it," said Peter, with a sly drollery about his mouth. "My sister has a notion that a young man and a young woman ought no more to be in propinquity than saltpetre and charcoal. She has been giving me a lecture on my blindness, and asking if I can't see this, that, and the other; but, besides being the least observant of mankind, I'm one of the most hopeful as regards whatever I wish to be. Now we have all of us gone on so pleasantly together, with such a thorough good understanding—such loyalty, as the French would call it—that I can't, for the life of me, detect any ground for mistrust or dread. Have n't I hit the blot, Conyers—eh?" cried he, as the young fellow grew redder and redder, till his face became crimson.

"I assured Miss Barrington," began he, in a faltering, broken voice, "that I set too much store on the generous confidence you extended to me to abuse it; that, received as I was, like one of your own blood and kindred, I never could forget the frank trustfulness with which you discussed everything before me, and made me, so to say, 'One of you.' The moment, however, that my intimacy suggested a sense of constraint, I felt the whole charm of my privilege would have departed, and it is for this reason I am going!" The last word was closed with a deep sigh, and he turned away his head as he concluded.

"And for this reason you shall not go one step," said Peter, slapping him cordially on the shoulder. "I verily believe that women think the world was made for nothing but love-making, just as the crack engineer believed rivers were intended by Providence to feed navigable canals; but you and I know a little better, not to say that a young fellow with the stamp gentleman indelibly marked on his forehead would not think of making a young girl fresh from a convent—a mere child in the ways of life—the mark of his attentions. Am I not right?"

"I hope and believe you are!"

"Stay where you are, then; be happy, and help us to feel so; and the only pledge I ask is, that whenever you suspect Dinah to be a shrewder observer and a truer prophet than her brother—you understand me—you'll just come and say, 'Peter Barrington, I'm off; good-bye!'"

"There's my hand on it," said he, grasping the old man's with warmth. "There's only one point—I have told Miss Barrington that I would start this evening."

"She'll scarcely hold you very closely to your pledge."

"But, as I understand her, you are going back to Ireland?"

"And you are coming along with us. Isn't that a very simple arrangement?"

"I know it would be a very pleasant one."

"It shall be, if it depend on me. I want to make you a fisherman too. When I was a young man, it was my passion to make every one a good horseman. If I liked a fellow, and found out that he couldn't ride to hounds, it gave me a shock little short of hearing that there was a blot on his character, so associated in my mind had become personal dash and prowess in the field with every bold and manly characteristic. As I grew older, and the rod usurped the place of the hunting-whip, I grew to fancy that your angler would be the truest type of a companion; and if you but knew," added he, as a glassy fulness dulled his eyes, "what a flattery it is to an old fellow when a young one will make a comrade of him,—what a smack of bygone days it brings up, and what sunshine it lets in on the heart,—take my word for it, you young fellows are never so vain of an old companion as we are of a young one! What are you so thoughtful about?"

"I was thinking how I was to make this explanation to Miss Barrington."

"You need not make it at all; leave the whole case in my hands. My sister knows that I owe you an *amende* and a heavy one. Let this go towards a part payment of it. But here she comes in search of me. Step away quietly, and when we meet at the tea-table all will have been settled."

Conyers had but time to make his escape, when Miss Barrington came up.

"I thought I should find you mooning down here, Peter," said she, sharply. "Whenever there is anything to be done or decided on, a Barrington is always watching a fly on a fish-pond."

"Not the women of the family, Dinah,—not the women. But what great emergency is before us now?"

"No great emergency, as you phrase it, at all, but what to men like yourself is frequently just as trying,—an occasion that requires a little tact.

I have discovered—what I long anticipated has come to pass—Conyers and Fifine are on very close terms of intimacy, which might soon become attachment. I have charged him with it, and he has not altogether denied it. On the whole he has behaved well, and he goes away to-night."

"I have just seen him, Dinah. I got at his secret, not without a little dexterity on my part, and learned what had passed between you. We talked the thing over very calmly together, and the upshot is—he's not going."

"Not going! not going! after the solemn assurance he gave me!"

"But of which I absolved him, sister Dinah; or rather, which I made him retract."

"Peter Barrington, stop!" cried she, holding her hands to her temples. "I want a little time to recover myself. I must have time, or I'll not answer for my senses. Just reply to one question. I 'll ask you, have you taken an oath—are you under a vow to be the ruin of your family?"

"I don't think I have, Dinah. I 'm doing everything for the best."

"If there's a phrase in the language condemns the person that uses it, it's 'Doing everything for the best.' What does it mean but a blind, uninquiring, inconsiderate act, the work of a poor brain and sickly conscience? Don't talk to me, sir, of doing for the best, but do the best, the very best, according to the lights that guide you. You know well, perfectly well, that Fifine has no fortune, and that this young man belongs to a very rich and a very ambitious family, and that to encourage what might lead to attachment between them would be to store up a cruel wrong and a great disappointment."

"My dear Dinah, you speak like a book, but I don't agree with you."

"You don't. Will you please to state why?"

"In the first place, Dinah, forgive me for saying it, but we men do not take *your* view of these cases. We neither think that love is as catching or as dangerous as the smallpox. We imagine that two young people can associate together every day and yet never contract a lien that might break their hearts to dissolve."

"Talking politics together, perhaps; or the state of the Three per Cents?"

"Not exactly that, but talking of fifty other things that interest their time of life and tempers. Have they not songs, drawings, flowers, landscapes, and books, with all their thousand incidents, to discuss? Just remember what that writer who calls himself 'Author of Waverley'—what he alone has given us of people to talk over just as if we knew them."

"Brother Peter, I have no patience with you. You enumerate one by one all the ingredients, and you disparage the total. You tell of the flour, and the plums, and the suet, and the candied lemon, but you cry out against the pudding! Don't you see that the very themes you leave for them all conduce to what you ignore, and that your music and painting and romance-reading only lead to love-making? Don't you see this, or are you in reality—I didn't want to say it, but you have made me—are you an old fool?"

"I hope not, Dinah; but I'm not so sure you don't think me one."

"It's nothing to the purpose whether I do or not," said she; "the question is, have you asked this young man to come back with us to Ireland?"

"I have, and he is coming."

"I could have sworn to it," said she, with a sudden energy; "and if there was anything more stupid, you 'd have done it also." And with this speech, more remarkable for its vigor than its politeness, she turned away and left him.

Ere I close the chapter and the subject, let me glance, and only glance, at the room where Conyers is now standing beside Josephine. She is drawing, not very attentively or carefully, perhaps, and he is bending over her and relating, as it seems, something that has occurred to him, and has come to the end with the words, "And though I was to have gone this evening, it turns out that now I am to stay and accompany you to Ireland."

"Don't sigh so painfully over it, however," said she, gravely; "for when you come to mention how distressing it is, I 'm sure they 'll let you off."

"Fifine," said he, reproachfully, "is this fair, is this generous?"

"I don't know whether it be unfair, I don't want it to be generous," said she, boldly.

"In point of fact, then, you only wish for me here to quarrel with, is that the truth?"

"I think it better fun disagreeing with you than always saying how accurate you are, and how wise, and how well-judging. That atmosphere of eternal agreement chokes me; I feel as if I were suffocating."

"It's not a very happy temperament; it's not a disposition to boast of."

"You never did hear me boast of it; but I have heard *you* very vainglorious about your easy temper and your facile nature, which were simply indolence. Now, I have had more than enough of that in the convent, and I long for a little activity."

"Even if it were hazardous?"

"Even if it were hazardous," echoed she. "But here comes Aunt Dinah, with a face as stern as one of the sisters, and an eye that reminds me of penance and bread and water; so help me to put up my drawings, and say nothing of what we were talking."

"My brother has just told me, Mr. Conyers," said she, in a whisper, "a piece of news which it only depends upon you to make a most agreeable arrangement."

"I trust you may count upon me, madam," said he, in the same tone, and bowed low as he spoke.

"Then come with me and let us talk it over," said she, as she took his arm and led him away.